BACK TO THE DIVIDE

From the Chicken House

I so wanted to go back to the world of *The Divide* that I'd almost have gone without Felix! Betony and Ironclaw's world is as funny, and dangerous, as ever. Old friends, old enemies and some surprisingly nasty twists, in this new tale. Elizabeth is a great storyteller.

Barry Cunningham
Publisher

BACK TO THE DIVIDE

Elizabeth Kay

Illustrated by Ted Dewan

2, Palmer Street, Frome, Somerset BA11 1DS

For Liv Emma

Text © Elizabeth Kay 2004
Illustrations© Ted Dewan 2004

First published in Great Britain in 2004
The Chicken House
2 Palmer Street
Frome, Somerset BA11 1DS
United Kingdom
www.doublecluck.com

Cover design by Ian Butterworth
Cover illustration by Ted Dewan
Designed and typeset by Dorchester Typesetting Group Ltd
Printed and bound in Great Britain

1 3 5 7 9 10 8 6 4 2

British Library Cataloguing in Publication data available.

ISBN 1 904442 27 7

✳ TO WHOM IT MAY CONCERN ✳
In the event of my death, please read.

Last year, that would have meant within the next few months. I used to have a heart condition, but now I'm completely better. I was cured by a spell in another world - an amazing place with no science, but lots of magic! The trouble is, when I came home, a couple of very nasty creatures from that world got into this one, and they could be seriously bad news. These creatures - an unscrupulous Japegrin called Snakeweed, and his horrible Sinistrom, Architrex - are here, somewhere.

This information is to help anyone who may have to deal with them, if, for whatever reason, I'm not around any more. This may mean seeking help from the other world.

Getting there
This is far from easy. In fact, it may be impossible without the spell that I was given and somehow lost from my notebook on the way back home ...

Snakeweed's world is in another dimension, beyond a magical crossing place called a Divide. I got there by accident via the Continental Divide in Costa Rica, but it might be possible to cross from a similar place, providing the geography is the same.
Once you've found a Divide, or watershed (A mountainous ridge dividing two river systems) you'll need to position your body, equally distributed across the line of separation, for the length of a heart beat.

THE WORLD ACROSS THE DIVIDE
Who to trust

TANGLE-PERSON
Elvex tanglus

DESCRIPTION
An elf. Blond hair - usually tangled, as if they've had the worst hair day ever. Slanting green eyes, pointy ears and green clothes.

BEHAVIOUR
Tangle-folk are herbalists, and their magic is all to do with healing spells and potions.

LOOK FOR
Betony, the best friend I ever made. Also, Ramson, Tansy and Agrimony. They live in tree houses in Geddon.

BRAZZLE
Aquila leonis

DESCRIPTION
A griffin. Its front half is like an eagle and it has feathery ears, like an owl. Its back half is like a lion and it's the size of a grizzly bear.

BEHAVIOUR
Brazzles are very clever, and live for a long time. The males guard hoards of gold, and are mathematicians. The females are historians.

LOOK FOR
Ironclaw - very useful! He worked out the spell that sent me home. Ironclaw can usually be found with his best friend Granitelegs, near his dirt-board on the peak of Tromm Fell. Thornbeak - his mate - works far from Tromm Fell in the library in Andria.

BRITTLEHORN
Equus cornis

DESCRIPTION
A unicorn. It has a silvery-white coat, blue eyes, and a twisted horn in the centre of its forehead the colour of old ivory.

BEHAVIOUR
Brittlehorns are wise and generally peace loving creatures that like meditating, but they can be very vague. They live in herds in a valley near Tromm Fell.

LOOK FOR
Milklegs, their ageing seer. Last I knew, the brittlehorns were mourning the deaths of Snowdrift and Chalky, the brittlehorns who were murdered by Architrex, Snakeweed's sinistrom.

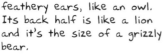

Who NOT to trust:

JAPEGRIN
Elvex irritans

DESCRIPTION
A pixie. Curly red hair, pointy ears, and green squinty eyes. Clashing purple clothes.

BEHAVIOUR
Japegrins can use simple magic, and they like practical jokes. They can be extremely nasty, and dominate all around them, though not all of them are bad.

LOOK OUT FOR
Snakeweed. Enough said.

WARNING!
EXTREMELY
DANGEROUS!
There are a number of unpleasant creatures to avoid, collectively known as shadow-beasts. These include worrits and vampreys but the scariest of all are sinistroms.

SINISTROM
Hyaenodonyx sorcerys

DESCRIPTION
A shape-changing shadow-beast, stored as a speck of energy inside a pebble. Most of the time it looks like a huge and particularly ferocious hyena.

It stinks - a cross between rotten eggs, unwashed armpits and decaying toadstools. It can disguise itself as a lickit, but the smell tends to hang around a bit. The lickit, Elvex cuisinus, is an elvish being that always dresses in white and specialises in delicious magical cookery.

BEHAVIOUR
Anybody can summon a sinistrom by rubbing its pebble, and it has to obey you. A sinistrom is returned to its pebble the same way. Once it has taken shape, it can be killed just like anything else, but its body completely disappears at the moment of death. The best way to ensure a sinistrom is immobilised is to dunk its pebble in fertle-juice. This reduces sinistrom and pebble to dark sticky treacle and as far as I know the sinistrom inside can no longer escape.

LOOK OUT FOR
Architrex. He's on the loose.

Felix

I

'I'll be perfectly all right,' said Felix, trying to keep his temper. 'A week's pony-trekking isn't going to kill me.'

His mother looked upset.

'Wrong phrase,' said Felix. 'Sorry.'

'We mustn't wrap him up in cotton wool any more,' said his father. 'It's not as if he can't ride. I've never known anyone learn so fast.'

Felix smiled to himself. His lessons at the local stables had been more of a refresher course – he'd learned to ride the previous summer, and his teacher had been a unicorn in a back to front world where mythical beasts were real, and *he* had been the legend.

'It's just habit,' said Felix's mother. 'Thirteen years of watching and waiting for him to ... to ... you know. And then a complete cure, and a real future. I still can't believe it.'

'Even after last week's check-up? They said he was one of

the healthiest kids they'd ever seen. Come on, the boy needs something exciting to do during his summer holidays.'

A ring at the doorbell interrupted the conversation, and Felix's mother went to answer it. 'She'll come round,' said his father. 'She was all right about the rock-climbing, wasn't she?'

'In the end,' said Felix. 'But I'm *fourteen*. She still treats me as though I'm six.'

Felix heard the front door close, and people talking in the hall. He listened harder, although he could only make out the occasional word. There was something horribly familiar about the voices. The living room door opened, and Felix felt as though someone had kicked him in the stomach.

'Hello, Felix,' said Snakeweed. 'Archie and I were just passing, you know, and we thought we'd drop in and touch base.'

Felix couldn't think of a single thing to say. Snakeweed wasn't human, although he looked it; he was a japegrin, and he had caused a lot of misery in his own world before he'd tricked his way into this one. He had a hat pulled down over his head to hide his pixie ears, but his eyes were still green and squinty and twinkling with malice. The white-suited figure beside him in the Panama hat had to be Architrex, the sinistrom who had killed two of Felix's friends. Sinistroms were shadow-beasts, and they had two alternative forms. The one Architrex had assumed at the moment was his two-legged lickit form. In his other guise he would be a devil-hyena.

Felix's mother was looking slightly bewildered. 'They say they met you last summer. But last summer we were in Costa Rica. …' She glanced at her husband.

Felix's father suddenly looked very interested indeed. 'Well, this is a pleasant surprise,' he said, extending his hand. 'How do you do.'

Snakeweed gave him a funny look. 'How do I do what?'

Felix's father went into his talking-to-foreigners mode. 'When last summer did you meet my son, exactly?' he asked, speaking very slowly and clearly.

'Augustus,' said Snakeweed.

'August? But … that's when Felix disappeared.'

This was getting difficult. Felix managed to say, 'What do you want?' although it was an effort.

'Your notebook,' said Snakeweed.

'It won't do you any good,' snapped Felix. 'The spell to cross the Divide was wiped out when I came back.'

'Really? Well, why don't you let me have a squint at it, and see if I can make the writing reappear?'

Felix's mother was looking even more confused. 'What are you talking about?'

11

'I think you'd better go,' said Felix to Snakeweed.

'Not until I get what I want.'

'Who *are* these people, Felix?' asked Felix's father.

'They're no friends of mine,' said Felix.

'Then I think you'd better do what my son says, don't you?' said Felix's father. 'Let me show you the door.'

'Seen it,' said Snakeweed. 'Didn't like the colour much.'

'Phone the police, David,' said Felix's mother.

Architrex stepped smartly over to the phone, and ripped the plug from its socket.

David Sanders seemed to grow in stature. 'I should warn you that I'm a black belt in karate,' he said, feeling in his pocket for his mobile.

'Karate? Well, *bake me a brazzle*, I thought we were in Wimbledon,' said Snakeweed, waving his hand in a figure-of-eight flourish. Then he muttered something under his breath, and Felix saw an expression of alarm cross his father's face as he tried to step forwards. It was as though his feet had suddenly become stuck in invisible mud. The colour drained from his face, leaving it white – not just pale, but as white as snow. He was now frozen to the spot. Then his hair turned white, and his clothes, and his shoes. He didn't seem to be breathing.

'What have you done to him?' shouted Felix, trying to keep the panic out of his voice.

'Turned him to stone,' said Snakeweed proudly. 'Though actually, it looks more like marble with those little grey

12

blotches and veins. Now then, how about that notebook? Or shall I create a matching pair?' He glanced at Felix's mother, who was already standing as still as stone, her eyes white-rimmed with shock.

Felix gritted his teeth. 'You'll turn him back again, if I give the notebook to you?'

'Of course.'

'It's in the summer-house.'

'Lead on, Macduff,' said Snakeweed cheerfully.

'It's *Lay* on, Macduff,' said Felix shortly, opening the French windows and stepping out on to the patio. He could see that the human expressions Snakeweed had picked up were going to irritate him no end.

'You too, Mrs Sanders,' said Snakeweed. 'Don't want you blowing the thistle and raising the alarm, do we?' He took her arm, and although she flinched she did as she was told – but she looked more as though she were sleepwalking than anything else.

Felix's house was a big detached one – and the garden was huge. The fence at the end backed on to a railway cutting, so it wasn't overlooked. There were a lot of fruit trees, some of which trailed their branches right down to the ground like crinoline skirts.

'It'll be all right,' said Felix desperately, as he walked along beside his mother. 'Look, I didn't lose my memory last summer. I crossed over into another world, and my illness was cured by magic. I knew that if I said that, everyone would think I was mad. But now you've seen a real spell being cast yourself, and you *have* to believe me. And there *are* countercharms. Dad will be OK, honestly.'

'It's a joke, isn't it?' said Felix's mother, her voice unnaturally shrill. 'He's an illusionist. I don't think it's very funny, though.'

'I'm a businessman,' said Snakeweed indignantly. 'I came over here to set up a potions business, but the paperwork was impossible. So I've decided to go back home. And your son has the magic ingredient.'

'I've *told* you,' said Felix. 'The spell's not there any more.'

'We'll see. That's the summer-house, is it?'

Felix opened the door. It was his own private place, where he kept his most precious possessions. His mineral collection and his chemistry set lived here – and so did anything connected with the previous summer, such as sketches of griffins and textbooks on mythology. Snakeweed grabbed the first notebook he saw. This was a field-guide Felix had been compiling about the otherworld creatures.

'Sinistrom,' Snakeweed read out loud. '*Hyaenodonyx sorcerys*. A shape-changing shadow-beast … Blah, blah, blah – can't read the writing.' He turned the page. 'Worrit. *Canis hystericus*. You've given them all Latin names. Pretentious, *toi?*'

'That's the wrong book,' replied Felix, taking the right one down from a shelf in the corner. Snakeweed snatched it from him, and flicked through it. Page after page was blank, all except for one – Felix's vocabulary notes. The golden brazzle feather he kept there spiralled down to the floor.

'What's this?' said Snakeweed, peering at the entries. 'Brazzle – griffin. Wise-hoof – centaur. Brittlehorn – umicorm.'

'Unicorn.'

'Your writing's atrocious. Flame-bird – plonker. Or is it phoenix? Japegrin – pixie. Is that what I'm called over here? A pixie?'

Felix nodded.

Snakeweed bent down and picked up the brazzle feather. He examined it, and then he laughed. 'Oh Felix,' he said. 'You've been *so* dim. You of all people ought to know how powerfully magical brazzle feathers are. Was this the one that was used to *temporarily* cure your heart defect?'

'No.' Felix gritted his teeth again, determined not to rise to the bait. It hadn't been a *temporary* cure, it had been permanent. Snakeweed was just trying to wind him up. He liked a joke, and he liked the cruel ones best.

'No matter. Look and learn.' Snakeweed turned to the next blank page, and brushed it with the feather. The writing gradually reappeared. He did the next page, and the next.

Felix felt like a complete idiot. Why hadn't he realized that the only reason the vocabulary notes had been visible was because he had kept the feather between the pages? He watched as Snakeweed carried on stroking the pages, one by one, knowing he would get to the Divide spell eventually.

'Ah,' said the japegrin. 'Here we are. A long string of numbers. Dear oh dear, your writing is a total disgrace. What's this?'

'A four.'

'And this?'

'A square root sign.'

Snakeweed felt in his pocket, and pulled out a personal organizer. 'Love these little electronic gadgets,' he said. 'Copy it out in here, so I can actually read it. And don't make any mistakes, or I'll send Architrex back to rip your throat out.' He snapped his fingers at Archie. The figure in white seemed to collapse in on himself, and turn into a three-dimensional puddle. Then he re-formed himself as a hyena – but one with extra-long fangs and a horribly intelligent expression.

Felix copied out the spell.

'I'm dreaming,' said Felix's mother. 'Yes, that's what this is. A nightmare.' She looked at Archie. 'I've seen you before. You were the hallucination I had last summer, in Costa Rica, when I had sunstroke.'

Snakeweed snapped shut the organizer, replaced it in his pocket, and smiled. 'Right,' he said. 'We'll be off, then.'

'If I'm dreaming,' said Felix's mother, 'I can do anything I want. I can pick up this cricket bat and hit you with it.'

She picked up the bat, and swung it. Snakeweed dodged the blow, and slipped outside. Felix's mother followed him. The devil-hyena snarled, both he and Felix tried to get

16

through the door at the same time, and found themselves wedged together. The sinistrom stench filled Felix's nostrils, and he felt sick. Snakeweed fended off another swing of the bat, and made that curious little movement with his hand. Then he started to mutter something under his breath. *Oh no*, thought Felix, struggling to push his way past the sinistrom's hairy body. Not my mum as well.

She had gone quite rigid, and the colour was leaching away from her hair. By the time Felix made it to the lawn, Mrs Sanders was a perfect marble replica of her former self.

'You promised!' shouted Felix. 'You promised you'd turn my father back once you'd got the spell, and now you've petrified my mother too!'

'You've got a short memory,' said Snakeweed. 'I never keep a promise. You ought to know that.'

'You can't just leave them!'

'Watch me,' said Snakeweed, and he and Architrex let themselves out of the side gate.

Felix ran after them. They had a Land Rover – sprayed japegrin purple – parked in front of the house. Snakeweed climbed into the driver's seat, and the sinistrom hopped in the back. Felix grabbed hold of the door-handle, but Snakeweed had locked it. The japegrin started the engine, and laughed. Then he accelerated away, and Felix had to let go or be dragged over the tarmac. He watched as the vehicle sped off down the road, turned right, and disappeared. He wondered for a moment why Snakeweed hadn't turned *him* to stone, too – but the answer was obvious. He hadn't been enough of a threat. He went back into the house, sat down in front of his father's statue, and despite valiant efforts to keep a grip on things he burst into tears.

After a while he pulled himself together, and tried to think logically about the situation. Snakeweed hadn't taken his notebook, he'd only taken the copy of the spell. Felix could now cross back over himself to look for the counter-charm – if he could find a Divide to do it on. The Pennines were the closest range of mountains. There would be a Divide up there, of course there would. A watershed, where all the water on one side flowed to the North Sea, and all the water on the other went to the Irish Sea. Was Snakeweed aiming for the Pennines, or did he think the spell only worked in Costa Rica? All Divides were magical places, but perhaps Snakeweed didn't know that.

Felix stood up, and went out into the garden. His mother looked surprisingly graceful beneath the plum tree, shielded by the overhanging branches and standing there as white as chalk, with a faint sheen to her. The angle of the cricket bat suggested that she was about to hit a six, and her face was a furious picture of concentration. 'Don't worry, Mum,' said Felix. 'I'll sort it. I'll find Ironclaw, he'll know what to do. A brazzle is a powerful ally to have.' A picture of his old friend flashed into his mind; half eagle, half lion, but three times the size. Ironclaw should have been an imposing figure, but he was very careless about his appearance and he

18

usually looked a mess.

As Felix went to kiss his mother goodbye, a fly landed on her shoulder. Annoyed, he made a move to brush it off – and stopped. The fly seemed frozen to the spot. As he watched, its colour changed from black to white. When its transformation was complete, it fell to the ground. Felix bent down and looked at it. The fly was now solid marble. There were other marble creatures down there, as well. A couple of ants, a mosquito, and a woodlouse. They were strangely beautiful, their tiny bodies white and lustrous. I ought to take one of them with me, thought Felix – a sample, to show Ironclaw so that we can work out an antidote. He reached out, and just in time he realized that he, too, would turn to marble if he touched one of them. It would be a skin thing, he thought, lots of spells rely on skin-to-skin contact. Better test it, though. He picked a leaf from the plum tree, and found a snail. Then he dropped the leaf on to his mother's marble shoe, and placed the snail on top of it. The snail did nothing for a while, and remained cream and brown. Then its head poked out and it moved off the leaf, leaving a silvery trail of slime behind it. After a few seconds it froze, and the same thing happened.

Right, thought Felix, as he went back into the house. He found some pliers and a matchbox, and he transferred the marble snail safely to the container. Just to be sure he wrapped the box in insulating tape, so that it couldn't open by accident. Then he packed a rucksack with useful things like a torch and a compass and some spare clothes and a water-bottle, cancelled the milk, changed the answerphone message to 'We've gone away for a few days', and set off for the coach station.

He had plenty of time to sit and think during the bus ride to the Pennines. Although he was desperately worried about his parents, he couldn't help feeling wildly excited as well. He'd never expected to be able to get back to the other world. Perhaps he would see Betony, the best friend he'd ever made. She was a tangle-child – an elf – and he did miss her. She was probably in Andria, a town by the sea, assisting Thornbeak in her historical research in the library. Thornbeak was a brazzle like Ironclaw, and although she was a bit intimidating Felix would never have found his cure without her. She was as smart and decisive as Ironclaw was untidy and forgetful. Her golden feathers were always immaculately groomed, and her talons and her claws always shone.

His mind drifted back to the marble statues at home, and the chain reaction they were causing. Supposing a bee landed on his mother, and took off again really quickly? How far would it fly before it turned to stone? Would a fox investigate it, and turn to marble itself? The knock-on effect could wipe out the entire wildlife population of the garden – and not just the garden. There were cats to consider, and cats' owners. It wasn't too dissimilar from messing about with genes – you could never predict all the results. The more he thought about it, the worse the possibilities became until he was considering the total annihilation of all life on earth. Was this ludicrously over the top? He didn't know. After all, a virus could travel on a breath of wind, as could a grain of pollen, and either of them could mutate into who knew what. It was quite clear that the sooner he found a counter-charm, the better.

When the coach finally reached the Pennines, Felix took a bus out of town and deep into the countryside. He knew he would have to hike the final part of his journey, and when he reached the last village he went into a shop and bought some bars of chocolate to give Betony, and a newspaper for Thornbeak. The brazzle would love to see something like that from Felix's world. Then he left the village and started to walk uphill.

He reached the peak he was aiming for at sunset. He had to wait for a couple of other hikers to leave, and in passing he asked them if they'd seen a purple Land Rover. They hadn't. Felix had mixed feelings about this – he knew that if Snakeweed had gone to Costa Rica, it would give him plenty of opportunity to warn everyone about his return. But if Snakeweed was the only one who knew how to restore his parents to normal, he needed him as quickly as possible.

When Felix had crossed back the previous time, Ironclaw had recited the spell for him. This time he had to do it himself. He checked that his rucksack was securely fastened round his shoulders. Then he stood on the highest bit of rock he could find, opened his water-bottle, and slowly started to pour the contents on to the ground. He was looking for the place where it only took the slightest movement of his hand to make the water trickle away in opposite directions – one lot would be bound for the North Sea, the other lot for the Irish Sea. *He* couldn't be divided like that, so after a moment – with the aid of the spell – he would be sent into the other dimension. It was several minutes before he saw a droplet of water land on a tiny ridge, hesitate, then split itself in half.

He had found the Divide.

He lay down across it, opened the notebook, took a deep breath and read out the numbers. When he came to he'd be on Tromm Fell, the rocky peak that was Ironclaw's home. The old about-to-pass-out feeling that had once been so familiar returned, and then ... blackness.

When Felix regained consciousness, the sun was just rising. He sat up, wondering how long he'd been out. He felt very cold and stiff, but otherwise perfectly OK. His rucksack was still on his back, and the notebook was on the ground beside him. He packed it away, and looked round.

The first shock was that he was not on Tromm Fell. He had never seen this place in his life before. He was on a ridge in the middle of some mountain range, and there were little patches of snow here and there. It was a miracle that he wasn't suffering from hypothermia. Could hypothermia run in families? His uncle had died on an expedition to

Mount Everest. It had happened before he was born, but nonetheless ...

The second shock was the track leading off downhill. It was similar to the one on Tromm Fell, but there was one huge difference. This one had tyre-marks on it. He swallowed. He must be in some other world entirely, one that had invented machines. Anything could happen, but he couldn't stop now. There was no cure for his parents in his own world; this one, wherever it was, had to be a better bet.

He headed off down the track. The fir trees didn't look quite like any he had seen before, and the birds were unfamiliar. There was a reassuring smell of pine in the air, though, and a faint trace of wood-smoke. He suddenly felt incredibly *alive*, every sense drinking in the atmosphere, his mind working overtime as he wondered who might have lit the fire. He smiled suddenly. These days, he could allow himself to feel brave and intrepid and heroic; his body wasn't going to let him down the way it had done in the past.

Snakeweed's comment about a temporary cure wouldn't quite go away, though. Supposing – just supposing – the cure reversed itself, once he re-crossed the Divide? He made himself stop thinking about it, and noticed as he carried on downhill that the smell of smoke grew stronger.

After he'd been walking for about half an hour the path divided. Felix decided to take the fork that didn't have tyre-tracks on it, and eventually he came to a valley. It was warmer here. A river meandered in a leisurely fashion through a meadow which was carpeted with purple flowers. There was a cliff with caves in it at one end, and a trickle of smoke was visible. Something obviously lived in one of the caves. Felix followed the path along the riverbank until he reached the cliff.

A semi-circular lawn lay in front of one of the cave-mouths, upon which a creature with a stripy fleece was tethered to a stake. It lifted its head briefly, and looked at him. Felix felt a thrill run through him; this was no sheep or goat. It was an animal from another dimension, it had to be. As if to confirm this the creature suddenly went cross-eyed, quacked like a duck, and waggled its ears. Then it went back to cropping the grass.

The fire in front of the cave-mouth had a spit above it, but the only thing hanging from it was a metal cooking pot, which was filled with steaming water. A piece of wood was propped against a rock, with the word 'Turpsik' burnt into it. Next to that was a pile of refuse; fish bones, vegetable peelings, scraps of paper, shards of broken pottery. Felix picked up one of the pieces of paper and looked at the writing. It was in English, which was a relief, but the handwriting was worse than his own. He thought – and not for the first time – how strange the whole language business was. Was English always the common tongue in other dimensions? It seemed as unlikely as a chimpanzee writing *Hamlet*. Or was he looking at it the wrong way round, and it was something to do with *him* – he could only cross into a dimension with which he had a particular affinity? He squinted a bit harder at the fragment of paper, and finally he made out a word here and there, and eventually a whole phrase – '*so fear each wand, and fear each boot …*'

Wands meant *magic*, and magic was what he needed to revive his parents.

He peered into the cave-mouth, and realized he could see a shape moving in the gloom. 'Hello?' he called. 'Anyone at home?'

'It's not ready,' came the reply. 'Try again tomorrow.'

Felix wondered what exactly wasn't ready. 'I haven't ordered anything,' he said.

'Not taking any new commissions at the moment,' returned the voice. 'Goodbye.'

'Can't I just talk to you for a minute?'

'Far too busy,' said the voice briskly. 'Waterfall's flooded the office. Lost five days' work.'

'I could help you clear up.'

There was a moment of silence. Then the shape became larger and more distinct, and the owner of the voice finally emerged from the cave.

Felix tried not to laugh. He'd met a lot of mythical creatures the previous summer, but he hadn't encountered one like this. It was taller than a man, but not ridiculously so. Its legs were goaty, like a faun's, and it had only one eye, situated in the middle of its forehead. However, it was wearing a dress. The dress was a faded coral pink, stretched tightly across an ample bosom that proclaimed the owner female, and there was a lace frill round the hem that had come unstitched in a couple of places. The unnaturally red hair was scraped back in a bun, and there was a pearly pink pin holding it in position.

'You're a cyclops,' said Felix.

'I'm a poet,' said the cyclops indignantly. 'Turpsik. Won the Creative Cursing Competition last year. Surely you've heard of me?'

Felix shook his head.

'Thought you were Pignut,' said Turpsik. 'Told him the anthem probably wouldn't be ready today, but he takes no notice. Look, if you really are offering to help me clear up there's a broom over there. Sweep the water out of the cave and into that little gully.'

To Felix's surprise, she showed no interest whatsoever in who *he* was. He picked up the broom and went into the cave. It was a mess. Papers were scattered everywhere, most of them soggy; the only area that had remained dry was an alcove that held a set of rickety shelves, filled with books of poetry. He started to sweep out the water, rescuing pages

26

every so often and collecting them in a pile. Turpsik busied herself clearing away the debris that had blocked the drainage channel beneath the tiny waterfall that was her plumbing system.

Eventually she said, 'That's enough for one day. Still got a few rhyming couplets to get done by tomorrow, and a refrain to compose.' She didn't thank Felix for his help, but she did offer him lunch. Felix accepted, although he had misgivings.

He needn't have worried. Turpsik's bosom hadn't reached its impressive size on just bread and water. The cyclops flung a few ingredients into an iron pan, chucked a couple of fish into another, and a delicious smell wafted across the mouth of the cave. Then she milked the sheepy creature straight into a jug, added a fruity mush, and stirred it in. The result was one of the nicest milkshakes Felix had ever tasted.

Turpsik talked non-stop all the way through the meal, and Felix had no chance to raise the matter that was uppermost in his mind – a countercharm for the marble spell. The only time the subject veered away from Turpsik's difficulties in making a living as a poet was when she asked Felix if he wrote poetry himself.

Felix shook his head.

'Can you sing?'

'Sort of.'

'Have a go at this for me,' she said, handing him a sheet of paper. 'Like to hear someone else perform it, so I can see how it sounds. It's an anthem.' She hummed the tune for him in a deep, rich contralto.

Felix cleared his throat, and sang:

'We shall replace what we have lost,
We don't give up, or count the cost;
We don't forgive, we don't forget,
We never make an idle threat.
So fear each wand, and fear each boot,
And know that we are resolute.'

'Hmm,' said Turpsik. 'Think it still needs a bit of work. Not sure I should have accepted the commission at all, really, but Fleabane always gets what he wants, doesn't he?'

'Fleabane?'

'Don't you know anything about current affairs?'

'I'm from another world,' said Felix.

'Oh,' said Turpsik. 'I'm from the north.'

Felix could hardly believe it. Wasn't she in the slightest bit interested in the enormity of what he'd just said?

'I can see that the north doesn't mean anything to you,' said Turpsik, sounding disappointed.

'I don't even know what *world* I'm in!' bridled Felix. 'Let alone anything about the geography or current affairs.'

'The north,' said Turpsik, as though he hadn't spoken, 'is the home of the one-eyes, to whom it is patently obvious I am related. It's a harsh land, but it's produced some fine poets, such as myself. There's something inspirational about ice and snow and seafood. We didn't have much to trade other than fish, so we didn't have a great deal of contact with the outside world. The first we knew of the great changes elsewhere was when one of the few traders who *did* call on us showed us something called a newspaper. Appalling prose-style, produced in unprecedented quantities by some new-fangled invention called printing. I spoke out against this abomination with considerable eloquence; hence my exile. Written some very powerful free verse on the subject ... Anyway, headed south, and ended up here. And then I heard that Tiratattle was in ruins, and—'

'*What?*' shrieked Felix.

Turpsik's one eye opened wide with astonishment. 'I'm impressed that you disapprove of vandalism that strongly.'

'Tiratattle,' said Felix, hardly daring to believe it. 'Did you say Tiratattle?'

'Yes.'

'Where are we now? At this moment?'

'In the Andrian mountains.'

'And there's a town called Andria, on the coast? With a library?'

'Of course.'

'I've been here before,' said Felix.

Felix's announcement was obviously of no interest what-soever, because Turpsik just carried on with her story. 'The japegrins who had previously occupied Tiratattle moved out in droves,' she said. 'And then they invaded Andria, because they'd read in one of those wretched newspapers how much nicer it was.'

'Betony was in Andria,' said Felix. 'Assisting Thornbeak.'

'Thornbeak? I've met Thornbeak. Helped her with some research on squintlefish shoal-songs. You're not that Felix Sanders by any chance, are you? The human boy?'

'Yes,' said Felix.

'*Synonyms and similes*,' said Turpsik. 'You're more famous than *me*.'

2

There was a moment of silence as Turpsik studied Felix. Then she said, 'If you've been away for a while, I'd better tell you what's happened since Snakeweed and his sinistrom disappeared. Apparently the King and Queen of Andria have abdicated, in favour of a president. Fleabane. He's set up his headquarters in the palace. His japegrins are all wearing kicking boots, and they're armed with heavy-duty wands. They've got an incendiary spell suspended over the library, and they're threatening to burn it down.'

'*Burn it down?*' Felix was horrified. '*Why?* It's unique.'

'Fleabane is having a few little problems getting the Andrians to see everything his way and he knows how much they care about their library. Nasty piece of work, this new president, even for a japegrin. Power mad. Big ideas and an even bigger temper, though he's only a little runt of a thing himself. Learnt his tactics from Snakeweed, back in Tiratattle. He needs a diversion, you see – some common enemy that can be overcome. And what better common enemy than Snakeweed himself? Everyone hates him, because he started all this with his unscrupulous business schemes. But Snakeweed found his way into *your* world, along with that especially nasty sinistrom Architrex, didn't he? Fleabane wants to bring him back. Then there will be a big trial – everyone invited – and Snakeweed will be sentenced to death and burnt at the stake. Fleabane's arrested everyone in the library – that'll include Thornbeak, of course, and her assistant – Betony, did you say her name was? He's forcing them all to look for the Divide spell. They won't find it, of course – it's not in a book at all, it's in a brazzle's head. Presumably you have it as well, or you wouldn't *be* here. How does it work?'

'You have to stand across the Divide so that your atoms – ittybitties – are equally distributed on either side. The spell freezes you in two halves, and makes sure you're in exactly the right position, moving you if necessary – it mustn't be too far. Then, after a pause the length of a heartbeat, it sends you across.' But all the time Felix was saying this, he was thinking – if the japegrins knew I was back, there would be a price on my head. He looked at Turpsik.

'Oh, I won't turn you in,' said the one-eye.

'What will they do to Thornbeak and Betony if they don't find the spell?'

'Don't know,' said Turpsik. 'Never met Fleabane, but don't like the sound of him. No respect for books or any of the arts.'

'He can't be worse than Snakeweed,' said Felix, and he told her what Snakeweed had done to his parents, and the chain reaction that had started to happen.

'Don't use magic myself,' said Turpsik. 'You need a proper sorcerer to sort that one out.'

'And I can't leave Betony a prisoner, either. I have to *do* something.'

'Fleabane's got a triple-head guarding the library,' said Turpsik. 'Have you ever *seen* a triple-head? They're huge. Three scrawny necks poking out of a bundle of grey feathers. The beaks have wicked hooks to them, and the talons are even worse. Wrote a poem about one once: *Blood-red cheeks, and a blood-red soul; each beak can swallow a japegrin whole.* Which reminds me, how come you speak the same language as me, if you're from another dimension?'

'I've often wondered that too,' said Felix, momentarily thrown off-course by Turpsik's question. 'But what I find even more remarkable is that nobody over here seems to speak anything else – in my world, there are loads of different languages.'

'We used to have lots of languages as well,' said Turpsik. 'Tangle, Brittlehorn, Lickit. About four hundred years ago we decided that was silly, and we'd be better off with just one.'

'So how did you hit on English?'

'You'd need to ask an historian that.'

Thornbeak. Thornbeak was an historian. This reminded

Felix of what they'd originally been talking about. 'There *must* be a way of rescuing Thornbeak and Betony,' he said.

'Can't smuggle a brazzle out under your coat, you know.'

'Is there another way out of the library?'

'Bound to be,' said Turpsik. 'There aren't any plans of the building because it's so old. No plans that survive from when it was built, that is. There have been others made since. Rumour has it there were tunnels all over the place – there was definitely one to the palace.'

'I thought Fleabane was using the palace as his headquarters?'

'He is. But there might be a tunnel to the beach, for instance. Very rocky along that coastline. Try exploring the caves; one of them might lead somewhere. Find someone with a bit of local knowledge. Ask around. Discreetly, mind.'

'And risk getting caught, and having the spell tortured out of me with those heavy-duty wands?'

'You need a disguise, and a good cover story. I could send you off with Pignut when he arrives, to sing the anthem to Fleabane. That would get you into Andria. Go for a walk on the beach afterwards.'

'And supposing there isn't a tunnel? Or it's been blocked up? Or it's being guarded?'

'Then you'll have to think of something else, won't you?'

Felix couldn't think of anything else. 'How can I disguise myself?'

'You'd be best off as a japegrin. I can run you up a little

purple number – dab hand with a needle and thread.'

'What about my hair?'

Turpsik patted her bun. 'I'm grey as a diggeluck, really,' she said. 'You can use some of my dye.'

The dye worked astonishingly well, and Turpsik curled his hair in such a way that it fanned out in a tangle of red, hiding his ears completely. The purple japegrin clothes fitted perfectly, and clashed with his hair in the approved manner. There was even a little hood in one of the pockets that buttoned on to the collar.

'Fernytickles,' said Turpsik suddenly.

'Sorry?'

'Fernytickles. Hold still.' She painted some freckles across his nose with the hair-dye.

Felix stared at his reflection in a puddle. Apart from his blue eyes, which should have been green and squinty, he looked totally authentic.

Turpsik spent the next hour making him sing the anthem over and over again, changing the tune a bit here and there until it was exactly the way she wanted it. Then she read him a few thoroughly depressing poems about grey skies and snowstorms and fish. After that they had cakes and more milkshakes, and just as they were finishing them Pignut arrived.

To Felix's amazement he was riding a wise-hoof. Wise-hoofs were academics, not beasts of burden, and they ran the library. When confronted by such an imposing creature in the flesh, Felix found the term wise-hoof came more naturally to him than centaur. The horse part was chestnut; the tail was a pale sandy colour, as were the hair and beard. Pignut dismounted, and Turpsik gave him a sheet of paper with the words to the anthem written on it. Then they haggled about the price.

As the haggling became more heated, Felix turned to the wise-hoof. 'Are you a librarian?' he asked.

'Yes,' said the wise-hoof.

'So why are you carrying a japegrin around?'

'You're a japegrin,' the wise-hoof pointed out.

Felix was torn between revealing his true identity so that he could ask the librarian about Betony, or keeping quiet. He tried a middle course of action. 'How many prisoners are they keeping in the library?'

'Twenty or so.'

'And are they all OK?'

The wise-hoof looked at Felix contemptuously. 'No,' he said, 'they're not all OK.'

'What do you mean?'

'Why are you interested?'

'We're not all thugs, you know,' said Felix desperately, remembering that there had been japegrins who'd sided against Snakeweed.

'There have been a few ... *accidents*, I think Fleabane called them.'

'Has anyone been killed?'

'Two of my colleagues. They tried to neutralize the incendiary spell hanging over the library, and got caught doing it. On-the-spot wand-execution. The screams went on for rather a long time.'

'I'm sorry,' said Felix.

'That doesn't really help,' said the wise-hoof.

Pignut and Turpsik reached an agreement, with Felix's forthcoming performance of the anthem thrown in as a special offer. The contract was sealed with a ritual slapping of hands and the exchange of insults. Pignut and Felix climbed up on to the wise-hoof, and rode out of the valley.

After a while Pignut said, 'I don't even know your name, song merchant.'

So Felix was a song merchant now, was he? But he couldn't call himself by his real name, it was far too memorable. 'Sam,' he said, which was the first alternative that came into his head.

'*Sam?*'

Bad choice, thought Felix.

'Short for Samphire, presumably?'

'That's right,' said Felix, heaving a silent sigh of relief. This was short-lived, however, as it started to rain. Then he remembered the hood, and put it on. The cagoule in his rucksack would have been more effective, but trying to explain fluorescent orange nylon would have been a nightmare.

'Met Fleabane before, have you?' Pignut asked him.

'No. What's he like?'

'Well …' The japegrin sounded unsure whether to continue. Then he seemed to cast caution to the winds and said, 'Between ourselves, he's not frightfully popular.'

'That's a bit of an understatement,' muttered the wise-hoof.

'In fact,' said Pignut, 'a lot of folk are beginning to think he's worse than Snakeweed. Snakeweed was a con artist, not a brute. Oh, I know he used sinistroms, but only when he had to.'

Felix could hardly believe he was hearing this.

'Kicking boots, heavy-duty wands, squawking-mad triple-heads, incendiary spells,' Pignut went on. 'Not to mention the disappearance of the king and queen. Gone on holiday, apparently.' He laughed grimly. 'If you believe that, you'll believe anything. Where's it all going to end?'

'It won't end,' said the wise-hoof. 'Whatever Fleabane gets, he'll just want more. That's the way he is.' He skirted a puddle, and nearly slipped over in the mud. The rain was getting heavier. 'People used to be satisfied with what they had before they started reading what everyone else had. Newspapers? Abuse-papers, if you ask me.'

Pignut turned his head and grinned at Felix. There was a drip of rain on the end of his nose. 'I bet you're glad you're a japegrin, and not a lickit or a tangle-child,' he said. 'It can't be much fun scratching a living in the outlying farmsteads they've all been sent to. Fleabane takes most of the produce in rent, and full stomachs are a thing of the past. Not putting you off, am I? You'll need to sing that anthem like a flame-bird if we're to impress his lordship. Do it well, and you'll get a gold coin. Do it badly, and you're not the only one in trouble. *I'll* get it in the neck for choosing the wrong poet to write the wretched thing.'

'I can't keep this up for much longer,' said the wise-hoof irritably. 'Carrying two people instead of one is no joke. It's getting on for dusk; are we going to stop somewhere for the night?'

'We'll find an inn,' said Pignut. 'A hot tub and dinner sounds like the best idea I've heard for a long time.'

They travelled for the next half-hour in silence, with just the splash-squelch of hooves for accompaniment. Then they rounded a bend in the road, and saw a wooden building on stilts. The area underneath was obviously stabling for cuddyaks, and as they drew closer Felix could hear them bellowing, and smell the manure.

'Oh great,' said the wise-hoof bitterly. 'I can't climb a ladder. I'm going to be in with the beasts of burden, aren't I?'

'It's just for one night,' said Pignut. 'And it'll be warm and dry. The only thing that's going to suffer is your pride. Actually, Andria isn't all that far away now. We could just keep going.'

'No thanks,' said the wise-hoof. 'I'll settle for the stable. The company will be an improvement, anyway.'

Later, as Felix sat drinking his fertle-juice and eating his mushroom omelette he felt alternately wildly elated at being back in the other world, and then worried sick about nearly everyone he cared about. The few seconds left in between were taken up with checking out how he was feeling, just in case his cure was fading away. So far, he felt OK. Which was more than his parents could say. He felt a sudden flare of hatred for Snakeweed.

The inn was packed with traders selling everything from lickit sweets to hand-made paper, for which there was now great demand. It was Felix who had brought printing to Betony's world, and he could see the evidence of his actions everywhere. Leaflets on the tables, advertising wailing courses in three-part discord. Tacky posters, promoting crystal ball parlours and giving their hygiene-rating. Advertisements on the backs of the menus, for toadstool suppliers. He'd wanted to come back so badly, but he hadn't expected what he'd found. Apparently there was a curfew, and roadblocks on every street leading out of Andria. The tangle-folk had been forcibly re-housed, miles from anywhere, and the king and queen had quite simply vanished. Everyone at the inn seemed a bit edgy, and quieter than might have been expected. The conversations kept to safe subjects like the weather, and magic.

And although Felix felt reasonably confident of his disguise – he wasn't anything like as weedy as he'd been the previous year – there were always the blue eyes....

40

Ironclaw fluffed out his feathers, scratched out a couple of numbers on his brazzle dirt-board, and thought for a moment. It was the best dirt-board on Tromm Fell, situated in a shallow depression close to the Divide, and protected from the wind on three sides by a rocky outcrop. He wrote a few more numbers in the sandy soil with his talon, hopped back, and surveyed the result. Elegant, that's what it was. All the best solutions were. He'd been working on a pyramid idea for cataloguing the books in the library by subject, which would make finding things less of a hit-and-miss affair. The first number would stand for the general area of interest – animals, say. The next number would specify whether it swam, flew, wriggled or walked. Then what? Whether it used magic or not? He ruffled his feathers again, and glanced at the sky. There was a speck in the distance – Granitelegs, maybe, dropping by with some lunch and a tricky little algebraic problem or two. He focused the magnification area of his eye on the speck. It wasn't a brazzle at all. It was a fire-breather, and it was carrying two passengers. As it got closer, it became apparent that the passengers were japegrins. Ironclaw waited until the fire-breather landed, using the footpath as a runway and skidding to a halt far too close to his dirt-board for comfort.

The japegrin with the most badges on his uniform jumped down and said, 'Are you Ironclaw?'

'Who wants to know?' asked Ironclaw cautiously.

'Never you mind,' said the japegrin. 'I'm one of Fleabane's

senior operatives.'

'And who's Fleabane?'

'President of Andria,' said the japegrin.

Ironclaw didn't like the sound of this at all.

The japegrin fiddled with his belt, so that the wand hanging from it was more visible. 'Granitelegs said we'd find you here.'

Ironclaw eyed the wand. 'What do you want?'

'The spell that crosses people over the Divide. You were the one who calculated it – and you memorize everything. It's common knowledge. Thornbeak told us.'

'*Thornbeak* told you?'

'She's one of the prisoners in the library.'

Ironclaw stiffened. 'What exactly do you mean by prisoner?'

'All the librarians and historians are under house arrest whilst they look for this dimension spell. You may not be the only mathematician to have worked it out.'

'Well I've forgotten it,' said Ironclaw. Although it was a lie, it still pained him to say it.

The japegrin drew his wand. 'We've had orders to, er ... persuade you if you seemed reluctant.'

'Really,' said Ironclaw, eyeing the wand again. It was an ugly thing, thick and blunt and black.

The japegrin tapped a rock with it, and a shower of sparks arced to the ground. 'I want you to send Toadflax here into the other world.'

The second japegrin stepped forward.

'Then I want him to come back again,' said the first japegrin, 'so I know you haven't sent him somewhere else entirely.'

'Go dunk your head in a cuddyak pat,' said Ironclaw.

The senior japegrin aimed his wand at Ironclaw's dirt-board, and flicked his wrist. A sheet of flame rushed across it, melting the sand into something resembling black glass. 'I can do the same to you,' he said. 'Or I can simply start by singeing your wing feathers, so that you can't fly.'

Ironclaw fought to suppress his fury. I can get rid of one of them, he thought. I could just recite the first part of my spell, and freeze Toadflax where he stands. And then I need to deal with the other one. I ought to peck his eyes out for ruining my dirt-board, but I can never summon up enough enthusiasm for that sort of thing. 'You win,' he said, which wasn't something he could remember ever saying before. 'I need freckle-face there standing with one foot on either side of the Divide.'

'The Divide?' queried Toadflax, looking round.

'The watershed,' sighed Ironclaw. 'Don't you know anything? It's right there, on the ridge.'

When everything was as it should be, Ironclaw recited the spell. Toadflax seemed to shift a little way to the right, and then he froze.

'What's the matter?' snapped the senior japegrin. 'Why hasn't he disappeared?'

Ironclaw scratched his rump with his hind leg and looked thoughtful. 'There's some sort of barrier preventing the spell from completing,' he said. 'Is he wearing a talisman?'

'No.'

'An amulet?'

'No.'

'Well, there's something strongly magical on his person,' Ironclaw announced, waiting for his adversary to come up with the reason himself.

Finally the light dawned and the japegrin said, 'It must be his wand. It's a heavy-duty one.'

'Oh, right,' said Ironclaw innocently, making a move to relieve the frozen figure of the offending item.

'Oh no you don't,' said the japegrin quickly, '*I'll* take charge of that, thank you,' and he stepped across the Divide himself.

Ironclaw gabbled the spell again as rapidly as possible, and the japegrin suddenly realised what was happening. He reached for his own wand, but his arm lost its momentum, as though it had changed its mind, and his fingers fixed in an empty grasp. A grimace of awful realisation froze, like a mask, on his face.

Nice one, thought Ironclaw, feeling pleased with himself. He turned to the fire-breather. 'I don't think your employers need you any more,' he said. 'I suggest you go back to Andria.'

The fire-breather looked fed up, but it got to its feet and

galloped down the path until it had enough speed to take off. Then it soared into the air, and headed off to the east.

Ironclaw knew that the japegrins wouldn't remain frozen for all that long, but at least they wouldn't have any transport now. He buried the wands, then flew over to Granitelegs to tell him his intentions. Ironclaw had known Granitelegs for nearly two centuries; they squabbled about everything, and mathematics in particular, but they were really rather fond of one another, although neither of them would ever have admitted it.

'You're going to do *what?*' squawked Granitelegs.

'Rescue Thornbeak and Betony,' repeated Ironclaw, strapping a crock of gold to his leg in case he needed to bribe someone.

'I'm sure Thornbeak's perfectly capable of rescuing herself,' said Granitelegs. 'She's terrifying. Can I use your dirt-board while you're away?'

'Feel free,' said Ironclaw.

Granitelegs gulped. He'd only asked as a joke. Ironclaw never let *anyone* use his dirt-board. When Ironclaw was just a little speck in the sky Granitelegs flew over to it. The dirt-board was as hard as stone and completely unusable. Typical, thought Granitelegs. Then he wondered whether he could invent a spell to return it to its former state. Ironclaw would be seriously impressed. He fluffed out his feathers, and toyed with a few figures.

'Anyone home?' called the flame-bird, peering into the cave.

'No!' shouted Turpsik, wondering how to rhyme *scum* without being offensive.

'I need to tell someone,' said the flame-bird.

Turpsik put down her pen. This sounded intriguing. 'Tell someone what?' she said.

The bird flew into Turpsik's cave, and settled on a pile of books. He folded his azure wings, and raised and lowered his scarlet crest a couple of times.

Turpsik glared at him with her one eye, hoping he was house-trained, and said, 'This'd better be good. Still got masses of work to do. Can't devote all evening to visitors, even if they are reincarnated ones.'

The flame-bird ruffled his feathers in a self-important way and said, 'You know the king and queen have disappeared?'

'*Everyone* knows that.'

'No, listen,' said the flame-bird. 'I met a carrionwing in the forest, and she said the oddest thing. That the king and queen were still alive, but that they could only be rescued by a mythical being. I asked her where they were, but she said she couldn't tell me, she'd signed a confidentiality agreement. Something to do with her job.'

'What is her job?'

'Refuse disposal.'

Turpsik was good at finding unexpected links between things, but she couldn't find one here. 'The king and queen are supposed to be on holiday,' she said.

'The carrionwing said they were resting.'

Turpsik glanced at the notebook in front of her, and the unfinished couplets. Then she sighed heavily, and said, 'You'd better tell me everything the carrionwing told you.'

3

When the first drops of rain fell, Ironclaw decided to stop for the night. He wasn't quite sure how far away Andria was, and he hated flying in the dark. There was a cliff below him that looked as though it might have a cave or two in it, so he spiralled down and landed on a little patch of grass.

There *was* a cave, and a very nice one, too, by the look of it – but it was already occupied. Someone inside was singing. Ironclaw peered into the gloom. He could just make out a two-legged figure, dancing as it sang. He listened. The words weren't wonderfully inspiring.

'Ice in the rigging, ice on the deck,
Frost on the tiller, snow down your neck.
Mallemaroking, mallemaroking,
Sing as you keep on shov'ling and stoking ...'

Ironclaw coughed politely.

The voice stopped singing, and a buxom figure in a pink dress emerged from the cave.

Well, polish my talons with a sinistrom stone, thought Ironclaw, stepping back a pace, it's a one-eye. What's *she* doing here?

Well, grease my hooves with cuddyak butter, thought Turpsik. A brazzle. What's *he* doing here?

'I'm looking for shelter for the night,' said Ironclaw.

'This isn't a bed and breakfast cavern,' said Turpsik, who felt that four lots of visitors in one day were four lots too many. 'Try somewhere else.'

Ironclaw squinted into the cave-mouth, trying to ascertain exactly how big the accommodation was. Then he noticed the plaque with the name *Turpsik* burnt on to it. 'Turpsik,' he said thoughtfully. 'Didn't you win the Creative Cursing Competition last year?'

The one-eye patted her horrible hair into place. 'Indeed I did. And you are?'

'Ironclaw.'

'Didn't you solve the dimension spell?'

Ironclaw had a quick preen. 'That's right.'

'Better come in,' said Turpsik.

'I liked the song,' lied Ironclaw, as he followed her into the cave. 'I've never heard anyone rhyme mallemaroking before.'

'Know what it means?'

'Carousing on ice-bound ships, obviously,' said Ironclaw.

49

'Doesn't everyone know that?'

'Surprisingly, no,' said Turpsik. 'Like some tripe? Run out of fish, sadly.'

'Don't mind if I do,' said Ironclaw.

'You're heading for Andria, presumably,' said Turpsik, dishing him up a plateful of mush from the cauldron, and pouring him a bucket of fertle-juice. 'Not the same Andria it used to be, not without a king and queen. Abdicated and gone on holiday, apparently.' She went on to tell him the slightly different account the carrionwing had given the flame-bird.

'So where are they?' asked Ironclaw.

Turpsik shrugged. 'Fleabane will know, you can be sure of that. Dreadful business all round. Using the library as a prison, as well. Already got one brazzle captive there – Thornbeak. Know her?'

'Yes,' said Ironclaw, feeling rather proud about the next thing he was going to say and lashing his tail to emphasize it. 'I'm planning to rescue her.'

'Know her well, then?'

'Not really,' said Ironclaw. 'She's the mother of my son.'

'Fine historian,' said Turpsik. 'Knows all there is to know about Flintfeather. *He* wrote poetry, you know.'

'I thought he was a mathematician,' said Ironclaw.

'Yes, well, that was a sideline.'

'A *sideline?*' squawked Ironclaw, incensed. 'It was the poetry that was the sideline.'

'Poetry is *never* a sideline,' said Turpsik, her one eye flashing. 'It deals with the fundamental issues of life.'

'As does mathematics,' said Ironclaw.

'Describe a triple-head in numbers, then.'

Ironclaw glared at her. 'I could give you its weight and its height and its peck-reach ...'

'But not its thought processes.'

'They're not important.'

Turpsik laughed. 'Typical cock, aren't you, Ironclaw? Never hear a hen say something like that. But if you want to get past the triple-head that's guarding the library, you'll need to understand how its minds work.'

I'd rather just peck its eyes out, thought Ironclaw. No I wouldn't.

'*Blood-red cheeks, and a blood-red soul,*' recited Turpsik. '*Each beak can swallow a japegrin whole ...*'

Ironclaw gulped. 'Is it partial to bribes?'

'Shouldn't think so. Not unless you've got some worrit kidneys, or a pickled vamprey. Bit of a gourmet, in its own way.'

Ironclaw remembered the cliff outside. There would be birds nesting there. 'Poultry any good?' he asked.

Turpsik looked dubious, and helped herself to some more tripe.

'Eggs, maybe?'

Turpsik laughed. 'Only if it's a really unusual one. Got a few stonecrake eggs in the larder, but they're common as muck.'

Ironclaw hated asking for advice, but he had no choice. 'What approach do you suggest, then?' he mumbled.

'Well,' said Turpsik, savouring the moment, 'I'd concentrate on the three heads if I were you. They always agree on things – or they always have up until now.'

'Logic problems!' crowed Ironclaw. 'Get it to argue with itself!'

'One of those rare occasions when a poet and a mathematician can actually collaborate,' said Turpsik.

'Pass the tripe,' said Ironclaw, 'and let's get started on a brain-teaser.'

Betony ran her finger along the dust-covered bookshelf. It came away filthy, so she wiped it on her tunic.

Thornbeak made a quiet clucking sound of disapproval, ruffled her immaculate golden feathers, and flattened them again.

'One more smudge isn't going to make any difference,' said Betony, wiping the finger again. 'Or two, even.'

'Keep your voice down,' hissed Thornbeak. 'You *know* this section of the library's out of bounds now. Getting caught in here is not a good idea.'

Betony clapped a hand to her mouth, rather too theatrically for the brazzle's liking.

'You're not taking this seriously enough,' reproved Thornbeak. 'We could be executed on the spot.'

Betony decided she'd better take it seriously. She began to scan the shelves for a book about lifting incendiary spells as rapidly as she could. She'd been working in the library with Thornbeak for the past year, doing historical research, and she loved the place. Now she was a prisoner in it. The thought of it being burnt to the ground by Fleabane's spell was dreadful – they *had* to find the countercharm.

The library was the oldest building in Andria, although no one quite seemed to know exactly *how* old. Huge and rambling, it was made entirely of wood. Despite being only one storey high, it had so many passages and rooms that, to Betony's annoyance, she still got lost from time to time – so hopefully the guards patrolling it could get just as lost too.

Suddenly, a jape-grin appeared from nowhere and said, 'What are you two doing in here? Fleabane ordered you to look for the Divide spell, not play with fire.'

A trickle of sweat made a sudden and uncharacteristic dash down Betony's spine. She hadn't heard him approaching, which was odd; kicking boots had metal studs on the soles, and they usually made a lot of noise on the wooden floor. They could hurt, as well. She glanced down. He was barefoot.

He made a wry face. 'My pair didn't fit very well. I've got blisters. Look, I've had instructions to keep everyone out of this section. Even you.'

Thornbeak raised a feathery eyebrow, and swished her tawny-tasselled tail.

'Oh, I know who you are,' said the japegrin. 'You're nearly as famous as Ironclaw, the brazzle who solved the dimension spell. Do you know him well?'

'Not really,' said Thornbeak. 'He's the father of my son.'

'I'm Betony,' said Betony, feeling that he should have heard of her as well, 'and I was trained as a herbalist. Let's have a look at those blisters.'

The japegrin seemed undecided for a moment – but Betony's voice had been bossy enough to tip the balance, so he sat down on the floor and let her examine his feet.

'I can sort this out,' said Betony confidently, pushing her blonde hair back behind her pointed ears so that she could see better. She waved her hand and recited the standard healing incantation, and they all sat and watched as the blisters popped, and then shrank to nothing.

The japegrin sighed deeply. 'Thanks,' he said. 'Listen, I don't like what Fleabane's doing any more than you do; he's ten times worse than Snakeweed. I'd never been to the library before. It's an amazing place, isn't it? Before all this invasion lark started, I used to grow flumpett flowers. I thought I had every variety there was, but I've found pictures of ones I'd never even heard of.' He smiled. 'I'm not stupid. I know what you're really after in here. And I hope you do find it. Burning this place to the ground would be a crime.' And with that, he left.

Betony and Thornbeak glanced at one another. Betony grinned, and they resumed their search.

A little while later Thornbeak said, 'How extraordinary.' She took a book from one of the shelves, and placed it on a leather-covered desk. A cloud of dust billowed off the binding and a musty smell issued from the pages, as though they hadn't been turned for a very long time. 'This volume contains the original plans of the building. I thought they'd been lost.' She flicked through the book with her talon until she came to something that interested her. Then she said, 'Thirteen. Logical.'

'Thirteen what?'

'Thirteen secret exits behind the bookcases.'

'*Fangs and talons!*' squealed Betony, her green eyes flashing with excitement.

'*Ssh,*' admonished Thornbeak. 'We're not leaving until we've neutralized the incendiary spell. I suggest we stop looking for demolition charms, and concentrate on fire-raising.'

They moved on to the room that dealt with fire and water. Thornbeak looked at the rows and rows of books, and groaned. 'They're not even divided into the two subjects,' she said. 'I wish someone would invent a proper system for cataloguing everything. We'll just have to pull them out one at a time.'

They carried on with their quest, flicking through book after book and replacing each with a sigh of disappointment. Then, just before sunset, Betony found a book called *Great Arsonists of the Past*. She stifled a yelp of delight, and passed it over to Thornbeak.

Thornbeak found what she was looking for in minutes. She nodded sagely and said, 'The countercharm has to be applied at sunrise exactly where the spell was cast, and that's the entrance hall. Fortunately, the only ingredient we need is a brazzle feather. We'll go back to our sleeping quarters like good little prisoners, and sneak out just before dawn.'

A different japegrin from the one they'd encountered earlier appeared in the doorway. 'Any luck?' he asked.

Thornbeak shook her head.

'Oh well,' said the japegrin, 'it's quite possible we won't need it. Fleabane's sent a couple of his militia to Tromm Fell, to torture the spell out of the brazzle who calculated it.'

Thornbeak froze, and Betony went white.

'It's curfew time,' grinned the japegrin, pleased with the reaction his statement had created. 'You'd better scuttle back to your storeroom.'

Thornbeak and Betony made their way back to their poky little sleeping quarters.

Thornbeak's yellow eyes were dark with misery. 'They don't *need* to torture Ironclaw,' she said. 'All they have to do is bet him he can't remember the spell, and his ego will do the rest.'

'I think you're underestimating him,' said Betony, see-sawing between believing it one moment, and being every bit as worried as Thornbeak the next.

Pignut woke Felix at some unearthly hour, and the wise-hoof was on the road before sunrise. 'It takes ages to get an audience with Fleabane,' the japegrin explained as they trotted along. 'We need to be first in the queue, or we could wait all day.'

The japegrin at the roadblock recognized Pignut, and waved them all straight through. Felix felt a surge of relief; he hadn't wanted anyone looking at him *too* closely.

'You seem nervous,' said Pignut.

Felix gave him a wan smile, wishing there were an easier way of getting into Andria than singing Turpsik's anthem to Fleabane.

Pignut peered at him a little more closely. 'You've got blue eyes,' he said.

'I had an eye infection,' said Felix, saying the first thing that came into his head.

Pignut looked sceptical.

He's not convinced, thought Felix, I need a better story. And then one came to him. 'Remember Global Panaceas?' he asked.

'Snakeweed's potions company?'

'Yes. My mother ...' He struggled for a moment with a sudden paralysis of the throat as his eyes watered, and coughed to cover it up. He'd had a sudden vision of himself, old and grey, still in Betony's world and still looking for the antidote to the marble spell whilst his parents' faces became worn and moss-covered, and their hands developed a crazy-paving of fracture lines. 'My mother bought one of their remedies for me,' he managed, after a moment or two, 'but it went wrong.'

As most of Snakeweed's cures had gone wrong when he'd been running Global Panaceas, Pignut simply nodded and said, 'Accidents will happen.'

'I was lucky not to go blind,' said Felix, feeling some elaboration was called for. 'The stuff really stung, you know? My eyes went all bloodshot, it was agony, and when the bandages came off my eyes had turned blue.'

'Oh well,' said Pignut, 'it could have been a lot worse. They might have turned brown, like a ragamucky's. They're still a bit watery, though.'

Andria was different from the way Felix remembered it. Everything looked a little bit smaller, a little more run-down, a little less jolly. The grass verges hadn't been cut, and there weren't any lickit stalls on street corners any more. They carried on past the lodging house he and Betony had stayed at, but the gate was teetering on its hinges, and there were weeds in the garden. The wise-hoof sighed heavily as they took the main highway to the palace, which was in the opposite direction from the road that led to the library.

Ironclaw could see a faint blue haze shimmering on the library roof as he circled above it. He had no idea what it was; some new sort of weatherproofing, maybe? It was so early in the morning that the only creature he could see in the grounds was the triple-head. Good, he thought, that makes my job a whole lot easier. He swooped down and landed on the grass.

The triple-head opened its six eyes. Then all three beaks squawked, 'Password!' simultaneously.

'I'm not stopping,' said Ironclaw. 'Just thought I'd drop by for a chat. *I'd* find it incredibly boring, sitting on a statue all day. Pay well, does it?'

'Cuddyak hearts with pukeberry sauce,' said Head Number Two.

'Devilled creepy-biters.'

'Sweet and sour vamprey wings.'

Ironclaw tried to look impressed. Then he said, 'I bet they haven't offered you flame-bird eggs. It just so happens that I've got one in my leg-pouch.'

All three heads became far more alert.

'You can have it if you solve a little puzzle for me,' said Ironclaw. He took the stonecrake's egg out of his leg-pouch. Turpsik had painted it red with her hair-dye, and it looked rather exotic. Number Two and Number Three glanced at one another, and smacked their beaks.

'Hang on a moment,' said Number One. 'Why would a *brazzle* want help with a puzzle?'

'Four heads are better than one,' said Ironclaw quickly. 'Now then. The problem goes as follows: two of you are guarding doors. Behind one of them is the egg.'

'No,' said Number Two, 'all three of us are guarding the door. And the egg's out here.'

'This is all hypothetical,' said Ironclaw. 'Imaginary. A pretend situation. Let's start again. Number One; you're guarding the left-hand door. Number Two; you're guarding the right-hand door. Number Three is the one who's trying to decide which door to choose. One guard always tells the truth; the other guard always lies. You can ask one question only, Number Three, to whichever guard you like. Get it right and you get the egg. Get it wrong, and you get beheaded.'

The concept of one head not being there any more was obviously a new one.

'That's worrying,' said Number One.

'I'm not sure we should go along with this,' said Number Two.

'It's my head that's on the block,' said Number Three.

Ironclaw clenched his toes in an effort to keep his temper. 'It's hypothetical. *Pretend.* I'm not really going to behead you.'

'That's all right, then,' said Number Two. 'Am I the one who lies, or the one who tells the truth?'

'The whole point is that we don't know,' said Ironclaw.

'We never lie to one another,' said Number Three.

Ironclaw was losing patience. 'All I want is the *question*,' he snapped. 'The question that will get Number Three the egg, whichever one of you he asks.'

'I don't think there *is* a solution,' said Number Two.

'Yes there is,' fumed Ironclaw.

'Well, if you know the answer already, why are you asking us?'

'I don't know the answer!' screeched Ironclaw, although naturally he did. 'I just know there is one! Flintfeather solved it, but the answer's been lost!'

'That's different, if it's Flintfeather,' said Number Three.

'We're sitting on his statue,' said Number Two. 'He was ever so clever.'

'Just like you, Number Three,' said Number One.

'In that case,' said Ironclaw, 'why don't you just get on and solve the problem for me?'

'OK,' said Number Three unexpectedly. 'Let's say that Number One is the liar, and Number Two tells the truth.'

'I think Number One ought to be the one who tells the truth,' said Number Two.

'It doesn't matter!' squawked Ironclaw, hopping up and down with impatience.

'Number One tells the truth, then,' said Number Three. 'If I ask him which door the egg's behind, he will tell me the right answer. If I ask Number Two, I'll get the wrong answer. So I'll ask Number One. Number One, which door is the egg behind?'

'We haven't decided that yet,' said Number One.

'No, you're quite right, we haven't.'

Ironclaw clenched his toes more tightly. He desperately needed them to start arguing. 'You haven't understood the problem at all, have you?' he said. '*One* of you lies, *one* of you tells the truth, but *none* of us knows which one. How can you find out which door the egg lies behind with only *one question?*'

'Oh, I see,' said Number Three suddenly. 'I just have to ask either of them what the other would say, and then do the opposite. If Number One's the honest one, and the egg's behind *his* door, he'll tell me Number Two will say it's behind *his* door. So it won't be, because Number Two would lie. If I ask Number Two, he'll say Number One will tell me it's behind Number Two's door, because he's lying about Number One's answer. So the answer is: If I asked the *other* guard which door the egg was behind, what would he tell me?'

Ironclaw's beak dropped open.

'Oh Number Three, that's quite brilliant,' said Number One.

'You're as clever as Flintfeather,' said Number Two.

'We'd like our prize now,' said Number Three.

Ironclaw passed them the egg, wondering what on earth he was going to do next. He had been looking forward to

Thornbeak's reaction when he strolled in, a picture of debonair nonchalance, ready to tell her that he'd got the triple-head too busy squabbling with itself to notice their departure.

'Hang on a minute,' said Number One, 'Flame-birds don't *lay* eggs, they're reborn from their own ashes.'

Oh *droppings*, thought Ironclaw. How was I supposed to know that? And then he had the most extraordinary piece of good fortune — a faint growling sound, that got louder and louder.

All four heads turned to look, but there were trees in the way. The triple-head obviously regarded the noise as a threat, as it dropped the egg and flew away to investigate. Ironclaw decided to have a good preen before he entered the library. Thornbeak was very particular about that sort of thing.

Just before dawn Thornbeak and Betony left their sleeping quarters, and tiptoed through the library until they arrived at the entrance hall.

'Right,' said Thornbeak. 'I need to place one of my feathers in the centre of the star on the floor. Then I recite the spell.' She took a pace forward, stopped, and glanced at her feet. Her front two bird legs were armed with golden talons. Although she could sheathe the claws on her hind paws, she wouldn't be able to move silently. 'My talons are going to make too much noise,' she whispered. 'I think you'll have to do it.'

Betony was instantly terrified, but at the same time felt terribly important and grown up. She could see the japegrins behind the desk, fast asleep, but she had never operated a spell a hundredth of the power of this one; it was a level thirteen. If she got it right, she would be able to boast about it for years to come – but supposing she got it wrong?

Thornbeak passed her the book. 'It's at the right page,' she said. 'Read it out loud after you've put this feather on the little black spot in the middle. Don't hesitate, and don't leave anything out.'

Betony took Thornbeak's feather, and looked at the spell. The words swam before her eyes, and she had to blink a few times before she could focus. Her heart was thumping, she could feel it, and her mouth was horribly dry. Come *on*, she said to herself, you can do it.

'Go *on*,' urged Thornbeak, with a lash of her tail. 'You can do it.'

Betony tiptoed across the floor. She put the feather in the centre of the star, and the ghostly blue haze on the ceiling rippled. Then she took a deep breath, and started to recite the countercharm. One of the japegrins mumbled something in his sleep, but he didn't wake. The sun was streaming in through a side window now; she could see the long shadows it was casting on the lawn outside. The rain clouds had gone.

She was about halfway through the spell when she heard the noise. She dug her nails into the palm of her hand, and kept going. Then, out of the corner of her eye, she saw the triple-head fly past the window. She almost hesitated – in flight, the bird was even more terrifying.

Thornbeak muttered under her breath, 'Call those beaks? Third rate nut-crackers.'

Betony suppressed a smile, and forced herself to concentrate on what she was reading. Only a few more words to go ...

And then Ironclaw burst through the door. The draught of air blew the feather across the hall, and Betony lost the thread of what she was saying. She grabbed the feather but it was too late; the blue glow amongst the rafters intensified, and there was a sudden smell of treacle. The doors slammed shut with a crack like a thunderbolt. The japegrins appeared to wake up with a start, but their eyes wouldn't open.

Ironclaw looked around him in alarm. 'What did I do?' he asked.

'Messed up the countercharm to the incendiary spell,' snapped Thornbeak. 'The fire risk has gone, but the doors will be glued shut with super-treacle, and so will a lot of other things. The only reason we aren't stuck fast is because we're brazzles, and the only reason Betony isn't is because she picked up my feather. What are you doing here, anyway?'

'Rescuing *you*,' mumbled Ironclaw. 'Made a bit of a cuddyak's ear of it, didn't I? I suppose I'm a prisoner as well now.'

'Not necessarily,' said Thornbeak. 'We know of a secret

exit. Fleabane won't be able to reinstate the spell for another moon or two – you can't apply something like that twice in quick succession, it simply won't take. I hope there's a tunnel to the beach that hasn't fallen in, because the penalty for neutralizing the spell is death. Grab that lantern, Betony, we're going to need it.'

It wasn't quite as simple as that, though. The bookcases behind which the exits lay were now glued shut with super-treacle.

'*Bites and stings*,' swore Thornbeak, 'I'm going to have to try and dissolve some of this stuff. It's a risky process, though – I could get stuck myself.'

'Then let me do it,' said Ironclaw gallantly.

'Sorry?' said Thornbeak, as though she couldn't believe her ears.

'I'll do it,' said Ironclaw, feeling brave and chivalrous and scared stiff.

Thornbeak looked worried. 'That's what I thought you said. Are you feeling all right?'

Ironclaw glared at her.

They went back to the first bookcase. Ironclaw rubbed his feathers along the crack as Thornbeak recited a quick melting spell. The treacle began to trickle away, forming a little puddle on the floor. The puddle got bigger and changed shape, piling up on itself like candle-wax. And then, with a sudden creak, the bookcase slid to one side and a long dark tunnel opened up before them.

Ironclaw led the way, and Betony followed. But as Thornbeak went to slide the bookcase back into position, she found she couldn't quite close it. The treacle that had solidified on the floor was in the way – and part of it was now shaped like a paw.

'I think we've just had a piece of really bad luck,' said Thornbeak. 'Treacle and sinistroms have always had a strong magical connection. Everyone knows that if you dunk a sinistrom's pebble in a glass of fertle-juice, it turns it into treacle. There must have been a little blob of shadow-treacle lying around somewhere. By changing the composition of *all* the treacle in the library, I've resurrected a sinistrom.'

'And it won't just be any old sinistrom,' said Ironclaw. 'If it had its pebble juiced, it will have been a renegade. I think we'd better get a move on, before it completes its transformation and decides to follow us. It may not have eaten for a few decades.'

Pignut, Felix and the wise-hoof were standing at the head of the queue outside the palace, waiting for an audience with Fleabane. Felix was feeling increasingly nervous at the prospect of singing Turpsik's anthem to the president. He adjusted the strap on his rucksack and picked at the sleeve of his purple tunic. Anything to take his mind off it. A murmur ran through the queue, and he glanced up.

People were shading their eyes with their hands, and staring up at the sky. A huge grey bird was descending, carrying something in its talons. It was far too big for a brazzle, and it only had two legs. The three heads made up for that, however. Felix felt his hair whip back from his face in the draught from a pair of enormous wings as the creature came in to land, and he pulled his hood back up to hide his ears. By the time he'd tucked away the problem, the bird was on the ground.

'Will you look at that,' said Pignut, pointing to the thing the bird had been carrying.

Felix felt his heart start to beat faster.

'It's one of those mythical vehicles,' said the wise-hoof knowledgeably. 'A tank.'

'Land Rover,' said Felix automatically, and then wished he hadn't.

'Remarkably well-read for a japegrin of your age, aren't you?' said the wise-hoof. 'I thought all you learnt at school was twistery and bigotry.'

Felix didn't reply, he was feeling too upset. Somehow, Snakeweed had managed to cross his Land Rover over the Pennine Divide, and no doubt he'd brought his sinistrom Architrex with him — in lickit form. This world really didn't need Snakeweed promoting the internal combustion engine; printing had been quite bad enough.

A japegrin with hair the colour of dried blood stormed out of the palace and strode over, with the clear intention of giving the triple-head a piece of his mind.

'Have you left the library unguarded?' he yelled.

68

The bird shifted awkwardly from foot to foot, and its three heads looked from one to the other and back again.

'Get back there and do your job!' shouted the japegrin.

The triple-head opened its wings and knocked the speaker flat with the rush of air as it took off. Three more japegrins appeared from inside the palace, and ran over.

The door of the Land Rover opened, and a japegrin stepped down on to the grass. He was followed by a lickit. A gasp went up from the queue.

'We're watching history being made here,' said Pignut to Felix. 'That's Snakeweed, Sam. Snakeweed himself.'

Felix wondered who Pignut was talking to for a moment – then he remembered that Sam was his alias. 'Is that Fleabane?' he asked, pointing to the japegrin with the dark red hair.

'Yes,' said Pignut. 'Curse his toenails.'

Fleabane wasn't a typical japegrin. He was small and tubby, and his hair was a dark Titian red, not ginger. His eyes were green – but a deep bottle green, rather than emerald. He clambered to his feet, and stared at Snakeweed as though he couldn't believe his eyes. 'Well, well,' he said eventually. 'Looks as though Catchfly got lucky on Tromm Fell. Remarkably fast work; I shall give him a commendation. I suppose I should congratulate the triple-head, as well.' He turned to another japegrin. 'Send that bird a cauldron of devilled creepy-biters.'

'Certainly, Mr President sir.'

'So, Snakeweed,' said Fleabane. 'My name's Fleabane; you won't remember me, I was a very junior member of your team in Tiratattle.'

'I was intending to visit the king and queen,' answered Snakeweed smoothly.

'They've abdicated,' said Fleabane. 'Andria's the japegrin capital now. And you're under arrest.'

'What's the charge?'

'We'll think of something,' said Fleabane. 'The burning's scheduled for next Thursday.'

'I demand a proper trial,' said Snakeweed.

'Oh, you'll get one,' said Fleabane. 'The more witnesses there are the better. Now then. Tell me how that vehicle works.'

'No idea,' said Snakeweed.

'Take him away,' said Fleabane to a japegrin with a thick, ugly wand. 'And make sure the closing spell on the door of his room is word-perfect.'

The white-robed lickit started to sidle away.

'Oy!' yelled Snakeweed. 'You're in this with me, Archie! Don't you dare slink off!'

'Not so fast, lickit,' said Fleabane. Then a strange expression crossed his face, as though he'd just smelt something unpleasant. The japegrin next to him seemed to have smelt something, too. It wouldn't be long before someone put two and two together, and came up with sinistrom stench.

The lickit glanced round. There were far too many japegrins for even the most energetic of killing sprees; he'd be better off out of it. He switched to his four-legged sinistrom form, banking on the surprise element to give him enough time to complete his transformation. Then he legged it, hoping that no one would have the presence of mind to aim their wand at him. He was nearly at the road when a shower of sparks singed his coat. But the main strike had been somewhere to his right; he took evasive action, and the next hail of sparks landed to his left. Then he was on the main highway, and out of range.

Fleabane signalled to two of his militia. 'After him,' he said.

The two japegrins looked at one another. It was clear that neither of them fancied the idea of hunting down a sinistrom in the slightest.

'Now, not next week!' shouted Fleabane.

The japegrins looked sheepish, and ran off towards the road.

Pignut laughed. 'They'll find the nearest bar, and down a flagon of fertle-juice,' he said to Felix. 'Who'd want to come face to face with a sinistrom? They've got the most powerful jaws of any living creature, and they don't mind if their food isn't quite dead when they start to eat it. First one I've seen, I'll be honest about it. What a morning. And to think we were here, on the spot! Just wait till I tell my nipper.'

4

If Felix hadn't been so nervous about singing the anthem to Fleabane, he would have found the next hour's wait quite amusing. A japegrin had been instructed to move the Land Rover, but he didn't have a clue how to go about it. The headlights came on, and went off again. The windows went up and down a few times, the indicator flashed, the windscreen wipers zipped from side to side and the washer sent up a jet of water. When the engine finally roared into life it became apparent that the vehicle had been left in gear, as it leapt forward like a startled gazelle and then stalled. The japegrin punched the steering wheel in fury, and the sudden blare of the horn made everyone nearly jump out of their skins.

Eventually Felix and Pignut were allowed into the palace, although the wise-hoof was told to remain outside.

'Right,' barked Fleabane. 'What's your petition? You get three minutes, and then I see the next in line.'

Pignut handed him the sheet of paper with the words on it and said, 'The anthem, your Excellency. Turpsik the one-

72

eye thought you might like to hear it sung.'

Fleabane leaned back in his chair, rested his hands on his portly stomach and said, 'Go ahead.'

'Sam's going to do it,' said Fleabane. 'He's a song merchant.'

Once again Felix wondered who Sam was for a moment before he remembered. He took a deep breath, and went for the first note. Nothing happened. He cleared his throat, and tried again. This time his voice obeyed him, but he was glad he knew the words off by heart – if he'd had to refer to the song-sheet, his shaking hands would have betrayed his lack of professionalism. He managed to finish the anthem without making any mistakes, and heaved a silent sigh of relief.

'Like it,' said Fleabane. 'Nice undercurrent of violence. It's arrived just in time for Snakeweed's trial, as well. Tell you what, why don't I give you free tickets for the front row, and then you can sing the anthem through so that everyone gets the feel of it.'

Pignut nudged Felix, and he realized he was meant to express his gratitude. 'Thank you,' he said, although he found the idea of Fleabane selling tickets for a trial unspeakable, even if it was Snakeweed's. Fleabane tossed him a gold coin, and they left the palace.

'The trial won't be today,' said Pignut. 'Do you have anywhere to stay?'

'I think I'll try Bedstraw's,' said Felix, remembering the name of the lodging house.

'Oh, right. See you in court, then.'

Felix tightened the straps on his rucksack, and headed off towards Bedstraw's. He might as well stay there as anywhere else whilst he was searching for a tunnel to the library, and the gold coin would buy him several days' board. He didn't think Bedstraw herself would recognise him; when she'd seen him the previous year, he'd been disguised as a tangle-child.

The lodging house was full of japegrins, but there was one room left. Over lunch, which was served at a communal table with bench seats on either side, Felix told the tale of the dodgy eye remedy over and over again. No one questioned it, and he began to feel more confident, and started asking about the coastline.

'You only just arrived, then?' asked someone, helping himself to another hunk of crusty onion-bread.

Felix thought quickly. 'Yes,' he said. 'I was quite ill with that eye problem, and I stayed with an aunt in the forest to recover.'

'Did she take you to the castle? My little'un's been on at me to take her there.'

Felix had no wish to display any further ignorance, so he simply said, 'No. She thought the sea air in Andria would be good for me.'

The japegrin laughed. 'The air round here is thick with discontent,' he said. 'I don't think it's very good for anyone. You see, nobody's seen the king and queen since the

74

announcement of their abdication. Now, you might say a tangle-king and queen are neither here nor there to *me* – being a japegrin – but they were harmless, and there are rumours that something nasty's happened to them....'

'There's no proof,' said another japegrin. 'No bodies. You can't go making allegations like that.'

The first japegrin decided to change the subject. 'The beach is worth a look,' he said to Felix. 'And there are some weird rock formations beyond it.'

'With caves and tunnels and things?'

'Yes, I believe so.'

'Have you been in any of the caves?'

'No – you can get lost. There's an old hermit down there, a brittlehorn. If he likes you he might give you a tour – the rocks grow in amazing shapes, like plants. But he won't show everyone. He has to like you first.'

A brittlehorn was very good news indeed. Brittlehorns had quite a store of magical knowledge – just like their unicorn counterparts – and even if this one didn't have an answer to the marble spell, he might know someone who did.

Rutherford Aubrey Tripp always walked the same way to Wimbledon station each morning, his umbrella under one arm, his briefcase under the other. Normally, he wasn't terribly observant – his head was far too full of protons and neutrons and quarks to bother much with the natural world. A herd of stampeding wildebeest could have galloped down the

High Street without attracting his attention. The only exception to this tunnel vision was the interest he took in his fruit trees. He had a passion for Victoria plums, beautiful, succulent, gorgeous Victoria plums, but this year the wasps had been a serious pest. They had badly damaged the crop, leaving it open to brown rot, and his mind turned over the pesticides he would be needing for the weekend.

Suddenly Rutherford came back to earth with a bump. He'd left his lab keys behind on the kitchen table, he was almost certain of it. He stopped and turned out his pockets, scattering coins and biros and computer discs on the pavement. As he bent down to retrieve them, he noticed a small white object next to a fallen plum. It looked remarkably like a dead wasp – except that wasps weren't white. He rummaged in his briefcase for his glasses, and by the time he'd found them another wasp had landed on the plum. He bent down to look, and as he did so the second wasp crawled across the first one.

After a moment it froze, and the colour seemed to leach away from its body as though it had been dunked in bleach. In less than a minute, it looked exactly like the first one. Someone's been spraying their plums with a very effective insecticide, thought Rutherford. I wonder what it is?

He wasn't a man to take chances with potential poisons, however, so he wrapped both the wasps and the plum up in a handkerchief, and put them in his briefcase. He'd ask someone at work to do a quick analysis for him. Doctor Emily Parsons, maybe.

When Felix left Bedstraw's lodging house a little later, he took everything with him in his rucksack – he didn't know what the outcome of his trip to the beach looking for secret passageways was likely to be. On his way out he sneaked into the garden shed, and found what he wanted quite quickly – a ball of twine, just like the one Theseus had used in the minotaur's labyrinth. He was going to make sure he didn't get lost in the caves.

He walked off down the road, and bumped into Bogbean, one of the japegrins he'd been speaking to over lunch.

'Guess what?' said Bogbean. 'Someone messed up the incendiary spell this morning. They couldn't get into the library for ages, the doors were glued shut with super-treacle. Eventually they found a locksmith who knew the melting spell, and when they got in there it was chaos.'

Felix fought to keep the anxiety from his face and said, 'What sort of chaos?'

'Couple of the militia blinded – not permanently – and several more glued to their mattresses. Plumbing's all bunged up, and some of the prisoners have disappeared. But that's minor stuff ...'

'Which prisoners?' interrupted Felix.

'Dunno exactly – a brazzle and a tangle-child, I think. Just vanished, apparently. No one saw them leave – and you can't really miss a brazzle, can you? But that's *nothing* – Harshak has been resurrected. Can you believe it? I never realized Harshak was a real sinistrom; I always thought he was just a folk-tale.'

'They don't even know where he is,' said another japegrin. 'He could be anywhere.' He glanced nervously behind him.

'Harshak ...' said Felix, as though the significance had momentarily slipped his mind.

'*Harshak*,' said Bogbean. 'Sinistrom to the king of the nomads, five hundred years ago. The biggest, fiercest shadow-beast there's ever been. Killed a brazzle in single combat, and when the king ordered him back to his pebble as a punishment he actually refused, turned on the king and ripped him to pieces. But the king's daughter was as bright as a riddle-paw, and she picked up the pebble and dunked it in her glass of fertle-juice. She presented the nugget of treacle to the library, where it supposedly remained on show for a couple of centuries. Then it was presumed lost, and my history teacher told me it probably never really existed.'

'Your history teacher will be lighting the wrong end of his candle now, won't he?' said the other japegrin.

Bogbean laughed, but Felix was feeling more depressed by the minute. Thornbeak and Betony had disappeared. Were they dead, or in hiding, or had they escaped somehow? And now there was a new menace – Harshak. And then he remembered that brittlehorns had ways of dealing with sinistroms, and he cheered up.

When he reached the seafront, he recalled the last time he'd been there. It had been night, and he'd been carried there unconscious. He'd been dying. And then Thornbeak had worked her magic, and he'd been cured, and everything had been wonderful. Perhaps he'd be able to repay her a little. He took a deep breath, but suddenly it didn't feel quite right – the air in his lungs was sharp and salty, like blood. The fear flooded back. Then he realized it was just the sea air, and he felt foolish. Bracing, that was the word. There was nothing wrong with him. He made his way to the end of the beach, and started to clamber over the rocks. Before long he came to the caves, but he decided to look for the brittlehorn first. Only if he couldn't find him would he venture in alone.

When he reached the ninth cave-mouth, he saw hoof-prints in the sand. He went over and had a closer look. They were too delicate for cuddyak prints; they had to belong a brittlehorn. Felix followed them into the cave, tied the end of the twine to a projection in the rock, and switched on his torch.

The cave branched into three tunnels, and the prints took the left-hand route. He followed them. After a little while the tunnel opened out again and the most amazing landscape lay before him, full of stalagmites and stalactites. Felix heard himself catch his breath. Twisted columns of stone rose before him, the colour of Jersey cream. Hourglass pillars, veined with turquoise; filigree arches, in pink and orange and rust. Mounds of pearl-grey rock formations, layered like puddles of candle-wax, and forests of tiny spikes as white as milk teeth.

At one end of the cave there was a pool of water, as motionless as ice. The stonescape was reflected in it, a perfect mirror image. Felix had been to the Cheddar caves once on a school trip and been seriously impressed, but this was phenomenal.

After a minute or two he realized that the hoof-prints led into the little lake, and disappeared. He took off his shoes, put them in his rucksack, rolled up his trousers, and waded in. It was quite shallow, and he thought perhaps he could see hoof-prints on the miniature beach the other side. The next moment he must have stepped in a pothole, because he was underwater. He thrashed wildly, fighting his way to the surface, and then he realised that his torch had gone out. Not only that; he'd let go of the ball of twine. He trod water, although it was difficult as the weight of the rucksack was dragging him down. Eventually his hands found the edge of the drop, and he hauled himself back into shallow water. He just sat there for a moment, getting his breath back. He was in a mess. It was pitch black in there. He didn't even know which way he was facing, and he was very cold. Eventually he stood up, and inched his way towards what he hoped was the bit he'd just come from. He just needed to be on dry land. The water got shallower and shallower, and then he was standing on a smooth stone surface and he felt ever so slightly better. He took off his clothes, and wrung them out. The water had only just started to penetrate the rucksack – his other clothes were almost dry, and the matchbox containing the marble snail was still zipped up safely in a side-pocket.

He dressed as well as he could in the dark and then he just sat there, wondering what to do next.

After an age, from out of the darkest darkness, Felix noticed a faint glow. Gradually, it intensified. It was coming towards him – and yes, he could hear the faint click of hooves. After a little while he could make out a four-legged outline, walking towards him with its head bowed, suggesting that its owner was elderly or infirm or severely depressed. It's the brittlehorn, thought Felix. He could see that its twisted ivory horn was glowing with an eerie green light, as though illuminated from within. Then it must have caught his scent for it stopped, raised its head and looked straight at him.

'Am I glad to see you,' said Felix.

'I can't really answer that,' said the brittlehorn. 'Not being you, you see.'

'I got lost,' said Felix, his words tumbling over themselves in his hurry to explain himself, 'and my torch went out and the twine slipped through my fingers and I thought I was going to die down here and then you—'

'First things first,' said the brittlehorn. 'My name is Pewtermane. Last year, a sinistrom by the name of Architrex killed my daughter, Snowdrift. Since then I have only wanted solitude, which is why I came here. And you are?'

Felix was momentarily lost for words. Snowdrift had been his friend, she had carried him through the Geddon forest the previous summer, only to be poisoned by Snakeweed's sinistrom. And this brittlehorn was Snowdrift's *father*? Just as he was about to tell Pewtermane who he was, there was a distant rumble. Volume isn't everything, thought Felix fleetingly. Some sounds are just sounds – but others hint at something more, like the rattle of a diamondback, or the hiss of an avalanche – and this is one of those.

A huge cloud of dust raced down the passageway; a tidal wave of it, billowing as it came. The brittlehorn started to cough. Its glowing horn faded into the haze, and disappeared – but strangely, there was more light now, not less. Once the dust was in the cavern it spread out, thinned, swathed everything in mist and then, after a minute or so, it started to settle. Breathing became easier and things gradually came into focus – there really was a lot more light, as though the sky had been allowed in somewhere. There's been a rock-fall further back, thought Felix, I wonder what caused it?

He didn't have to wonder for long, because the scruffy dirt-encrusted brazzle that dashed out of the tunnel was undoubtedly Ironclaw. And the slightly cleaner one that followed him was almost certainly Thornbeak. And the tangle-child behind *them* was definitely Betony, carrying a lantern.

'Busy down here all of a sudden,' said the brittlehorn. He closed his eyes, rested a hind leg, and appeared to doze off.

'Betony!' yelled Felix, wanting to jump for joy. 'It's me!'

He heard Thornbeak say, 'What's this, Betony? I didn't know you were friends with a japegrin.'

Felix remembered his red hair and his purple clothes.

Betony said, 'I'm *not*. I don't know who he is.'

Ironclaw suddenly angled his head the way he did when he used his magnifying vision. '*Well knock me down with an eggshell*,' he said. 'It's Felix! Just the person we need.'

Betony's mouth dropped open. Thornbeak picked her up unceremoniously in her beak, carried her across the water and dumped her in front of Felix.

She scrambled to her feet, and just looked at him. Her face seemed older; she'd grown. But not as much as he had – he was now taller than she was, by a couple of inches. He noticed she was still wearing the necklace he'd made her the previous year. Then she grinned and the smile was just as infectious as ever, and her eyes were just as green as he remembered. Green like chips of malachite; not a human colour at all. 'I've missed you,' he said.

'I've missed you too.'

They both laughed.

'You've turned up at exactly the right moment,' said Ironclaw. 'You see, the king and queen have been taken—'

'There's no time for that now,' said Thornbeak. 'There's a sinistrom after us, and I don't think he's had anything to eat for a while.'

'About five centuries,' said Felix. 'His name's Harshak.'

'*Slashes and gashes!*' swore Thornbeak. 'I thought that monster was just moonshine. They said his remains were somewhere in the library, but I didn't really believe it.'

'Come on,' said Ironclaw. 'We ought to leg it. Even I

83

know Harshak killed a brazzle in single combat, and history's hardly my strong point.'

'What about Pewtermane?' queried Felix, pointing to the brittlehorn.

Pewtermane opened one eye. 'Sinistroms don't mess with brittlehorns as a rule, and I'm only after Architrex,' he said. Then he closed the eye again, and went back to sleep.

Although the final tunnel was big enough for a brittlehorn, it was a different matter for a brazzle. 'You two go first,' said Thornbeak, ushering them in. Felix and Betony started off down the passageway. They could see proper daylight ahead of them now, and hear the faint rumble of the sea.

'I'd better go last,' said Ironclaw. 'I'm the biggest, and the most likely to get stuck.'

'How come you've suddenly acquired such good manners?' queried Thornbeak. 'I'd have expected you to be off down that tunnel without a second's thought for anyone else.'

Ironclaw looked hurt.

'Oh, I'm not complaining,' said Thornbeak, ducking as she entered the passageway.

Ironclaw watched her shapely hindquarters disappear into the gloom. Then he backed into the tunnel himself, so that anyone following him in would have his beak to contend with rather than his backside. I'll peck his eyes out if he tries to have a go at me, thought Ironclaw. I *will*.

5

When Harshak actually entered the tunnel, Ironclaw felt sick. He could see the sinistrom silhouetted against the opening, and he was big. Very big. Ironclaw carried on shuffling backwards, feeling the ceiling of the passageway scrape against his back. Harshak was shortening the distance between them far too quickly. At least if he kills me, thought Ironclaw, my body will block the tunnel and the others will get away. And then he felt terribly noble, like someone out of one of Turpsik's epic poems. Harshak's eyes were glowing an irritating green; they were quite close now. And then the head was right there in front of him, and almost as a reflex action he fended it off with his beak. He'd put some force behind that swipe, and he heard Harshak thump against the wall of the tunnel. He shuffled back a few more steps, and suddenly he was sure that Thornbeak wasn't behind him any more – the air on his behind was just that fraction cooler. Good, he thought, she's out of the tunnel. She'll be able to get away now, and she'll take the youngsters with her. He felt a stab of pity for himself, tinged with pride.

And then the sinistrom was at him again, his lips drawn back in a snarl, strings of saliva hanging from his jaws and whipping from side to side as he launched himself into the air. This time Ironclaw got a proper peck at him. He felt his beak connect with something, but it was yielding and furry. Not the eyes, then. He couldn't in all honesty say he was sorry. And then he realized he was stuck.

He wriggled, but only succeeded in getting more stuck. The horrible slurpy sounds from in front of him meant that the sinistrom was licking his wound. That wouldn't last long. Ironclaw tried to dig at the sand on the floor of the tunnel, but he was too tightly wedged to do much good. This is it, then, he thought. His mind drifted back to the problems he'd solved, the mathematical victories he'd won. He hadn't done badly. Not badly at all. He'd produced a fine son, and he'd even seen him as recently as six months ago. He'd chosen the right hen, no doubt about it. Or had she chosen him? He thought back to their brief and acrimonious courtship. He'd helped build the nest, hadn't he? Or had he? He remembered getting deeply involved in a particularly juicy probability problem.... Had he actually taken back those branches he'd collected?

The snarl came just before the leap. Ironclaw jolted himself back to the present, did a lightning calculation as to where the sinistrom's belly would be, and sliced upwards. He missed the precise target, but he felt his beak connect with something, and he knew he'd done some damage. He heard Harshak hit the tunnel wall again, and heard a strangled yelp as he landed. And then he could feel something, down by his feet. Someone was digging from behind him. He had more movement already. Thornbeak hadn't gone after all; she was digging with all four legs, her talons loosening the sand, her paws scooping it out. He started to scrabble with his own claws, and it became easier and easier. And then he was squeezing through the final bit of the tunnel, and at last he was in the cave.

'Pretty impressive,' said Thornbeak, glancing behind him at Harshak. The sinistrom was out for the count, lying on his side, his tongue lolling from his mouth. Ironclaw fluffed out his feathers and looked smug and completely forgot to thank her for her assistance.

'I think we'd better get away as quickly as we can,' said Thornbeak. 'Harshak could come round at any moment, and if you go back to finish him off you might not be so lucky a second time.'

'*Lucky?*' screeched Ironclaw.

'Where are we going?' asked Betony.

'Geddon,' said Thornbeak. 'Andria strikes me as a very unhealthy place to be at present. I'll take you, and Ironclaw can take Felix. Tromm Fell's only a short flap away from Geddon.'

'About the—' said Ironclaw.

'Not now,' said Thornbeak.

'If I cross the Divide on Tromm Fell to get back home,' said Felix, 'I'll find myself in Costa Rica, without a ticket or a passport, and there's a spell I have to find, and....'

'We can always bring you back here again,' said Thornbeak. 'Come on, let's *go*.'

Felix climbed on to Ironclaw's back, and settled himself just where the hair turned to feathers. The brazzles took off, but they circled Andria as they didn't want to be seen. And then they were flying towards the mountains, and Felix started to tell them what Snakeweed had done to his parents. It was only as he was finishing the story that he remembered Betony's parents, too, had been turned to stone by a spell that went wrong.

'There isn't a countercharm,' said Betony bitterly. 'You just have to wait for it to wear off.'

'How long does that take?'

'Twenty years.'

Felix bit his lip. He'd be nearly the same age as his parents by the time he could speak to them again. How weird was that? And what would happen to him in the meantime? He'd have to stay with relatives, and at the same time keep the statues safe somehow. The difficulties were multiplying like bacteria in a petri dish, and threatening to overwhelm him. And supposing the twenty year thing didn't apply in his world? He'd lose them for ever. What a reversal of fortunes. This time the previous year, his parents had been facing losing *him* for ever. Whichever way round it was it felt horrible – the poison just had a slightly different flavour.

'Permission to squawk now?' asked Ironclaw, with a sideways glance at Thornbeak.

'Oh, go on then,' said Thornbeak.

'I've had a bit of inside information about the king and queen,' said Ironclaw. 'I think they're still alive, but they're being held prisoner somewhere.'

'Oh,' said Felix dully.

'Apparently,' said Ironclaw, 'they can only be rescued by a mythical being.'

'Don't you see, Felix,' said Betony, 'you couldn't have arrived at a better time. We just have to find out where they are.'

'I don't see why they're so important,' said Felix, so overcome by his own misery that he couldn't contemplate anyone else's. 'They don't do anything.'

'Of course they do!' squealed Betony. 'They lead the dancing!'

'Yeah, right, that's really crucial.'

'You don't understand, do you? The king and queen exist to remind everyone that there's more to life than mixing potions and mining gold. They're in charge of *fun*. Fleabane's idea of entertainment is public trials and executions. I'd rather have a dance festival, personally.'

Felix didn't reply.

'I think you've forgotten something,' said Betony. 'Who gave us the book containing the spell that cured you?'

'The queen,' said Felix, shamefaced. 'Yes, of course I'll help.'

'You may question the prisoner now, Squill,' said Fleabane irritably, picking a strand of dark red hair from the sleeve of the purple presidential robe he'd had made. When the young song merchant hadn't shown up for the trial, he'd had to get Pignut to sing the anthem instead. Pignut's voice had sounded like a cuddyak with indigestion.

Snakeweed had laughed more than anyone, and not just at the anthem. This trial was a ramshackle affair compared to the legal battles he'd seen on otherworld television. The court had been set up on the raised bit of ground on the lawn outside the palace which was used for dance festivals, and the prosecuting japegrin was none other than Squill, Snakeweed's old advertising director.

'I've got quite a list of victims here,' said Squill. 'Two brittlehorns, Chalky and Snowdrift ...'

'Oh, *bake me a brazzle,*' said Snakeweed. 'The brittlehorns died miles away from where *I* was at the time. How am I supposed to have killed them?'

'You used sinistroms.'

Squill flicked through some papers. 'I have written affirmations here that you kept two sinistrom pebbles in your safe.'

'I'm not denying I had a couple of sinistroms,' said Snakeweed. 'I'm just denying that I ordered them to kill anyone.'

'Why did you keep them, then?'

'I used to take them hunting,' said Snakeweed. 'They were very good at it.'

There was a ripple of laughter from the crowd.

'Architrex exceeded his authority,' continued Snakeweed. 'When I was arrested he ran out on me, and sinistroms don't do that. I submit that – somehow or other – Architrex has developed free will. I was not responsible for his actions. There *is* a precedent. Harshak.'

Another murmur ran through the crowd; everyone knew Harshak had been resurrected.

Fleabane beckoned Squill over, and they discussed it in whispers. Snakeweed heard Squill say, 'But if we drop the murder charge, what's left? Magical malpractice?'

He smiled to himself. Things were going his way – and they'd go his way even more if he could whisper a little illusion spell, and use a bit of magic to sway his audience. He put his hand over his mouth so that no one could see what he was doing, and crossed his fingers.

Eventually Squill stepped down and said, 'Snakeweed will

now be tried for the indirect murder of twenty-three diggelucks, a flame-bird ...'

'Indirect murder?' scoffed Snakeweed. 'There's no such thing. You've just invented it.'

'Do you deny that you marketed a number of potions that caused the death of the beings who took them?'

'I'm not responsible for people disobeying the instructions on the label,' said Snakeweed.

As most of the potions that had backfired were those for diggelucks and tangle-folk, the japegrin audience nodded in agreement. They nodded rather more enthusiastically than might have been expected. Snakeweed suppressed a smile. His whispered illusion spell was working, although the effects wouldn't last all that long. But then, they only had to last long enough to get him off the hook.

'You employed diggelucks to mine for gold to finance your operation, using drilling spells,' said Squill, an edge of desperation creeping into his voice. 'But you didn't pay any attention to the normal safety procedures. And then you sold them cough remedies that hadn't been tested – remedies that had serious side-effects.'

'I looked into that,' replied Snakeweed. 'It seems that the labelling of the potion was at fault. The labels were the responsibility of my advertising director. And my advertising director was *you*.'

'Fix!' shouted someone.

Fleabane stood up. 'It's clear that the accusations levelled against Snakeweed are without foundation,' he said, with a venomous glance at Squill. 'Nevertheless, Snakeweed should pay for some of the misery he ... er ... inadvertently caused. We'll take the otherworld vehicle as compensation. And to demonstrate his remorse, he can help to restore our wonderful library to its former state. I sentence him to one month's community service.'

A great cheer went up. One month's community service was a doddle compared to being burnt at the stake. Not everyone was equally as thrilled with the verdict, however; a lickit in the back row got up and left in disgust.

Fleabane felt pleased with himself. Freeing Snakeweed altogether would have been a dangerous move – this way he could still make himself popular and keep him prisoner. And perhaps a little accident could be arranged.

However, the very next day posters began to appear, demanding a proper presidential election. Someone started a Daft Party, pushing for a fire-breather as president, but one of the most popular suggestions appeared to be a brittlehorn called Pewtermane.

The sinistrom posing as Architrex trotted along the mountain path, reflecting – not for the first time – that Architrex was a much nicer name than his *real* one.

Grimspite had been pretending to be Architrex for a whole year now, but his dreams still took him back to the centuries he'd spent as a speck of energy inside a pebble.

He'd been a slave, at the beck and call of whoever owned his stone at the time. When he'd crossed the Divide the first time his pebble had been lost, so he no longer had a master. And what had he done? Attached himself to Snakeweed, who was still convinced he was Architrex.

Snakeweed would have made a lousy master whatever world he was in. He had no idea how to treat a sinistrom – he had ordered Grimspite around as though he had employed a second-rate hired killer, instead of a highly sophisticated shadow-beast with a real flair for rearranging intestines. As the year had progressed, Grimspite had hated Snakeweed more and more. He kept his identity secret, looking forward to the moment when he would reveal himself to Snakeweed, and Snakeweed would realize that there was nothing to stop *this* sinistrom from tearing him to pieces. He kept putting it off, however. On the one hand, anyone who spoke to him the way Snakeweed did deserved all he got. On the other hand, sinistroms didn't do that sort of thing to a master. On the third hand – or paw, possibly – Snakeweed wasn't his real master. And on the fourth paw, he was losing interest in extreme violence. It was all very confusing.

When they'd crossed the Divide the second time Grimspite had come round before Snakeweed, so he'd rifled through Snakeweed's pockets for Architrex's sinistrom pebble and thrown it as hard as he could into the undergrowth. His cover would have been blown if Snakeweed had tried to imprison him in it, as the spell wouldn't have worked.

Snakeweed had noticed the stone's absence before long, and had sworn loudly. 'There are some places I can only take you in a pebble, Architrex,' he had fumed. 'I couldn't smuggle a fully functional sinistrom into the palace, for instance, should I want to get rid of the king and queen.'

Grimspite had looked seriously alarmed.

'A sinistrom with a conscience?' Snakeweed laughed. 'Whatever next?'

Is that what I've acquired, Grimspite wondered? A conscience? How can I tell whether I've got one or not? He sniffed himself, but he still smelt the same. He licked his backside, but it still tasted the same.

'You'll be telling me it's unethical to rip things apart next,' chuckled Snakeweed.

That had been a bit of a poser. Ripping things apart had always been Grimspite's goal in life, although he hadn't done much of it recently. How did he feel about that? He didn't know.

'And I don't want you getting any big ideas, now I've mislaid your pebble,' Snakeweed had said. 'In fact,' he added, drawing his wand, 'I'm going to make sure you don't.' And before Grimspite could react, he threw a blocking spell over him that could only be lifted by a brittlehorn. There was now no way at all that Grimspite could physically hurt him.

Grimspite had been absolutely furious. You just didn't *do* that sort of thing to a sinistrom. It was the worst insult imaginable. He had to get the spell lifted urgently. Then he would make one exception to his new policy of non-violence.

Grimspite carried on along the mountain track, wondering what to do next. After he'd run out on Snakeweed outside the palace he'd spent a few days searching for the brittlehorn hermit he'd heard about, in the hope that he could lift the blocking spell, but he hadn't found him. Then he'd gone back for the trial – which he'd witnessed in two-legged lickit form, from the back row – and he'd seen the Land Rover confiscated. This was bad news. The manuscript of the book he'd been writing while he was in the other world was still inside it. He wished he'd had the sense to grab it whilst he could. This needed some thought.

A thin trickle of smoke in the distance seemed to be worth investigating, so he made his way to a little valley with a river, and trotted over to the cave at the far end. Someone was singing a song about fish, and there was a pile of fishbones and vegetable peelings near the entrance.

Grimspite tapped politely with his paw on the sign that said *Turpsik*.

The singing stopped and a voice yelled, 'Go away! I'm working!'

Grimspite sighed, and went away. Then he had an idea. He loped over to the river, caught a very fine gobblerfish, and carried it back proudly in his jaws. He placed it on the ground outside the cave, and tapped on the sign again.

'Go away!' repeated the voice.

'I've brought you a present,' called Grimspite. 'A

gobblerfish.'

There was silence for a moment, and then a large figure in a pink dress emerged from the cave. When she saw the sinistrom, she stopped dead.

Grimspite decided to try and look friendly, but it wasn't something that came naturally. How did you do it? He put his head on one side in what he felt was an engaging fashion, and experimented with a little whine. Nope. It sounded like a vamprey's attack squeak. Perhaps the direct approach was best. 'Look,' he said, 'I don't *like* being a shadow-beast any more than you like seeing one. I don't even like disembowelling things these days. I prefer talking to people.'

Turpsik glared at him with her one eye. 'You don't expect me to believe that drivel, do you?'

'I suppose not,' said Grimspite. 'I'll leave you the fish, anyway.' He turned, and walked off back down the valley.

Turpsik eyed the fish. Then she picked it up and sniffed it. It was fresh, all right, and she couldn't smell any unorthodox additions such as poison. She glanced down the valley. The sinistrom wasn't even trotting – he was walking quite slowly, with his head bowed. 'Thanks!' she called after him. He stopped, and turned round. There was such a hopeful expression on his ugly face that Turpsik didn't have the heart to tell him to go away again. 'All right!' she shouted. 'You can stay to dinner!' You're going to regret this, she thought to herself. Sinistroms have hearts of granite.

But the only thing she regretted was not being able to get

a word in edgeways. Grimspite talked and talked and talked about what had happened to him over the last year. He told her how much he despised Snakeweed, and the way Snakeweed still thought he was Architrex. 'And what's more,' he finished, 'I've been writing a cookery book.'

'Who ordered you to do that?'

'No one,' said Grimspite, perplexed.

'*You*, a sinistrom, made a decision to do something *you* wanted to do?'

'Yes.'

'Extraordinary,' said Turpsik.

'And I'll tell you something else,' said Grimspite. 'I think it's just possible I'm developing a conscience.'

Turpsik's mouth dropped open.

'My pebble got lost, you see, when I crossed the Divide,' said Grimspite.

'So you're a free agent. How interesting. I was always led to believe that sinistroms just wasted away without a master to instruct them.'

'I think it was something to do with crossing the Divide,' said Grimspite. 'It kind of cut all the ties between me and my stone.' His brows drew together. 'It's an uncomfortable sort of business, a conscience. Ripping things apart is what sinistroms do best. But I haven't done much of that over the last year – I've been kind of happier messing about with recipes. But … well, I do miss having a proper mission.'

'I can see that,' said Turpsik. 'You could make getting

your manuscript back a sort of mission. Let's discuss it after dinner.'

'OK,' said Grimspite. 'I'll wash up.'

'Splendid fish,' said Turpsik, wiping her plate with a hunk of bread and handing the utensil to him. 'But tricky things to catch.'

'I'll get some more for you if you like,' said Grimspite, licking the plate clean.

'That'd be nice,' replied Turpsik, wondering whether to explain about hygiene. Grimspite started on the cutlery, and she decided against it. Helping with housework was obviously uncharted territory, and she didn't want to put him off.

When he'd stacked everything away, Grimspite studied his paws for a moment. Then he looked up and said, 'Are we friends?'

Turpsik smiled. There was something rather endearing about him if you ignored the knife-like canines. 'Reckon so,' she said.

Grimspite had a really good scratch to celebrate.

'Need to decide on a plan of action regarding your manuscript,' said Turpsik, wondering if Grimspite had fleas. 'Be retching with rage if I lost any of *my* work.'

'It's called *Dining Out on Mythical Beasts*,' said Grimspite. 'Good title.'

Grimspite had never been congratulated for anything except extreme violence before. It felt good. He started to tell Turpsik about triangle-fins and sword-noses. Not that he'd caught either of those last two himself, but he'd been to a couple of classy restaurants with Snakeweed and he remembered the menu with affection.

Turpsik made a few suggestions about the names he'd chosen for various dishes. *Berk buk-a-buk* didn't have the right ring to it, and the otherworld name – *chicken* – had nothing going for it. *Cluck-bird* sounded better.

The next morning he slipped out early, and caught another gobblerfish for breakfast. As they ate, they talked. Talking was such fun. He told her all about Snakeweed's trial, and how he'd witnessed it from the back row.

'Sounds like a complete fiasco,' said Turpsik. 'Fleabane isn't nearly as clever as Snakeweed.'

'And you should have heard the anthem,' said Grimspite. 'It was a hoot.'

Turpsik stiffened.

'Honestly,' said Grimspite, warming to his theme, 'the tune was totally unsuitable, and the words were just plain stupid ...' He trailed off. 'What's the matter?'

'Nothing,' snapped Turpsik. 'I've just got a lot of work to do today. Now shove off and leave me in peace.'

Grimspite felt devastated. What had he done? This friendship business was so complicated, there seemed to be rules all over the place that he just didn't understand.

'It *was* funny,' he said lamely, trying to make her laugh. 'When Pignut got to the *fear each wand and fear each boot* bit, he pointed to them just like a children's entertainer. Fleabane looked absolutely furious, I think the anthem was meant to be all sort of solemn and—'

'Can't stand around gossiping all day,' said Turpsik sharply. 'Goodbye.'

The journey to Geddon was a two-day flight, and when the brazzles stopped for the night Felix raised the matter of his parents again. 'I thought maybe *you'd* be able to calculate a spell,' he said to Ironclaw.

Ironclaw shook his head. 'You need a proper sorcerer to sort that one out, Felix. I don't think even a brittlehorn could do it. We could do with a proper sorcerer to locate the king and queen, as well.'

'If there'd been a solution to petrification spells,' snapped Betony, 'don't you think we'd have found it by now? My brother and sister did try, you know. They wanted to bring me up even less than I wanted to be brought up by them.'

'This isn't the same thing at all, Betony,' said Thornbeak. 'Your parents were turned to stone by a spell that went wrong. Snakeweed must have quite cold-bloodedly used a specific chain-reaction hex, and the implications are very serious.'

Betony scowled.

'He may not have known it was a chain-reaction hex,' said Ironclaw. 'Magical theory was never his strong point.'

'Consider this, Betony,' said Thornbeak. 'Eventually the

infection will spread outside Felix's garden, and people will start to notice. There is no magic in Felix's world; from everything he's told me, its arrival would be a disaster. What's a good thing in one place may be a bad one in another.'

'They'll want to find out how it works,' said Felix. 'Scientists will be desperate to analyze what's going on, and if they succeed they'll use magic for all sorts of dreadful things. Snakeweed was a total amateur compared to the businessmen in *my* world.'

'Hardly anyone understands the principles behind magic,' scoffed Betony. 'It's too difficult.'

'I understand the basics,' said Ironclaw, and he started to explain, emphasizing the importance of something he called a twisty-strip. It wasn't until he said that it had only one side and one edge that Felix realised he was talking about the Möbius strip, a curious mathematical figure with all sorts of intriguing properties he'd once seen demonstrated at school. He'd been presented with it as a thin ribbon of paper, joined together at the ends, but with one half-twist in it.

Perhaps, thought Felix, that's what magic is – physics with a different twist to it. My world just hasn't discovered the twist.

6

Nearly four thousand tangle-folk lived in Geddon, the closest town to the rocky peak of Tromm Fell, and Betony's home. Most of the dwellings were treehouses with small plots of land to one side, and only in the centre did the wooden buildings crowd together at ground level along narrow streets, Elizabethan-style. There was a square right in the middle, which was used for story-telling sessions and wailing concerts. There was also a market, a school, several lodging-houses and a livery stable, but no landing strip for the fire-breathers. They had to use the main road to take off and land, and there was a bell that someone rang to clear the way whenever necessary. Each treehouse had a yard beneath it, and some of them had been turned into gardens. At dusk, dozens of varieties of evening flumpett saturated the air with their fragrance.

The brazzles landed as the shadows were lengthening and the stabber-birds were screeching lullabies at their chicks.

Betony leapt off Thornbeak's back and ran over to the rope ladder that hung from the family treehouse. The ladder was still anchored to the statues of her parents. She noted that someone had polished them recently – her elder sister Tansy, probably. Her brother, Ramson, had never polished anything in his life except his sickle.

'Tansy!' she yelled, cupping her hands round her mouth and aiming her voice up at the treehouse. 'Ramson! It's me, Betony, I'm back!'

Tansy's plain, pointed little face appeared on the balcony. 'Betony!' she squealed. 'We were so worried about you! We heard about what's happened in Andria – Ironclaw dropped by last week to tell us he was going to rescue you.' Then she noticed Felix. 'Who's that japegrin with you?' she asked suspiciously.

'It's Felix,' said Felix.

'The blue eyes,' said Tansy. 'Of course.'

'I think I'll be off,' said Ironclaw. He glanced at Thornbeak. 'What are *you* going to do?' he asked.

'I'm not sure,' said Thornbeak. 'I used to spend every day in the Andrian library, but that's out of the question now.'

Ironclaw studied his talons. 'You could come back to Tromm Fell with me if you liked.'

'And just what, precisely, am I supposed to do on Tromm Fell?'

'The perching rocks need a good clean, and it would be nice if someone else did the hunting because I've got this

104

fascinating little number series I ...' said Ironclaw, but he didn't get any further because Thornbeak pecked him.

'I thought hens liked that sort of thing,' muttered Ironclaw, rubbing the affected area with his hind leg and making far more of it than necessary.

'Cleanliness, yes,' said Thornbeak, ruffling her immaculate feathers and flattening them again. 'Cleaning, no.'

'I suppose I could pay someone else to smarten up the perching rocks. Even Granitelegs said they were getting a bit whiffy.'

'Ramson's looking for a job,' said Tansy. 'He failed his herbalist finals, so he can't work in Dibber's printing business, writing spell-books.'

'What sort of job?' asked Ramson, sauntering into the yard. 'Oh, hello, Betony.' He looked at Felix. 'And who are you?'

'Felix.'

Ramson peered a little more closely at Felix through his tangle of blond hair. Then his mouth dropped open and his Adam's apple bobbed in and out a couple of times. '*Blazing feathers!*' he exclaimed. 'So it is!' Then he added, 'You've grown. Can't say I go a bundle on the ginger hair, though.'

Thornbeak told Ramson about the job.

'Scrubbing brazzle rocks?' said Ramson, horrified. 'I'm a herbalist.'

'No you're not,' snapped Tansy. 'Not until you've retaken your exams. I don't want you lounging round the place all day, playing the same old tunes over and over again on that lute. He'll take the job, Thornbeak.'

Ramson looked fed up, but he didn't argue.

'And he'll start immediately,' Tansy added.

'*Blazing feathers*, Tansy ...'

'Climb on,' said Ironclaw, 'we're leaving.'

Felix watched as the brazzles became specks in the sky.

'I've got a throat lubricator to deliver,' said Tansy. 'See you in a bit.' She put a purple gourd into a basket, and hurried off down the lane.

'You can have Ramson's room,' said Betony. 'Come on, I'll show you round.'

Felix had never been to Betony's home. The statues of her parents at the foot of the rope ladder were a forcible reminder of his own situation. He could see the family likeness, particularly in Betony's mother. He ran his finger over her. At least she wasn't dangerous, the way his own parents were. He shivered. His own parents had turned into a time-bomb, relentlessly ticking away in another world. He decided to try and stop thinking about it, as there was nothing he could do until he found a sorcerer.

The ladder led up to a platform, which went all the way round the tree trunk. There were three rooms on the first floor; a living room, a storeroom, and a dispensary for preparing potions. Sawn-off branches made a spiral staircase to the next floor, which had two tiny bedrooms and a bathroom. A barrel stored rainwater for showers, and drained on to the garden below. Above that there was another floor, with two more bedrooms. The kitchen was in a covered area on the ground, where the stove was. The living room was the only room that had been properly finished; the floor was sanded and varnished, and there were colourful cushions scattered around to sit on. Candles stood in lots of little niches and the door was a curtain, made of some thick blue material. There was a painting of some toadstools on one of the walls, and a weird and wonderful plant was growing in a blue ceramic pot on the window ledge. It looked like a succulent of some sort – a desert plant, anyway. Its stem was thick, bulbous, swelling out like a beer belly beneath rolls of pale green flesh. If it had possessed a head instead of a coronet of spiky leaves it would have looked like a football-sized statue of a sumo wrestler, or a jade Buddha. In the middle of the coronet sat one bright red flower.

'Hello Socrates,' said Betony to the plant. 'I haven't seen you for ages.'

'Socrates?' queried Felix.

'What's wrong with Socrates?' demanded the plant. 'Good old-fashioned mythical name. Betony, I'm as dry as a fire-breather's backside. Tansy's awfully forgetful.'

Felix's mouth dropped open.

Betony watered the plant, and then she went around lighting candles with a wave of her hand, muttering the incantation. 'Don't fight; flame, light; ignite; burn bright.'

Felix remembered trying to prove that he could do magic

in his own world by trying the same spell, and being bitterly disappointed. He realized he'd got the words in the wrong order, so he tried again. This time the candle burst into flame immediately, and he felt so pleased with himself that he started lighting as many as possible, and racing Betony to reach them.

'Hey,' said Betony, 'you've really got the hang of this now, haven't you? Have to get you out of those japegrin clothes, though. They're frightful.' Felix emptied out his rucksack, found some relatively clean stuff, and changed into it. Then he dismantled his torch, and dried each bit separately. When he put the pieces back together again and the torch worked, he felt like Einstein.

Betony decided to smarten herself up as well. Her clothes were still covered with the dust from the tunnel, and it was a relief to get shot of them. She'd had to leave all her stuff behind in Andria, but when she tried on some of her old things she found that they were too small. She borrowed a plain sludge green dress of Tansy's, but it didn't do a thing for her and she kept tripping over the hem. I know, she thought, I'll see if Agrimony will lend me something. She told Felix she wouldn't be long, and that Socrates would keep him company for a bit. Then she climbed down the ladder, leaving out the last few rungs and jumping nimbly to the ground. Although Agrimony had been a bit of a pain at school she'd behaved rather well the previous year, and she had gone up in Betony's estimation. She'd been brave and unselfish, and she'd even admitted there was more to life than dancing the star squirm or the dusk hop, or coming top in toadstool tests. Betony was really looking forward to seeing her – would the improvement have lasted, or had it been just skin-deep?

'Oh, hi, Betony,' said Agrimony, with a disbelieving glance at the dress.

'I know,' said Betony. 'Can you lend me something? I left everything behind when I was running away from Harshak down a collapsing secret passage after heroically saving the library from an incendiary spell.'

'I don't think anything of mine will fit you.'

'I can't wear what I came in. Reciting a *level thirteen* spell makes you perspire like anything, and then I got some dust and some sinistrom blood on me as well.'

'I've grown more than you have,' said Agrimony, flicking through her wardrobe. 'Everything I've got has a bust these days.'

'They actually had a triple-head guarding the library, Agrimony. *A real live triple-head.* It was huge. It flew off when it saw Snakeweed drive past in an otherworld vehicle. A *self-propelled* thing.'

'Try this,' said Agrimony, pulling out a slinky embroidered little number. 'It's last year's style, I don't wear it any more.'

'Thanks,' said Betony flatly, putting it on.

'I have to think about my appearance,' said Agrimony. 'When I got back from Andria last year I became quite a hit at the storytelling sessions. It's not just having something exciting to tell, you know, it's the way you do it. I'm a natural, apparently. I'm going to be apprenticed to the chief storyteller.'

'Betony darling!' screeched Agrimony's mother Grisette, appearing the doorway. 'How lovely to see you!'

'Thornbeak and I saved the library from an incendiary spell,' said Betony.

'That's nice,' said Grisette, looking at Betony appraisingly, 'but I think the bodice is a little full for you. I could put a couple of tucks in it.'

You can see where Agrimony gets it from, can't you, thought Betony.

Felix lay back against the cushions, and leafed through *Moss, Moulds and Mistletoe – a Herbal Primer*. It was an old-fashioned schoolbook, handwritten by a scribe. Some of it was quite unpleasant: *First, rot your toadstool until the smell makes you vomit. Scrape off the pink mould, mix it with an equal quantity of your own blood and let it fester for two days.* He put it back on the shelf, and chose another: *Fire-breathers: Structure and Function*. It was fascinating; he hadn't realized that fire-breather dung was red-hot, and was used to get an oven going. Nor had he known that elderly fire-breathers who had retired from commercial flying still worked part-time – they stripped paint for decorators, operated kilns for potters and ran beach barbecues in the summer. He put the book back, and selected another. *A Child's Book of Shadow-beasts and Scourges*. He looked at the pictures of sinistroms and worrits, remembering his own encounters with them. The last section dealt with creatures that weren't shadow-beasts, but could be big trouble nonetheless – cutthroats and carrion-wings and brandees, things he hadn't even heard of. There was an anecdote about someone called Leona, who was half-lion and half-amberly (whatever that was).

... and the worrit found himself up against the best magical mind he'd ever encountered. Leona twisty-stripped him – she reversed the worrit's own magical powers, and told him jokes until he laughed himself to death.

The best magical mind he'd ever encountered? Was Leona an historical figure, or was she still alive?

'Are you just going to sit there reading, human?' demanded Socrates, dropping a dead leaf. 'I thought I was going to have some interesting company for a change.'

Felix grinned. 'Is Leona a real person?' he asked.

'She's a riddle-paw.'

'What's that?'

Socrates described Leona, and Felix realized that Leona was almost certainly a sphinx. This was definitely worth investigating; an accomplished sorceress was precisely what he needed.

'Why do you want a sorceress, anyway?' asked Socrates.

Felix told him everything. His visit to Betony's world the

previous year, the need to find the reverse-marble hex, the japegrin takeover in Andria, and the disappearance of the king and queen.

'Hmm,' said Socrates, re-arranging a petal, 'you've got a couple of root-tangling posers there, haven't you? But Leona's supposed to be very clever, she probably knows a royalty location spell.'

'And the marble thing?'

'Worth a try.'

'It's not very clear from the book where she lives.'

'That's because she doesn't live in one place. She chooses a town, and terrorizes it for a while.'

'So she could be anywhere?' said Felix, feeling depressed.

'Oh, I know the general area,' said the plant. 'Well, more or less. I originally came from a king's garden, you know, in a city west of here. The fruit trees used to talk about her. It's a long way, though. You'd have to fly.'

No problem, thought Felix. I'll speak to Ironclaw tomorrow.

'He didn't get very much done, did he?' said Thornbeak, surveying the small area of rock that Ramson had cleaned. She pecked at it, and another shower of dirt fell off. 'I'm not sleeping on this until it's decent, Ironclaw.'

'I haven't got time for housework,' said Ironclaw. 'My dirt-board was ruined by a japegrin, I've got to make another one.'

'Can't you sort out the old one?'

'No,' snapped Ironclaw.

'Let's see it, then.'

They flew over to the little hollow in the rocks. Ironclaw's beak dropped open. The dirt-board had been restored to its former glory, but it was covered with calculations.

'I see,' said Thornbeak.

Ironclaw wasn't listening. He put his head on one side and studied the figures. After a moment or two he saw a mistake. 'Granitelegs,' he said. 'He never could get the hang of probability. The second half of all this is rubbish.'

'You said the dirt-board had been ruined.'

'Granitelegs must have reversed the spell,' said Ironclaw. 'Well, this is excellent.' He started to erase some of the numbers.

'Hold on,' said Thornbeak, 'you can't just rub out all his work.'

'Why not? It's no good.'

'Granitelegs has done you a favour,' said Thornbeak. 'The least you can do is give him a chance to copy down the correct part.'

Ironclaw glared at her. 'But I've got something really important I want to work on.'

'What?'

'It's a present. For you.'

Thornbeak looked sceptical. 'What is it, exactly? A distribution graph for prey animals? I'm not doing all the hunting, Ironclaw, however easy you try and make it for me.'

'It's a cataloguing system for the books in the library.'

Thornbeak stared at him. 'But I can't use the library any more.'

This obviously hadn't entered Ironclaw's head.

'Oh never mind,' said Thornbeak. 'Tell me about it.'

Ironclaw told her.

'That's really sweet of you,' said Thornbeak, when he'd finished. 'And if the library is ever open again, I shall get it up and running. It's a splendid solution. Let's have lunch.'

Ironclaw watched as Thornbeak sliced up a haunch with her beak. She could even do that elegantly. She was quite a hen – and her hindquarters were still the most attractive he'd ever seen.

They were just finishing their meal when Felix and Betony appeared over the ridge. Betony was wearing her old tunic and trousers, which she'd washed. She'd left Agrimony's dress behind; it was totally impractical.

'We've got a result,' said Felix.

Ironclaw looked astonished. 'I didn't know you were working on anything.'

Felix laughed. 'It's just an otherworld expression. I've found out where we have to go for both a royalty-location spell and a countercharm to the marble thing.'

'Where?'

'West. We need a riddle-paw.'

'A riddle-paw?' Thornbeak looked surprised. 'I didn't

114

think there were any left in this part of the world.'

'Her name's Leona,' said Felix. 'Socrates told me about her.'

'Riddle-paws are dangerous,' said Thornbeak. 'They won't even enter into a conversation until you've solved one of their puzzles.'

'What happens if you get it wrong?' asked Betony.

'They eat you.'

Ironclaw laughed. 'I've yet to find someone who can set *me* a puzzle I can't solve.'

'Excellent,' said Felix. 'You'll take us there, then?'

Ironclaw looked from Felix to Thornbeak and back again. He'd been so excited about getting back to his dirt-board he'd forgotten all about the need to find the king and queen, and he certainly hadn't bargained for *this*.

'I think you asked for that, Ironclaw,' chuckled Thornbeak. 'Yes, Felix, of course we'll take you.'

'We've packed our rucksacks already,' said Betony.

'No one knows exactly what lies to the west,' complained Ironclaw. 'There's forest on the slope of Tromm Fell, but beyond that there's desert. And beyond that ...'

'Sheer adventure,' said Betony, her green eyes sparkling with anticipation.

'Hmph,' said Ironclaw.

It took them a little while to get organized, as Thornbeak insisted on Ironclaw taking some of his gold with him.

Eventually both brazzles strapped on bulging leg-pouches, and they were off. The flight wasn't terribly arduous, as they were gliding downhill most of the time, but before long the sun turned crimson and sank beneath the horizon. They would have to camp in the forest for the first night; the following day they would be flying across the desert.

They found a glade carpeted with dusk-flowers that nodded their heads in time to the evening bird-chorus. The trills and warbles were rather unusual – Felix could swear that one bird was singing a definite tune, and another was practising arpeggios. Moonbeam moths were performing synchronized aerobatics as Betony lit a fire, and started to toast some bread and cheese. Ironclaw and Thornbeak went off to hunt before it got too dark, and Felix and Betony settled themselves comfortably against their rucksacks, and had supper.

'How did you feel, when *your* parents were turned to stone?' asked Felix.

'Fed up,' said Betony. 'Tansy's a lousy cook, and Ramson's useless at housework.'

'Didn't you miss them?'

'Not really,' said Betony, poking the fire with a stick. 'They always seemed to be busy in the dispensary, mixing potions and stuff.'

Felix looked shocked.

Betony glanced sideways at him. 'Well, maybe a bit. Tansy was the favourite, you see, because she was so interested in all that. I was the naughty one. And after all, they'll come back to life in what – sixteen years' time. I'll be a famous historian by then, if the library's open again. I shall astound them.' She poked the fire once more, causing a tiny fountain of sparks. 'No one else in my family has ever done anything interesting. What about yours?'

'I had an uncle who climbed mountains.'

'Why?'

Felix laughed. 'Because they were there, I suppose. He died before I was born. My parents may not be as exciting as he must have been, but I think I prefer them that way.'

Betony's expression suggested she thought otherwise. 'It's a pity your parents were too heavy to bring with you,' she said. 'You need a specific countercharm really, otherwise you'll have to try lots of different broad-based ones. Ramson turned Socrates into a sickle when he was little, and then tried to reverse it. Poor old Socrates changed into a toadstool and then a stink tree before my father intervened. Ramson *nearly* managed it, you see – all vegetation, but not precise *enough*. Your parents could turn into humungallies or river-fatties before you hit on the right spell.'

Felix imagined his garden inhabited by a pair of elephants or hippopotamuses. It didn't bear thinking about. Then he remembered the matchbox in his rucksack. 'I brought a sample with me,' he said, taking it out.

'You chiselled a bit off one of your parents?' cried Betony, aghast. 'It'll stay amputated, Felix, you won't be able to re-attach it.'

Felix laughed. 'I'm not that daft,' he said. 'I brought one of the little creatures that crawled over the statue. A snail.'

'A snail?' said Betony. 'What's that? Oh, let's see, Felix, please, I'd love to have a look at one of your world's creatures.'

Felix unwound the insulating tape, hoping it would stick back again, and very carefully opened the matchbox. The stark white *wrongness* of the snail took him by surprise for some reason, and hit him hard. How many animals in his own world were like this now? Had the contagion spread across London? Across the Channel? Or further still – to Africa, Asia, America?

'Wow,' said Betony, staring at the little marble gastropod. 'That's seriously weird.'

Felix forced himself to concentrate on the here and now and said, 'Don't you have anything similar?'

Betony shook her head. Then she stiffened.

Felix looked round. 'What is it?'

'I heard something.'

'What?'

'A squeak.'

Felix grinned. Surely Betony wasn't frightened of mice – or whatever this world's equivalent was? He suddenly noticed that the birds had stopped singing. All that remained was a deep, velvety silence; it was as though the landscape itself were holding its breath. Betony was sitting very still, her head slightly on one side, listening. Perhaps

118

her ears are sharper than mine, thought Felix, and his smile widened. The tops of them certainly were; delicate little elfin points.

Betony swallowed. Her spine had begun to prickle, and her customary bravado was wearing very thin all of a sudden. She kept on listening, as hard as she could. The eerie silence was broken once by the distant call of a night-hawk, then it closed round them again. She threw another handful of twigs on to the fire – but they must have been damp, because instead of blazing up they nearly snuffed it out, and a cloud of smoke billowed out instead.

Felix heard the high-pitched attack squeak a split second before he saw the dark shape dive out of the trees towards Betony. She raised her hands above her head, and tried to ward it off. Felix had no idea what the creature was; to him, it just looked like a large bat. Then, to his amazement, Betony burst into tears.

The shape hovered above her, its leathery wings beating, waiting for another chance to strike. Then it dived again, squeaking, its nasty little face creased with excitement, its fangs clearly visible, even in the gloom. As it skimmed past her it stuck out its tongue, and licked a tear from the end of her nose. Betony stood up, flailed her arms wildly around her head, and caught it a glancing blow.

The creature fluttered to the ground, and Felix got his first real look at it. It was an ugly little thing. Its face was dark grey and leathery, its fangs very white by comparison.

The face wasn't bat-like, though – it was almost human, apart from the glowing red eyes. The ears were out of proportion, huge; the skin inside was so creased and folded they looked more like flowers than ears.

'It's a vamprey, isn't it?' said Felix, leaping to his feet. 'A shadow-beast.'

Betony had edged round to the other side of the fire. She was still crying, which wasn't like her at all. 'Vamprey attacks are very rare,' she sobbed. 'I don't know what to do.'

I do, thought Felix, and he seized a branch and swung it as hard as he could at the tiny target. He missed. The vamprey slithered to one side, took off again and vanished into the gloom.

'*Fangs and talons*,' wailed Betony. 'I wish I'd paid more attention to shadow-beast studies. I know vampreys bite you, and drain your blood – but they're very fussy about who they feed on, like worrits. Worrits won't eat anything that hasn't died laughing, and vampreys won't kill anyone who … oh, *why* can't I remember? They always come back, you see. And it might bring the rest of the colony with it.'

She tried to recall what her teacher had said, but all she could see was the title of the essay she'd written – *Countering Shadow-beasts*. She'd copied half of it from Agrimony when Agrimony wasn't looking, and got into trouble.

'I think I can guess,' said Felix. 'You hardly ever cry, Betony, and the vamprey was trying to lick your face. I bet *that's* what it wants; tears.'

Betony wiped her eyes with her sleeve, and sniffed. 'Thirteen out of thirteen,' she said. 'I remember now. They're the opposite of worrits – and that's the whole *point* of the attack squeak. They need you to know that they're about to sink their vicious little teeth into you, so that they can lap up the tears before they start on the blood. *That's* what I learnt in class; whatever you do, you mustn't cry.'

'OK,' said Felix, handing her a tissue. 'Smile.'

Betony looked at the tissue, perplexed. 'What's this?'

Felix started to explain, but his explanation was cut short by a whoosh that rapidly increased in volume as hundreds of vampreys swept out of the trees and homed in on them. The chorus of attack squeaks filled the air with shrill piercing cries, and countless leathery wings were suddenly beating around their heads.

7

Felix took a firmer grip on the branch he was holding, lashed out at the vampreys with it and yelled, 'Why is grass dangerous? Because it's full of blades!' He managed to fell one vamprey with the fore-stroke and then another with the back swing, and he felt very pleased with himself.

Betony forced a wobbly grin and said, 'What happened when the sinistrom fell down the well? He kicked the bucket.'

'Why is history for fruit cakes? Because it's full of dates!'

The jokes were appalling, but they were doing the trick. The vampreys were just flitting aimlessly about the glade now; they weren't diving down to attack.

'Why did the creepy-biter swallow a candle?' gabbled Betony. 'For light refreshment!'

'Which shadow-beasts are the most artistic?' added Felix, trying to adapt his own world's jokes as best he could. 'Vampreys! They're good at drawing blood!'

Wrong joke. The smile left Betony's face.

The vampreys swooped towards them again, but then, suddenly and inexplicably, they turned in mid-air and left.

Felix glanced up, and saw two dark shapes descending rapidly, with occasional forays to snap at something. Ironclaw and Thornbeak landed in a flurry of fur and feathers, firing anxious questions at them, and asking whether either of them had been bitten.

Betony had regained her composure as quickly as ever. 'Nope,' she said breezily. 'We're fine; we just told each other jokes.'

Thornbeak looked impressed.

But Felix was looking gutted. 'The matchbox,' he said. 'It's gone.'

'Are you sure?' said Betony. 'We might have kicked it or something.'

'What's a matchbox?' asked Ironclaw.

Felix described it, and told them what was in it. The four of them then searched the glade, but to no avail.

'Why would a vamprey want a marble snail?' said Felix. 'It doesn't make sense.'

'They collect things,' said Thornbeak. 'No one knows why.'

No one knows why jackdaws collect things, either, thought Felix. Then something occurred to him. 'Surely,' he said, 'the moment the vamprey touched the snail, it would turn to marble as well?'

'Remember, a vamprey's a shadow-beast,' said Thornbeak. 'Ordinary spells don't work on them.'

'I *need* that snail,' said Felix desperately. 'What am I going to do?'

Thornbeak and Ironclaw looked at one another.

'Someone's going to have to enter the vamprey's roost-cave, aren't they,' said Betony, 'and get it back.'

Ironclaw sighed. 'I suppose it'll have to be me, won't it? Brazzles are meant to be immune to vamprey bites; something to do with our feathers. I've never put it to the test, mind you.' Being heroic seemed to be an ongoing requirement rather than a one-off event, which was depressing.

'We'll do it in daylight,' said Thornbeak, with an uncharacteristically fond glance in Ironclaw's direction. 'No sense in taking unnecessary risks. I'll fly up high just before daybreak – then I'll be able to see them streaming back to their roost like smoke, and we'll know where to find them.'

Felix and Betony curled up under Thornbeak's protective wing, and went to sleep.

Early the next morning Thornbeak circled above the forest, using her magnifying vision to scan the trees below. There was a pale streak of pink in the sky to the east – dawn was imminent, and she didn't have long. A sunrise-bird started to sing somewhere; then another and another. She clenched her talons with impatience, and widened her search. The sky was getting lighter all the time. Suddenly, all the birds fell

124

silent. A grainy shadow was crossing the canopy, dividing and reuniting like a shoal of fish. That's them, thought Thornbeak, and she hovered above them, watching. The leading edge of the smudge sharpened to a point. Then the whole shadow changed shape like a leech, squeezed itself through what was presumably a crack in a rock-face, and disappeared.

Thornbeak spiralled down, so that she could memorize a few landmarks. A skeleton tree, victim of some thunderstorm; a great grey crag, criss-crossed with fissures; a pool, its surface still and dark and oddly menacing. It wasn't a cheerful sort of place. She landed in front of the rock-face, and surveyed it.

The vampreys' entrance crevice was clear enough, from all the droppings fanning out beneath it. That was the good news. The bad news was that it was far too narrow for a brazzle to negotiate. She went over to it and peered through the chink into the gloom, hoping she would be able to see another exit. It was too dark to see anything much, although she could hear the rustle of leathery wings as the creatures settled themselves on their roosts to sleep away the daylight. There couldn't be another exit, there wasn't enough light.

A rush of air made her jump, as a straggler tried to skim past her and make it home. She caught a glimpse of its vicious little face; Snakeweed on a bad day, but with red eyes instead of green. She snapped at it, but it was too fast for her, and it slithered through the crack with a triumphant squeak.

Thornbeak took off, and flew back to the camp with a heavy heart. It was too narrow. One of the youngsters was going to have to venture inside; she could donate a feather or two, which would help, but plucked feathers wouldn't be as powerful as ones that were still attached to their owner. In the end it was going to depend on the strength of mind of whoever accepted the challenge.

Betony immediately assumed that *she* would be the one who would have to retrieve the snail. Felix had been so ill the previous year that she was used to taking charge. 'Right,' she said, 'I'll tuck the brazzle feathers into my cap, so I'm protected from above, and—'

'Hold on a minute,' said Felix. 'This is *my* problem.'

Betony stared at him.

'The snail was *my* responsibility.'

'But ...'

'Not only that,' Felix went on, 'you have a lifetime's dread of vampreys – I don't. I'm far more likely to be able to laugh at them than you are.'

'You'll be saying that boys don't cry next.'

'No I won't. I don't think crying's a sign of weakness, as it happens. It shows that you *feel* things. I've done plenty of crying in my time – let's face it, I had plenty of reason to – and I'm not ashamed of it. But I do think I stand a better chance of fighting back the tears this time than you do.'

'He's right, Betony,' said Thornbeak. 'I think we'd better have breakfast. I want the sun high in the sky before we attempt this – vampreys won't come out in daylight, so they won't pursue him.'

Betony wasn't quite sure how she felt about all this. She skewered some mushrooms on a stick and held them over the fire, watching them darken and shrivel. On the one hand she was relieved; the prospect of entering a cave full of vampreys was very scary. But on the other hand she had her pride to consider, and the wonderful story that would now be Felix's, not hers. A smell of burning interrupted her thoughts, and she had to throw the mushrooms away and start on another lot.

Thornbeak gave Felix two of her feathers, so Ironclaw gave him four. Felix smiled to himself; Ironclaw just couldn't help being competitive. He stuck them in his cap, and Betony handed him a skewerful of mushrooms. He'd forgotten how good they were – clotted cream on a stick, with a hint of paprika and lemon. He followed this with a drink of water from a nearby stream; then he washed his face and hands and fastened his rucksack.

Ironclaw fluffed out his feathers, glanced at the sky and announced, 'Well. We can't just sit in our droppings all day. Let's go.'

They took off. They hadn't been in the air for very long before Thornbeak called out, 'That's the tree ... and there's the cliff!' She started to descend.

It seemed to get colder the lower they got, which didn't make sense. When they landed by the cave the sun had gone in, and everything looked drab and depressing.

Betony glanced at the pond, and shivered. The water was dark, too dark; it looked very deep. There were no plants growing on the banks, but there were a lot of bones scattered around. She didn't look at them too closely.

'OK,' said Felix. 'No point hanging around.'

'What's wrong with you if your nose runs and your feet smell?' asked Betony.

Felix looked blank.

'You're built upside down!'

Felix burst out laughing – more from Betony's attempt to protect him than from the joke itself. Then, whilst the smile was still on his face, he slipped through the crack in the rock.

There were tiny red lights dotted all over the cave's ceiling. For a moment it just seemed bizarre; then a couple of them moved, and he realized they were eyes. He switched on his torch. A vamprey was hanging upside-down on the rock wall just above his head, watching him, its claws hooked over a tiny ledge. It opened its mouth and snarled, but as it was upside-down the snarl looked more like a grin. Felix grinned back, and the vamprey seemed to lose interest in him.

OK, thought Felix, I can handle this. He swept the beam round the cave, and was amazed to see piles and piles of junk on the floor, spattered with filth. At least, it looked like junk at first glance. Broken pottery, a dented chalice, a bent arrow. A rusty spoon, a chipped crucible, a tangle-cap … He shuddered, and the vamprey on the wall turned its head towards him. He forced his mouth back into a smile, and the vamprey turned away again. He started to pick his way through the bits and pieces, noting that not everything was junk. A nugget of gold, a silver necklace, a copper brooch ... it was going to take for ever to find one tiny matchbox. The place stank; the dirt was a century's worth of vamprey droppings, some old and dry, some black and tarry and smelling pungently of ammonia. He took a tissue out of his pocket, and fashioned it into a mask by making holes in it and threading a bit of string through it. If he breathed in too much of the stuff he might start sneezing, and his eyes would water.

Another chalice, a belt studded with bronze stars, a little book ... He picked it up. It was an instruction manual for something called a storm-oracle. He let it drop. A splintered wooden sheath for a scythe, a shoe; something that resembled a miniature crystal ball, with a brass band round the middle. There was some lettering on it, although most of it had worn away. A,C, L, E ... The last part of the word *oracle*, maybe? He put it in his pocket, and went back for the booklet. He could study it later; anything involving magical theory would be interesting.

A jade bracelet, a leather strap that looked like part of a cuddyak bridle, yet another chalice ... a matchbox. He heaved a sigh of relief, and bent down.

It was empty.

The vampreys overhead began to stir, their leathery wings rustling like dry leaves. A small shower of the disgusting black droppings rained down, and Felix wiped them off as best he could and put the matchbox in his pocket. It's just a setback, he said to himself, nothing more, don't get upset about it. If the matchbox is here it's almost certain that the snail is, too. With the mask on the vampreys could no longer see whether he was smiling, so he made himself laugh out loud. The laugh sounded hollow and insincere.

Not insincere enough, however. He saw the movement out of the corner of his eye, and swung the beam of the torch towards it, his heart suddenly beating a lot faster. A big black dog stepped out of the shadows at the far end of the cave. It couldn't be a dog, of course – it had to be a worrit. He had another shadow-beast to deal with, one that would try to make him laugh himself to death.

Checkmate, thought Felix. If I laugh, the worrit will get me. If I cry, the vampreys will.

The worrit looked even sillier than the one he'd seen the previous year. It had the mis-matched eyes – one yellow, one green, but its black fur was decorated with polka-dots, and the hair on its head was arranged in lots of daft little plaits that stuck out at right-angles. It was wearing a ruff round its neck, which kept springing out of position and tickling its nose. To counteract this, the worrit blew at it every so often. Felix felt the giggles start to rise within him, and the ominous rustling of the vampreys died away again.

Felix suddenly remembered the way the riddle-paw had dealt with a worrit. What had the book said? *She told him jokes intil he laughed himself to death.*

'Hi,' said the worrit.

'Not particularly,' he countered. 'In fact, I'd say meeting you was the low point of the day so far.'

The worrit hesitated.

Felix ripped off his makeshift mask, stuck out his tongue, spread his hands palm-forwards either side of his ears and wiggled his fingers. 'What's this?' he asked.

'A vamprey with indigestion?'

Felix had to struggle not to double up with laughter, for that was probably exactly what he *did* look like. He started to back away towards the cave entrance. He couldn't win here, the best thing was just to get out. The worrit took a couple of steps forward, tripped over its own feet and fell down. When it got up, it had a diamond bracelet hanging over one ear.

Felix fought to control himself. Then he said, 'Where can you find a lot more diamonds than that?'

The worrit's furry black eyebrows drew together in an expression of consternation.

'In a pack of cards,' said Felix. Only a few more steps to go, now. Then he realized that the worrit didn't have the faintest idea what a pack of cards *was*. It started to do a dance that Felix remembered was called the star squirm. He mustn't laugh, mustn't laugh. He dug his nails into the palm of

131

his hand, but he did it so forcibly that the tears sprang to his eyes. A sound like breakers on a beach swelled from above, as the vampreys smelt the salt and prepared to attack. Felix turned and ran. As he sprinted for the exit he saw something small and white on the ground, half-hidden by a dagger. It was the snail. He let his sleeve drop down over his hand, bent low mid-stride, knocked the dagger out of the way, and seized hold of the snail. There was a sudden rush of wings, but the brazzle feathers in his cap acted like a force field round his head. The vampreys would have to find another area of unprotected skin, and they flittered round him, confused. Then he was squeezing himself through the gap, and the air outside was sweet and clean and his friends were waiting for him.

'Did you get it?' asked Betony, before he'd even had time to catch his breath.

Felix held up the snail to show her. He felt perfectly all right, he wasn't turning to marble, his sleeve had protected him. Everything had worked out OK.

'You're bleeding,' said Betony, pointing to Felix's hand. She looked far more upset about it than was strictly necessary.

Thornbeak stiffened. 'Let me see,' she said.

Felix put the snail back in the matchbox, rolled up his sleeve and looked at his hand in astonishment. The blood had trickled down his wrist, warm and wet and sticky. He hadn't felt anything bite him, but the rush of adrenalin as he'd raced for the exit could have had a numbing effect. 'Are vampreys poisonous?' he asked, feeling weak all of a sudden.

Ironclaw started to say something, but Thornbeak stamped on his foot.

'*Tell me*,' said Felix, turning to Betony.

Betony bit her lip, and looked at Thornbeak.

'Wash it in the pool,' said Thornbeak. 'I need to see if there are any puncture marks.'

Felix rinsed his hand in the cold dark water, and held it up for her to inspect. The blood started to well out of the cut again immediately – but it was a cut, not a couple of tiny holes.

'*Blazing feathers*, that's a relief,' said Thornbeak.

'The snail was lying under a dagger,' said Felix, remembering. 'I must have caught the edge of the blade as I pushed it aside. What would have happened to me, if it *had* been a vamprey bite?'

'Vampreys thrive on blood, sweat and tears,' said Ironclaw cheerfully. 'But they're only tiddly little things really. If they attack in a group, they can drain your blood fast enough to kill you straight away. If it's one on its own, it has to wait for the bite to take effect. The wound won't heal, you run a fever, start sweating, feel as limp as a waterlogged feather, and burst into tears. Starters, main course and pudding – all in one.'

'Thank you for that, Ironclaw,' said Thornbeak dryly.

'Come here,' said Betony to Felix, with a relieved smile.

133

'I can fix that.' She wrapped a curious ribbed leaf around the afflicted finger, and recited the standard healing incantation. Then she washed his shirt for him in the pool, and wrung it out. Felix took another one out of his rucksack – the wet one he tied to a strap by one sleeve. It would billow out and dry off when they were in the air. Five minutes later the cut had healed and they were on their way west once more, in their hunt for news of a riddle-paw.

The forest gave way to foothills and scrub, and then to proper desert. It was starkly beautiful; dune after dune of red-gold sand curved into interlocking crescent moons, with corrugated plains of it between, the ripples splitting and converging and dividing into complicated patterns. Now and again they flew over bare rocky outcrops. These jagged formations rose out of the desert like sets of molars, the red stone striated with parallel streaks of purple. They stopped for lunch beneath one of them, taking advantage of the shade. It was still incredibly hot, however, despite the wind that raised little eddies of sand, and they got through rather more of their water than they'd have liked. No one was particularly hungry.

'Hotter than a fire-breather's backfire,' observed Ironclaw, fanning himself with a wing.

'You do have a way with words, don't you Ironclaw?' said Thornbeak acidly.

'Oh, thanks,' said Ironclaw, the sarcasm totally lost on him.

'Talking of words,' said Felix to Thornbeak, 'there's been something I've been meaning to ask you. Turpsik said that before you settled on one language for everyone you used to have lots of languages, like we do.'

'That's right,' said Thornbeak. 'There were dozens ... Tangle, Japegrin, Brazzle ... You, presumably, have humungally and bottle-nose and human being?'

'Elephants and dolphins may well have their own languages,' said Felix, 'but we haven't deciphered them yet. It's only human beings who use words in my world. What I want to know is how you decided on English.'

'English?'

'That's what I speak.'

'Do you know,' said Thornbeak, 'I take everyone speaking the same tongue so much for granted that it never occurred to me how odd it was that you spoke it too.' She laughed suddenly. 'Oh, *I* see. *Blazing feathers*. Well well well.'

'Well?' said Betony.

'Well?' said Felix.

'Well?' said Ironclaw.

'When different communities started trading with one another,' said Thornbeak, with a dry chuckle, 'the guilds all got together and decided that one language would be a sensible idea. But they couldn't agree which one it should be – every single species argued the case for its own tongue. The most distinguished sorcerer at that time was a lickit by the name of Sugarcrust, who was said to have invented time-travel. He offered to go shopping for a language that had fallen into disuse, or hadn't yet been invented, so that *everyone* had to learn it from scratch. What he came back with was – what did you call it? English?'

Felix nodded. Then he smiled. 'He wasn't time-travelling at all, was he?' he said, following Thornbeak's train of thought. 'He'd discovered the Divide spell, and he'd been to England.'

Thornbeak nodded. '*Sugarcrust* thought he'd travelled into the future, though. He stored all the words he'd learned in a jinx-box, which was a bit silly, as jinxes are notoriously unreliable, and the storage was far from perfect.'

'So that's why we call a rhinoceros a river-fatty, and a pixie a japegrin,' said Betony, showing off.

'Fascinating as all this is,' said Ironclaw, who obviously wasn't fascinated in the slightest, 'I think we ought to get going.'

They took off again, but it wasn't until the sun was nearing the horizon that they began to see vegetation again. The plants they saw were like the cacti of Felix's own world; the tall branching saguaro, familiar from Westerns, and the paddle-shaped prickly pear. They weren't identical, though – the flesh of the saguaros was a dusky violet colour, and that of the prickly pears pale lemon. Some of them were in flower – huge, extravagant blooms of bright scarlet and peacock blue.

The sand here was firmer, interspersed with gravelly bits and boulders. There was a range of mountains in the distance, but they weren't anything like as high as the Andrian mountains. The brazzles looked for somewhere to camp that would be sheltered, for the wind was blowing more strongly and no one wanted to be sandpapered all night long. Eventually Ironclaw spotted a dried-up riverbed, and they landed.

Felix wondered whether to say anything. He knew that a dried-up riverbed was called a wadi, and his geography teacher had told him that people who camped in wadis could get swept away in the middle of the night by a wall of water. The sky was clear, though, and it didn't look as though it had rained in this area for years. They settled themselves down, and had supper. This time it was Ironclaw alone who did the hunting – Thornbeak wasn't going to leave the youngsters on their own again, not after what had happened the last time. He returned with some gazelle-type creature, and he and Thornbeak retired to a polite distance to eat.

Felix looked up at the sky. The stars were coming out, with that extraordinary brilliance peculiar to deserts. They munched on their bread and cheese, and squealed every time they spotted a shooting star. Felix suddenly remembered the things he'd brought in his rucksack, so he got out the newspaper, and gave it to Thornbeak, and then he passed the chocolate to Betony.

'Weird,' she said, as she rolled it round her mouth. 'We don't have anything remotely like this. I suppose it's quite nice.'

It had never occurred to Felix that chocolate might be an acquired taste.

'Hey, look,' said Betony, pointing.

Felix glanced over towards the mountains. Lightning was forking down from the sky, silhouetting the peaks in front of it. The storm was so far away that they couldn't hear any thunder at all. It was like a firework display just for them, and they watched it, enthralled.

'*Fangs and talons*,' swore Thornbeak suddenly.

The others turned to look at her.

'What sort of a world do you live in, Felix?' said Thornbeak, glancing up from the newspaper. 'I assume that these journals place things in order of importance?'

'Well, yes,' said Felix nervously.

'The front page is all about the result of a game of something called football. The second page is about some people called film stars. It's only as we get further in that there's a report about an earthquake, and a scientific breakthrough. Am I missing something? Is football a way of settling international disputes, perhaps?'

'No,' said Felix miserably.

'Listen to this,' said Thornbeak. '*The centre forward's amazing new hairstyle is already being adopted by teenagers up and down the country. ...* That's page one. And then, on page seven: '*Doctor Emily Parsons has upset environmentalists again. Her company's latest discovery is likely to make the Greens turn red with anger. ...*' What discovery? They don't even tell us what she was working on.'

'They probably think it's too difficult for their readers to understand.'

'I see. So newspapers are just for people who aren't very bright. Television is more challenging, I imagine. Which programmes are the most popular?'

Felix told her about soaps and reality-shows, feeling desperately ashamed of his own species.

Thornbeak looked more and more horrified. 'Is this what mass communications lead to, Felix? World-wide brain-death?'

'There are some good things,' said Felix, and he explained about the Royal Institution Christmas lectures, and documentaries. But he had to add that not that many people watched them.

'I can see why you're so worried about the principles of magic leaking into your world,' said Thornbeak. 'This is a very important quest, isn't it? I can just picture it – magic as mass entertainment, making fools of people for a cheap laugh. Or magical weapons, to turn enemies to stone. And that'll lead to more experiments with magic, and effects no one's capable of really understanding because they haven't studied it for long enough. It's not just your parents we'll be saving, it's your whole civilization. If I can grace it with such a title.'

8

Rutherford Aubrey Tripp bumped into Emily Parsons in the canteen at work. It was an up-market sort of canteen, as it was an up-market sort of company. It served unpleasantly healthy food that didn't fill you up, and garnished it with seaweed and samphire and salsify. Rutherford was poking miserably at his herb salad, and wondering why it tasted of fish, when Emily sat down at the next table. She had brown hair and an olive skin, and dark eyes that were set a little too closely together. She was slightly built but very intense, and most of Rutherford's colleagues thought she was a bit scary. He watched her for a moment or two, admiring the way she sliced up her avocado. She wielded her knife like a scalpel, and dissected the flesh with confidence and precision. The last time he'd found an excuse to talk to her she'd demolished one of his latest theories in one sentence, and then laughed at his tie. She was a difficult person to impress.

Suddenly Rutherford remembered the marble wasp, so he fished it out of his briefcase. It would be far better to get *her* to approach *him*, so he unwrapped it and just sat there, looking at it.

After a while she glanced across, and her dark eyes widened in surprise. 'Didn't know you were into sculpture, Rutherford,' she said. 'That looks like a really classy acquisition, which is mildly astonishing, considering your taste in ties.'

'It's not a sculpture,' said Rutherford. 'It's what happens to a wasp when it's zapped by a new insecticide.'

'Wow,' said Emily. 'Something that effective will be quite a little money-spinner. Not on the market yet, though, is it? How did you get hold of it?'

'By accident.'

'Oh yes?' She smiled. 'Oh, I see. A bit of industrial espionage. If you can analyze it before it goes on sale, you might be able to make a cheaper competitor. How are you doing?'

'It's not really my field, is it?'

'True,' said Emily. 'But it is mine.'

Rutherford smiled.

It was surprisingly cold once the sun had disappeared, so Felix and Betony curled up under Thornbeak's wing for the night as Ironclaw's snoring increased in volume. It was Felix who woke first. It took a moment or two to register what was happening, as he was still half-asleep and he was vaguely aware of a warm dampness. His first thought was that he'd had an embarrassing accident, which was something he hadn't done since he'd been cured of his illness. Then he realized that there was far too much water for that; it had reached blood-temperature because it had picked up heat on its long journey from the mountains. The wadi was flooding, and the river was getting deeper with a frightening rapidity.

Thornbeak woke up, and squawked with alarm. Then everything seemed to happen very quickly. It wasn't a sudden wall of water, like a tidal wave, but it was much faster than a tide coming in, and it was carrying twigs and branches that knocked against him as he stood up.

'What is it?' gasped Betony, now also on her feet.

'The river!' yelled Felix. 'We've got to get out!'

The side of the wadi was quite steep. By the time they reached it the water was up to their waists and it was getting hard to make any progress, especially with the rucksacks on their backs. Thornbeak seemed to be in trouble; her feathers had been soaked from beneath. Rain always ran off her with no trouble at all, but this was different. She flapped her wings and screeched for Ironclaw, but he was having the same problem himself. The deeper the water got, the faster it seemed to flow. Felix got a toehold on the bank, climbed up a little way, and stretched his hand down to Betony. Hauling her out was harder work than he'd have thought possible – every muscle seemed stretched to breaking point, and both their hands were slick with mud. He could see her face in the moonlight, twisted with effort, and for a while there was just pain and panting and slipperiness. Then she was out, and the two of them scrambled up the bank on their

142

hands and knees and out of danger.

Felix turned his attention to the brazzles, and his eyes widened in horror. The river was in full spate now, and it wasn't just carrying twigs and branches any longer – whole tree trunks were tumbling along, catching on promontories, and freeing themselves again. Ironclaw was trying to reach Thornbeak, but he was no swimmer. Then one huge uprooted tree appeared, travelling very swiftly in the middle of the river, and veering straight towards them.

Both Felix and Betony yelled at the tops of their voices, but there was nothing anyone could do. They watched in disbelief as the tree hit both brazzles head-on, and carried them away and out of sight. It all seemed to have happened in an instant. They both ran along the bank for a little way, but the water was moving much faster than they were, and pursuit was futile.

'It's all my fault,' said Felix bitterly. 'I should have said something.'

'Said what?'

'That wadis can flood really suddenly. I'm such a feather-brained *idiot*, I should have realized. All that lightning we saw in the mountains. Our own personal firework display? Yeah, right. Although it wasn't raining *here*, it must have been pelting down up *there*. What on earth are we going to do?'

'I don't know,' said Betony. Her clothes were sodden, and she was shivering.

'Do you think they could survive something like that?'

'I don't know,' said Betony again.

Felix put his arm round her and they sat on the bank for a while, not speaking. The river rushed by, regardless, and he saw the corpse of some animal pass them. He didn't comment, and he didn't know if Betony had seen. She didn't remark on it, anyway.

After a while he said, 'We're not going to get any sleep after what's happened, so I suggest we start walking downstream. The river will slow down eventually.'

'When it reaches the sea,' said Betony.

'Long before that,' said Felix. 'Come on.'

They trudged on until dawn, one weary footstep after the other. The river was more sluggish now, and they were able to refill their water bottles. Gradually it got shallower and narrower, and piles of debris began to appear, washed up on the newly exposed sandbanks. Felix saw the bodies of two of the gazelle-like creatures, and another animal he couldn't identify, but there were no brazzles.

'Maybe they got out,' he said. 'Maybe they're holed up somewhere, waiting for their feathers to dry.'

'And maybe they're at the bottom of the river.'

The grief was so all-enveloping that it actually numbed him; his face felt abnormally rigid. The gravity of the situation itself was just too enormous for tears. And now they were stranded in a desert, with no hope of retracing their journey – they'd be dead by the evening, in that heat. They just had to go on until it became too hot to walk, find some shelter for the day, and hope.

They carried on walking until the heat became too much, then they selected one of the rocky outcrops, and sat down in the shade. They drank some of their water; not quite enough, really, but they had to ration it. The sky was an unbroken gradation of blue, from cyan at the horizon to ultramarine above, and the silence was complete. Felix looked at Betony and realized that she had been crying, but so quietly that he hadn't noticed. 'I'm going to climb to the top of this crag,' he said, 'before the stone gets so hot it blisters my feet through my shoes. See if I can spot anything of interest.'

'It's almost a sheer face, Felix.'

'I'm not the same person I was this time last year,' said Felix, 'I've got muscles.' He flexed his arm, trying to make her smile. She didn't react. He let his arm drop again and said, 'I've done some rock-climbing. I can see a route up.'

Betony just nodded in a lack-lustre way.

Felix scrambled up the outcrop, thinking his way up it; planning each handhold, testing each tiny support before he put his weight on it. Eventually he made it to the top and stood there for a moment, breathless and triumphant. Then he wondered whether the breathlessness was a sign of anything else. A cold wash of fear went through him, and he sat down so abruptly that he jarred his spine. He sat there for some time, waiting for the dizziness, waiting for that old about-to-pass-out feeling. Gradually his breathing returned to normal. He felt silly and irritated with himself; he was perfectly all right. He stood up again, shaded his eyes, and scanned the landscape. In the distance, a little column of dust was rising. He wished he'd had the sense to bring a pair of binoculars with him – then he wished Ironclaw had been there, with his magnifying vision. And then he did have a good cry, but he made sure he'd finished it before he climbed down to Betony and told her what he'd seen. 'There's a dust column moving in a straight line towards us, at a regular speed,' he said. 'Someone riding some sort of animal is my guess.'

'Yes, but what sort of someone?' said Betony.

After a while, a shape began to emerge from the murk. As they watched the outline did take on the form of an animal, with a rider. If the person was hostile there was nowhere to run anyway, so they stood their ground and waited.

The creature was the same sandy colour as a camel. It had humps, too – but four of them, and the rider was mounted in the middle, although he was almost entirely hidden by his clothing. He had a fierce tanned face, with a tattoo on one cheek and slanting dark eyes. He was wearing a curved scabbard, and there was a spear slotted into a leather loop beside him. Felix swallowed nervously, and tried to appear calm and in control.

'He's a nomad,' whispered Betony. 'I've heard of them, but I've never met one before. And the animal's called

146

a quaddiump.'

'Greetings,' said the nomad. 'This meeting must be as welcome to you as a puddle. What are you doing, all alone on the Skeleton Plain?'

Felix told him what had happened, although he kept quiet about looking for the riddle-paw.

'I have seen no brazzles,' said the nomad. 'But I can take you to the nearest oasis.' The breeze was quite strong, and for a moment the material that swathed his head was blown to one side and a pointed ear revealed itself. He's a member of the elf family, thought Felix, but a different sort of elf to Betony. His skin is brown, his eyes are brown, and his hair is black. The nomad leant down and offered his hand, and Felix climbed up beside him. Betony did likewise, and then they were on their way. The quaddiump moved with a peculiar swaying gait, and it took a while for Felix to acclimatize to it. They didn't stop for lunch – but the nomad shared his gourd of fresh water with them, and some bread and dried fruit.

The sun was sinking low in the sky when they reached the oasis, and the little stone buildings cast long deep blue shadows in the sandy streets. There were palm trees here, proper palm trees with dates on them, and the houses looked like those Felix associated with Moroccan or Tunisian villages, except that they were circular, not square. They eventually came to a halt, and the quaddiump went over to a waterhole and drank deeply.

Betony and Felix thanked the nomad, who directed them to an inn, and said goodbye. The inn was called The Offal House. It was one of the circular buildings, rather larger than the others. The rooms would have made a pattern like the segments of a bisected orange, but with the middle missing, for in the centre was a garden. Low tables and cushions were placed in between little palm trees and flowering plants, and people were sitting on the cushions eating and drinking.

Felix and Betony copied what the others were doing, and found themselves faced by a totally unfamiliar meal, consisting of a rice-like cereal, with vegetables and slivers of something liverish. It was a bit on the slimy side, but it filled them up. 'Paying for this is going to clean us out,' said Betony. 'Ironclaw ...' Her voice faltered. She swallowed, took a deep breath and went on, 'Ironclaw and Thornbeak had the gold in their leg-pouches.'

The next morning, Betony handed over the last of their money to the innkeeper.

'Don't despair,' said Felix. 'I'm going to sell my torch.'

Betony stared at him, aghast. Then she said, 'But Felix, it's scientific. You've always said that you don't want any scientific things on the loose over here, any more than you want magical things in *your* world.'

'The battery will run out eventually. And then it won't work any more.'

'I hope you know what you're doing.'

148

'You've got a better idea, have you?'

Betony scowled. 'No. If we're going to find the brazzles we need transport.'

'Find them? You're optimistic. Shouldn't we look for them first?'

Betony bit her lip, and her eyes brimmed with tears. She wiped her hands angrily across her face, and looked away.

'That came out wrong,' said Felix. 'I'm sorry. We mustn't give up hope.'

'I haven't,' sniffed Betony. 'It's just that I lost my necklace in the wadi, too.'

Felix felt even guiltier. He'd had no idea that the shells he'd strung together on a silver chain the previous year had meant that much to her. 'I'll get you another,' he said. 'I promise. One that will make Agrimony emerald with envy.'

'It'll cost you,' said Betony, with watery smile. 'Agrimony's envy doesn't come cheap.'

They made their way to the market, and offered the torch to one of the traders. He asked a lot of questions about it, and Felix felt he had to come clean and explain that the torch wouldn't work for ever.

'It is like a glass offal-dish, then,' said the trader. 'Once it is broken it cannot be mended. How much do you want for it?'

Betony took a deep breath. 'Ten gold pieces.'

'Ten gold pieces?' squealed the trader. 'Would you beggar me? It is better to itch all over than endure the worries of poverty. Five.'

'Eight,' said Betony. 'And it's worth twice that. It's a scientific instrument.'

The haggling went on for a while longer, but eventually they settled on seven gold pieces. As they were about to leave, Betony asked the trader where they might find a riddle-paw.

His eyes widened. 'No idea.'

'No idea at all?'

'Go to Kaflabad. It's the biggest town for miles, someone there may be able to help you.'

'Thanks,' said Betony, stuffing the coins deep into her pocket. 'Right,' she said, as they walked back across the market square, 'if we're going to look for Ironclaw and Thornbeak first, quaddiumps aren't going to be much use. We need something that can fly.'

'A fire-breather?'

'Yes. Let's find the stables, and see what they've got.'

But there weren't any fire-breathers; the stables were just for quaddiumps. They found a café and sat at one of the tables, drinking a herbal infusion and wondering what to do next. A nomad noticed Felix's blue eyes, and asked his name.

'Felix,' said Felix.

'Felix what?'

'Felix Sanders.'

'Felix Sanders what?'

'Just Felix Sanders.'

'We have three names,' said the nomad. 'I am Fettle Fottle F'dal.'

'I have a middle name,' said Felix. He didn't like it much, so he always abbreviated it. 'It's Matt.'

'Ah,' said Fettle. 'We, too, often name our children after a beloved possession that has died.'

Felix had to think about that for a moment – then he realized that Fettle was probably referring to a magic carpet. Suddenly, he remembered the one he'd encountered the previous year, which had been employed as a lift at the conference centre in Tiratattle.

'Did your parents replace their carpet?' asked Fettle.

'No,' said Felix, not really concentrating as he was wondering whether a magic carpet might be the answer to their transport problem. 'They got a car.'

'Ah,' said Fettle, 'a *car*. Is this a big car-pet?'

'Not exactly,' said Felix.

'And did it have a good sense of humour? A carpet is like an onion: it can make you laugh or make you cry.'

'It broke down on a level crossing once,' said Felix. 'I suppose you could call that having a warped sense of humour.'

Betony kicked him on the ankle.

'Sorry,' said Felix, 'I'm a bit preoccupied. Is there somewhere you can buy magic carpets round here?'

Fettle gave them directions, and they finished their drinks and made their way to the bazaar.

Betony cheered up a bit. She'd never ridden on a magic

carpet, and they were doing something positive about finding the brazzles. They went to a storeroom, and surveyed the selection of floor-coverings on show.

'Is the only difference their size?' asked Betony.

'Certainly not!' answered a high female voice indignantly.

Felix gulped. The speaker seemed to be a small red and cream mat.

'Some of us have enhancements,' said a deeper voice. This came from a multi-coloured rug the size of a double bed.

'And some of us, no names mentioned, are second or even *third*-hand,' said a rush mat.

'Experience of life is an added bonus, not a disadvantage,' replied the multi-coloured rug gravely.

Reject that one, thought Felix. No sense of humour.

'I'm a racer,' boasted a long thin carpet with a short pile. 'Came second in the T.T. last year.'

Felix's mouth dropped open. The T.T. was the name of a motorcycle race on the Isle of Man.

'The Textile Trophy,' explained the racer.

'You need a licence to pilot a racer,' said Betony, pointing to a notice on the wall.

'You don't need one to fly *me*,' said another carpet. This one was a beautiful cherry red, with an intricate blue and cream design in the centre, and its fibres were so silky that they gleamed when the light caught them. There was a white fringe of tassels at either end.

'Let me introduce myself,' said the rug, its voice

emanating from different bits of its surface. 'I'm brand new, and I'm the very latest design. Top of the range. My name is Nimblenap; Nimby for short.'

For the first time since the brazzles' disappearance, Felix burst out laughing.

The rug rippled with displeasure. 'What's wrong with Nimby?'

'It's an acronym,' said Felix. 'Not In My Back Yard.'

'I can land just about anywhere,' said the carpet, offended. 'From the smallest back yard to the most inaccessible mountain ledge.'

'Felix is from another world,' said Betony, not wishing to waste time in explanations.

'*Well, shuttle my weft,*' exclaimed the rug in an awe-struck voice. 'What an honour it is to meet you.'

'Creep,' said the rush mat.

'Smarmy git,' said someone else.

'We'll take the polite one,' said Felix, pointing at the cherry red rug.

The haggling took a long time, but eventually a price was agreed: four gold pieces in exchange for the rug known as Nimby.

The carpet undulated with pleasure, and followed them outside like a hovercraft. They climbed aboard. Felix was a little apprehensive – although Nimby was large enough for them both to lie down if they felt like it, a tilt of more than thirty degrees was going to be bad news.

Their purchase took off, and the oasis rapidly became a tiny speck. 'Where to?' he enquired.

'There's a big wadi to the east. Can you find it, and fly along its length? We're looking for a couple of brazzles.'

'Your wish is my command,' replied Nimby. 'Hey, I've

been wanting to say that for ages. You're my very first masters, you see.'

Felix suddenly realized that the rug was going to have to bank sharply to go in the right direction, but there was nothing to hold on to. He needn't have worried. The sides of the carpet bent upwards, so that they were travelling in a sort of cup. The rug completed its manoeuvre with commendable smoothness, and flattened out again. Felix heaved a sigh of relief.

'I can even create a roof for you, if it rains,' said Nimby proudly. 'Not that it ever does round here, of course.'

It was a depressing reminder of the storm in the mountains, and conversation ground to a halt.

They found the wadi with no difficulty. The water level had dropped considerably, and they followed the course of the river until it dried up completely. Nothing.

'I think we'd have seen *something* if they'd drowned,' said Felix, trying to be optimistic. 'Brazzles are huge, and the water's not very deep any more. We'd have seen a couple of humps, surely?'

'Well what's happened to them, then?'

'They're probably looking for *us*.'

'Maybe something's eaten them.'

'It would have had to make quick work of it,' Felix pointed out.

'A pack of somethings, then. I don't know what scavengers you get in deserts, but I bet there are some.'

'There certainly are,' said Nimby, trying to be helpful, and he described a creature that sounded more like a sabre-toothed tiger than anything else – except for the fact that it had two heads, and six legs.

'Shut *up*,' said Betony. 'We don't need to hear things like that right at this moment.'

'Oh dear,' said the carpet. 'Have I put my fringe in it? I

should have added that there haven't been any seen round here for ages. Where do you want me to go now?'

'Kaflabad,' said Felix.

'Oh, how excellent,' said the carpet. 'I'm really going to see the world with you two, aren't I?'

'How *do* you see things?' queried Felix. 'You don't have eyes like us.'

'Sensory receptors all over the place,' said the carpet proudly. 'Woven in. Oh, by the way, you mustn't let me get too wet, or I lose my voice.'

Felix stifled a giggle. A carpet that could catch a cold?

'I speak with my fibres, you see,' the rug explained. 'By rubbing them against one another.'

Betony gritted her teeth and scowled, 'Are we just going to abandon all hope of finding Ironclaw and Thornbeak, then?'

'Of course not,' said Felix. 'But they won't know where *we* are, so they'll try and find the riddle-paw, because that's the only rendezvous that makes sense.'

It did make sense, and Betony nodded.

9

The carpet had to cross the mountains to reach Kaflabad, but it wasn't anything like the ordeal for Felix that crossing the Andrian mountains had been the previous year. Pale green crystalline formations protruded from frost-shattered rocks, sparkling in the sunlight and dazzling the eyes with their brightness. They were like no other mountains Felix had ever seen – staggeringly beautiful but impossible to climb, with their razor-sharp pinnacles of clear olive-green crystal. Once on the other side of them, they could see Kaflabad in the distance.

'The buildings are enormous,' breathed Betony, as they drew closer. 'Bigger than the palace in Andria, even.'

Felix could hardly believe his eyes. The buildings rose like wedding cakes, tier upon tier, each level slighter smaller than the last, clearly visible above the city wall. Some were rectangular, some were square, and some were pyramid-shaped. Narrow ramps wound their way up the walls, and he could just make out people – and quaddiumps – toiling their way to the top. The number of tiers varied considerably, but one of the buildings was absolutely enormous. They're ziggurats, he thought, just like the ones the Ancient Sumerians built. I saw a picture once, in a Bible.

'I probably ought to land in the main square,' said Nimby. 'There will be a carpet rack there somewhere. Nobody can steal me, of course – I belong to you, and I won't unroll for anyone else.' He began his descent, and Felix saw other carpets flying around with people sitting on them, although none of them was as big or luxurious as Nimblenap. Most of them were just doormats, really.

The buildings in the square were mainly two-tiered, with a balcony running all the way round. The carpet rack was clearly visible; a set of glass shelves, with a transparent roof of some sort over the top. As soon as they disembarked, Nimby rolled himself up, and they placed him on one of the shelves.

'Parking costs one silver piece per day,' said the stallholder, bustling over. He would have been good-looking in any world; hair as black and glossy as a raven's wing, skin the colour of runny honey, features as fine and chiselled as a Greek statue's. A faint perfume seemed to follow him – nothing cheap or tacky or flowery; sandalwood, maybe. He wasn't a kind of being with whom Felix was familiar.

Betony passed over a gold coin, and the stallholder gave them their change.

Felix glanced round the square. Apart from a few nomads, which he identified by their plain bright clothes and the scarves concealing their faces, all the people were the same race as the stallholder. 'What *is* he?' Felix whispered to Betony.

'An amberly,' she whispered back.

The women were tall and slim, and they moved with a flowing grace. They wore turbans made of the same patterned material as their clothes, and they held themselves very straight and carried all sorts of things on their heads. Their wrists, ankles and necks were festooned with jewellery, which, appropriately enough, seemed to be made almost entirely of amber and silver.

'They're all so beautiful,' said Felix admiringly. 'I think they may be what we call peris. I've been reading up on mythology since I visited your world, and the Persian fairy — the peri — seems the best fit.'

'Really,' said Betony in an offhand voice. 'Anything else you'd like to lecture me about whilst you're at it?'

Felix blinked. What on earth had he said to upset her? Maybe she felt out of place amongst the beautiful people of Kaflabad. She was very conspicuous, with her blonde hair, her slanting green eyes and her grubby tunic. Most of the red dye had washed out of Felix's hair in the wadi, and it was now back to its normal brown. For once *he* was the one who attracted the least notice. On the other hand, it might have nothing to do with her appearance — she could simply be

159

upset about the brazzles.

'Let's hit the town,' he said, trying to cheer her up. There was no point moping about; they needed to get some information. 'Where shall we start?'

'The bazaar, I suppose,' said Betony. She glanced down at her tunic. 'We could get some new clothes.'

This seemed like a good idea. Kaflabad was very hot, and what they were wearing wasn't terribly practical, as well as being unusual. They made their way to the market, bought a flowing robe each – blue for him, and green for her – and changed into them immediately. Betony swirled the long skirt around her ankles, and perked up. When they'd added headscarves to the outfits, wrapping them round their faces to protect them from the dust, like the nomads, neither of them attracted a second glance.

'Lunch?' suggested Felix.

Betony nodded enthusiastically, and they treated themselves to a slap-up meal in a restaurant. When they'd finished, Felix casually asked the waiter whether he'd heard of any riddle-paws in the vicinity. The waiter looked at him as though he were completely insane, and shook his head. They left the restaurant and tried asking a few passers-by, but they drew a blank every time. It was only when they were passing a stall selling little carved statues that Felix noticed one that did look a bit like a sphinx. He went over, and started to haggle for it.

'That's Leona herself,' protested the stallholder. 'Sculpted from life, so I'm told. The artist must have risked his neck to carve that one. Two gold pieces, come on, you know it's worth it.'

Leona herself? This was a bit of luck. Felix gave in, bought the little statue, and asked where he might find the sculptor.

'Down by the dye-market,' said the stallholder, rubbing the coins together as though he couldn't believe his good fortune.

'You were telling the truth, weren't you, that he carved this from life?'

The stallholder grinned, his teeth very white against his brown skin. 'That's what he told me.' All of a sudden, he didn't sound the least bit convincing.

Felix and Betony headed off for the dye-market. They found the sculptor with no trouble at all, treading some skeins of wool in a vat of gorgeous purple-blue liquid. 'It's just a sideline, the carving,' he said. His legs were blue to the knees.

'But did you see her?'

'Who?'

'Leona. The riddle-paw,' said Felix, keeping a grip on his temper with difficulty.

The sculptor sucked his breath in between his teeth. 'The riddle-paw,' he said. 'Now, there's a creature to conjure with. I expect you want to know what they're really like, that's what I get asked all the time. And seeing as you obviously have taste – you bought one of my statues, after all – I'll tell you. Big, but not as big as the tales that are told of them. Their hair is brown – but sometimes it's black, or red, or blonde. And they have deep voices – well, the males have deep voices but the females don't – apart from the old ones, that is. They eat their food raw. Or cooked. And they ask riddles. That do you?'

Pathetic, thought Felix. 'Where is she?' he asked.

'Who?'

'Leona.'

'Oh, miles away. She's terrorizing the town of Sebeth at the moment.'

'Where's that?'

'West,' said the sculptor vaguely. 'Can I interest you in a statue of a triple-head?'

'No thanks,' said Felix. 'Do you know anywhere we might be able to buy a map?'

'There's a bookshop on the other side of the main ziggurat,' said the sculptor. 'You could try there.'

They found the bookshop easily, but to their astonishment only a few volumes were really expensive – the old ones. The rest were very cheap. Betony picked one up, and leafed through it. 'It's been printed,' she said, amazed.

'Hot off the press, that one,' said the amberly bookseller.

The knowledge of printing has spread like wildfire, thought Felix; is there anywhere in Betony's world that hasn't taken it up?

'Delivered by triple-head, only last week,' said the bookseller. 'We've got our own press up and running now, of course. What can I do for you?'

'We'd like a map of the area,' said Betony.

'Certainly,' said the amberly, handing one over. 'How about a newspaper as well? All the latest news from Andria.'

'OK.' Felix passed him two silver coins in payment, and they went outside. Before they turned their attention to the map they leafed through the paper, which turned out to be two days' old. It had been printed in Kaflabad, and said things an Andrian paper would never have got away with. *'Concern deepens over King and Queen of Andria,'* Felix read out loud. *'There have been no sightings of either monarch since the abdication, and ugly rumours are circulating. Most people suspect Fleabane of foul play, but the lack of evidence rules out further action. The current thinking is that whilst the king and queen were still alive they could be reinstated, and that their complete removal was the only way to ensure that this didn't occur.'*

'Depressing,' said Betony. 'I liked the king and queen, even if they were a bit wet. I hope Ironclaw's information was correct, and they *are* still alive. Let's look at the map, then.'

For the first time Felix saw Betony's world laid out in front of him. There was Andria, by the sea; Tiratattle, Geddon, Tromm Fell – and Kaflabad. Beyond Kaflabad was just a mountain range, with the word 'Unexplored' printed across it. There were many other places to the north and south he'd never heard of, but Sebeth just wasn't there. Felix went back into the bookshop and complained.

'There are no maps west of here,' said the bookseller. 'Everyone knows that. And no, you can't have your money back.'

They had a brief and spirited argument that got them nowhere, so they walked back to the main square. As they approached the carpet rack, they heard the occupants talking amongst themselves. 'Ssh,' said Betony, grinning. 'Let's eavesdrop.'

'... and his name's Felix,' Nimby was saying.

'You must think I was woven yesterday,' scoffed a thread-bare little rug.

'A human being? Don't talk such rag-rot.'

'You think you're so up-market, don't you, with your three hundred knots per square centimetre? Well, it doesn't impress *us*.'

'You're spinning us a carpet worker's yarn.'

'No I'm not,' said Nimby indignantly. 'I've got the most exciting owners ever – we've been looking for brazzles already, and ...'

'Brazzles? Pull the other thread.'

'I'm telling you the truth. We've got to find a riddle-paw and ask it something, as well.'

'Riddle-paws just *love* brazzles,' said the rug. 'They regard them as a challenge. You'll be lucky if there's anything left of them apart from a few feathers by the time you get there.'

'What do you mean, *by the time I get there*? I could out-fly any of you any day.'

'Oh yeah?'

'Yeah.'

'Come on then, show us.'

'I can't, I have to wait for my owners.'

There was a chorus of sarcastic laughter.

'All right then,' said Nimby, and before Felix or Betony could do anything about it their carpet had rolled itself off the shelf, and shot into the air.

The little threadbare rug did likewise, and the two of them zoomed off in the direction of the ziggurat, followed by yells of, 'You show him, Drugget!'

'He'll bring him down a warp or two,' observed a striped mat. 'If I know Drugget, he'll fly low over the railings by the king's garden, and make that swanky floor-mop snag himself on one of the spikes. He won't fly in a straight line again for a week!'

'I don't *believe* this,' said Felix despairingly.

But Betony was thinking far more quickly, and she'd hailed a chariot, drawn by two of the gazelle-like creatures. 'Come on!' she yelled, leaping on board. Felix followed suit, his headscarf suddenly unravelling and revealing his face.

As he tried to wind it back round his head again he heard the mat exclaim, 'Well, *brush my pile with a cactus!* His master really *was* a human being!'

Then Betony was shouting, 'Follow that carpet!' and they

165

were off, galloping through the streets and scattering pedestrians right and left.

It was hard to keep Nimby in sight; he and Drugget swooped and dived and swerved, neck and neck – or whatever the carpet equivalent was. Passers-by glanced up with horrified expressions and a quaddiump shied, throwing its rider into the gutter. 'Take us to the main ziggurat!' yelled Betony, and the chariot took a left-hand bend on one wheel.

'Make your mind up!' bellowed the driver.

A few minutes later the chariot slid to a halt in a cloud of dust, and its passengers piled out and paid the fare.

'The garden's on the fifth level,' said Felix, looking up. 'We'd better hurry.'

They ran up the ramp, pushing their way past people coming the other way. By the time they reached the fifth level all they could do was stand there panting, their hearts in their mouths. After a moment or two the carpets came into sight, flying low and fast. Drugget was slightly in the lead; at the last moment he zipped down behind the railings, skimming the rosebushes and scattering petals.

'Nimby!' screamed Betony and Felix, as one.

The carpet obviously heard them because he braked sharply, his front end flipping upwards. Drugget tried to loop the loop to find out what had happened to his rival; he misjudged it, thumped into the wall of the ziggurat, and fluttered to the ground.

Nimby landed none-too-gracefully beside the children.

'I've been a bit of a dish-cloth, haven't I?' he said. 'I'm really sorry. That was a stupid thing to do. Do you want to beat me? They sell carpet beaters in the bazaar.'

'No,' said Felix. 'Just don't do anything like that again, will you?'

'He won't get the chance!' shouted an amberly, from the level below. 'You're both under arrest, for dangerous driving!'

'But neither of us were aboard!'

'Immaterial! You are responsible for the behaviour of your vehicle!'

Another amberly appeared, walking down the ramp from the level above. 'Your carpet's impounded,' he said, and he raised some sort of weapon, which he fired straight at Nimby. A jet of fermented fertle-juice hit the rug dead centre, and a dark stain spread outwards like blood. Nimby hiccoughed, and flapped his fringe a couple of times. Shortly after that he stopped moving, and started to snore. Felix and Betony looked at one another. There was nowhere to run, and it was clear that their carpet had been disabled. Felix clenched his fist, and hit himself on the thigh with annoyance. Andria – and the Divide that would take him back home – suddenly seemed a very long way away indeed.

Squill entered Fleabane's office in the Andrian palace. 'Snakeweed's been put up as a candidate in the elections,' he said. 'He's made a lot of friends with his de-gluing work in the library.'

'I know,' replied Fleabane. 'It's time for that little accident, I think.'

'I'll see to it,' said Squill. 'Oh, there's a lickit outside.'

'Send him in.'

'You've got three minutes,' snapped the president, when the lickit appeared. 'I'm a very busy being.'

Grimspite took a deep breath. He didn't particularly enjoy being in lickit form, he much preferred his four-legged guise. 'Do you have any use for that manuscript in the Land Rover?' he enquired.

Fleabane gave him a sharp look. 'How do *you* know it's a Land Rover?'

'It says so,' said Grimspite. 'On the back.'

'It does, actually,' said Fleabane's secretary.

'The manuscript seems to be a cookery book,' said Grimspite. 'And I'm a cook.' He smoothed his white lickit robe to emphasise the point.

Fleabane told his secretary to fetch it, and then he leafed through it. He started to read some of the recipes out loud, until he was laughing so much he could hardly carry on. 'Listen to this bit,' he spluttered. 'First, disembowel your berk buk-a-buk ...'

Grimspite wanted to protest that the wording was clear and sensible, but he couldn't. He had to stand there whilst Fleabane carried on making fun of his recipes.

Fleabane's secretary was having hysterics; his reaction was

way over the top, presumably to impress his president. 'It's even funnier than Turpsik's anthem,' he shrieked.

Grimspite stiffened. *Turpsik* had written the anthem? *Liver and kidneys*, that explained everything. He'd insulted her in the worst way possible.

'There wasn't anything wrong with the anthem,' snapped Fleabane. 'It was just the way it was sung.' He turned to Grimspite. 'OK,' he said. ' You can have it. But there'll be a charge – you can cook for the people restoring the library. You get the manuscript when the job's finished.'

Grimspite went to the palace kitchen to pick up a brazier, feeling awful. He understood – rather too well, now – exactly how much his sarcastic comments about Turpsik's anthem must have stung. He had to find a way of apologizing to her.

In the entrance hall of the library, Snakeweed continued to work at the desk. A lickit arrived at some point, set up his cooking equipment just outside and used the other desk as a kitchen table. Then two militia came in and ordered Snakeweed to show them where the books on sea monsters were. The ocean section was hardly ever used, and the rooms were deserted. When they reached their destination Snakeweed looked at the muddle of books and grinned. Where the sea monsters were was anybody's guess.

One of the japegrins drew his wand. 'We don't want a book,' he said nastily.

'A power-surge in a heavy duty wand is rare, I grant you,'

said the other with an evil smile, 'but accidents do happen and Fleabane's sent us to take care of you.'

'You have a really good way of expressing yourself,' said Snakeweed admiringly. 'If I became president, you could make a lot more money as my press officer.'

'What would the holiday entitlement be like?'

The sinistrom attack came like a bolt from the blue, and, despite the faint whiff of rotten eggs, took them all completely by surprise. The elder japegrin was on the floor and out cold almost instantly. Before the other one could unfasten his wand he, too, was flat on his back and comatose. Snakeweed turned and ran, aiming for the entrance hall, but he knew he'd taken a wrong turning when he found himself in the Ancient History section. There was no other exit; he was cornered, and there was nowhere to hide. He grabbed the biggest and heaviest book he could from the shelves.

'Oh for goodness' sake,' said the sinistrom, appearing in the doorway. 'It's me, Grimspite.'

Snakeweed gripped the book a little more tightly.

'It's *me*,' the shadow-beast repeated. 'I was the lickit in the entrance hall, cooking for the people in the library.'

'And your name's Grimspite?'

Oh, dunk my paws in custard, thought Grimspite, I'm meant to be Architrex. Why is life such a bother these days? 'I meant Architrex,' he said. 'Grimspite was what my mother used to call me.'

'You didn't have a mother.'

170

'No,' said Grimspite, 'and I'm beginning to wonder whether that isn't highly significant. I mean, the way we sinistroms have turned out, you know? Bloodthirsty, callous, psychopathic, cruel ...'

'This is veering off the point,' said Snakeweed. 'First of all you say you had a mother, then you say you didn't. If you didn't, who called you Grimspite?'

'My first master – well, mistress,' said Grimspite, feeling even more irritated with Snakeweed than usual, and making it up as he went along. 'I was just a cub, really ...' It went against the grain, it really did, having to rescue someone you fully intended to kill at a later date. If Snakeweed died before the blocking spell had been lifted, all sorts of unpleasant things could happen to Grimspite, a lot of them involving treacle.

Then suddenly there was the tramp tramp tramp of kicking boots, and nowhere to go.

'Well, well,' said Fleabane, standing in the doorway, flanked by two japegrins. He looked from Grimspite to Snakeweed and back again. 'You weren't a lickit at all, were you? You were Snakeweed's sinistrom. And you've disabled two of my militia. Can't have that.' He nodded genially to one of the two japegrins accompanying him – but he had never encountered a sinistrom in the flesh, so he seriously underestimated Grimspite's speed.

Grimspite launched himself at the japegrin on Fleabane's left. Snakeweed threw the book at the one on Fleabane's right, and caught him squarely on the head. Fleabane was fumbling for his own wand now, but he was far too slow. Grimspite glanced at Snakeweed.

'Kill him,' said Snakeweed, so Grimspite did. Following a direct instruction was still second nature to him – if he'd had time to think he might have chosen differently.

He felt a bit odd afterwards. He'd now killed two jape-grins in quick succession, and it hadn't given him the buzz he was used to feeling. It all seemed a bit tacky, somehow. He'd been rather proud of himself for the restraint he'd shown with the first two. They'd need some stitches, true – but he'd done them a favour; scars were the height of sophisticated elegance. Well, they were for a sinistrom.

He looked at the bodies. The trouble with *dead* was that it was so irreversible. 'What are we going to say now?' he asked.

'Get yourself back into lickit form, and don't worry your pretty little head about it.'

Grimspite knew that his head was neither little nor pretty. Snakeweed's remark was extremely offensive.

'We'll stagger outside,' Snakeweed added, 'looking dreadfully upset, and say that Harshak has had a bit of a killing spree.'

'That's clever,' said Grimspite.

'When I tell everyone how I tried to defend Fleabane, they'll ask me to become acting president – I even hit Harshak with this very book, you see, and drew blood.' He smeared it a little more obviously over the cover. Then he ripped his clothes a bit and the two of them limped to the entrance hall, and went outside.

The triple-head squawked with alarm when it saw the state they were in, and a couple of the militia came running over.

Snakeweed did a distressed hero impression, and the jape-grins practically fell over themselves to suggest that Snakeweed took Fleabane's place. As they left for the palace in a cuddyak cart, the triple-head called after Grimspite, 'You will remember to give me a signed copy of your cookery book when it's published, won't you?'

'Of course!' Grimspite called back. The triple-head had been really helpful when he'd been grilling things on his brazier, and it had given him all sorts of ideas for new recipes.

It quickly became clear that Betony and Felix were going to have to climb to the very top of the ziggurat. Finding an antidote to the marble spell seemed to be slipping away from them again, and Felix felt thoroughly frustrated. The sheer misery at the loss of the brazzles ran along underneath, like an icy cold underground river. The guard who'd arrested them was quite pleasant once he realized they weren't going to try and escape – there was no point – and he talked all the way up.

'The king has his palace at the summit,' he explained.

'The court's in session there every afternoon, so you'll be dealt with promptly.'

'What's the penalty for dangerous driving?' asked Felix, imagining a fine – or, at the very worst, a period of hard labour. The ziggurats took some building. They seemed like a bit of a waste of time, really – it wasn't as though you could live inside them. The bases were made of solid brick, and only the terraces and the tops were usable.

'Depends what sort of mood the king's in,' said the guard. 'Last week someone got buried alive for overtaking on a blind corner. The week before that, someone else was ordered to stand on his head for half an hour for the same offence.'

This was not reassuring news.

'Then there's all that stuff about the king and queen of Andria,' the amberly went on. 'That's had an adverse effect on him. No monarch likes to hear about another one being overthrown, and when they just *vanish* afterwards … I don't think he's been sleeping too well.'

Felix was quite sorry that the ramps zigzagged up each time – he would have liked to walk along the terraces, and look at them properly. He was pretty sure, now, that he was seeing something very similar to the Hanging Gardens of Babylon. The retaining wall on the edge of each terrace must have been quite deep, as the beds of earth were big enough to support fully-grown fruit trees. The railings were there to stop people falling over the side, although some of them were so swathed in climbing flowers they were invisible. These flowers were bright purples and pinks and reds, not unlike bougainvillea, and they cascaded downwards like frozen waterfalls of colour.

The palace turned out to be quite small. The king was seated on a throne in the middle of a courtyard, and he was listening to someone defending himself against a parking infringement.

'I was unloading barrels of ink,' said the defendant. 'I was only there for a couple of minutes.'

'Surely you could have parked in the approved place, and rolled them there?'

The defendant looked worried. 'You're so clever, your Majesty, I'd never have thought of that.'

'Hmm,' said the king, banging his gavel on the arm of the throne. It was severely dented on one side. 'I'm going to fine you one left shoe for the parking offence, and sentence you to six months' gardening for the illegal use of flattery in court. Next.'

The guard nudged Felix and Betony, and they stepped forwards. 'Pull down your scarves,' he hissed. 'No covered heads in front of the king.'

Betony and Felix unwound their headscarves.

The king peered at them. 'A tangle-child and a mythical being,' he said. 'How exciting.'

'Speeding offence, your Majesty,' said the guard, with a swift and disbelieving glance at Felix's ears. 'An unsupervised carpet — a big one, as well. More witnesses than leaves on a tree.'

'There's far too much of this sort of thing these days,' said the king. 'I need to make an example of them. Being a mythical beast is no excuse.'

Felix and Betony looked at one another in alarm.

'The death penalty seems appropriate. Any cutthroats in the area?'

The guard shrugged.

'Well, what else can I throw them to?'

A wonderful idea popped into Felix's mind. 'I hope he doesn't sacrifice us to a riddle-paw,' he whispered, loud enough for the king to hear.

The king brightened. 'I heard that,' he said. 'What a marvellous solution. I owe the king of Sebeth a favour for that flowering shrub he sent me. Tell me; is Leona still causing him problems? I heard she ate his chief accountant last year.'

'I believe so, your Majesty, though no one ever knows exactly where she is. There are several rocks she uses when she's lying in wait.'

The king turned to Felix and Betony and banged the gavel on the arm of his throne again, deepening the dent. 'I sentence both of you to be sacrificed to a riddle-paw. Well, maybe sacrifice isn't quite the right word. If you solve enough of her riddles she may get bored and let you go. Next.'

The guard looked faintly disgusted, although he tried to

hide it. He cleared his throat. 'Er … one small problem, your Majesty. How do we get them there? No one knows exactly where Sebeth is, it's a hidden city; you need a Sebethian guide to find the place.'

'Well find one, then.'

'You need a guard to enforce the penalty, as well.'

'Consider yourself nominated, Jahim.'

The guard looked seriously cheesed off. 'We'll need a carpet big enough to carry four people.'

'Well, use theirs, then. Put a temporary change-of-ownership hex on it. What's next? Not another parking offence?'

Jahim saluted, and led the children away. Felix wanted to laugh out loud. If they survived Leona's riddles, and got the marble spell, they'd have their carpet back again and be able to cross the desert. Best of all would be a scenario where the brazzles were waiting for them at Sebeth; if anyone could solve Leona's riddles, Ironclaw could.

It took them a good twenty minutes to walk all the way back down the ziggurat. They were put into custody whilst Jahim went off to look for a guide and get the change-of-ownership hex applied. Custody was unexpectedly pleasant; they were given cool sherbet drinks, and a sort of bean-mush to eat, sprinkled with seeds. Provisions for their journey were also produced – legs of cold meat, a loaf of bread, some quaddiump cheese and a pot of honeyed sweets. It was clear that the king wanted them to reach their destination alive and well. There were blankets, too.

10

It was mid-afternoon by the time Nimby arrived, carrying Jahim and a surly-looking nomad. The guide had no luggage of his own, but his clothes billowed around him revealing odd shapes now and again, as though he had a lot of hidden pockets in which he carried a variety of things.

'*Bobbins and bodkins*,' said Nimby, 'this is a turn-up, isn't it? Sent to the very place—'

'Shut up, Nimby,' said Betony.

'What exactly happens when we get to Sebeth?' asked Felix quickly, worried that the sentence might be changed if the king got to hear that he'd given them exactly what they'd needed – a guide.

'My orders are to fly down low and tip you off,' said Jahim. 'There's no way I'm landing next to Leona. Then we hover for a bit, watch what happens, and report back.'

'Or take us back,' said Felix.

178

'Er ... yes,' said Jahim. It was quite clear that he didn't expect them to live.

The children climbed aboard, and Nimby took off. He obeyed every flight-sign to the letter, keeping to the speed limit and flying in an anti-clockwise direction round big ziggurats. It was only once they'd left the city walls behind that he gained more height, and accelerated to a decent cruising speed.

Although Jahim was quite talkative, asking a lot of questions about Felix's world, the guide didn't say a word for some time. He just sat there, his scarf wound round his head so that only his dark eyes were visible. Now and again he indicated a slight change of direction with his hand, obviously using wadis and rocky outcrops as landmarks.

'Is Sebeth like Kaflabad?' Felix asked him.

The guide shook his head.

'Any ziggurats?'

The guide shook his head again.

'Well what *are* the buildings like?'

'They are excavated into the rock.'

'Will we get there tonight?'

The guide shook his head again, and Felix gave up trying to get information out of him.

They had to camp right out in the middle of the desert. Jahim turned Nimby into a tent, opening out a telescoped pole he'd brought with him, and they had supper. Felix had always been very litter-conscious and he buried the remains

of their meal a little way off, knowing it was all bio-
degradable: date stones, the bones from the cold meat, fruit
peel. He looked at the expanse of sand stretching away before
him, silver in the moonlight. No chance of getting washed
away here, he thought, returning to the tent, and they all
settled down to sleep.

He was woken at some stage during the night by the sound
of something digging. He listened. Scrape, scrape; then the
pitter-patter of a shower of sand. He sat up. Something was
unearthing their rubbish. Scrape, scrape … pitter-patter. A
pause; then a crunch – the crunch of bone. He nudged Jahim.
Jahim rolled over without waking and pulled his blanket over
his head. The crunching went on for a minute or two, and
then stopped. Another pause. Felix listened as hard as he
could, hoping whatever it was had gone away.

The next thing he heard was a sniff – right next to him,
on the other side of the carpet. Then three more sniffs, in
quick succession. It was something big – the sniffs weren't
low to the ground, they were waist-height. Felix felt the
adrenalin rush through his body like a forest fire. He nudged
the guide. The nomad woke instantly, and took in the situation straight away. Very quietly, he produced a candle from
one of his hidden pockets, and lit it with a wave of his hand.
Then he wrapped his headscarf round his scimitar, and set
fire to it. The impromptu torch flared up, and Jahim and
Betony awoke with a start. Felix put his fingers to his lips,
and they stared wide-eyed as the guide flung back the car-

pet.

Two of the most terrifying creatures Felix had ever seen leapt backwards. Nimby shrieked, woken by the guard's action and the heat of the flames. Jahim drew his dagger with one hand, white-faced, and tore off his headscarf with the other. He copied what the guide had done, and a second torch flared up. The creatures retreated to a safe distance, but they didn't go away. They were the closest things Felix had ever seen to sabre-tooth tigers – except for the fact that they had two heads and six legs each. The legs weren't arranged like those of an insect, however – the front end had two pairs of front legs beneath the heads, then the bodies seemed to merge into one, so that the back half of the body was standard lion issue, with just one pair of hind legs, although the tail was shorter. They were more heavily built than the aver-

age lion, though, and their fangs projected well below the line of their jaws. They didn't have manes, and their eyes glowed as green as a sinistrom's, but their faces were nothing like as intelligent.

'We can't stay here,' said Jahim. 'We don't have enough to burn, and fire is the only thing that will keep them at bay.' He grabbed his blanket, and motioned to them all to do the same and step outside. Then he grabbed the pole, and telescoped it back to the size of a small truncheon. Nimby flattened himself out on the ground, but he was shivering, and things kept rolling off him.

'Keep still,' hissed Jahim, 'unless you want to get shredded to cushion-stuffing by those fangs.'

'What *are* they?' asked Felix.

'Cutthroats,' said Jahim shortly, hefting their gourd of water on to the carpet and making sure the stopper was secure. 'They prey on travellers.' His torch was burning down now; it wouldn't last much longer.

They all scrambled aboard. The torch flickered one last time, and died. The cutthroats took a couple of paces forward.

'Come *on*, Nimby,' said Jahim. 'You can take off now.'

'I've been singed,' wailed the carpet. Part of the fringe at Nimby's rear end was now just blackened stubs.

'*Zithers and ziggurats*,' swore Jahim. 'That doesn't stop you flying, does it?'

Nimby made a gulping sound, as though he were fighting back the tears. The cutthroats broke into a run.

'*Fly*, curse your fibres!' shouted Jahim, and Nimby took off rather shakily. He wasn't quick enough; one of the cutthroats came level, and leapt into the air. The beast caught the guide's clothing with one of its four forepaws. The nomad was dragged to the edge of the carpet, and the weight of the cutthroat prevented Nimby from rising any further. Jahim swept his dagger round in an arc, but only managed to slice off a handful of hairs. Felix and Betony were clinging on for dear life; the carpet was shuddering and jerking, trying to pull away.

The nomad seemed to be fumbling in his clothing for something. His dagger's in his *belt*, thought Felix, why doesn't he draw it? Nimby lurched to one side, in another attempt to shake off the cutthroat, and tilted alarmingly. The guide tumbled to the ground and the carpet shot up a couple of metres, like a balloon suddenly released from its moorings, and then steadied.

Felix and Betony watched in horror as the guide scrambled to his feet. The second cutthroat had arrived now, and it looked as though the pair of them had decided to play with their victim, like a cat with a mouse. The first one patted the nomad with its paw, and he staggered a few steps. The second one did likewise, and this time the nomad *ran*. The sudden break into a sprint delighted the cutthroats; they roared with approval and bounded round in a circle, ready to cut him off.

The guide had now found whatever it was he had been looking for. He pulled it out of his clothing, and held it aloft. It was a brass lamp. As the children watched, the nomad's feet left the ground and he streamed into it, like a steaming kettle in reverse, and disappeared. The lamp tumbled to the ground.

The cutthroats sniffed the lamp with their four noses, and looked at one another.

'He wasn't a nomad at all,' said Jahim wonderingly. 'He was a brandee.'

'What's a brandee?' asked Nimby.

'Beings that live in magical lamps,' said Jahim.

'In our world, he'd have been one of the jinn – a genie,' added Felix.

'This isn't your world,' said Betony shortly. 'He was our *guide*, Felix, and now we've lost him.'

'We'll come back later, when the cutthroats have gone, and pick him up. When the sun rises his lamp will shine like a beacon. Then one of us simply has to rub the lamp, and he'll reappear.'

'Where are we going to spend the rest of the night?' asked Betony. 'It's not safe down there.'

'We need to put some distance between ourselves and those monsters,' said Jahim. 'Otherwise they'll just hang around, hoping we'll land. We'll fly on for a bit, and then hover until morning.'

'I can't hover at night!' yelped Nimby. 'Hovering uses up

far too much energy.'

'Tough,' said Jahim.

'You don't understand,' said Nimby. 'I have to twisty-strip sunlight, and I can only store so much of it. That's why carpet racks are made of crystal – to let the light through.'

Wow, thought Felix. He's a bit like a solar panel.

'We'll find somewhere to land, then,' said Jahim. 'But we'll all stay on board, and take it in turns to keep watch.'

They flew for another fifteen minutes or so, and then they touched down. Jahim took the first watch, and Betony the second. By the time it was Felix's turn, dawn wasn't far away. He sat cross-legged on the carpet, his blanket wrapped around him, but he was still cold. He saw a strange long-legged mousy thing that bounced across the sand like a grasshopper, but that was all. When the others woke up they had breakfast. Then they had to wait until mid-morning before Nimby had absorbed sufficient energy to fly.

When they were halfway back to where they'd camped, Jahim suddenly stiffened. Felix followed his gaze, and saw a long low cloud on the horizon. After a moment or two he realized it was coming towards them, and quite quickly, too.

'We need to land,' said Jahim urgently.

'It's a sandstorm, isn't it?' said Felix.

Jahim nodded.

Betony looked interested. 'Can't we fly above it, and watch?'

'No,' said Jahim. 'It could be hundreds of metres high.

185

We must shelter.'

Nimby lost height, and settled himself gently on the sand. 'I'd better make another tent,' he said. 'Only this time I'll make sure it's pile inwards.'

Betony laughed. 'You vain thing,' she said. 'Worried that a bit of sand between your fibres will make you look scruffy?'

'I'd like to still *have* some fibres, thank you,' retorted Nimby. 'My underside is more resilient than my pile.'

Betony grinned.

'This isn't funny,' said Jahim. 'The sand will be blowing fast and hard; you won't be able to see a metre in front of you. Everything will get dark. A sandstorm can take the glaze off a pot, so wind your scarves tightly around your heads. Breathing will become difficult. I do not know how bad this one is likely to be.'

'I might,' said Felix, suddenly remembering the little crystal ball he'd found in the vamprey cave. He pulled it out of his pocket, and felt around for the tiny instruction manual.

'A storm-oracle!' said Jahim. 'We are fortunate. I know how to work it.'

Felix handed it to him, and Jahim cupped it in his hands and peered into it. The clear transparency of the crystal clouded, and turned yellow. The yellow deepened to orange, then red. After a moment or two it became clear that it was going to remain red.

'A bad storm,' said Jahim, 'but not the worst. The worst

is purple. These instruments are valuable, Felix. If ... when we get to the riddle-paw ...'

'If I don't survive you can have it,' said Felix wryly, anticipating Jahim's request.

The three of them huddled together beneath the carpet's canopy, sitting on his in-folded edges to prevent him blowing away. When the storm arrived it howled like a banshee, and despite their efforts to weight him down a corner of the carpet flicked up. It was as dark as evening out there, and they could see nothing except swirling sand which dashed against the exposed parts of their faces like flicks from a wire brush. Jahim got the corner anchored once again and they sat there in the dark, sneezing occasionally.

'Won't it bury us?' asked Betony, sounding worried now that she'd appreciated just how violent a sandstorm could be.

'Only on the windward side,' said Jahim. He didn't sound quite as confident as Felix would have liked.

The storm didn't last all that long, however, and after a while the noise died away.

Jahim lifted a corner on the lee-side, and they could see the long low cloud barrelling away from them in the distance. They scrambled out, and dug the other side of Nimby free.

'Can you give me a shake?' asked the carpet, so Felix and Jahim seized him by one of his edges, and shook the sand from his pile.

'Right,' said Betony, 'we'd better find that lamp now,

hadn't we?'

Jahim looked at her as though she were mad.

'The sandstorm will have buried it, Betony,' said Felix. 'We haven't got a hope of finding it.'

The colour drained from Betony's face. 'What will happen to the brandee?' she asked.

'He will sleep until one day the sand blows away and reveals his lamp again,' said Jahim. 'Sand dunes are like boils. They come and they go.'

Betony made a face. 'And what are *we* going to do? We don't have a guide any more.'

'We know the general direction of the hidden city,' said Jahim. 'We fly on, and hope we can spot it from above.'

They took off, and flew for what seemed like ages across the flat plain below. Eventually some rock formations appeared in the distance, patterned gold with sunlight and violet with shadow. As they drew closer they realized that the terrain was very rugged indeed, but there was no sign of a city. They crossed the highlands, noticing gorges and ravines and canyons. On the far side the landscape changed dramatically. This was where the rain fell; the bare rocks were suddenly clothed with rich tropical vegetation.

'We've come too far,' said Jahim. 'We'd better go back, and try again.'

They flew down the ridge, concentrating on the arid side of it, but they still didn't see anything. 'They were right about it being a hidden city,' said Felix. 'It doesn't have a spell on it, does it, so that it can't be seen?'

Both Jahim and Betony burst out laughing. 'Magic doesn't work like that,' said Betony. 'There's no such thing as an invisibility spell.' She stopped laughing. 'Is that something you can do with science, then?'

'No,' said Felix.

Jahim suddenly looked interested. 'You know about science?'

'Not much,' said Felix warily.

'But you have flown in balloons, and you have lamps that are lit by gas?'

Felix was about to remark that those things had been replaced by aeroplanes and electricity, but he thought better of it. 'Balloons and gas-lamps are things in story books,' he said.

Jahim looked disappointed. 'I thought you said the things in *our* world appeared in *your* legends, and *our* legends were real in *your* world?'

'Only some things,' said Felix.

'So you don't have metal bridges, or under-water boats, or tall houses with shiny windows that gleam rose-red in the sunset?'

'That's it!' shouted Felix.

'*What's* it?' asked Betony.

'Rose-red. *"The rose-red city, half as old as time."* It's a quote from a poem about Petra, a town cut into the rock that could only be reached along a narrow winding chasm. I bet this city's similar – we need to look for an opening.'

Betony's eyes strayed to the escarpment that stretched away into the distance in either direction, creased and folded like crumpled material. 'It would be like looking for a flea on a cuddyak.'

'The trick, then,' said Jahim, 'is to make the flea jump.' He studied them both for a moment. 'Tell me,' he said, 'you seem unaccountably anxious to find Sebeth, when meeting the riddle-paw will probably end in your death. *Why?*'

'Tell him,' said Betony.

'This all started when a japegrin turned my parents to marble,' Felix began, and he gave Jahim a potted version of his story.

When Felix had finished Jahim said, 'You think the brazzles have survived, don't you? I have to hope for your sakes that they have. You are a noble creature, human, and I shall assist you in every way I can. I didn't like the idea of just tipping you off and watching Leona devour you – it lacks honour. The King of Kaflabad has been far too influenced by newspaper reports about the new president of Andria.'

Felix and Betony glanced at one another. '*New* president?' queried Felix.

'He is called Snakeweed.'

'I don't *believe* it,' said Betony, her face suddenly scarlet with fury.

'Oh, it is true. I have read about it myself – it was the very latest news, just before we left. Snakeweed is using a triple-head to distribute his newspapers, as they can fly long distances at great speed. The old president – Fleabane – was killed by a renegade sinistrom.'

'Harshak, presumably,' said Felix.

'You are very well informed,' said Jahim.

'Snakeweed was the japegrin who petrified my parents,' said Felix.

'*Well, give me an underlay and tack me down*,' Nimby piped up. 'You do know some famous people, don't you?'

Felix scowled. 'Infamous rather than famous, I think.'

'We need to get back to the problem in hand,' said Jahim. 'How do we make our flea jump, and become visible? A city cannot exist without trade – not a city bordering a desert such as this. But we have not seen any convoys of travellers – we have seen no one. This is perhaps not surprising, considering the cutthroats. However, the citizens of this city must eat, and you cannot transport great quantities of food by carpet.'

'Maybe they get their supplies from the other side of the highlands,' suggested Betony.

Jahim nodded. 'In which case, there must be a road. That's what we must look for – we've been flying too high, hoping to spot a city, when what we need is a narrow highway through the mountains.'

Nimby gradually lost height, and they started to fly at a lower altitude. The details of the scenery were now much easier to pick out; spurs and gullies, cairns and corries. They saw a goaty thing, similar to the one outside Turpsik's cave, which sprang from rock to rock in alarm as their shadow passed over. A flock of twittering birds lifted out of the scrub, and something that resembled a tiny pink ankylosaurus lashed its armoured tail and retreated into its shell. The flowering cacti grew here in clumps, twisted into strange interwoven designs, and once in a while they saw bushes covered with pear-shaped orange fruit.

'Remember I can't fly at night,' said Nimby. 'We'll have to make camp before too long.'

And then they saw it. A narrow path that wound its way between the rocks – and shortly after that, a line of heavily-laden quaddiumps, roped together. The leading rider looked up, saw them, and waved. This was so cheering that they all waved back, and Nimby had to be reminded that he couldn't loop the loop when he had passengers. After that it was easy. They followed the trail until it zigzagged down to level ground, and ran along the escarpment for a little way until an opening appeared, dark against the honey-coloured rock.

The carpet slowed to a walking pace, as the cleft was narrow. 'Hang on,' said Felix, as Nimby was about to enter it. 'I thought Leona would be lying in wait on a rock somewhere?'

'Maybe there's another entrance,' said Betony.

'It's not very good terrorizing practice to stay in the same place indefinitely,' said Jahim. 'People tend to abandon cities they can't enter. No, she'll wander off from time to time, looking for ideas for new riddles. I think we should go into

192

Sebeth, and find lodging for the night. Nimby could probably do with a shampoo, as well.'

'Yuk,' said the carpet, just like a small boy with a strong aversion to soap and water.

'What's that?' asked Felix, pointing to some symbols etched into the stone next to the opening.

'No idea,' said Jahim.

They all looked at it, wondering whether it was some sort of notice in a strange language. 'There's a whole list of symbols that seem to have been crossed out,' said Felix. 'All we're left with is that.' He pointed at the line which read:

$$\text{III} \triangle \quad \square \quad \infty \triangle$$

'Only open between certain hours?' hazarded Betony.

'Keep left?'

'A speed limit?'

'Choose Fettle's Livery Stables for the best quaddiump care in Sebeth?'

'Maybe it's simply a decoration,' said Felix. 'Oh well. Let's go.'

Nimby turned into the chasm and flew sedately along its length, passing some merchants going the other way.

The narrow passageway opened out quite suddenly, and the children gasped with astonishment. Wonderfully ornate facades and gateways were sculpted on the rock face, with interiors that went deep into the hillside. No wonder it had been impossible to locate the city from above – there was very little to see. The network of canyons would simply look like a network of canyons. You had to be down on the same level to realize that a thriving city lay within. The streets bustled with people – but during the day they would be in shadow, and practically invisible. It was evening now, and the streets were lit with torches. Delicious sugary smells wafted from braziers; buskers played weird stringed instruments and wailed incomprehensible songs. There was a crystal rack near the entrance to the city, and above it a sign read: *No carpets to be flown beyond this point.*

The amberly attendant scurried over, and gave Nimby a disbelieving glance. 'You can't park that carpet here unless it's been cleaned,' he told Jahim. 'Three silver pieces for the full treatment – shampoo, triple-rinse, and a thorough brushing. Two silver pieces for the standard cold wash, or one silver piece for the budget beating. I wouldn't advise the budget in this instance. I can also do a quick repair job on the burnt fringe for just one silver piece extra, if you go for the de-luxe wash.'

Jahim handed over four silver pieces, and Nimby made a strangled sort of noise.

'He'll look like new,' said the attendant.

'Hello, stranger,' said a silky little rug. 'My name's Hearthmat. You look as though you've had some pile-raising adventures.'

'Nimblenap,' said Nimby, cheering up. 'And yes, I've had rather an exciting time, as it happens ...'

Betony grinned, and she, Felix and Jahim went off to look for an inn. Sebeth was fascinating. The shops were so different. One of them only sold blue things, another red. There was one place entirely devoted to fragrances – not just perfumes, but cooking spices as well. There was a bathhouse and a musical instrument shop and a pottery, as well as several inns. They wandered along, looking for one that took their fancy.

'Oh, look,' said Felix. 'A riddle shop.'

You never know when you might meet Leona, read the sign in the window. *Don't think it won't happen to **you**, because it just might. Be prepared! We have all the latest riddles, and their solutions. Come into Doddal's Riddle Shop and browse.*

'I think we'd better take a look,' said Jahim.

They went inside. The shop was very big, with lots of caverns branching off in different directions. By the entrance to the third cave there was a huge placard, with a linear design and some symbols on it.

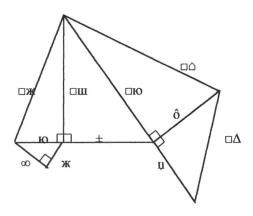

Next to this a notice read: *Twenty gold pieces for whoever can solve this key. Leona's last puzzle has beaten the best riddling minds in Sebeth. Come up with the solution, and your fame will last for ever.*

'They're the same symbols that were etched into the stone at the entrance to the chasm,' said Felix.

'It's a simple as stepping in a cuddyak pat,' pronounced a familiar voice from the next cave.

'Ironclaw!' yelled Felix and Betony together, and they rushed through the doorway, flung themselves at the brazzle and hugged him.

'Where in the name of Flintfeather did you two get to?' asked Thornbeak, stepping out from behind a bookcase.

'Oh, Thornbeak,' said Betony, 'we thought you were both dead.' And with that, she burst into tears of relief.

II

'Twenty gold pieces, I believe!' squawked Ironclaw, jumping up and down with excitement and rattling the objects on the shop shelves.

'Ironclaw,' said Thornbeak severely, 'we've got plans to make.'

'First things first,' said Ironclaw. 'I want my reward, not to mention the everlasting fame that goes with it.'

'Let's hear the answer, then,' said Doddal, the riddle-shop owner, although it was clear he didn't think for one moment the brazzle had actually solved the puzzle. 'That figure is the key to what Leona's been scratching on the rock face outside the city. Each symbol represents a letter, presumably.'

'They're not letters,' said Ironclaw. 'They're numbers.'

'*Numbers?* How do you know?'

'Oh, it's obvious,' said Ironclaw. 'Five triangles, joined together like a pointy hat with flaps, and all of them right-angled. So we just use Bronzepinion's Rule.'

Doddal looked blank.

'Bronzepinion's Rule. The box of the tilty side is equal to the sum of the boxes on the other two sides.'

'Oh,' said Doddal.

'Then it's easy,' said Ironclaw. 'If we assume that the smallest triangle is a 3, 4, 5 triangle, as that's the only one where all three sides have single digits, we know the symbols for three of them.'

Doddal raised his eyebrows. 'A 3, 4, 5 triangle?'

'The tilty side is 5. The box of 5 is 25 – five fives. Three threes are 9, four fours are 16, 16 plus 9 is 25.'

'Oh, I *see*,' said Thornbeak.

Ironclaw cast her a disbelieving look. 'So the 5 side must *also* be part of a 5, 12, 13 triangle,' he went on. 'We know that's a 3, so the other symbol must be 1. Therefore the number base is ten.'

'I *do* see, actually,' said Thornbeak. 'The 12 side is part of a 9, 12, 15 triangle as well. And *they're* all multiples of 3, 4 and 5.'

Ironclaw looked stunned.

'And the fifteen is part of a 8, 15, 17 triangle.'

Ironclaw looked even more stunned.

'And the last triangle has to be a 6, 8, 10 triangle. And now you have all the digits, plus zero. Am I right?'

Ironclaw nodded, speechless.

'I don't think that *can* be right,' said Doddal. 'The symbols on the rock are meant to be a message. And you're saying they're a line of numbers? I can't release the twenty gold pieces for something that doesn't make sense.'

Ironclaw looked furious. 'I know I'm right!' he screeched.

'Well, what have we got?' asked Felix reasonably.

Doddal handed him a sheet of paper with the five symbols on it :

$$\text{III}\triangle \quad \square \quad \infty\triangle$$

'Two, seven, one, four, zero,' said Betony.

Ironclaw glared at Doddal. 'You only said come up with the solution,' he snapped. 'You didn't say it had to be *used* for anything.'

'Why are they grouped like that?' asked Thornbeak. 'Couldn't it be twenty-seven, one, forty?'

Ironclaw shrugged. He was clearly sulking.

'Hang on,' said Thornbeak. 'How many people has Leona killed?'

'Twenty-seven,' said Doddal, suddenly looking a lot more interested.

Thornbeak laughed. 'That's why there are so many crossings-out. It's a tally. If you say it out loud you get: Twenty-seven won for tea. She's won twenty-seven riddles, and eaten the losers for tea.'

'Well, *riddle me ragged,*' said Doddal.

'Brilliant,' said Felix.

'Ten gold pieces each, then,' said Doddal. 'Seeing as you solved it together.'

Ironclaw looked miffed, but Thornbeak simply said, 'Dinner's on us,' and led the way out.

Felix introduced Jahim to the brazzles. Betony told Thornbeak how they'd bought a magic carpet, and Thornbeak explained how she and Ironclaw had hauled themselves out of the wadi. As they had been swept along, Ironclaw had calculated the probability of hitting each promontory he saw ahead of them, until a reasonable chance presented itself. He had then used Thornbeak as a landing stage, by climbing over her and hooking his beak into the mud. She had hung on to his tail, and he'd pulled her out.

Betony grinned. 'Doesn't sound like a bundle of fun.'

'It wasn't,' said Thornbeak. 'It's the only time I've let Ironclaw walk all over me, and it won't happen again in a hurry.'

After a few enquiries the little party found a restaurant that catered for raptors. The triple-head had cleaned the kitchen out of rump steak before it flew back to Andria, but there were plenty of other things to choose from.

'I'm surprised the triple-head came this far,' said Felix.

'Oh, we're very up-to-date here these days,' said the waiter, filling a trough for Thornbeak. 'Heard all about that new president Snakeweed and Harshak.'

Betony helped herself to some peribott-sauce. 'What exactly have you heard about Snakeweed and Harshak?' she asked.

'Snakeweed found his pebble in the library and got rid of

him,' said the waiter. 'He's frightfully popular as a result of it.'

'Got rid of him? How?'

'There are a few of today's newspapers on the tables,' said the waiter. 'I'll get you one.'

'I wonder how the triple-head found its way here?' mused Felix. 'We had enough problems ourselves. Come to think of it, how did you two get here?'

'Followed the road, of course,' said Ironclaw.

'It does help having magnifying vision,' Thornbeak pointed out.

Then the newspaper arrived and they all tried to pore over it, although there wasn't really enough room. Ironclaw's wings kept getting in the way.

'Here we are,' said Thornbeak. 'There's a long report about it. I'll read it out loud:

"By Inkhorn, our correspondent in Andria.

"As the sun sank behind the trees there was an air of expectancy outside the palace. There was a slight breeze, just enough to lift the occasional feather off the grass, which had been grazed to perfection by a team of cuddyaks earlier in the day. Snakeweed was standing on the stage with his hands in his pockets.

"There was a flurry of activity on the road, and a moment later Harshak appeared, travelling at an easy lope. There were gasps from the crowd – I don't think anyone realized quite how

big this sinistrom was going to be.

"Snakeweed showed the crowd a pebble he had in his hand; then he started rubbing it against his trousers, nice fluid action, with Harshak getting closer all the time. By the time the sinistrom entered the arena everyone had moved out of the way. Harshak started to slow down; he was resisting. Snakeweed's face was a picture of concentration, he was rubbing that pebble for all he was worth and reciting a shadow-spell at the same time. Harshak stiffened his legs and dug his claws into the grass, but you could see the force that was dragging him forwards. It was an astonishing feat of sorcery, quite extraordinary. Once the sinistrom was onstage he started to shimmer, his outline getting a bit blurry, and the crowd went mad. He grew smaller, then completely shapeless. Finally he shrank to a speck of light, which shot straight into the sinistrom stone. The applause was deafening.

"Snakeweed raised his hand for silence, and beckoned to a lickit who brought him a glass of fertle-juice. Snakeweed held up the pebble for everyone to see, and then he dropped it smack-bang in the centre of the juice. The pebble turned to treacle, and the crowd went berserk again. I could see a japegrin with tears in his eyes … two wise-hoofs hugging each other … what a triumph."

'And that's it,' Thornbeak finished. 'The ultimate publicity stunt.'

'So that's the end of Harshak,' said Felix.

'Good riddance,' said Ironclaw. 'He was known as the Nastiest of the Nasty, I believe. And he killed a brazzle in single combat. Have you two finished your dinner?'

'Certainly not,' said Betony, pushing her plate away and picking up the pudding menu. 'Oh *yes*,' she enthused. 'Got to have a slice of sparkle-meringue. Why don't you have the glitter-bomb, Felix, then we can fizz together.'

This sounded like fun. When the puddings arrived, they looked delicious – frothy and creamy with a crust of caramelized sugar on the top. Betony grinned. 'You first,' she said.

Felix took a spoonful, and tasted it. The flavour was a bit like vanilla, but as he removed the spoon from his mouth a shower of silver speckles exploded around him, and he yelped with surprise.

Betony had hysterics. Then she started on the sparkle-meringue, and a glittery starburst of pink enveloped her head. 'It's lickit cooking,' she said. 'Magical recipes. I haven't had one of these since I was little.'

They shovelled the puddings into their mouths as fast as possible, giggling as the silver and the pink collided, producing flecks of other colours which shot off at angles and then disappeared like sparks burning out.

'I think we'll head off to the perching rocks,' said Ironclaw, bored. 'See you in the morning.'

Felix and Betony finished their puddings, and left with Jahim. They found a very nice inn, and arranged to have their other clothes washed and pressed. Then they snuggled down in comfy feather beds, and fell asleep immediately.

The next morning they all met up by the carpet rack. Nimby looked like new again, and was regaling the other rugs with stories of his exploits in the desert.

'You've got more fibre than any carpet I've ever met,' Hearthmat was saying. 'Fancy actually going to *look* for Leona.'

'Morning, Nimby,' said Betony. 'This is Ironclaw, and this is Thornbeak.'

'Told you we were going to meet up with some brazzles, didn't I?' hissed Nimby, and the other rugs whispered amongst themselves and sounded overawed.

'Does this mean we don't have to carry you any more?' Ironclaw asked Felix. 'That'll be nice.'

'Oh good,' said Nimby. 'I was worried you wouldn't want me once you'd got your transport back.'

Ironclaw looked offended at the word 'transport', but before he could protest Thornbeak said, 'Right. I've made a few enquiries, and I know the location of five different rocks Leona uses. We'll start with the one by the diagram; if she's not there, we'll try the others. It may take some time, so I've packed a bag with some food and drink.'

'What sort of food and drink?' asked Betony suspiciously.

'Raw meat and water,' said Thornbeak.

'But ...'

Thornbeak laughed, her bright yellow eyes twinkling

with merriment. 'Plus some gobblerfish patties, a crusty nut loaf, a punnet of thunderberries and a gourd of rainbow-juice.'

Nimby unrolled himself, and Betony, Felix and Jahim climbed aboard. They flew back down the passageway, keeping to the speed limit, and once outside they went straight to the diagram. Leona wasn't there – nor had the twenty-seven been crossed out and turned into twenty-eight.

'The next one is a little way along the mountain trail,' said Thornbeak, so they took off again and found the loaf-shaped boulder with no difficulty. Leona wasn't there either. The trail got a little more difficult after that, with twists and turns and narrow stretches between rocks with overhangs where the brazzles had to walk rather than fly. Nimby was also too wide for the path, so he rolled himself up and Thornbeak carried him under one wing.

Although they'd started out cautiously, they became more *blasé* as time went on and there was no sign of the riddle-paw. They had lunch, and by the time they reached the fourth rock, Ironclaw was teaching them a raptorial song that involved some wing-flapping during the chorus. Betony and Felix were using their arms, and trying to get the right sort of squawk to go with it when they rounded a boulder – and there she was.

Leona was as big as a brazzle, but much more scary. She unsheathed her claws immediately, with a click that sounded like a flick-knife opening. Jahim stopped dead, and the others bumped into him.

Although Felix knew that Leona wasn't an Egyptian sort of sphinx – he'd bought a little statue of her, after all – he still felt his eyes widen in surprise. Half amberly and half lioness, with a few extras ... and extremely beautiful. She had jet-black hair, bound back in a Grecian style, and sloe-black eyes. Her skin was a flawless ivory, and she had high cheekbones and an aristocratic nose. The extras were rather noticeable canines, a dragon's tail, and a pair of rudimentary wings. The wings reminded Felix of those of an archaeopteryx – they didn't look powerful enough to give her the sort of flight the brazzles were capable of, but she could probably glide downhill, and use the occasional thermal to gain a little height and extend her range.

She studied them all from her vantage point on a rock, and then she said, 'I don't think you're going to give me much trrrouble, if the song you've been singing is anything to go by.' Her voice was low and menacing, like the distant rumble of a sleeping volcano. There was a hint of a purr to it

206

now and again, and an occasional suggestion of cat. *Big* cat.

Jahim gulped, and grabbed Nimby from Thornbeak. Nimby unrolled himself with unprecedented speed, and Jahim scrambled on to him.

'Jahim's only come along for the ride,' said Felix, determined not to be intimidated or to show any weakness. It wasn't as though he was ill any longer – he was a force to be reckoned with these days, although sometimes he had to remind himself of this. He stood a little straighter, and looked Leona in the eye. 'The rest of us want to ask you a couple of questions,' he said.

Leona raised her eyebrows. '*You* want to ask *me* questions? I think you'll find it's the other way round.' She flicked her armoured tail back and forth. It grazed the rock upon which she was lying, and struck sparks.

'We need two spells,' said Felix, undeterred. 'And we've heard that you're a sorceress of the first order. How many riddles do you want us to solve before you'll answer these two queries for us?'

'Depends on what they are,' said Leona thoughtfully, retracting and then extending her claws again. 'I'm intrigued, I have to admit it. No one's ever trrried to bargain with *me* before – I have to admire your nerve. Which spells do you need?'

'The king and queen of Andria are being held captive somewhere,' said Betony, 'and we know a mythical being is needed to rescue them.'

'Well, you've got the most difficult ingrrredient,' said Leona, glancing at Felix.

'We don't know where they *are*, though,' said Betony.

'A royalty location spell,' purred Leona. 'Yes, I can do that. And the other one?'

'Someone turned my parents to marble,' said Felix. 'It happened in my world – another dimension. It's a chain-reaction hex – anything that touches the statues turns to marble itself. I'm a human being, as I think you've realized, and my name is Felix.'

'And very appetizing you look too,' said Leona. Her eyes sparkled for a moment, and she licked her lips.

'My world hasn't discovered magic,' Felix went on, his voice steady and his gaze unflinching. He wasn't going to let Leona get the better of him, even though he was scared stiff. Her claws looked as unforgiving as flint arrowheads. 'For it to leak out like that in my world would be a complete disaster.'

Leona shook her head. 'Sorry. I can't give you anything specific without a sample of the marble.'

'I've got one,' said Felix, undoing his rucksack. He brought out the snail, and placed it on the rock in front of Leona.

'What an extrrraordinary crrreature,' Leona said, peering closely at it and sniffing it thoroughly. Then she said, 'It's clear you're telling the trrruth, human child. Very well. There *is* a countercharm that would work. The prrrice for both spells is the solution to three riddles.' She stretched herself out like a cat, sleek and well-groomed, her muscles rippling under her skin. Then she returned to her sitting position, and smiled. 'I can't believe I just said that, it's dirt-cheap by any standards.'

'Give us the first one, then,' said Ironclaw, fairly bristling with anticipation.

Leona laughed, although in some ways it sounded more like the yowl of a midnight alleycat. It made the hairs on the back of Felix's neck stand on end. 'Very confident, aren't you, brrrazzle?' she said. 'All right. What is the minimum number of weights you need to weigh every number up to thirteen on a pair of balancing-scales – you know, the ones that have a pair of dishes? Assuming each weight is a whole number?'

Felix looked at Ironclaw. 'It's four, isn't it? One, two, four and eight?'

Ironclaw shook his head. 'Three. One, three, and nine.'

Betony's brows drew together. 'How do you get two, then?'

'You put the Three in the empty dish. Then you put the One in the other dish, which holds the object being weighed. Three from one is two – you need to use subtraction as well as addition. The answer's three, Leona.'

The riddle-paw looked surprised. 'Not just an empty eggshell, are you?'

'I don't think you know very much about brazzles,' said Ironclaw.

'I thought they were all historians.'

'Only the females,' said Thornbeak. 'The males are mathematicians.'

'Let's try a psychological riddle, then,' purred Leona. 'Thrrree sorcerers have an argument, to be settled with heavy-duty wands at dawn, firing in rotation until only one is left alive. We'll call them Useless, Average, and Excellent. Useless knows he can only ignite his target one time out of three. Average always manages two out of three, and Excellent sends his target up in smoke every single time. Useless is allowed first strrrike. What should he do?'

'Hit a tree,' said Ironclaw. 'Next.'

Leona looked even more surprised.

'*Why?*' said Jahim from his vantage point on the carpet, a little above their heads.

'Because if he gets lucky and sends Average up in flames, Excellent will get him next shot. If he manages to hit Excellent, Average has a one-in-two chance of getting him. But Useless only has a one in three chance of hitting Excellent. Far better to let the other two battle it out, and leave Useless with first strike when there's only one adversary left.'

'You're good, brrrazzle, I'll give you that,' said Leona. 'It will almost be a pity to devour you. So now you can try the puzzle that *no one* has been able to solve.' She stood up, and scratched five symbols on to the rockface. Then she started to draw the diagram that was the key.

'Don't bother,' said Ironclaw. 'The answer's twenty-seven won for tea.'

Leona looked very angry for a moment. Her tail flicked back and forth, sending up showers of sparks, and her claws gouged long white grooves in the rock.

Felix took a pace back. The riddle-paw was a sorceress of the first order, she was capable of anything. He could almost feel her hot breath on his neck, her teeth digging into his shoulder, stripping away the flesh. Even Thornbeak had moved away slightly, although Ironclaw was standing his ground. He was quite clearly too pleased with himself to contemplate being plucked and consumed.

Suddenly Leona laughed. Her tail stopped twitching and she said, '*Well, set me a stiff one*, I shouldn't get upset. If I'd eaten you, brrrazzle, the world would have lost a great problem-solver.'

Ironclaw had a quick preen. 'You're pretty hot stuff yourself, Leona. We ought to thrash out a few equations together sometime.'

'I might take you up on that,' said the riddle-paw. 'I adore puzzles, but no one round here is interested, so I got ... well, annoyed. Ate a few people. Magical theory, now, that fascinates me. I know things that would make your feathers curl.'

'Please may we have the spells now?' interrupted Felix.

'Of course,' said Leona. 'The marble spell is mainly a recitation. But it does need one other element.' She wrote down the spell in Felix's notebook.

'What other element?' asked Felix, his heart sinking.

'A sprrrinkling of water from a prrrediction pool.'

'Like the one the brittlehorns use?'

'Prrrecisely.'

Thank goodness for that, thought Felix. We can stop off at the brittlehorns' valley. He turned to Betony, smiling with relief. Her face was expressionless. She noticed him watching her, and turned away. Felix felt confused. Surely she ought to be as pleased as he was? Then the penny dropped. 'Leona,' he said, 'would the countercharm work on Betony's parents? They were turned to stone when a bone-setting spell went wrong.'

'No,' said Leona.

'That's it? Just *no?*'

'I think you heard me correctly,' replied Leona, swishing her tail and looking annoyed. 'The countercharm is very specific. I can undo a spell cast prrroperly but not one that was just cast by someone completely incompetent!'

'You ought to memorize that marble incantation,' said Ironclaw hurriedly, before Felix could irritate Leona any further.

Felix sighed. 'I really don't have the same sort of memory as you, Ironclaw. I can't remember abstractions. I need pictures.'

'How strange,' said Ironclaw. 'You need a mnemonic, then. There's a mnemonic for my favourite trifle.'

'How come we've got on to cookery?' asked Nimby.

'We haven't,' said Leona, and Felix remembered that trifles were weird numbers like pi.

Ironclaw looked up at the sky and recited: 'Yes, I know I think admirably of myself. Cocky – but right! Problems? Ironclaw's supreme.'

'How does that work?' asked Felix. 'The initial letters don't make sense.'

'It's nothing to do with initials,' said Ironclaw. 'Each word has the right number of letters in it.'

'Oh, I see,' said Felix. '*Yes* – that's three letters. *I* – that's one. *Know* – that's four. Three point one four ... wow.'

'That mnemonic takes it to thirteen places, which is really all that's needed for most magic.'

'Oh, do shut up,' said Betony, getting impatient. 'What about the royalty location spell?'

Leona smiled. 'I need a brazzle feather.'

Both Ironclaw and Thornbeak plucked feathers from their breasts immediately. Leona was about to take Ironclaw's feather when she changed her mind, and selected Thornbeak's instead. Ironclaw looked put out.

'I need a clean one,' said Leona. She placed it on the ground so that it curved upwards, and was able to swivel. Then she closed her eyes and recited, '*Show the way, shaft of brazzle, seek the crown's bejewelled dazzle.*'

The feather stayed exactly where it was, motionless.

'Hmph,' said Leona, her tail flicking back and forth with annoyance.

'Why isn't it working?' asked Betony.

'I think the king and queen are asleep at the moment,' replied the riddle-paw. 'The feather *will* point to where they are, as soon as they wake up. You'll just have to keep trying.'

'Supposing they're not asleep? Supposing they're dead?'

'They're not dead. The feather would have vanished if they were. Just keep trying, and sooner or later you'll get a reading.'

'We ought to be on our way,' said Thornbeak.

Leona looked disappointed.

'We can't fly back now,' said Ironclaw. 'Sunset's only an hour away, and Nimby can't travel far in the dark. I think we should camp here, and leave first thing tomorrow morning.'

'Excellent idea,' said Leona, and they all busied themselves collecting brushwood. Leona lit a fire with a wave of her paw, and they settled themselves around it and had supper.

Ironclaw and Leona threw a few brain-teasers at one another, and were mightily impressed with each other's performance. Betony yawned, so Thornbeak asked Jahim about the history of Kaflabad, which interested Betony far more than logic. Nimby rolled himself up and went to sleep.

'I'd like to hear a bit about magical theory,' said Felix to Leona, when he could get a word in edgeways.

'Know anything about ittybitties?' asked Leona.

'I think we call them atoms,' said Felix. 'They join together to make molecules.'

'Oh, well when ittybitties join together, we call those ittybitty-twists. They can be either left-handed, or right-handed, or neither. And they can be huge.'

'That's like DNA,' said Felix. 'Twisted into a double-helix, and the basis of life itself.'

'You know quite a bit about it, then. Twist something one way, and it's one thing. Twist it the other way, and it's something else entirely, although it may look exactly the same. But give it a half-twist, and the unexpected *really* starts to happen. The twisty-strip effect.'

'We have things we call mutations – when DNA reproduces itself, and doesn't get it quite right.'

'Magic does something similar, except we control the not-quite-right part of it.'

'How?'

'With force fields. Wands give off force fields.'

'I once used magnetism to open a magic lock.'

'What's magnetism?'

Felix explained.

'Hmm,' said Leona. 'That's one I haven't heard of. We have others.'

Ironclaw started to explain. Twirl-force was obviously centrifugal force, and sticky-force was probably van de Waals' force, the one that enabled geckos to run across ceilings – but there were others that were far stranger, and Ironclaw lost Felix very quickly with the mathematics involved.

'The thing I don't understand,' said Felix, 'is how spells work when they're just spoken – when you don't exert another force. Like lighting a candle.'

'The wave of the hand is the other force employed there,' said Ironclaw. 'But suggestion is very important with person-to-person spells. Suggestion's a force too.'

Hypnotism, thought Felix. No one really knows how it works. Hypnotism with a half-twist could be very powerful indeed. By the time they all settled down to sleep, his head was spinning. It was clear that magical theory *could* be understood, right down to the fine details. He wanted to get back to his own world as fast as possible now, before one of the marble creatures got into the hands of someone who was capable of analyzing it.

The next morning Betony tried the royalty location spell again, but the king and queen still seemed to be asleep, as the feather remained unresponsive. Leona and Ironclaw decided to stay in touch through the new triple-head postal service that had recently been established. Now that Leona had someone she could swap riddles with she'd stopped feeling quite so resentful towards the Sebethians, and had decided to go back to eating less controversial game. Jahim, Felix and Betony climbed on board their carpet, which soared exuberantly into the air, and cruised alongside Ironclaw and Thornbeak.

'Felix,' said Betony, 'thanks for asking Leona about my

parents.'

'I'm sorry she couldn't do anything,' said Felix. 'It seems so unfair.'

'It's weird,' said Betony. 'Half the time I want them back, and half the time I'd rather things stayed the way they are.'

'I don't think anything about parents is straightforward,' said Felix, smiling.

They reached Kaflabad at sunset. Jahim reversed the change-of-ownership hex on Nimby, and they all said goodbye. Jahim was rather looking forward to reporting back to the king. His Majesty's face would be a picture when Jahim told him that the riddles had all been solved, and Leona had promised not to eat any more of Sebeth's inhabitants.

Nimby was parked on the crystal rack again – but he was a carpet of the world now, and his tales of high adventure earned him a lot of respect.

The brazzles found some suitable rocks outside the city walls.

Felix and Betony walked down one of the narrow streets, looking for an inn. As they passed a doorway, a dark figure jumped out and threw his arm round Felix's throat. 'Don't try anything, tangle-girl,' he growled at Betony, 'or I'll break the human's neck.'

Betony put a hand to her mouth, and stood transfixed.

'You left me to die, didn't you?' hissed the figure.

Felix couldn't speak; he could hardly *breathe*.

'I'm sorry,' said Betony in a small voice. 'The sandstorm

covered you completly. We wouldn't have been able to find you.'

Felix twisted his head, and got more air. What was Betony talking about? Then he felt something metal pressing against him, and he managed to glance down. It was a brass lamp.

'As you can see,' said the voice, 'the sand released me again. A triple-head saw me shining in the sunlight, praise its six eyes, and it brought me here.'

It's the brandee, thought Felix. He's out for revenge. I've had it.

'What do you want?' asked Betony shakily.

'I want to go to the human's world,' said the brandee. 'There might be a scientific way of turning me into a proper being.'

'What do you mean,' queried Betony, a little more confidently, 'a proper being?'

'How would you like to spend your life as a gas until some idiot summons you? It's always the same, they either want wealth beyond their wildest dreams, or the most beautiful female of their species. No imagination.'

'What happens if you're summoned by a female?'

'No idea. It's never happened to me.'

'So what would you do if you were human, and free?'

The brandee grinned. 'I'd go for wealth beyond my wildest dreams, and the most beautiful woman in the world. Put my lamp in your rucksack, boy, and take me with you.'

'You'd better let him go then, hadn't you?' said Betony.

'Sorry,' said the brandee, releasing Felix.

Felix coughed a couple of times, rubbed his neck, and opened his rucksack. The brandee streamed back into his lamp and Felix put it away, wrapped in some clothing. He gave Betony a look that said, *You know and I know I must never take that lamp across the Divide.*

Betony nodded again.

'I'll throw it away,' Felix mouthed at her, miming the action in case the brandee was listening.

Betony nodded for a third time, and giggled.

They found an inn, asked for the *à la carte* lickit menu and ordered the most expensive things on it – they could pay for them now that they had pocketfuls of brazzle gold once more. And what with the fruity fizzings and frothings and flashbangs that followed, they forgot all about the lamp in the rucksack.

The next morning they took off once again, and headed back across the Skeleton Plain for Geddon. By late afternoon the desert was behind them; they were in the foothills, and they would reach Tromm Fell the following day.

'I can't wait to see Agrimony's face when I turn up with my very own magic carpet,' said Betony. 'Sulphur's the *family* fire-breather, not Agrimony's own personal one.'

'And whose gold paid for him?' muttered Ironclaw.

Betony bit her lip, and glanced at Thornbeak.

219

'Oh, take no notice,' said Thornbeak, angling her golden head and peering at the scrubland beneath them. Suddenly she banked sharply, broke away from the others and went into a dive.

'Where's she going, Ironclaw?' asked Betony.

'No idea,' said Ironclaw. 'The workings of the female mind are way beyond even my considerable capabilities.'

They watched the little gold dot that was Thornbeak land in a patch of scrub, and then they were over the next outcrop and she was out of sight.

'Shouldn't we wait for her?' asked Betony.

Ironclaw raised one of his feathery eyebrows. 'Why?'

'It's polite.'

'It's OK, I can see her now,' said Felix. 'She's not far behind – but she's carrying something in her beak.'

'Looks like a branch,' said Betony.

'A *branch?*'

'Maybe she decided the perching rocks were too far gone.'

12

Rutherford Aubrey Tripp had forgotten all about the white marble wasp he'd passed on to his colleague, Emily Parsons. When she rang him he had no idea what she was talking about.

'Rutherford!' she shouted. 'You really are the limit! You ask me to do something in the spare time I don't have, and I assume it's something important. It now appears it was *so* important it's slipped your mind completely.'

'Ah,' said Rutherford, desperately trying to remember what it could possibly have been.

'You still don't know, do you?' fumed Emily. 'I've a good mind to keep this to myself.'

'Keep what to yourself?'

'This extraordinary petrification effect. You might have warned me. It's sheer chance I didn't turn to marble myself.'

A picture of the little white insect flashed into Rutherford's mind. 'Has someone invented the insecticide to end all insecticides, then?' he asked.

There was a grim little laugh at the other end of the line. 'You could say that, Rutherford, you could say that. I think we ought to meet up. There's a lot here that I don't understand. I'd like to investigate it further, but I want to be certain I'm not treading on any important toes.'

'You can tread on mine as much as you like,' said Rutherford, wishing he had the nerve to ask her out.

'I didn't mean yours, you idiot,' snapped Emily. 'I'm talking about MI5, the CIA, the FBI, the KGB or whatever combination of letters and numbers is appropriate these days. Do you get my drift?'

Rutherford gulped. 'I think so,' he said.

Not all the japegrins had been enthusiastic about Snakeweed becoming president, but as the only popular alternative had been Pewtermane, they hadn't argued. Better a japegrin than a brittlehorn. With a brittlehorn in charge they'd all be sent to philosophy classes, and urged to take up meditation.

Snakeweed had known something flamboyant was needed that would win everyone over. He'd got Grimspite to sniff out Harshak's sinistrom pebble in the library, and the public juicing of it had gone remarkably well – he'd made sure that the best reporters had been there, writing it up. The newspapers would be all over the known world by now, and he would be a hero. He hadn't really destroyed Harshak's pebble, however. He'd palmed it, and substituted another. He

222

kept the pebble in his safe, and admired it from time to time.

Snakeweed finished one of his gloating sessions, shut his safe with a closing spell, and summoned his secretary. 'What I need now,' he said, 'is a one-eye. I want an epic poem to commemorate Harshak's ... er ... demise. Apparently there's one in the Andrian mountains, an exile of some sort. She wrote that appalling anthem for Fleabane, but the style's exactly what I want. Nice undercurrent of violence. I've sent for her.'

'Right you are, Mr President, sir.'

Snakeweed smiled. 'I've got big plans. I've got some diggelucks dismantling the Land Rover, to see how it works. Otherworld Vehicles – I could set up a company, and market them. I've learned a lot about big business in the last year. You move your production line from place to place, wherever the labour's cheapest. And you don't have to pay vehicles a salary, the way you do triple-heads or fire-breathers. I've got a spreadsheet in my personal organizer, I've worked it all out.'

'Oh,' said Snakeweed's secretary. 'I forgot to tell you. We couldn't arrest Pewtermane because he's left the area. Gone back to the Geddon Forest apparently, to rejoin his herd.'

'Oh well,' said Snakeweed, 'that's even better. I won't have the tiresome job of thinking up a charge. And with Pewtermane gone, I have no serious opponents in the elections any more.'

Turpsik shrugged off the japegrin who tried to usher her into the palace, marched into Snakeweed's office, and regarded him contemptuously with her one eye.

Snakeweed looked up. 'I've got a little proposition for you, Turpsik. Write me an epic poem about the death of Harshak, and you can have a series of poetry readings here at the palace.'

Turpsik wondered how serious Snakeweed was. 'Need to think about it,' she said cautiously.

'Don't take too long,' said Snakeweed. 'I can always get hold of another one-eye.'

'But not one as distinguished as myself,' said Turpsik. 'There's an awful lot of rubbish being written at the moment.'

'How true,' said Snakeweed. 'You'll let me have an answer by this evening then, will you? I'm offering you a whole hour, once a week, and the best performers gold can buy.'

'I recite my poetry myself,' said Turpsik sharply.

'Whatever,' said Snakeweed.

Turpsik went to the library, where she could work at her leisure. Just as she was jotting down a few ideas a couple of japegrins walked past. Turpsik's hearing was very acute, so when one of them nodded in her direction and said, 'You know who that is?' she angled her head to hear better. Would they pluck up sufficient courage to ask her for her autograph?

'Turpsik,' said the second japegrin.

Turpsik patted her vile red hair into place, and waited.

'You'll never guess what Snakeweed said about that anthem of hers,' said the first japegrin.

Turpsik smiled to herself.

'He said a cuddyak could have done better, and the gassy backfires would have added a bit of light relief.'

Turpsik shut her notebook with a bang. The sooner she was out of Andria, the better. She marched out of the library, ignoring the japegrin at the information desk. The triple-head was being fed something disgusting.

'This is a choice bit of tail,' said Head Number Two to Head Number One. 'Can I offer you a peck?'

'How generous,' said Number One. 'Would you care for a beakful of liver?'

'Hold on,' said Number Three, catching sight of Turpsik. 'There's a one-eye trying to leave the library.'

'Been told you have to have an escort,' said Number One.

'Need to wait for one of the militia from the palace,' said Number Two.

The first arrival from the palace happened to be Grimspite, in lickit form, stuck with his two-legged guise until Snakeweed gave him his manuscript back. The only advantage was that he didn't smell quite as high as he usu-ally did; it was becoming clear that people noticed that sort of thing, and his personal hygiene had improved no end. As soon as he'd got his book he intended to go off and look for a brittlehorn to lift the blocking spell so he could get rid of Snakeweed once and for all. He glanced at Turpsik, who was sitting on the grass scribbling in a notebook. 'What are you doing?' he asked her.

'Writing a poem telling Snakeweed exactly what I think of him.'

Grimspite could see that Turpsik was unlikely to survive her next meeting with the president in one piece. 'I'll escort her,' he said to the triple-head.

'Password!' squawked Head Number One immediately.

'*Fangs and talons.*'

'We've got a new one now.'

'Oh,' said Grimspite, 'that's nice. What is it?'

'*Vamprey.*'

'Vamprey,' said Grimspite.

'It has to be one of the militia, though,' said Head Number One. 'Even if you do know the password.'

The other two heads emerged from the feathers, and they all spent a few minutes discussing recipes. Then Grimspite said, 'You work very long shifts.'

'We get time off.'

'We quite like guarding things, actually.'

'There are more interesting jobs,' said Grimspite. 'The new letter delivery service, for instance. It has two triple-heads working for it already, but they want more. You'd see the world, *and* get paid for it.'

'We like foreign food,' said Number Three. After a brief

discussion with the other heads the bird took off, and the only sign it had ever been there was a pile of white droppings on the statue of Flintfeather.

'Come on,' said Grimspite to Turpsik, 'let's get moving.'

'Go choke on a fish-bone,' said Turpsik.

Grimspite sighed. 'You don't recognize me, do you?'

'One lickit looks pretty much like another to me.'

'It's me. Grimspite,' he said, sounding disappointed. 'Look, I felt really bad about what I said about your anthem. When Snakeweed insulted my cookery book I understood exactly how you felt. Helping you escape was the best way I could think of to say sorry.'

'I suppose I shouldn't expect a sinistrom to know all that much about rhyme and metre,' said Turpsik. 'Let's face it, most beings can't tell a fish-saga from a fishing-song. Apology accepted.'

'Really?'

'Really.'

'Oh, *thank* you,' said Grimspite, with feeling. 'I've been trying so hard to learn about friendship, and all I seem to do is mess it up.'

'You'd make a lot of friends if you got rid of Snakeweed,' said Turpsik. '*Pukeberry eyes and a rancid smile, Snakeweed's face was etched with bile.*'

'I can't touch him,' said Grimspite, 'much as I'd like to. He cast a blocking spell on me.'

'Need a brittlehorn to lift that. Listen – I need to get

away from Andria. A long way away. Don't have the legs for it any more, though.'

Grimspite glanced down. Turpsik's goaty knees were rather podgy, and her ankles were far too thick to be athletic. 'You could nick a fire-breather,' he said. 'I have access to Snakeweed's one.'

A smile spread across Turpsik's face. 'There's a brittlehorn herd near Geddon,' she said. 'Why don't you come with me?'

'What about my manuscript?'

'Steal it.'

'But it's in Snakeweed's safe.'

'Haven't you ever heard him recite the opening spell?'

'Well ... yes. But I'm not sure I can remember all of it....'

'Cracked a few safes in my time,' smiled Turpsik. 'Poetry can be a dangerous profession. Tell me what you remember, my friend, and I'll see if I can fill in the gaps.'

Grimspite felt a warm glow envelop him. He was friends with Turpsik again, and it felt great.

Turpsik grabbed hold of Grimspite rather tightly as the fire-breather galloped down the runway, and Grimspite tightened his hold on his newly-retrieved manuscript.

Turpsik hadn't been on a fire-breather before, but she found the cold rush of air once they reached cruising speed delightfully bracing. There was a poem in this, somewhere. She watched the landscape unfold beneath her like a tablecloth. The Andrian mountains gave way to foothills, then to a vast ochre plain with scrubby little bushes and the occasional herd of lyre-horns. She saw the smudge of Tiratattle away to the north, and then they were over a dark mass of forest, interlaced with silvery rivers. At one point they passed over a strange stone building with a hedge round it, but it was too far below her to make out any detail. They stopped for the night by a wide river that wound its way between fields of flowers. Turpsik told the fire-breather how to fish with its wings, using them as a sort of umbrella. It learnt very quickly, gulping a few down as it went, and throwing the rest on to the bank. When it had caught enough it stepped out of the water, barbecued a couple of fish for Turpsik and Grimspite, and ate the rest itself. After that it burped, for rather a long time. Turpsik loosened the waistband of her pink dress and sighed with pleasure.

Before long the fire-breather dozed off, and Turpsik leant against its warm body and toyed with a few stanzas about leathery wings and favourite things. And then she was asleep.

Snakeweed stood in front of his safe, vaguely aware that something was missing and realizing that he had a cash-flow problem. There were only two crocks of gold left – perhaps he'd copied the Roman Emperor style of government a little too closely. Bread and circuses had impressed the Romans; cheap toadstools and free wailing concerts had worked just as well in Andria, but they'd been more expensive than he'd anticipated. The idea came to him as he stood there, staring at Harshak's pebble. Brazzle gold.

'You're a genius, Snakeweed,' he said out loud to himself. All male brazzles hoarded gold, even though they weren't that interested in making more of it. They just liked hanging on to what they'd got. There would be enough money on Tromm Fell to solve all his problems. He could take Harshak's pebble, summon the renegade sinistrom on arrival, and use him to force Ironclaw into revealing the whereabouts of his gold. He'd need some assistance to load it on to his fire-breather, however ...

Grimspite looked down as he and Turpsik circled above Geddon on Snakeweed's fire-breather. 'Can't land a fire-breather this size down there,' said Grimspite. 'They don't even have a proper runway, they just use the main road.'

'Fly on, then,' said Turpsik. 'If there's a brittlehorn herd there'll be a brittlehorn valley, and that'll be big enough.'

Snakeweed made his way to the livery stables accompanied by two of his militia, Pepperwort and Stonecrop. He pushed open the stable door, and stopped dead. 'Where's my *Whopper?*' he shouted.

Pepperwort looked blankly at Stonecrop, wondering what on earth Snakeweed was talking about.

'Never flown before, Pepperwort?' observed Stonecrop,

with a slightly superior expression. 'Fire-breathers come in several sizes – *Bigguns, Biggeruns,* and *Whoppers.*'

Pepperwort wrinkled his nose, wishing he had a cold so that he couldn't smell his surroundings quite so strongly. This was his first experience of a livery stable, and he didn't like it. The pungent aroma of red-hot dung mingled with the smell of cuddyak entrails, which lingered long after the offal itself had been eaten. Some of the overhead beams were singed and blackened, and a row of iron hooks on the wall trailed thick leather harnesses. There were several fire-breathers asleep in their stalls, little puffs of white smoke punctuating their deep, regular breathing. The stall directly opposite them – and the focus of Snakeweed's attention – was, however, quite empty.

'Someone's nicked it,' said Snakeweed indignantly. 'How *dare* they.'

Pepperwort and Stonecrop looked around for the proprietor, but there was no one in sight.

'We'll just have to take someone else's,' said Snakeweed. 'Pity there aren't any other *Whoppers.* Pepperwort, go and saddle up Number Five.'

Pepperwort beckoned to Stonecrop to help him lift down the saddle, a four-seater with a business-class luggage compartment.

'Get a move on,' said Snakeweed.

Pepperwort took a deep breath, but he didn't rush it. He approached the stall with extreme caution, and unfastened the fire-breather's halter.

The fire-breather carried on snoring.

'Er, excuse me,' said Pepperwort.

The fire-breather carried on snoring.

'Oy!' yelled Pepperwort.

The fire-breather awoke with a start, and looked round nervously. Then it had a good cough.

'Come on,' said Pepperwort, 'you're taking us to Tromm Fell.'

A pained expression crossed the fire-breather's face, and it slowly got to its feet. It had another good cough, and shook itself. A couple of scales hit the ground with a dull clunk. It followed Pepperwort rather stiffly out into the yard.

Stonecrop and Pepperwort placed the saddle on the creature's back. Number Five promptly sat down, which made fastening all the straps a bit of a chore. Stonecrop sighed. Snakeweed's fire-breather had been the only decent one in the stable – all the rest should have been pensioned off years ago.

Eventually the fire-breather stood up again, and they all mounted. It took a long time to get to the runway, but once there Number Five seemed to perk up a bit. It broke into a gallop, but didn't pick up enough speed to take off at its first attempt. With a heavy sigh it came to a halt, trudged all the way back, turned round and had another go. This time it managed to catch an updraught, and they rose slowly into the air. It banked sharply a couple of times, and Pepperwort could hear its laboured breathing as it searched for a thermal.

It was clear that they would have to stop several times for a rest and refuelling.

Felix and Betony changed out of the flowing robes and back into their normal clothes as soon as they reached Tromm Fell. Then they had a quick drink and a bite to eat, and Betony tried the royalty spell again, but the king and queen were obviously having a lie-in.

Thornbeak looked worried. 'I hope it does something soon,' she said. 'Felix wants to get home now he's got what he originally came for – but we need him to rescue the king and queen first, and we still don't know where they are. I've got a hunch they're not too far away, though – flame-birds don't fly west of here, and it was a flame-bird who brought the information. It's a pity there aren't any other mythical beings available to break the spell.'

'Wrong,' said Felix, delving into his rucksack.

'Oh!' said Betony. 'The snail!'

'Brilliant,' said Thornbeak. 'I won't apply the counter-charm to it until I need to, though. It'll be easier to transport as marble. Ironclaw will continue the search, leaving you free to go home, Felix.'

Betony's face clouded over for a moment, at the mention of Felix's departure. Then her chin lifted slightly. 'I'm going to go to the Andrian Divide with Felix,' she announced. 'I'm going to say goodbye there. I'll find out what's happening about the library, as well. For all we know, Snakeweed may have it up and running again.'

'Only if he can charge people to use it,' said Thornbeak sourly.

'There's something else that's bothering me,' said Felix. 'That Land Rover. If Snakeweed found a way of producing petrol, I bet he'd start manufacturing the things – and it wouldn't stop at vehicles. Eventually you'd get a pollution problem like the one we have in my world.'

'We'll see what we can do,' said Thornbeak.

Felix and Betony said goodbye to the brazzles, and climbed aboard their carpet.

'Where to, then?' asked Nimby.

'East,' said Betony. 'We need to collect a phial of water from the brittlehorn prediction pool for Felix's countercharm to work.'

The carpet rose into the air, and once again Felix and Betony were on their way. As they left the peak they caught a last glimpse of Ironclaw and Thornbeak. They were heading into the forest for some reason, arguing. Felix laughed.

Pepperwort sighed with relief when at long last his feet touched the ground again. The flight to Tromm Fell had not been a pleasant one, and Stonecrop had been sick. The fire-breather had developed a sort of judder when they were halfway there, and it had had a few near misses with particularly tall trees. The landing itself had been horrible. The fire-breather was now lying sprawled across the path, completely exhausted.

Pepperwort glanced round. This was a bare, lonely place. There were hardly any bushes, and he couldn't see any brazzles anywhere.

'We'll split up,' said Snakeweed. 'I'll start looking for the gold up here, and you two can head off downhill, looking for brazzles.'

Pepperwort felt he'd got the short straw. He did a precautionary wand-test and exploded a couple of bushes. Then he and Stonecrop set off down the hill, in the direction of Geddon.

The brittlehorn valley wasn't difficult to spot from above, and Grimspite landed Snakeweed's fire-breather without any difficulty. There was a waterfall at one end, tumbling down into a deep turquoise pool. He could see little groups of brittlehorns grazing, and a couple of foals chasing one another. Grimspite caught his breath at the sheer beauty of the scene. He suddenly realized that he had never thought of anything as beautiful before. *Tasty* was the most appreciative adjective he could ever recall using. After that he decided that what he wanted more than anything else was a good roll in some dung, and there was plenty of that around. He changed to his four-legged form, and got on with it. Turpsik re-pinned her hair into its horrible bun, and the fire-breather had a good scratch and let out a jet of flame. One of the brittlehorns turned to look, and neighed with alarm. Completely forgetting that he was in sinistrom form, Grimspite loped towards them. The whole herd turned and galloped to the other end of the valley, and disappeared inside a cave.

Grimspite sat down, feeling depressed. He knew he had to be very careful about this – brittlehorns could freeze sinistroms for short periods. It was back to the same old thing, how could he look sweet and unthreatening? If he crept forward on his belly, looking suitably submissive, it could be interpreted as a preparation to spring. He went as far down the valley as he dared, and stopped a little way from the cave. Then he rolled on his back and waved his paws in the air, glancing to the side from time to time to see if there was any reaction. Eventually a colt emerged, his curiosity overcoming his caution. Grimspite heard his mother whinny to him – but the colt was obviously showing off to his friends, for he took no notice and came closer. The whinny started to get more urgent.

'Hello,' said Grimspite. 'I don't mean anyone any harm.'

'I'm not falling for that,' said the colt. He took a deep breath, glanced at the other colts who were crowded together at the cave entrance and said, 'Stone you were, and to stone you will return as long as ... *oh bother.*'

'You've forgotten the rest of the shadow-spell, haven't you?' said Grimspite. 'But you don't need it, because I ...' He stopped. An ancient brittlehorn had emerged from the cave, and walking beside him were the human boy and the tangle-child.

'Hello, Architrex,' said Felix. 'I wouldn't do anything stupid if I were you, because Milklegs here will freeze you on the spot.'

'I'm not Architrex!' howled Grimspite. 'My name's Grimspite, and I hate being a sinistrom!'

Felix and Betony glanced at one another.

'*Please* listen,' said Grimspite. 'I got separated from my pebble, and I've got a conscience, and I prefer cooking to butchery. Turpsik will back me up. She's my friend.' He glanced down the valley. Turpsik had wandered over to the river than ran through the middle of it, and was gazing hopefully into the water .

'Turpsik?' said Felix. 'I know Turpsik. Turpsik's OK.'

'I think we'd better take him to the leader,' said Milklegs. 'He'll want to hear this.'

So they all went to the leader's cave, and Grimspite told his story. The leader stood there with his eyes shut, nodding every so often, although it was hard to tell whether the nods were nods of agreement, or a prelude to dropping off.

When Grimspite had finished Felix said, 'Actually, I believe him. When he's a lickit he does look a bit different to the way I remember Architrex's lickit.'

'Belief isn't proof,' said the leader.

'Let's have a look in the pool,' said Milklegs. 'You never know, it might come up with something.'

They went over. Neither Felix nor Betony could see anything except clear blue water, but Milklegs stiffened sharply, and peered more closely.

'What?' demanded Betony.

'This is completely off the point,' said Milklegs, 'but if the pool thinks something's important,

it overrides everything else. Snakeweed's up on Tromm Fell, peering into caves and looking behind boulders. I think he's looking for Ironclaw's gold.'

'Where are the brazzles?' asked Felix.

Milklegs shrugged. 'No idea. They're not up there, anyway.'

They all looked at one another.

'I don't know what to do!' cried Felix. 'I ought to hurry back to my own world to help my parents, but Ironclaw may be in trouble....'

Grimspite decided that a thoughtful and concerned expression was called for, but wrinkling his nose didn't feel quite right, somehow. It revealed rather too much of his canines.

'Excuse me,' said one of the mares to the leader. 'We mothers aren't too happy about having a sinistrom around.'

Grimspite deleted the thoughtful and concerned expression, and hung his head.

'I don't think this is a typical sinistrom at all,' said the leader. 'He has no pebble, therefore he has no master. Without a master he has no mission. When he crossed the Divide the first time, his psychopathic streak got left behind in his pebble, and he's developed a conscience to fill the gap. I think we should give him the benefit of the doubt.'

Grimspite looked at the leader with something approaching hero-worship in his eyes. Betony suddenly felt really sorry for him, so she patted him on the head. Nothing like a pat had ever happened to Grimspite before, and he felt a sudden and overpowering urge to please absolutely *everyone*.

'I know,' he said, 'why don't *I* go and look for Ironclaw and Thornbeak, and warn them?'

'There you are,' said the leader. 'Funny how things sort themselves out, isn't it?'

Grimspite trotted off down the valley, holding his head high. He had a proper mission now, one he'd *chosen* to accept.

'So what are *we* going to do?' asked Betony. 'Just sit here, doing nothing?'

'Sometimes doing nothing can be remarkably productive,' said the leader. 'However, in this instance I think you should fly off to the Andrian mountains and do what you were going to do all along.'

'Without knowing what's happening on Tromm Fell?'

'That's right,' said the leader. 'That's how it is, sometimes.'

Grimspite was halfway to the peak before he remembered that he hadn't asked anyone to lift the blocking spell. There was no point turning back now; he'd gone too far. When he'd fulfilled his mission, he'd be able to ask for it without feeling as though he were requesting a favour. He brightened up, and quickened his step.

13

Desperate to be off, and wriggling with enthusiasm, Nimby watched Felix fill a little phial with water from the prediction pool, stopper it, and place it in his rucksack. The carpet was full of energy after his brief sunbathe in the brittlehorn valley, and eager to impress – he wanted to show his owners that there were things a carpet could do that a brazzle couldn't.

Once they were on the move he decided to demonstrate some acrobatic low-level flying, following the path at speed and keeping just a couple of metres above the ground. It was really good fun, dodging tree-trunks and zipping along beneath overhanging branches. It required skill to do it properly, and he nearly made a mess of it when Felix suddenly hissed, 'Stop, Nimby!'

The carpet braked sharply, only just remembering to tilt his front end upwards so that he didn't tip his passengers off into the undergrowth. Then he subsided as gracefully as he could into the foliage.

'Listen,' whispered Felix.

'Don't you *care* that Snakeweed's stealing your gold?' a japegrin was asking.

Betony looked at Felix, wide-eyed.

'Move forward a bit,' hissed Felix, and Nimby wriggled forward until he found a tree to hide behind, so that his passengers could see what was going on in the glade in front of them.

A japegrin was holding Ironclaw and Thornbeak at wand-point in the middle of the clearing. 'I don't believe you,' Ironclaw was saying. 'The gold's rather well-hidden.'

'Not well enough.'

'In that case you'll be able to tell me precisely where Snakeweed found it.'

'Up there,' said the japegrin vaguely, indicating the peak of Tromm Fell with his head.

Ironclaw laughed. 'So why bother to come and tell us?'

There was a moment of silence.

'You can't answer that one, can you?' said Ironclaw. 'You thought I'd be so incensed I wouldn't stop to think, I'd just go flapping up there like a pullet. The only reason you want me up on the peak is so that Snakeweed can prise the real location out of me. You must think I fledged yesterday.'

Thornbeak had sidled round so that she was nearly within striking distance, but unfortunately the japegrin noticed, and he sent a shower of sparks shrieking across her feet. She made a funny little squeak of pain, and hopped backwards. The feathers on Ironclaw's neck stood up, and his eyes blazed with fury. He took a step forwards, and the japegrin gave him the same treatment.

'Ouch,' said Ironclaw, glaring at him.

'You'd better tell *me* where your hoard is then,' said Pepperwort.

'You won't be able to get at it,' said Ironclaw. 'I hid it in the other dimension, across the Divide.'

Felix gulped.

'Hey,' whispered Betony, 'that's really clever.'

Hundreds of crocks of gold, just lying in a jungle in Costa Rica? Felix couldn't begin to imagine the consequences of someone finding it.

'You're joking,' said the japegrin.

'I'm not,' said Ironclaw. He looked extremely pleased with himself.

'Well in that case you'll just have to cross us both over, and bring them back.'

'Go sit under a vamprey.'

Pepperwort smiled a rather horrible lopsided smile. 'Do you know what happens when the death sentence is passed on a brazzle? No? They're plucked. From head to toe.' He fingered his wand. 'This little beauty can remove a single feather if I switch it to narrow beam. Let me show you.'

A thin shaft of light shot out of the wand, and one of Thornbeak's golden feathers spiralled gently to the ground.

'See?' said Pepperwort. 'But I don't intend to pluck *you*, Ironclaw. I'll strip Thornbeak here, until she's just skin and bone.' There was another streak of light, and a second feather drifted lazily down.

Ironclaw screeched with fury, spread his wings and drew back his head like a swan about to deliver the peck of all pecks. The japegrin raised his wand in self-defence – and that might have been the end of Ironclaw if Felix hadn't yelled, 'No!'

The japegrin spun round, and sent a sheet of flame shooting across the undergrowth. The carpet tilted violently to one side, and deposited Felix in the bushes. Suddenly there was smoke everywhere, and he couldn't see anything at all. He blundered about, bashing his arm against a tree-trunk and coughing. His eyes were stinging, and his throat felt as though someone were trying to push a hedgehog down it. He could hear Nimby screaming, and Ironclaw shouting, 'You win, curse your entrails! I'll take you across the Divide. Just leave Thornbeak and the youngsters alone, will you?'

Then the smoke cleared, and Felix found himself facing Pepperwort's wand. This must be what it's like looking down the barrel of a gun, he thought, and his knees suddenly turned very weak.

Betony was standing a little to his left, ashen-faced, and Nimby was smouldering on the grass. 'I stamped out the flames,' said Betony, 'but he's badly burned.'

Nimby gave a faint moan, and Betony made a move towards him.

'Leave that carpet where it fell and get moving,' said Pepperwort.

'Brazzles can't walk the distances you can,' said Ironclaw. 'They're not built for it. They're built to fly.'

'All right,' said Pepperwort. 'You can carry me, and Thornbeak can carry the others.'

'What about the—' Thornbeak began.

'Do as he says,' interrupted Ironclaw.

Felix and Betony clambered on to Thornbeak. Pepperwort climbed rather nervously on to Ironclaw, and glanced round as though he expected to find a seatbelt somewhere. Realization slowly dawned that this was going to be very different from a scheduled flight on a fire-breather, and he grabbed hold of Ironclaw's feathers.

'Don't do that,' said Ironclaw. 'It spoils my concentration.'

'I have to hold on somehow,' snapped Pepperwort.

'Grip with your knees,' said Ironclaw, rising into the air. 'Don't you know anything?'

The brazzles climbed steeply above the tree canopy, their powerful wings whipping up the sort of wind that bent branches.

Then Thornbeak banked hard to the left, out of Ironclaw's way, and called, 'All clear!'

'All clear for what?' yelled Pepperwort.

'His dropping-like-a-stone impression,' screeched Thornbeak, and Ironclaw furled his wings and plummeted.

There was a high-pitched scream from Pepperwort. He parted company with Ironclaw, and landed somewhere in the tree canopy.

'That was as easy as a trifle,' said Ironclaw, and both he and Thornbeak laughed so hard that Thornbeak nearly unseated *her* passengers.

Felix joined in, out of sheer relief.

'We need to get Nimby,' said Betony sharply, so the brazzles circled round and headed back to the glade.

'I suggest that, after that, we go back to the brittlehorn valley and see if the rug can be repaired,' said Thornbeak. 'And whilst we're there, Milklegs can consult the pool and tell us whether Snakeweed's given up and gone back to Andria yet. I don't particularly want to fly back to the perching rocks if *he's* still there.' She looked at Ironclaw, who nodded in agreement. Then her attention was taken by a fallen branch that was curved in an elegant S-shape.

'I'll pick it up later,' said Ironclaw.

Betony looked at Thornbeak, perplexed.

'Those brazzle rocks are still terribly uncomfortable,' said Thornbeak. 'A perching branch would be an improvement. That's why we were in the forest. Shopping.' But she didn't look Betony in the eye as she said it.

By the time they picked up Nimby from the glade, he was only semi-conscious. He kept calling Felix 'Master

Weaver', and telling him to even up his selvedge.

'What are we going to do?' wailed Betony. 'He can't fly us to the Andrian mountains in this state.'

'He needs a first-class seamstress,' said Thornbeak. 'Someone who can do invisible patching.'

'Well we're not going to find one in the brittlehorn valley, are we?' snapped Betony. 'We'll have to go back to Geddon.'

'One thing at a time,' said Thornbeak.

Felix groaned inwardly. It was one thing after another, not one thing at a time. He needed to get back to his own world, and everything was conspiring against it.

'Can't *you* take us to the Andrian Divide?' he asked.

'I don't really feel up to a long flight,' said Thornbeak unexpectedly. She glanced at Ironclaw.

'Er ... nor do I,' said Ironclaw.

Betony's face creased into a frown. 'So what about the king and queen? You're meant to be looking for them.'

'I can't do anything until the feather responds, Betony,' said Thornbeak reasonably.

As soon as they landed in the brittlehorn valley it became apparent that there was some sort of celebration going on. A fire-breather was curled up a little way off on the bank of the river, fast asleep, its breath rising into the air like smoke signals. Oatcakes were laid out on the grass, and a stone trough had been filled with fermented fertle-juice. A group of colts were galloping around, deaf to the shouts of their mothers to calm down. Every so often one of them would sneak up to the trough and slurp down a mouthful of juice, until someone noticed and chased them away again.

'*Well, whisk my rump with a bunch of twigs,*' said Milklegs, when he saw the brazzles. 'Pewtermane's fame stretches far and wide. There were a lot of people wanted him for president of Andria, you know.' He glanced toward the mud wallow. Several brittlehorns were rolling around in it, but they were so mud-bespattered that they were unrecognizable.

'There's Granitelegs,' said Ironclaw, waving a wing.

Granitelegs seemed a little unsteady on his feet, and nearly fell over as he squawked a greeting.

'Too much fermented fertle-juice,' said Thornbeak disapprovingly.

'Is that Pewtermane, over there?' asked Felix.

'It is,' said Milklegs. 'We're celebrating his return. Have an oatcake.'

To Felix's surprise, Thornbeak had one too. 'I thought you were completely carnivorous?' he said. The oatcake didn't really taste of anything much, and he had to chew it for ages.

'Just fancied it,' said Thornbeak, and she had another one.

'Well well,' said a familiar voice. 'If it isn't Thornbeak. That squintlefish research you did for me was first rate.'

'Turpsik!' cried Thornbeak. 'What a delightful surprise!'

'Quite a party,' said Turpsik, surveying the others.

'I forgot to tell you about Turpsik nicking Snakeweed's

248

fire-breather,' said Felix to the brazzles, but before he could explain about Grimspite a really good idea came to him. 'Turpsik,' he said, 'I've just thought – you're brilliant with a needle and thread, aren't you?'

Turpsik smoothed her pink dress over her ample bosom and smiled. 'But not quite as good as I am with a dactyl and trochee.'

Betony looked blank.

'They're poetry terms,' hissed Thornbeak.

'Could you mend a magic carpet?' asked Felix.

'Never tried,' said Turpsik. 'Don't see why not, though.'

'I'll get him,' said Betony, and she went off to fetch Nimby.

Thornbeak turned to Milklegs. 'We've got a favour to ask,' she said. 'We want to know what's going on back up on the peak. Could you do a pool-check for us?'

Milklegs hiccoughed. 'All right,' he said.

Betony returned with the carpet tucked underneath her arm. Turpsik sucked in her breath, and let it out again. 'That's quite a job,' she said.

'But you could do it?'

'It'll take me a while.'

'Wipe your feet somewhere else,' muttered Nimby. 'I only lie down for royalty.'

'He's delirious,' said Turpsik. 'I'd better get started before any more of him becomes unravelled. Good job I always carry my sewing kit with me.' She took a battered little box

249

out of one of her pockets, along with the filleting knife she used as scissors.

'I'm getting something,' said Milklegs. 'Snakeweed's still up there, sitting on a rock. And Stonecrop's just arriving.'

As soon as Snakeweed saw Stonecrop he looked annoyed and snapped, 'Where's Pepperwort?'

'We split up,' said Stonecrop. 'We couldn't find the brazzles anywhere.'

'Well it's a good job I don't need them any more, isn't it?' snapped Snakeweed. 'You see, I know where Ironclaw has hidden his gold.'

'Where?' asked Stonecrop.

'Where I would have hidden it, if I'd been in Ironclaw's position. On the other side of the Divide.'

Stonecrop laughed, as though this were some kind of joke.

'Can you think of a better place?'

Stonecrop blanched. 'Are you suggesting we cross over there ourselves, and bring it back?'

'That's right. I can't carry it all on my own, and we'll need several trips. I don't fancy taking the fire-breather across, it's too noticeable. They don't have fire-breathers in the other world.'

'Supposing Ironclaw returns,' said Stonecrop, 'and tells our fire-breather to get lost? If he dismisses our transport, getting the gold back's pointless. We couldn't carry it.

Perhaps I should stay behind and guard the beast of burden.'

'Good point,' said Snakeweed. He rummaged in his pocket. 'But you're not staying, I need you. I'll leave Harshak in charge.'

'Harshak?' whispered Stonecrop. 'But ... but you destroyed him.'

'You think I'd surrender the best weapon I've ever had?' laughed Snakeweed. 'No no no.' He showed Stonecrop Harshak's pebble, and then he started to rub it between the palms of his hands. Stonecrop's eyes widened in horror; then he went very white, and grabbed hold of a rock to steady himself.

The pebble started to glow, giving off a foul smell as Harshak slowly materialized, gradually losing transparency until he was a solid being. His snout was criss-crossed with scars, his knife-like canines were a dirty yellow and he had appeared mid-snarl. There was a fresh scar on his stomach, but it was healing quickly, the way sinistrom wounds always did after a good licking. Stonecrop made a sort of strangled sound in his throat.

Harshak was glaring at Snakeweed as though he really didn't like him very much. Snakeweed stared back, his green eyes level and steady, and Harshak's snarl slowly faded away.

'That's better,' said Snakeweed. 'Now. See that fire-breather over there? The one that looks as though it'll shortly be shoe-leather? I want you to guard it.'

Harshak's eyes widened, and he looked outraged. 'Is that

251

all? You summon me here – me, Harshak, the most terrible of the terrible, and all you want me to do is guard a geriatric vehicle?'

'That's right,' said Snakeweed.

Harshak went over to the fire-breather. The fire-breather opened one eye, and let out a smoke-puff of alarm. 'I have no instructions to harm you,' said Harshak contemptuously. 'I, Harshak, the most gruesome of the gruesome, am your body-guard.'

The fire-breather made a face at the smell, opened his other eye and gave Snakeweed a look of disgust. Then he went back to sleep.

'Come on then,' said Snakeweed, beckoning to Stonecrop and walking over to the Divide. The two of them straddled the ridge as Snakeweed flipped open his personal organiser, and started to recite the numbers of the spell out loud.

'Blazing feathers,' said Ironclaw, as Milklegs told them what he'd just witnessed. 'I didn't expect Snakeweed to guess where I'd hidden the gold.'

'What are we going to do?' asked Betony.

They all looked at one another.

'I think I'd better follow them across the Divide,' said Ironclaw. Gold was a serious matter.

'I think I should come too,' said Felix. 'Brazzle gold shouldn't be in my world at all. It's nearly as worrying as marble statues.'

'It's inert,' said Ironclaw. 'It doesn't respond to magic. That's why it's used as currency.'

'Gold has a disturbing effect on human beings,' said Felix. 'It makes them reckless, as well as ruthless. Listen – Snakeweed won't have Harshak to defend him, and he won't be expecting us – so we could jump him, disarm Stonecrop, and retrieve Harshak's pebble. Then we bring back the gold, and destroy Harshak for good.'

'I want to go, too,' said Betony. 'I'd love to see Felix's world – even if it is just for an hour or two. And I can help carry the gold.'

'What are you going to do about Snakeweed?' asked Turpsik, glancing at Ironclaw. 'Didn't you once say you wished you'd pecked his eyes out?'

'It's just a figure of speech,' said Ironclaw uncomfortably.

'I'd do it myself,' said Thornbeak, 'but ...'

'No you won't,' interrupted Ironclaw. 'In fact, I don't even think you should cross the Divide.'

Betony expected Thornbeak to come out with a sharp reply, but she didn't. She merely said, 'No, it probably wouldn't be a good idea. Things to do.'

Felix and Betony climbed on to Ironclaw again, and he spiralled up and out of the brittlehorn valley. Before long the rocky peak came into view, along with two tiny columns of smoke. Ironclaw swooped down low and skimmed the rocks like an aircraft evading radar, and Felix suspected that he was just as good at it as Nimby. He could see the ground rushing by beneath him – Ironclaw's dirt-board, the perching rocks, the path, then a pile of brushwood, as though someone had been collecting fuel.

They crested a small outcrop, and there was the fire-breather. Harshak was lying down next to it, his head on his paws. Ironclaw landed close to the Divide, and Felix and Betony leapt off.

Harshak was on his feet and charging towards them before they had time to get themselves organized. Felix and Betony banged into one another, trying to get away, and fell over. Harshak crinkled his upper lip into a concertina, baring scimitar-fangs the colour of old ivory, and a deep rumbling growl erupted from his breast. He went straight for Ironclaw's throat, but the brazzle side-stepped him. Harshak skidded to a halt in a cloud of dust like a cartoon character, all four legs held rigidly out in front of him at forty-five degrees.

'Hang on …' said Ironclaw.

Harshak didn't give him the chance to finish – he leapt into action once more, all snarl and muscle. Ironclaw simply lifted into the air a little way and let him charge past underneath.

Harshak slid to a stop again, his brain eventually catching up with his legs. He wasn't going to defeat something that could fly without a considerable improvement in his tactics. He decided to try a bit of taunting and ridicule. 'I know you, you flea-bitten old mathematician,' he said. 'You nearly disembowelled me, in that tunnel back in Andria. Sheer luck, naturally.'

'I'll have you know that was a very skilful piece of beak-work,' squawked Ironclaw indignantly, settling back on the ground again and fluffing out his chest feathers.

Harshak took a couple of paces forward. 'Didn't have the guts to finish me off though, did you? Turned tail and ran for it. Call yourself a brazzle?'

Ironclaw flapped his wings, beside himself with fury. 'It wasn't like that, you mindless hairball!'

'Mindless hairballs aren't honoured with a title like *the meanest of the mean*, they're not imaginative enough,' declared Harshak. He was now close enough to try again, but he misjudged Ironclaw's speed and found himself hanging on to the brazzle's tail as he lifted into the air again. As his jaws were now full of fur he couldn't use insults any more, which was a drag. But Ironclaw could neither peck him, nor scrape him off with his talons, so there would be no winners until he landed again.

Ironclaw was finding it difficult to steer without his tail to help him. His original plan had been to dash Harshak's brains out on a rocky promontory, but as he got within striking distance he realized he couldn't control his descent, so he had to overshoot and land right next to the fire-breather. Harshak was at him again in a flash, and Ironclaw only just managed to scramble to one side and evade the sinistrom's attack. Harshak wheeled round for another go, and this time

Ironclaw sidestepped him very neatly, stuck out his leg, and brought him crashing down. Before Harshak could regain his footing Ironclaw had him pinned to the ground with his talons.

The fire-breather was looking increasingly nervous, and it let out an involuntary jet of smoke.

'I won't let him steal you,' snarled Harshak to his charge, twisting this way and that and getting nowhere.

'We're not after your moth-eaten fire-breather,' said Ironclaw. 'Use your head. Why would a brazzle *need* a fire-breather?'

Harshak snapped at the dust for want of anything better to snap at.

'Oh for goodness' sake,' said Ironclaw, his foot tightening its hold.

Harshak twisted his head to face Ironclaw's. 'Let me up, will you? I'm not going to attack anyone. I have no quarrel with *you*, not if you don't want the fire-breather, despite that little episode in the tunnel in Andria. I'm a professional killer, I can't be bothered with petty feuds.'

Ironclaw thought about it for a moment – but he wasn't going to be able to cross the Divide whilst he was in physical contact with Harshak, not unless he wanted to take the sinistrom with him. He decided to risk it, and released him.

'I can't say I rate Snakeweed much as a master,' said Harshak, shaking the dust from his coat. 'He has no idea how to treat a sinistrom of my seniority – I'm Harshak, the vilest of the vile. But I've been treacle for the last five hundred years, so I've no idea what's been going on. Perhaps sinistroms don't have the status they used to.'

Ironclaw, Felix and Betony straddled the Divide, and Ironclaw started to recite the spell.

'Hold on,' said Harshak. 'What are you doing?'

Ironclaw gabbled the numbers as quickly as he could.

'What are you doing?' persisted Harshak. 'That sounds like the Divide spell that Snakeweed used.'

Ironclaw completed the incantation. There was that odd little jump sideways, and then the darkness.

When Felix came to Betony was lying on the ground beside him, her mouth half-open, her eyes shut, her white-blonde hair spread out in a halo around her head. She looked angelic when she was asleep. When she was awake her face was far more impish. She opened her eyes, and sat up immediately. 'Are we here?' she asked. 'Is this your world?'

'Yes,' said Felix. 'Only it's not the part I live in. This is Costa Rica, where I crossed over the Divide the first time.' He glanced around, smiling, relieved to see that the butterflies were still colourful and fluttering and air-borne, not white and motionless on the ground. 'It's a year since I was last here, but I remember everything – the trees, the flowers, the humming birds. … It's much hotter here than England, which is where I come from.'

'Where did you hide your gold, Ironclaw?' asked Betony.

'Down there,' said the brazzle, nodding his head vaguely at the trees.

Felix made a face. The terrain wasn't ideal. 'We need to get off the main path,' he said. 'If anyone sees us we're in big trouble.'

Ironclaw led the way, pushing the undergrowth aside with his sheer bulk. Felix took a compass reading, just to be on the safe side – getting lost would be disastrous. The canopy would make it almost impossible for a brazzle to take off, which would be the quickest way to get back to their start-point.

Suddenly Ironclaw stopped dead, his head on one side, and looked intently at the leaf litter on the ground. Felix followed his gaze. For a moment he saw nothing unusual – then there was a slight movement, as though the forest floor were unzipping itself. A sinuous grey-brown shape with paler diamond markings slithered away.

'Oh, wow!' said Betony. 'What an amazing creature,' and she moved towards it.

'No!' yelled Felix. 'It's poisonous!'

Ironclaw acted like lightning, seized the snake in his beak and cracked it like a whip, breaking its neck. Then he swallowed it whole.

'Delicious,' he pronounced.

'That was a fer-de-lance,' said Felix, feeling a bit shaky. 'It would have killed you.'

Betony looked astounded. 'I didn't think you had shadow-beasts over here.'

'It's not a shadow-beast,' said Felix, and he explained about snakes and poison arrow frogs and tarantulas, and how it was best not to approach anything strange that she saw.

Betony was looking less entranced with Costa Rica by the minute, so Felix pointed out a humming-bird and an orchid and a column of leaf-cutter ants. She cheered up slightly, and when they came to a crystal-clear waterfall tumbling between mossy butterfly-speckled rocks she was back to her usual bouncy self.

'Not far now,' said Ironclaw.

Just as he finished speaking, a loud bang rang out.

'What's that?' asked Betony.

'The branch of a tree breaking off, probably,' said Ironclaw.

'I think it might have been a shot,' said Felix, but before he could explain they heard voices.

'Let's get a bit closer,' said Ironclaw. It was amazing how silently he could move when he had to. Felix and Betony followed where he trod, and after a couple of minutes they found themselves at the edge of a glade, where they could watch unobserved from the undergrowth.

Snakeweed and Stonecrop were standing there with their hands raised above their heads. Two men were pointing rifles at them, and arguing in Spanish. Next to them stood two mules, their panniers full of Ironclaw's crocks of gold.

'If you're going to kill us, at least have the decency to tell us that in English,' said Snakeweed, as cool as ever.

'How you know about El Dorado?' demanded one of the men. He had beady black eyes, and a thick moustache.

'El Dorado?' Snakeweed raised a ginger eyebrow.

'Don't play the clever with me,' said the man. 'José, here, he kill you just like that.' He snapped his fingers.

José's mouth smiled, but his eyes didn't.

'El Dorado,' said the man with the moustache. 'The ruined city, where the king he was painted with the gold-dust. Your Walter Raleigh, he not find it. Nobody find it till now.'

Behind the screen of foliage, Felix grinned. 'El Dorado was meant to be in Brazil, not Costa Rica,' he whispered.

Snakeweed glanced at Stonecrop. Then he gave a slight nod, and bowed his head so that his hat fell off. His pointed ears poked up through the tangle of red hair like demonic identity tags, and he uttered what he hoped sounded like a devilish cackle.

José's mouth dropped open, and he just stared. The other man turned his head to see what had alarmed his companion, and his hesitation was just long enough for Stonecrop to draw his wand. An arc of purple light hit the rifle, which flew across the clearing and landed in a bush. José spun round, levelled his own rifle and fired. The wand shattered with a sound like breaking glass. Snakeweed had drawn *his* wand by now, however, and he hit José's rifle a split second later. The weapon bit the dust, and José screamed and clutched his arm.

'Freeze them,' said Snakeweed, handing his personal organizer to Stonecrop. 'Use the first bit of the Divide Spell – we're close enough to the ridge for it to work.'

Stonecrop read it out.

'Very considerate of them to load all this on to pack animals,' said Snakeweed, patting one of the mules on the rump. 'We'll take them back with us.' The object of his attention laid back its ears and watched him suspiciously from white-rimmed eyes.

'All done,' said Stonecrop, handing back the organizer.

The two humans stood side by side among the flowers, their eyes shut, completely motionless. Felix thought they looked as though they were drinking in the beauty of the place; listening to the birdsong, smelling the vegetation, feeling the sun on their faces through the tracery of leaves. It was only after a while you realised there was something slightly wrong about them – they weren't breathing.

'Let's go, then,' said Snakeweed, and the party headed off along a little trail that would take them back up to the Divide.

'What shall we do now?' hissed Betony.

'Follow them, and take them by surprise,' said Ironclaw.

This was easier said than done, however, as Ironclaw was far too big to remain unnoticed unless they kept a fair distance from their quarry. When the path forked, it was several minutes before they realized they'd taken the wrong turning. They had to retrace their steps, and, hurry as they might, they knew they were now much further in the rear than they'd have liked.

14

'Well, *multiply my age by an imaginary number*,' said Granitelegs, landing in a cloud of dust on Tromm Fell and finding himself faced by Harshak. 'Who in the name of algebra are *you?*' He'd had rather too many fermented fertlejuices at Pewtermane's coming home party, and had decided to nip back to the peak and see if Ironclaw's dirt-board was free for a quick calculation or two.

'I am Harshak, the ghastliest of the ghastly.'

'Oh,' said Granitelegs, unimpressed.

'I have been given the menial task of guarding this arthritic vehicle. However, as you have wings of your own I doubt that you will have much use for it.'

'Never used to see shinistroms round here,' said Granitelegs. 'Now you're all over the place. Apparently there was one in the brittlehorn valley earlier today, one that had been sheparated from his pebble, if you can believe such a thing. I thought shinistroms just withered away and died if that happened.'

Harshak stiffened. 'What do you mean, separated from his pebble?'

'It got losht when he crossed from one dimension to another,' Granitelegs said.

'He doesn't have a master any more.'

'Is that so,' said Harshak thoughtfully, his brows knitting together until the black spots ran into one another, giving him temporary eyebrows. Then he gave that peculiarly manic sinistrom laugh and said, 'My pebble's in Snakeweed's pocket. And Snakeweed is in another world. Therefore I, Harshak, the most callous of the callous, am a free agent too.'

'Grimspite dishcovered he had a conscience, apparently,' said Granitelegs. 'He became a much nicer shadow-beast as a result.'

Harshak got to his feet. 'That was *his* choice,' he said. '*My* choice is somewhat different. I am now at liberty to kill at will, to maim, to torture, to spread terror wherever I go.' He glanced contemptuously at the fire-breather. 'No more second-rate missions for me. I shall fulfil my true potential – become the worst scourge this world has ever known. It's been a few centuries since I had some real fun.' He snapped at the fire-breather's hind leg, which opened up in a great gash.

The huge beast woke with a start, bellowed with pain, and coughed up a jet of flame.

'You're free to go,' said Harshak.

The fire-breather pulled itself to its feet, limped to an overhang, and launched itself into the air. It circled once, gaining a bit of height, then flew low over Harshak and relieved itself with a satisfied grunt. Red-hot clinker showered over the sinistrom, who yelped with pain and rolled in the dust to stop his coat catching alight. As the fire-breather winged its way off towards Tiratattle, Granitelegs could hear it laughing.

Rutherford Tripp met Emily Parsons in a discreet little café, close to where they both worked. He had never seen her without a lab-coat on before, but there wasn't really all that much difference. She was wearing a white silk shirt and a cream linen skirt, and she looked as no-nonsense as ever. Despite the fact that Rutherford had been to the café many times before, and the checked tablecloths and plastic daffodils were familiar eyesores, he felt on edge. He couldn't help glancing round from time to time, to see if anyone was watching them.

'Oh for goodness' sake, Rutherford,' said Emily. 'You're looking more like an international terrorist with every passing minute.'

'You made me nervous, with all your talk of the CIA and the KGB.'

Emily placed a tiny transparent plastic box containing the marble wasp on the table. Then she added another one, containing a white marble frog. Then a third, which was larger.

This held a starling – also white, also marble.

Rutherford heard himself catch his breath. 'The effect isn't limited to insects, then,' he said.

'No.'

'It can petrify any living thing?'

'Yes.'

'So what exactly was in the plum – some sort of systemic poison?'

'There was nothing in the plum.'

'*What?*'

'It's a chain-reaction thing.'

'That's not possible.'

'That's what I'd have said this time last week.'

'Are you thinking what I'm thinking?'

'I doubt it,' said Emily, 'but try me.'

'That this is a weapon that's being developed by a top secret laboratory, either here or abroad. And that if anyone knows we've got it, they'll want to get rid of us rather sharpish. Is there an antidote?'

'I haven't found one,' said Emily.

'It could be the end of all life on earth,' said Rutherford, the implications suddenly hitting home.

'Don't be silly,' said Emily. 'There are ways of containing it.'

'Foolproof ways?' He ran a hand nervously through his thinning sandy hair.

'Who needs foolproof?' said Emily. 'Good enough is all

that's required. And stop abusing your hair, or you'll have none left.'

Rutherford fiddled with his glasses instead. 'Good enough never lasts for ever,' he said.

'I don't care if it doesn't last for ever.'

'What about your children?'

'I don't have any children, Rutherford.'

'But ... it could mean the total extinction of the animal kingdom.'

'Not necessarily,' said Emily. 'The effect weakens the more links you have in the chain. Whatever turned your wasp to marble must have been a primary agent. I've been using fruit flies, infecting one from another in a sort of domino experiment. Eventually the fly only stays in its marble form for a few minutes. But the wasps you gave me are still exactly as they were. For all I know, they're going to stay like that for years.'

Rutherford glanced round again.

'Oh, for heaven's sake,' said Emily. 'If this was an accidental leak it's quite possible that no one even realises it's happened.'

'What do you mean, *if*?'

'I'm not so sure this phenomenon is man-made.'

Rutherford shook his head. 'You're not making sense.'

'I've been doing a lot of tests,' said Emily. 'This marble is seriously weird. So weird that it ... well, if someone told me it had come from another planet I might even believe them.'

Rutherford laughed.

Emily's dark eyes narrowed. She was not someone people laughed at. 'I want to know exactly where you found this,' she hissed. 'I need to locate the primary source. And then we start to think about what we're going to do with it. We're talking serious money here. Riches beyond your wildest dreams, if a cliché is the only thing that's going to get though to you.'

'I'd better take you to the garden in question, then, hadn't I,' said Rutherford, beginning to spend his fortune in his head. A house in the Seychelles, a yacht in the South of France, a racehorse or two ... 'We're going to have to keep this very quiet, aren't we?' he added.

'Obviously.'

'Kind of limits who we can mix with afterwards, doesn't it?'

'What are you getting at?'

'Well ... who could I marry, apart from you?'

Emily nearly choked on her herbal tea. 'When I said wildest dreams, Rutherford, I didn't expect you to go *that* far.'

Snakeweed wasn't the most patient of muleteers. It didn't take him long to decide that things could be speeded up with the aid of a whip, so he broke off a small branch and whacked it across the rump of the closest mule. The animal stopped dead immediately, rolled its eyes and kicked out at him. Snakeweed swore, and lost his balance. The slope was very steep here, and once he lost his footing he couldn't regain it. He teetered on the edge of the path for a moment before falling, and then he was sliding down and he couldn't stop.

Stonecrop looked over the drop, and gulped. Snakeweed had completely disappeared, although there was a long trail of crushed vegetation and mud showing the direction he'd taken. There was no way Stonecrop would be able to follow him down there. The mules didn't seem to like the narrow pathway very much at all, and were getting restless. Stonecrop decided to carry on before he was kicked over the edge as well, and wait for Snakeweed at the Divide.

Harshak shook the Tromm Fell dust from his coat, and attended to a small burn on his leg with his tongue. When he looked up again, he realized that Granitelegs had gone, so he checked the rest of himself over. Everything seemed to be in order. He was ready to maim, torture and terrorize whatever crossed his path. The choice was his, and his alone. He was going to take to this free will business like a creepy-biter to a lickit's big toe.

Before he decided which direction to select, he had a good sniff. There wasn't much to the west – the land was probably barren. The south smelt mainly of forest, with the odd whiff of nut-nibbler, and faint traces of vamprey and worrit. There were unlikely to be many settlements in an area with such a high shadow-beast population. The east was more promising, with a tang of tangle-folk and candle-wax and wood-smoke. However, there was a stronger smell of brittle-horn, which seemed to be between him and the tangle-folk village – and something else. He focused his nose more precisely, and was instantly beside himself with excitement. He could smell a one-eye. One-eyes were delicious, and they were such fun when they were terrified. Their goaty legs were no match for a sinistrom's, and apart from their liking for filleting knives they were more or less defenceless.

Harshak left the ridge and started to make his way east, avoiding the main path and slinking through the brush-wood. It felt great to be stalking things again, even though the one-eye was still a long way off. He dodged behind rocks, pounced at shadows, and snarled at tree-trunks.

And then he smelt brazzle.

Harshak stiffened, remembering how Ironclaw had pinned him to the ground, and he became more cautious. He'd killed a brazzle or two in his time, but brazzles should-n't be underestimated. There were only fifty-seven of the original one hundred and sixty-nine sinistroms left now, and Harshak didn't want to be the one to make it fifty-six. As the brazzle scent intensified Harshak circled round so that he was upwind, and crept forward on his belly. He peered over the next boulder, and saw the most amazingly complicated construction of twigs and branches. The dwelling was dome-shaped with a large entrance hole on one side, and despite its ramshackle appearance it was spotlessly clean. Harshak sniffed again. The smell of brazzle was very strong, but it was slightly stale. The other smell was far more exciting. Harshak licked his lips, and peered at the sky. There was nothing wheeling up above, waiting to swoop down and pounce, so he stopped trying to be inconspicuous and simply trotted over to what he now realized was a nest.

He peered inside. It took a moment or two for his eyes to adjust to the gloom, but the delicious smell was much stronger now, and he was slavering with anticipation. A huge white egg lay in the middle of a small depression, which had been lined with golden feathers. He patted it with his paw, and it rolled first one way, and then the other. He patted it harder, but it wasn't as fragile as it looked. How to get at the contents? His jaws weren't wide enough for him to get his mouth right round it and bite down; he'd have to get it outside and smash it against something. There was always the option of assuming his lickit guise, picking it up and dropping it over a cliff. It might be fun to bat it about a bit first, though. He had rather more difficulty than he'd anticipated getting it out of the nest – every time he rolled it to the entrance it seemed to give him the slip and slide back down into the depression again, but eventually he managed it.

Once he'd got the egg outside on the sand he treated himself to a game of ball, slapping it with his paw and chasing it. He became so involved in this new-found form of entertainment that the feathered bolt that hit him from above came as a complete surprise. He was knocked sideways with such force that the breath left his body with a loud grunt, and he did a couple of head-over-heels before he fetched up against a boulder. Before he had time to collect himself the attack was renewed, and he felt a talon rake across his shoulders. He twisted round and snapped, but he was too late. The brazzle was hovering above him, poised to strike again, and there was pure murder in her bright yellow eyes.

Was one stupid egg worth getting his eyes pecked out? He dodged her next assault, decided that discretion was the better part of valour, and legged it. The rocky ground suddenly turned sharp-edged and treacherous, and he realized he'd reached an area full of crevices and gullies that were small enough to conceal his progress. Just before he jumped down into one of them he glanced back. The brazzle had picked the egg up in her talons, and was returning to her nest with it.

Ironclaw, Felix and Betony were following a path that zigzagged uphill beside a little Costa Rican stream.

'What happens if they cross the Divide before us?' asked Betony. 'Supposing they've loaded all the gold on to the fire-breather and flown off before we get there?'

Ironclaw made a strangled sound in his throat – and then he cocked his head. Felix listened as hard as he could, and after a moment or two he made out a sort of rushing sound that was getting louder. A couple of seconds later he could hear someone saying '*Ow!*' and '*By all that glitters!*' and shortly after that Snakeweed landed at their feet, covered in mud. His clothes were torn, and his wand was missing.

'Well, *peck me where it hurts*,' said Ironclaw. 'It's Snakeweed.'

Snakeweed stared at them for a moment as though he couldn't believe his eyes. Then he scrambled to his feet and felt for his wand.

'Lost something?' asked Ironclaw innocently.

Snakeweed realized his wand was missing, and his eyes narrowed. His hand went to his pocket, and his expression became faintly alarmed. He rummaged in his other pocket, and then he turned both pockets inside out. He glanced up at the hillside he'd just slid down.

'What have you lost, apart from your wand?' Betony asked Snakeweed.

'His personal organiser?' guessed Ironclaw. 'His heart? His integrity? No – he lost that ages ago.'

'Rather my integrity than my heart,' said Snakeweed, with a sly glance at Felix.

'I think we need to get everyone back across the Divide as quickly as possible,' said Felix, ignoring him, 'before anything else magical gets mislaid.'

'The chances of his wand surviving intact are pretty remote,' said Ironclaw. 'And a broken wand has no magical properties whatsoever.'

'Let's hope it got smashed to bits, then,' said Felix. 'Hang on – does a magic carpet also lose its magic when it gets damaged?'

'No,' said Betony. 'Don't worry, Turpsik will be able to mend it. As long as she doesn't drink too much fermented fertle-juice at Pewtermane's welcome-home bash.'

When Felix's party negotiated the next hairpin bend, its members could see the trees thinning out and a lot more sky. They emerged on the rocky ridge of the Divide, where Stonecrop and the mules were waiting. The moment Stonecrop saw them Ironclaw shouted, 'Hands in the air, or I'll peck Snakeweed's eyes out!' He leant his great head next to Snakeweed's and clacked his beak a couple of times to illustrate the point.

Stonecrop shrugged, and raised his hands. 'I don't have a wand any more anyway,' he said.

'Oh, all right then,' said Ironclaw, and Stonecrop dropped his hands again.

'What are we going to do with him, when we get back?' asked Betony, indicating Snakeweed.

Ironclaw looked worried. 'I've no idea,' he said.

'I think Grimspite wants to deal with him,' said Felix.

'Oh good,' said Ironclaw.

They all straddled the Divide – although it took a while to get the mules to co-operate – and Ironclaw recited the spell.

They all came to more or less together. Granitelegs was sitting on a nearby rock, watching them. The mules showed the whites of their eyes and brayed a few times, and Ironclaw started to count his gold to make sure it was all still there. Felix stood up slowly.

'Feeling a bit wobbly, Felix?' said Snakeweed cheerfully. 'I told you the cure was only temporary.'

'I feel fine,' said Felix curtly. Once you started wondering how you felt, you noticed everything from a bruise to an insect bite.

'Tromm Fell never used to be this popular,' said Granitelegs, eyeing the mules.

'Oh, hello Granitelegs,' said Ironclaw, totting up his crocks. 'If you think you're using my dirt-board, you've got another think coming.'

'Just got a bit bored with the party,' said Granitelegs, who had sobered up since he'd encountered Harshak. Sinistroms had that sort of effect on people. 'You know how it is. All fermented fertle-juice and silly jokes. No one wants to talk about solid geometry. Even Thornbeak left early, said she had some project or other.'

Felix looked round. 'Left for where?'

'Oh, she'll be around,' said Ironclaw vaguely.

'Doing what?'

'Sitting.'

'Sitting?'

'Sitting on an egg.'

'*What?*' squawked Granitelegs.

Ironclaw looked uncomfortable.

'Are you mad?' said Granitelegs. 'It's only forty years since she laid the last one. You are the father, I take it?'

Ironclaw studied his toes. 'Yes.'

Betony grinned. 'When's it due to hatch?'

Ironclaw looked irritated. 'How should I know? It's hens who remember all that stuff.'

Snakeweed was standing there, his hands on his hips, looking annoyed. 'Where's my fire-breather?' he demanded, as though he still had a right to everyone's unquestioning obedience. 'And where's Harshak?'

'Gone off to terrorize things,' said Granitelegs.

Ironclaw stiffened. 'Which way did he go?'

'Who?'

'Harshak.'

'That way,' said Granitelegs, pointing a wing.

Ironclaw gave a piercing shriek of dismay and yelled, 'Stash my gold for me, Granitelegs!' Then he lifted into the air, and flew off at top speed.

'How peculiar,' said Granitelegs.

'But terribly convenient,' said Pepperwort, emerging from behind a rock with his wand in his left hand. His right arm was in a sling, and his clothes were torn. He cast Granitelegs a venomous look. Being tipped off Ironclaw's back into the tree canopy had provoked a hatred of *all* brazzles.

'At last,' said Snakeweed. 'An employee who acts with a bit of initiative. All we need now is a fire-breather. Then we transfer the gold to it, and go back to Andria. I've had enough of Tromm Fell to last me a lifetime. It's uncivilized.'

Pepperwort waited for Snakeweed to enquire about his arm. After a moment or two it was clear that this wasn't going to happen, so Pepperwort said, 'Your fire-breather's in the brittlehorn valley. Your original one, not the replacement. I saw it after I escaped from Ironclaw, fell into the tree canopy and sprained my wrist.'

'Wicked,' said Snakeweed.

Pepperwort looked understandably confused by this remark, and despite the gravity of the situation Felix felt himself smile.

'Well then,' said Snakeweed, 'it just remains for me to immobilize the brats and the brazzle, and we can be on our way. Your wand, Pepperwort.' He held out his hand, and Pepperwort passed his wand to Snakeweed.

Felix looked at Betony. Betony had gone very pale.

'Hang on,' said Granitelegs.

Snakeweed laughed, and aimed the wand in Granitelegs' direction. A shaft of purple light hit the brazzle on the head, and a cloud of feathers fell like autumn leaves after a sharp frost.

Pepperwort applauded.

Granitelegs was too shocked to even squawk.

Felix didn't know whether to laugh or cry – the brazzle

looked like something out of a cartoon. His head was completely bald; pink and pimply. His neck was bald, too – thin and scrawny and wrinkled, just like a Christmas turkey.

Pepperwort sniggered – but Snakeweed was having hysterics, until the tears ran down his cheeks. He raised his wand a second time.

'Stop it!' shouted Betony.

Snakeweed shook his head, too convulsed with laughter to speak. Another beam of light shot out of the wand, and this time Granitelegs lost all the feathers on his wings. He sat there, panting, his beak slightly open, his eyes dark with despair.

'Stop it!' yelled Betony again, and she launched herself at Snakeweed, ridiculously and pointlessly brave – fists flying, face contorted with fury.

Snakeweed murmured something, and flicked the wand like a fly swat. Felix watched Betony freeze – and as Snakeweed turned to face him, he knew that he was next.

When the spell hit him, he could actually feel it taking effect – the coldness seeping through his veins, settling round his bones and cooling his flesh from the inside. His eyes fixed in one position, so that he could only see straight ahead, and everything grew misty and vague. He couldn't swallow any more. The feeling of powerlessness was very scary, and the moment he stopped breathing was the worst of all.…

And then, darkness.

15

'You're sure you're all right?' Ironclaw asked Thornbeak, for the fifth time. He was half in and half out of the doorway to the nest; it wasn't big enough for both of them.

'Perfectly all right,' said Thornbeak. 'Harshak's long gone. Have you just abandoned those two youngsters up on the peak with Snakeweed?'

'Granitelegs is in charge,' said Ironclaw. 'He'll hide my gold, and then he'll take Betony and Felix to get their carpet. Neither Snakeweed nor Stonecrop have wands any more; they won't be a problem.'

'What's going to happen to Snakeweed? We don't want him going back to Andria and picking up where he left off, gold or no gold.'

'Grimspite wants to deal with him,' said Ironclaw. 'He's got a few old scores to settle.'

'Good,' said Thornbeak. 'And have you tried the king and queen again?'

'Yes. Still no response.'

'Obviously time for their afternoon nap,' said Thornbeak sourly. 'Now then. All this sitting's making me a bit peckish.'

'Right,' said Ironclaw. 'One prime haunch coming up,' and he backed out of the nest, and flew off to hunt.

Before he'd gone very far, however, he'd started to compile a mathematical puzzle in his head for Leona. It was a tricky little thing involving prime numbers, and he wanted to scribble a few of them down. He needed his dirt-board – it wouldn't take long, and he could hunt on the way back. He changed direction, but when he arrived at the shallow depression in the sand there was a stranger there. For a moment he didn't even realize it was a brazzle – the pimply pink skin looked all wrong, and the creature was just sitting there, shivering. He hopped over, about to give whoever it was a piece of his mind about trespassing on other people's dirt-boards when he realized it was Granitelegs. He just stared, open-beaked.

'Snakeweed,' whispered Granitelegs. His voice was very weak. 'Up on the peak. I was trying to get …'

'Don't talk if it's too tiring,' said Ironclaw. 'I'll go and fetch someone.'

'But you need to know …'

Ironclaw waited as Granitelegs tried to summon up sufficient energy to finish his sentence. He didn't manage it. He took a deep breath – then he simply keeled over on to his side. Ironclaw just sat there for a moment, paralyzed – then he realized that Granitelegs was still breathing, so he covered him up with some leaves. After that he headed off for the brittlehorn valley. Perhaps the brittlehorns knew of a potion that would help. It wasn't as if he'd been *completely* plucked, either – it was just possible he'd survive. Puzzles by post with Leona were all very well, but they were no substitute for beak-to-beak brain-buster battles with Granitelegs. Should have pecked Snakeweed's eyes out while I had the chance, thought Ironclaw. Mind you, Grimspite would like to disembowel him. And Pewtermane will want to skewer him through the heart when he finds out he was behind his daughter's death. Not standard brittlehorn behaviour at all, in my humble opinion, but I suppose he has his reasons. There are people with a much greater claim on Snakeweed's life than *me*.

When Ironclaw arrived at the brittlehorn valley, Milklegs was very helpful and went off to mix a potion straight away. Turpsik was just putting the finishing touches to Nimby – the job hadn't taken as long as she'd expected, and she was feeling very pleased with herself. She was singing a song that celebrated mending nets encrusted with all sorts of disgusting things. Nimby was joining in every so often, although he kept getting the words wrong and annoying Turpsik no end. Ironclaw suspected he might be doing it deliberately.

'Ought to take him for a test flight before long,' Turpsik said. 'He's getting far too full of himself.'

'I expect Thornbeak would like a visitor,' said Ironclaw. 'She's sitting.'

'I know,' said Turpsik.

Ironclaw's eyes widened. 'Have you been looking in the prediction pool or something?'

'It doesn't always take a mathematician to put two and two together, Ironclaw. Collecting branches and eating oat-cakes, it was pretty obvious. Brazzles don't have to sit for long though, do they? The chick hatches very quickly.' She tied a knot in Nimby's fringe. 'Right. That'll do, I think. I'll tell her you'll be back shortly, shall I?'

'Er … yes,' said Ironclaw, suddenly remembering he was meant to be taking her a haunch.

Nimby dipped rather violently when Turpsik placed her considerable weight on him, but he recovered quite quickly and the two of them departed for Thornbeak's nest.

When Turpsik arrived at the dome-shaped construction, she ducked her head and stepped inside. Thornbeak was sitting at the edge of the shallow depression in the middle, and watching the egg intently. It wobbled slightly, and a brief staccato of tapping issued from within.

'It's hatching,' she said softly.

Turpsik had the feeling that a baby brazzle wouldn't be the most endearing of infants. It would be practically bald, squawk a lot, and peck at anything within range.

There was another burst of tapping, and the shell cracked a little. The tip of a golden beak poked through the hole.

'It's a female,' whispered Thornbeak.

'What are you going to call her?'

The shell split a bit further, and the beak went back inside the shell and started pecking again. Another crack opened up, and Turpsik could see pimply pink skin.

'I'd thought about Thornclaw,' said Thornbeak. 'But Ironclaw wanted Ironbeak. We had the same argument last time, which was why we ended up with Stonetalon.'

The shell cracked right the way across, and Turpsik saw the head for the first time. It was covered with dark grey streaks, which were presumably sodden feathers. The baby blinked a few times, and rubbed her beak against the edge of the shell.

'Got to have some sort of name,' said Turpsik.

'Hello,' said Thornbeak to the baby, the tone of her voice completely different from the usual clipped delivery that was her trademark. The baby kicked the eggshell clear, and tried to stand on four very wobbly legs. The front half of her body was lightly dusted with a grey-brown fuzz of down, and the back half had a thin covering of tawny hair.

Thornbeak gently lifted up the pieces of shell with her beak, and threw them outside with a toss of her head.

'Cheep,' said the baby.

'Isn't she cute,' cooed Thornbeak.

'Name?' persisted Turpsik.

'I'll just call her Fuzzy until I can discuss it with Ironclaw,' said Thornbeak. 'He should have been here for the hatching. That's the second time running he's missed it.'

'He said he wouldn't be long,' said Turpsik.

'Hello, little Fuzzy,' crooned Thornbeak. 'Who's gorgeous then?'

Fuzzy, mused Turpsik. If it sticks she won't be too pleased about it when she grows up. Brazzles always take powerful names.

'Cheep cheep,' said the baby.

'She's really pretty, isn't she?' said Thornbeak.

The chick opened her beak wide and squawked, revealing a glistening red interior and a purple tongue. The squawks were very loud and insistent.

'What does she want?' asked Thornbeak, looking slightly panicked.

'Food, of course,' said Turpsik.

'Oh,' said Thornbeak. 'Right. I'd better go and hunt something. This ought to be Ironclaw's job, you know.' She scrambled out of the nest, and flew away. The chick shut her beak for a moment, as she watched her mother go.

'Hello Fuzzy,' said Turpsik, as soon as Thornbeak was out

of sight. 'Who's a pretty girl, then?'

Fuzzy looked at her first with one eye, then the other. Then she started squawking again. It was a highly unpleasant sound, raucous and demanding, and she showed no signs of stopping.

Sonnets and similes, thought Turpsik. I'm no good at this sort of thing. She started to stroke the chick's scrawny head, and sing it a soothing song. By the time Thornbeak returned, the chick had learned her first word.

Fish.

'*Fish?*' hooted Thornbeak. 'Where am I going to find fish round here?' She dropped the nut-nibbler she'd caught at the chick's feet. Fuzzy eyed it suspiciously, but eventually she ate it.

'Ought to make a move,' said Turpsik. 'Felix will be wanting his carpet. Worried about that marble curse spreading. There's a poem in that.'

'Bye,' said Thornbeak vaguely.

Fuzzy burped.

Emily Parsons scraped a plum skin off the sole of her boot, looked at the high stone wall over which the plum tree hung and said, 'Are you saying we've got to climb that?'

Rutherford nodded.

'Why can't we just ring the doorbell, and say we're investigating a claim that this garden ought to be made a triple SI?'

'A what?'

'Oh, for heaven's sake, Rutherford, a Site of Special Scientific Interest.'

'Because there won't be anyone in, Emily. I tried. Then I looked them up on the electoral roll, and got their phone number from directory inquiries. There's an answerphone message saying they're away for a few days.'

'OK,' said Emily, 'I'm impressed.'

'I could give you a leg-up.'

'All right,' said Emily. 'It's a secluded area, and the street's completely deserted.'

They walked to the corner, where the wall was lowest, and she scrambled to the top of the wall with a surprising athleticism. Then she leant down, and gave Rutherford a hand. After that they both dropped down on to the grass, and looked round.

It was a big garden, with shrubberies and winding paths, and it was apparent that the lawn hadn't been mown for at least a couple of weeks. The grass was dotted with daisies and dandelions, and it was going to seed and creeping into the flowerbeds. Hips and haws were swelling on the rose bushes, which badly needed deadheading, and there were even some mushrooms here and there. On closer inspection, not all of them were mushrooms. One of them was a white marble toad.

Emily tucked her trousers into her boots to make sure that there were no exposed areas of skin, and put on a pair of

285

surgical gloves. Rutherford did likewise, and they started to explore.

It was like visiting the statue section of a garden centre. To begin with, apart from the toad, there was just the occasional invertebrate. Then Emily spotted a squirrel, and Rutherford tripped over a hedgehog and narrowly avoided being spiked by it. He shivered when he realized how close he'd come to being turned to marble himself.

'There's a summer house over there,' said Emily. 'Let's take a peek.'

The door wasn't locked, and they stepped inside.

'Looks like it belongs to a kid,' said Rutherford, flicking through a pile of comics and running a gloved finger over a particularly fine example of rose quartz.

'Nothing much here,' said Emily, leafing through some notebooks and papers. 'Hang on, what's this? *Canis hystericus?*' She laughed, but nevertheless she slipped a few things into her pocket, just in case there was some useful information. Then she noticed a bright golden feather lying on the floor. She picked it up, and looked at it. There was something odd about it, so she put it in one of her plastic envelopes, and they both went outside again.

'Oh my,' said Rutherford.

'What?'

He pointed at the statue of Felix's mother, standing beneath the plum tree in her chalk-white blouse and skirt, cricket bat poised to hit a six, an albino blackbird perched, motionless, on her head. The ground around her was frosted with insects.

'Looks like the primary source,' said Emily, prodding some milky bees thoughtfully with the toe of her boot.

They both studied Felix's mother, but there was nothing more remarkable about her than any of the other marble statues.

'I wonder why she decided to play cricket in those clothes,' said Rutherford. 'They're highly unsuitable.'

Emily laughed. 'You're priceless sometimes, Rutherford, do you know that? She wasn't playing cricket. She was defending herself – look at the expression on her face.'

Rutherford suspected that a lot of sportsmen looked murderous in the heat of the moment, but he kept his thoughts to himself. 'Defending herself against what? A swarm of bees?'

'Ah,' replied Emily, 'two bees or not two bees, that is the question.'

Rutherford laughed. It wasn't because the joke was funny, but because he'd never known Emily make one before.

She scowled for a moment, as though she regretted doing it. Then she went over to Felix's mother and squinted down the garden with her close-set dark eyes, working out the trajectory of the statue's gaze. 'Human-sized, whatever it was,' she concluded.

'Let's try the house,' said Rutherford.

Neither of them was really surprised to find that the back

door was open – everything here was weird. They found a stone cat in the kitchen and a mouse in the hall, but the living room was full of marble people.

The man by the fireplace had his hand halfway out of his pocket, caught in the act of pulling out a mobile phone. Next to him stood two teenage boys, wearing baseball caps. Beside *them* stood a man wearing a balaclava helmet. He was carrying an empty holdall in one hand, and a vase in the other.

Emily started to laugh.

Rutherford stared at her. 'What's the joke?'

'Oh, can't you see?' giggled Emily. 'The man with the phone lived here. He didn't have a cricket bat to hand, so he was going for his mobile. The woman in the garden was presumably his wife, and she ran for it and got cornered under the plum tree. But the two teenagers and the balaclava man came along later. They're burglars – the back door was wide open. They probably came in separately, and made the mistake of touching one another. It must have been the first intruder – or set of intruders – who actually broke in. There were chips of wood on the kitchen floor.'

'None of this really helps us to get to the heart of the matter though, does it?'

'No. But there's one thing we do know – this isn't MI5, or the KGB, or the CIA, or the FBI. They wouldn't have left the evidence here like this.'

'So?'

'Well, unless you can come up with anything better, I'm plumping for aliens. This technology is going to be priceless, if we can only understand it. Our people would pay a lot of money for something like this.'

Rutherford glanced around nervously. 'Aliens? They might come back.'

'And you might get knocked down by a car, and I might have a heart attack, and the Earth might get hit by a meteorite. I'm going to work flat out on this, Rutherford. Are you with me, or not?'

A house in the Seychelles, a yacht in the South of France, a racehorse or two ... 'I'm with you,' he said.

Grimspite was feeling rather put out that he hadn't been able to find the brazzles. He'd tracked them to a clearing, but then they'd obviously taken off because the scent had vanished. He'd had a proper mission, one that he'd chosen, and he'd failed. He was now nearing the top of the peak, and he'd drawn a complete blank.

He rounded a promontory, and stopped dead in his tracks. Felix and Betony were standing there, completely immobile. It was obvious that someone had put the freezing spell on them, and who else could it have been but Snakeweed? These spells usually wore off fairly quickly, though, especially if you used music. It would be the friendly thing to do, and then he could ask Felix and Betony what, exactly, had happened.

Grimspite sat on his haunches, raised his nose into the air and started to howl *Jaws, Paws and Claws*, which was the only song he knew off by heart. When he got to the bit that went *Crunch that spine and make it mine, I won't decline, it looks divine,* he wondered whether it was quite the thing – but shortly after that he saw Felix blink; then Betony yawned, and after that they both stretched themselves and flexed their fingers and started to laugh.

'I'm glad you're both OK now,' said Grimspite, although he was wondering why they found melting back to normal so funny. 'What's the joke?'

'Nothing,' said Betony. She glanced at Felix and had another fit of the giggles.

Felix bit his lip, he knew he shouldn't be laughing at Grimspite's singing, but he just couldn't help himself.

Grimspite's brow furrowed. It looked as though he'd been wondering whether he'd been out of time.

Betony suddenly creased up again, but suddenly the smile left Felix's face. A picture of Granitelegs sitting there shivering had just flooded back through his mind.

He told Grimspite how Ironclaw had flown off; how Pepperwort had appeared from nowhere, complete with wand, and what Snakeweed had done to Granitelegs. 'What I don't understand,' he finished, 'is why Snakeweed only froze us. Why didn't he kill us?'

'His wand was probably running low on power,' said Grimspite. 'You have to use a re-charging spell on heavy-duty ones every so often. Look, I know you've got other things on your mind. You need to get back to your world, and you need to cross over in the right place, too. You head back to the brittlehorn valley, and pick up your carpet. I'll sort out Snakeweed.' He put his nose to the ground and sniffed. 'Looks like we're travelling the same way for a bit, though,' he said.

'Suits us,' said Betony, and the three of them headed off down the hill.

The mules negotiated the rocky path down from Tromm Fell with no difficulty. 'How are we going to get the fire-breather out of the brittlehorn valley?' asked Pepperwort. 'They're not going to let us just take it, are they?'

'Bribery,' said Stonecrop. 'We've got enough gold to buy Andria.'

'You can't bribe a brittlehorn,' said Snakeweed. 'There's nothing much they want.'

'Well, what are we going to do, then?'

'We'll take a hostage,' said Snakeweed, 'and swap it for the fire-breather.'

'We should have brought that tangle-child with us.'

'She'd be troublesome,' said Snakeweed. 'I've had a much better idea.'

Pepperwort and Stonecrop looked at one another, but neither of them could imagine what the better idea might be. They all carried on walking, and Snakeweed scanned the sky from time to time, his hand shading his eyes. After a while he spotted what he wanted, and pointed.

'It's a brazzle,' said Pepperwort nervously, taking cover.

'It's a brazzle going off to hunt,' said Stonecrop, even more nervously, pulling the mules beneath an overhang. 'Look at the way she's going up on a thermal, so that she can use her magnifying vision to pinpoint her prey.'

'She's gone over the other side of the peak now,' said Pepperwort eventually. 'That's a relief.'

'Certainly is,' said Snakeweed, and they set off again. A few moments later they rounded a bend and saw a great mound of twigs and branches in front of them.

'It's a brazzle nest,' said Stonecrop.

'Yup,' said Snakeweed. 'And where there's a nest there's going to be an egg. And an egg is far less trouble to kidnap than a tangle-child. Empty one of those panniers – you can re-distribute the gold amongst the other three.'

Pepperwort and Stonecrop set to work, whilst Snakeweed ducked his head and entered the nest.

It was spotlessly clean. But where a large white egg should have been, there was now a round fuzzy chick with a semi-bald pink head. There were pale grey quills stippled around just beneath the skin – only a few of which sported straggly grey feathers – and the eyes were an unpleasant acid yellow. The beak, however, was pure gold. A hen chick, then. She regarded Snakeweed for a moment, and then she said, 'Fish.'

'OK,' said Snakeweed, 'I'll take you to a river where we

can find some fish.' He picked her up, and she wiped her beak on his sleeve and burped. Snakeweed held her at arm's length, carried her outside and dumped her unceremoniously in the empty pannier.

'Fish,' said the chick.

'That's not an egg,' said Stonecrop. 'It's a chick.'

'Oh, thirteen out of thirteen,' said Snakeweed sarcastically.

They started off down the track, which quickly led into the forest. 'That's a relief,' said Pepperwort, glancing up at the tree canopy above them. 'We want as much overhead cover as we can get.'

'Want a fish,' said the chick. Brazzles learned to speak very quickly indeed, and Fuzzy was no exception.

'What's the magic word?' asked Pepperwort. 'Want a fish *what*?'

'Want a fish *now*!' screeched Fuzzy.

'*Please* is the word I was looking for,' said Pepperwort.

Fuzzy raised herself up on her hind legs, flapped her pink pointy wing-stubs for all she was worth, and just squawked.

'Shut up,' said Snakeweed.

'It's a good job they don't fledge as quickly as they learn to speak,' said Stonecrop dryly.

'They don't get their wing-feathers for ages,' said Snakeweed. 'She can't escape.'

Fuzzy regarded them with her savage yellow eyes, but it was impossible to work out what she was thinking. The mule had a good idea, however, as the pong that started to come from the bottom of the pannier drifted nose-wards.

'What's a blocking spell?' asked Felix as he, Grimspite and Betony followed the stony track down from the peak of Tromm Fell.

'A spell that stops me harming Snakeweed,' said Grimspite, 'and it can only be lifted by a brittlehorn. I was kind of hoping Pewtermane would do the honours. I haven't met him, but you say he's the father of Snowdrift. Snowdrift was poisoned by Architrex, on Snakeweed's orders, so Pewtermane might quite like to help. I was really looking forward to the expression on Snakeweed's face when he realized I'd fooled him into thinking I was Architrex for over a year. After that I was going to kill him. Turpsik said it would make me lots of new friends. And then I was going to renounce extreme violence for ever.'

'Won't Pewtermane want to kill him?' asked Betony.

'I'd have to give him the choice, of *course*,' said Grimspite. His brow furrowed. 'Harshak will probably want to kill him as well.'

'You can't *all* kill him,' Betony pointed out.

'I know,' said Grimspite. 'It's a bit bothersome, really.'

It became even more bothersome when they rounded the next bend, and found Thornbeak outside her nest jumping up and down and shrieking, 'I'll kill him! I'll peck his eyes out so hard they'll come out the back of his head! My baby! Snakeweed's taken my baby!'

'Another would-be executioner for the list, then,' said Grimspite.

'Oh, Thornbeak,' said Betony, 'whatever's happened?'

'Kidnapped,' said Thornbeak. 'A harmless little chick. How *could* he?'

'How do you know it was him?'

'Look,' said Thornbeak, pointing to hoof-prints outside her nest. 'Those weren't made by any creature from this world. They have to be those mule-things Ironclaw told me about. And where *is* he when I need him?' She glanced towards the forest, which was very dense just there. 'That's where they've gone. I can't look for her, I'm too big.'

'*We* can,' said Grimspite. 'Snakeweed will be making for the brittlehorn valley, so that he can grab the fire-breather and take the gold back to Andria. You go there, and wait for us.'

'I feel so helpless,' said Thornbeak. 'My poor little baby. She'll be so frightened.'

Ironclaw landed next to his dirt-board with the potion Milklegs had mixed for Granitelegs suspended from his beak. He placed it on the ground and said, 'Come on then, you old fraud. Sit up and take your medicine like a cock.'

There was no reply.

Ironclaw flapped his wings to blow away the leafy quilt he'd used to cover Granitelegs, and nudged his friend with his foot. He suddenly realized that Granitelegs was very cold

– far too cold. He looked more closely at him.

The brazzle's eyes were closed, and there was no movement – he wasn't breathing.

Ironclaw felt a lump rise in his throat. He was too late. Granitelegs was dead. He poked him with his talon, in the vain hope that he'd been mistaken, but there was no response. The body was stiff as well as cold.

Ironclaw just stood there, feeling gutted. His rivalry with Granitelegs had lasted nearly two centuries, and he knew he was going to miss him dreadfully. They'd had their arguments, lots and lots of them, and Granitelegs had never really got on with Thornbeak. Well, Ironclaw hadn't either, a lot of the time, if he was honest about it. He remembered the first time he'd brought Thornbeak back to Tromm Fell, and Granitelegs having a bit too much fermented fertle-juice and saying, 'Did you hear the one about the brazzles who couldn't agree on a name for their chick? When the brittlehorn asked them why they couldn't discuss it, the hen said the cock hadn't spoken to her for two years. "Why not?" asks the brittlehorn. "Well," says the cock, "I didn't like to interrupt her."' Granitelegs had had hysterics, and Thornbeak had pecked him.

Ironclaw swallowed, but the lump wouldn't go away. Granitelegs had been tactless and clumsy and irritating, but he'd been Ironclaw's best friend. Life would never be the same again.

Suddenly, Ironclaw remembered that this was all Snakeweed's doing. The anger rose within him like no anger he had ever felt before. He took off and climbed steeply, using his magnifying vision to look for his quarry. Then he thought that he'd better let Thornbeak know what he was up to, so he swooped down to the nest.

He could hardly believe his eyes – the nest was completely empty. Both Thornbeak and the egg had gone. I'll kill him, thought Ironclaw, as he spotted the mules' hoofprints outside. This time, I'll definitely kill him.

16

Harshak ducked into the undergrowth as the carpet whizzed past him, zigzagging along the forest track like a demented bird of prey. It looked as though something was giving it a test-flight. As he watched it disappear it left an undulating trail of scent behind it. A faint hint of charring tickled his nose, as though the rug had once been burnt; soap, as though it had recently been washed – and delicious, scrumptious, yummy one-eye. A one-eye test piloting a magic carpet? How odd. Harshak licked his lips, and followed the smell.

Before long he came to the brittlehorn valley. He skulked at the forest edge for a while, just watching. A fire-breather was asleep on the riverbank. It was totally different from the beast he'd had to guard, up on Tromm Fell – young, muscular, smouldering with vitality. At the other end of the valley a group of mares were clearing up after what looked like a party. There were fragments of oatcakes all over the grass, as well as wisps of hay and puddles of fermented fertle-juice. A trough had been knocked over, and the prediction pool had dead leaves floating on it. Someone had decorated the mud-wallow with branches of fire-tree that were now the worse for wear, drooping into the mire and shedding their brightly coloured cones everywhere.

A group of colts were lying down, fast asleep and snoring. The mares were talking quietly to one another as they worked, and Harshak could see that the carpet had landed close to a cave entrance. The one-eye was no longer on board – she must have gone into the cave.

Hmm, thought Harshak, I'm not sure I want to risk barging in there. Brittlehorns can freeze sinistroms in their tracks. Maybe I'll just wait for a while.

He curled himself up under a tree, and dozed off. Even the most menacing of the menacing needed their ugliness sleep.

The most extraordinary braying noise woke him up. He sat bolt upright, and listened. Voices. He sniffed. Japegrins – and something that smelt a bit like brittlehorn, but not quite. He wriggled underneath a fallen log, and waited. Two mythical no-horns came walking down the path, loaded up like cuddyaks. They were accompanied by three japegrins. Harshak identified Snakeweed immediately, and his lips drew back in a soundless snarl. Snakeweed had treated him with the utmost contempt – he, Harshak, the most brutal of the brutal. Ripping his throat out would be a pleasure – except for the fact that Snakeweed was his master. Or was he? Harshak still felt remarkably free to maim, torture and terrorize whatever crossed his path without precise instructions from anyone. Perhaps his pebble had got left behind in the other world. Go for it, he thought, and stepped out on to the path in front of the no-horns.

They didn't react the way cuddyaks would have done. Cuddyaks would have stood shoulder to shoulder, and lowered their heads so that their bony brows were the first point of contact. These creatures panicked immediately and galloped off in opposite directions, making that disagreeable hee-hawing noise. One of them seemed to be squawking, as well, which seemed unlikely – but then, these were other-world creatures, so anything might be possible.

Snakeweed wrenched Pepperwort's wand from his belt, and held it out in front of him. Harshak had encountered Snakeweed's sorcery before, and he was well aware that he knew some shadow-spells. However, they weren't going to work if he didn't have Harshak's pebble. Pepperwort and Stonecrop took one look at Harshak, turned, and ran.

'Lost something, Snakeweed?' said Harshak. 'A pebble, maybe?'

'My hostage, stink-fur,' said Snakeweed insolently. Then, suddenly, he looked past Harshak, out into the brittlehorn valley.

Not falling for that one, thought Harshak – then he heard the sound of beating wings, and he couldn't help looking out there himself. The female brazzle who'd attacked him up on the peak was landing in the middle of the grass, and the one-eye had come out of the cave. The one-eye was adorably plump and juicy, and Harshak licked his lips. Then a second brazzle appeared. Ironclaw. Harshak watched him land, and heard the excited exchange of squawks, although he was just too far away to make out exactly what was being said. After that, an elderly brittlehorn followed the one-eye out of the cave, then another. Popular place, this valley, thought Harshak, and he turned back to Snakeweed.

The japegrin had vanished.

Harshak felt really annoyed with himself. He'd been looking forward to killing Snakeweed. The one-eye was now surrounded by brazzles and brittlehorns, so she wasn't a very sensible target, but Harshak's hearing was very acute, and he could hear footsteps approaching. He decided to wait, and see who it was.

Felix saw Harshak first, and he stopped dead. Betony went very pale, and grabbed him by the arm.

Oh well, thought Harshak. They're little more than a morsel, but I suppose they'll do. Mind you, I am meant to be maiming, torturing and terrorizing, so it wouldn't do to kill them straight away. And then another sinistrom appeared.

Harshak just stared for a moment – this was the last thing he'd expected. 'Grimspite?' he said finally. 'It *is* Grimspite, isn't it?'

'Yes,' mumbled Grimspite. He didn't like the way Harshak was looking at him – with undisguised contempt.

Harshak was a very senior sinistrom, and he was perfectly within his rights to punish Grimspite for un-shadow-beast actions. Being friends with a tangle-child and a mythical beast was about as un-shadow as you could get.

'I remember you,' said Harshak. 'You always were a bit of a runt; a mite soft-hearted, and far too fond of your food. It's ironic that you survived, and Architrex didn't.'

Felix frowned. 'What do you mean, Architrex didn't?'

'Architrex is dead.'

'How do you know?'

'His energy's missing. Pity, he was an excellent sinistrom. Spiteful, vindictive. One of the best.'

'What happened to him?' asked Betony.

'Who cares?' said Harshak. 'He's history.'

'I care,' said Betony. 'He killed two brittlehorns, friends of mine.'

'That was clever of him,' said Harshak admiringly. 'Tricky targets, brittlehorns.'

'Well?' persisted Betony.

'All I know is that it was something sudden,' said Harshak. 'Like being struck by lightning.'

I know what happened, thought Felix suddenly. I know what happened to Architrex. When he and Snakeweed crossed over to my world, last summer, they got separated. Architrex killed some livestock, and ended up getting shot – I remember the hunting party. When Snakeweed met up with Grimspite, who'd got into my world by accident, he just assumed he was Architrex.

All of a sudden Harshak noticed something out of the corner of his eye, and he spun round to see better. The rest of the party followed suit. The scene before them was so extraordinary that they all just stood and watched it for a moment.

Snakeweed had caught one of the mules, mounted it, and was galloping flat out for the fire-breather. At the far end of the valley Thornbeak and Ironclaw gaped with astonishment; then they lifted into the air together, and collided. They landed on their backs on the grass, winded.

'Oh no you don't, that japegrin's *mine*,' growled Harshak, and he shot off after Snakeweed.

The moment the sinistrom was out in the open the old brittlehorn spotted him, lowered his head, and broke into a gallop. The colts woke up, whinnied to one another and set off in pursuit, their mothers neighing at them to come back *immediately*.

Grimspite hared off after Harshak and Felix and Betony followed, rather more slowly. 'I wish I had some binoculars,' panted Felix, knowing that neither he nor Betony were fast enough runners to get close to the action.

Betony put her fingers to her lips, and let out a piercing whistle. As Nimby rose into the air Turpsik flung herself aboard, obviously not wanting to miss any material she could turn into an epic poem. Nimby tilted alarmingly; then he steadied, and flew towards them at top speed.

Snakeweed reached the fire-breather before anyone caught up with him. It had scrambled to its feet, and was puffing out jets of smoke; two sinistroms heading towards it were enough to make any being with wings want to take off. Snakeweed didn't waste time unbuckling the panniers carrying the gold – he simply cut them with two strokes of his wand. Harshak and Grimspite were belting towards him, but Felix could see that Pewtermane was going to intercept them before they made contact. Then Nimby arrived. Felix and Betony scrambled on to the carpet beside Turpsik, and Nimby took off again and headed across the valley. Ironclaw and Thornbeak had now recovered themselves, and were back in the air.

Harshak didn't see Pewtermane come at him from the side. The brittlehorn caught him a glancing blow mid-stride, and Harshak rolled over and over, and eventually came to a stop. Pewtermane slid to a halt and stood over him, his flanks heaving, the tip of his horn red with blood. Grimspite couldn't stop in time, and he cannoned into him. Pewtermane staggered backwards, and struggled for a moment to regain his footing.

'*Why*, brittlehorn?' hissed Harshak. 'You are peaceful beings; you freeze enemies, you don't gore them. I am Harshak, the deadliest of the deadly, but I have no quarrel with you.'

'Oh bother,' said Pewtermane. 'You're not Architrex, then? My eyes aren't what they used to be.'

304

Snakeweed had loaded the panniers on to the fire-breather, and was now standing with his back to it, his wand at the ready. Then the brazzles landed, making a take-off for the fire-breather impossible.

'Architrex!' yelled Snakeweed to Grimspite. 'Clear a run-way!'

'So *you're* Architrex!' neighed Pewtermane. He whirled round like lightning, lowered his horn, and lunged. Grimspite dodged sideways, but the horn passed so close to him that it shaved a few hairs off his flank. Barely pausing to draw breath, Pewtermane pirouetted and stabbed again.

'I'm *not* Architrex!' yelped Grimspite, taking evasive action once more.

Pewtermane took no notice. He was going at it hell for leather now, jabbing with his horn, then spinning round and kicking with all his might.

'Architrex is dead,' said Harshak.

Pewtermane skidded to a stop. 'What?'

'That's Grimspite,' said Harshak. 'A very junior sinistrom indeed.'

'It was *Snakeweed* who ordered Architrex to kill Snowdrift,' shouted Felix, as Nimby came level and hovered above the mêlée.

The fire-breather had the river behind it, which cut off escape in that direction. In front of it there was now a semi-circle of hostility – Harshak, Grimspite, Pewtermane, Ironclaw, Thornbeak, Felix, Betony, Turpsik, Nimby – and a nervy bunch of colts, each trying to outdo the others in bravado.

Grimspite stepped forwards. He had been waiting for this moment for a long time. 'I'm not Architrex, Snakeweed,' he said.

Snakeweed looked sceptical.

'You heard Harshak,' said Grimspite. 'Harshak has no reason to lie about this. The sinistrom known as Architrex has been dead for some time. My given name is Grimspite, and I am a free agent. You have treated me like dirt for the last year. I am bound to no one, least of all *you*.'

For once, Snakeweed looked totally and utterly astounded.

'Which one of us gets to kill him?' enquired Pewtermane. 'He was responsible for the poisoning of my daughter.'

'He's kidnapped *my* daughter,' said Thornbeak, 'and I don't know where she is.'

'He murdered my best friend,' said Ironclaw.

'He turned my parents to stone,' said Felix.

'He treated me with contempt,' said Harshak. 'Me, Harshak, the most horrible of the horrible.'

'He insulted my poetry,' said Turpsik.

Snakeweed had recovered his composure by now, and he laughed at her. 'You don't have the guts to kill anyone.'

Turpsik produced a knife from her pocket, and drew it from its sheath. The blade was long and thin, and it looked fearsomely sharp. 'Wrong,' said Turpsik, 'it's *you* who won't have the guts by the time I've finished. This is my favourite filleting knife, I take it everywhere. Never know when it might come in handy.'

'You can't *all* kill him,' said Nimby.

Snakeweed raised his wand a fraction. 'How true. And I'll take as many of you as I can with me.'

No one seemed to know what to do. Although some of them would have liked to go ahead whatever the consequences, they didn't want to endanger the others. Felix thought it looked as though someone had freeze-framed the whole scene – there was an air of unreality about it. Then the lid of one of the panniers behind Snakeweed began to lift, and a pink pimply head appeared. Still nobody moved, although Thornbeak's eyes widened.

'I suggest you simply let me go,' said Snakeweed smoothly. 'Then nobody gets hurt.'

Fuzzy stretched her neck to its fullest extent. Then, like an elastic band snapping, she aimed the most vicious of pecks at Snakeweed's wand-arm. The wand tumbled to the ground, and broke into thirteen pieces. The scene un-froze, as everyone made a move towards Snakeweed.

'You promised me a fish!' Fuzzy squawked, her wing-stubs flapping with fury.

Snakeweed whipped round, grabbed Fuzzy by her scrawny neck and held her at arm's length. Everyone stopped dead again – except for Harshak, who didn't give a bent wand about the chick's safety.

'No!' shrieked Thornbeak, and she leapt at Harshak, seized him by the scruff of his neck with her beak, lifted him high into the air and shook him violently from side to side.

Felix heard the snap of his spine – and then, quite suddenly, the sinistrom simply wasn't there any more. He had just vanished, the way all shadow-beasts did when they died.

'She's killed him,' said Betony, in an awe-struck voice. *'Thornbeak's killed Harshak.'*

'That's one less, then,' said Snakeweed. He was now on the fire-breather, Fuzzy tucked underneath one arm, her neck still grasped in his hand. 'Let me leave, or I'll strangle her.'

'Let him go,' said Thornbeak.

The semi-circle parted in the centre, and the fire-breather broke into a run. They all just stood and watched as it reached take-off speed, spread its leathery wings, and launched itself into the air. It banked sharply, and headed off in the direction of Andria, rapidly becoming a dark speck against the heavy grey clouds that were gathering in the east.

Everyone looked at Thornbeak.

'We'll let him get a bit of a start, so that he thinks he's got away, and then we'll follow,' she said. 'There's a storm brewing, and my feeling is that it's going to be a bad one.'

'Hang on,' said Felix, remembering the storm-oracle in his pocket. He took it out and cupped it in his hands the way he'd seen

Jahim do it, but it obstinately refused to co-operate. He gave Betony the little manual.

'You've got to get the right finger movements,' she said, and gave him step-by-step instructions.

At last the crystal clouded, and changed colour – but this time it went right through the red until it reached the purple.

'Snakeweed won't be able to fly through *that*,' said Thornbeak. 'He'll have to land and take shelter, and that's when we'll strike. He'll have to let go of Fuzzy at some point – he has to eat and drink and sleep ...' She broke off, too choked to go on.

'Fuzzy's quite something, isn't she?' said Ironclaw proudly. 'Fancy going for Snakeweed like that. She really can peck, can't she?'

Thornbeak brightened slightly. 'It's thanks to her that Snakeweed doesn't have a wand any more. That's going to help. But I'm afraid that Ironclaw and I are too large to creep up on them.' She looked at Grimspite.

'It'll be a pleasure,' said Grimspite. He turned to Pewtermane. 'I know you wanted to dispatch Snakeweed yourself, but it isn't practical now. Will you lift the blocking spell from me, and allow me to act on your behalf?'

Pewtermane dipped his silvery head in consent. 'I will,' he said, and recited the incantation.

The leader came over and gave his neigh of approval, which made the raising of the spell permanent. Afterwards he studied Grimspite for a little while. Then he said, 'Tell me, sinistrom, what are you going to do after all this is over?'

Grimspite shrugged. 'I don't really know. I'd like to finish my cookery book … but after that, I'm not sure. I don't think I'd want to write another one. It's not really … well …'

'Challenging enough?'

Grimspite nodded, and looked embarrassed.

'I think you'd be ideally placed to offer some interesting insights into free will. After all, you've seen it from both perspectives – not having it, and then getting it. Would you like to live here? We could teach you some meditation techniques.'

Grimspite gulped. 'Yes please,' he said.

The leader turned to Turpsik. 'We could do with a good poet here, too. The colts would benefit from some proper instruction on assonance and alliteration.'

Turpsik beamed. 'You offering me a cave here as well, then?'

'There are more than enough to go round.'

'Then I accept,' said Turpsik. She glanced at the river. 'Get a lot of fish in there, do you?'

'Shoals beyond your wildest dreams.'

Turpsik sighed with pleasure.

'Right,' said Thornbeak, 'now all that's settled, I think we should make a move.'

'Grimspite, you can ride on Nimby, with us,' said Felix.

'We're all going in the same direction, aren't we? I've got the phial of water from the prediction pool, and I've got the spell – but I would like to know that Fuzzy was safe, before I went back to my own world.'

'I'm really not at all sure about the name *Fuzzy*,' said Ironclaw to Thornbeak. 'It's a bit wet for a brazzle. How about Ironbeak?'

'We've been through all this before,' snapped Thornbeak.

'Granitefuzz,' suggested Betony. 'In memory of Granitelegs.'

'Granitefuzz it is,' said Thornbeak.

Ironclaw turned his head away to hide the wobble his beak had suddenly developed.

Felix reckoned they were a quarter of the way to Andria when the storm hit. To begin with, the passengers on the carpet just noticed the tree canopy swaying more vigorously than usual. Then their hair began to whip across their faces, and the brazzles started to do interesting tilts with their wings to remain on course. The sky darkened to slate-grey, tinged with a sickly yellow towards the horizon. The clouds raced westwards, piling up one upon the other until there was no definition between them any more and the faint moaning of the wind became a howling gale. The slate-grey darkened to charcoal; then suddenly it was rent in two by a brilliant streak of lightning. A moment later, there was a loud crack of thunder.

'Going down!' called Nimby, as he began his descent.

Grimspite was lying with his head on his paws, his stomach flat against the pile of the carpet, and Betony thought he looked a bit ill. She saw Thornbeak perform an acrobatic manoeuvre out of the corner of her eye, her primaries spread out like fingers. The sky lit up, mimicking a plant's root system as the lightning forked and forked and forked again, and the thunder crackled malevolently as each streak earthed itself somewhere in the great groaning forest.

Betony clutched at Felix as the rain drove at them in big fat drops that almost blinded them. It was going to be difficult to find somewhere to land – the brazzles needed a clearing. The lightning illuminated everything once again, and Felix saw a lake below them, its surface whipped to a frenzy of waves. There was an open sandy area beside it, and the brazzles touched down moments before the carpet.

Nimby rolled himself up as quickly as possible, before he became too wet to speak, and Grimspite slunk a little way away from everyone so that he could throw up in peace.

'It's going to be too late to fly any further once the storm abates,' said Thornbeak. 'And it's too dangerous to shelter in the forest.' As if to illustrate this a huge branch on a nearby tree split away from the trunk, and fell to the ground with a resounding thud. The wind continued to shriek through the trees like a convocation of deranged eagles.

The brazzles settled themselves on the ground, and beckoned to Felix and Betony to come under their wings. Then they tucked their heads under their wings as well, and just let the water roll off their well-oiled feathers. After a little while Grimspite joined them, complaining about the fact that he couldn't smell anything as the rain was washing away every scent except water. They all made the best of a bad job, and went to sleep.

Snakeweed's fire-breather had finally rebelled against its master's wishes, and landed by a lake. Travelling in these conditions was ridiculous – visibility was so poor that you could fly into a mountain before you knew it. It didn't look like there was going to be any supper, either, and the brazzle chick wouldn't stop squawking.

Snakeweed fastened down the lid of the pannier, but it didn't make much difference to the racket that issued from within. 'Shut up!' he shouted.

'Want a fish!' shrieked the chick.

After a while Snakeweed realized he wasn't going to get any sleep, despite being fairly snug against the warmth of the fire-breather's belly. It was tempting just to wring the chick's neck – but without a wand he might still need a hostage, so he decided against it. However, he could do with something to eat himself, and fire-breathers were adept at barbecuing things. He glanced at the lake. The fire-breather was looking at the lake as well.

'You any good at fishing?' asked Snakeweed.

The fire-breather lashed its tail and nodded. It had just

been remembering that it had been taught to fish by Turpsik.

'Wonders will never cease,' said Snakeweed, so he unsaddled it and watched it waddle down to the water's edge.

The rain was easing off. The fire-breather waded into the shallows, and spread its wings like a stabber-bird. After a moment or two its head darted downwards and came up with a fine gobbler fish, which it swallowed in one gulp. It repeated this several times until Snakeweed became impatient and yelled, 'You're meant to be fishing for *me*.'

The fire-breather gave him a filthy look, and carried on feeding. Eventually it had its fill, tossed a fish on to the bank, and started to wade back to the shore.

'*And* one for the chick,' called Snakeweed.

The fire-breather gave him an even filthier look, but it did as it was told.

The fish was a bit big for the chick, and Snakeweed roared with laughter as she struggled to swallow it. Once she'd succeeded she went straight to sleep, and there was peace and quiet at last. The fire-breather grilled Snakeweed's own fish for him with a few jets of flame, and by the time he'd finished it and was ready for sleep himself, the storm had passed.

17

Felix was the first to wake the next morning. He had been lying awkwardly against Betony, and his foot had gone to sleep. He scrambled out from beneath Thornbeak's wing, and looked around. Ironclaw was still dead to the world, with Grimspite's hind leg poking out from beneath his feathers as though it had been painted there by Salvador Dali. The previous night Thornbeak had quickly volunteered to shelter both the youngsters *and* the carpet, leaving Grimspite and his smell to Ironclaw. Ironclaw never noticed things like that.

The lake was shrouded with mist, and the tops of the trees on the other side rose out of the fog like brooding giants. It wasn't a cheerful place. They'd have to wait for the sun to break through before Nimby could be dried out properly. Felix stamped his foot, trying to hurry along the horrible pins-and-needles sensation and get it back to normal. There were some big black birds perched high up in the treetops –

at least, they looked like birds, but he no longer took anything for granted in this world. And was that a curl of smoke? The mist was obscuring whatever was causing it, but a dwelling of some sort seemed the likeliest answer. He tried the royalty location spell once more, but without luck – was probably far too early in the morning for the king and queen to be up. It was a pity they hadn't been able to try it the previous evening, but you couldn't use a feather in a storm.

Felix had travelled through this forest the previous summer – but he had been going to Tiratattle, which was more to the north, and not directly to Andria. Betony had traded the toadstools they'd collected for bread and cheese in the villages they'd passed. He would have expected a settlement of some sort here, for the lake was obviously teeming with fish, but it looked as though there would only be the one house when the mist cleared.

The feeling was back in his foot now, so he decided to go for a walk and see if he could find any edible fungi. Betony would be impressed if he'd remembered the right ones to gather. There was a path that skirted the lake – but whether it was used by sentient beings or wild animals he had no idea. The rain had washed away any footprints there might have been. He was feeling fairly cheerful. Andria was only another day's journey; soon, he would be back in his own world, and applying the countercharm to his parents. And then the explanations would have to start. Would his mother recall what had happened to her – or would she think Felix had gone round the twist? Supposing neither of his parents remembered anything? There would be a couple of missing weeks to account for – that couldn't just be glossed over. There would also, presumably, be a lot of wildlife to unfreeze. This was assuming the pollution hadn't got outside the garden. The one thing he *did* know was that it hadn't got as far as Costa Rica. But supposing, when he returned, Wimbledon was just a marble theme park? No, that was silly. Even the Great Plague hadn't affected everyone. There would always be a few people and creatures who were immune, surely?

He suddenly noticed he could see a lot more on the other side of the lake. A watery sun had broken through the thin cloud, and steam was rising from the drying foliage of the forest. He still couldn't make out the source of the smoke, but he could now see that there were two tiny columns of it, close together, as though there were two chimney pots. Then he spotted a clump of pink and white toadstools, and he was as certain as he could be they were the ones Betony used for mushroom omelettes. Maybe he could trade some of them for a loaf of bread with whoever lived in the house with the fire. He took off his jacket, and tied it into a sort of bag. Then he filled it with toadstools and carried on along the path, which, shortly after, divided into two. The right-hand path continued along the border of the lake, and the left-hand one went into the woods.

A small headland obscured the view for a while, but when he arrived at the other side of it he had a shock. The smoke was issuing from a fire-breather, and not a house at all. It only took a moment to establish that it was Snakeweed's fire-breather, and Snakeweed himself was curled up next to it, fast asleep.

What an opportunity! He could sneak up to the fire-breather, open the pannier, and rescue Fuzzy. He would be a hero. He, Felix Sanders, the kid who just a year ago had been unable to do anything, *he* would be the one to save the day. He felt his heart – his *healthy* heart – start to beat faster. What a way to repay everything he owed the brazzles. It would leave Ironclaw free to look for the king and queen again.

He needed to go into the woods so that he could approach his quarry unseen, from behind, so he retraced his steps to where the path divided, left his jacket-bag of toadstools at the fork, and took the left-hand track.

For a while he could still see the lake through the trees. Then the wood grew denser, and he lost sight of it. He took a compass reading, to make sure he was still going in the right direction, and quickened his pace. There was some-thing unpleasant about this part of the forest, something dark and rank and vengeful. He could smell the sour stench you got on disused footpaths when it had been raining, where everything had become so overgrown you couldn't separate one plant from another.

A thorny strand caught at his ankle and it took him a while to untangle it, for it seemed to have an active and spiteful life of its own. Then it happened again, and it was even more difficult to extricate himself. He started to keep a lookout for that particular plant, and avoid stepping on it. An image from a television documentary popped into his head, a speeded up sequence of a bramble growing. Pale green tendrils looping themselves around other plants, their thorns catching hold of their victims in a vice-like grip, tightening around them until they strangled them. In fast-mode, a bramble had a lot in common with a predatory animal.

At last the trees thinned again, and Felix realized he had come out of the wood exactly where he'd wanted to – right behind the fire-breather. He could hear it snoring, which was all to the good, and what was even better was that the pannier he wanted was on the side closest to him. He could see the wickerwork bulging from time to time, as the chick moved around inside it.

He crept up to the pannier, and started to unfasten the strap. A sharp little beak suddenly thrust itself through the rushes, and pecked him. It was as much as he could do not to cry out, but he bit his lip and swore silently inside his head.

'Fuzzy,' he whispered, 'I'm a friend of your mother's. A friend of Thornbeak's. I've come here to rescue you.'

The movements inside the pannier ceased. Felix hoped

this was a good sign, and had another attempt at the strap. This time he managed to unbuckle it unscathed, and he lifted the lid as quietly as he could. A pink pimply head shot out and tilted sideways, so that the owner could study him with one of her bright yellow eyes.

'Ssh,' said Felix, putting his finger to his lips. Then he held out his arms, and Fuzzy scrambled out of the pannier. She was heavier than he'd expected, and the claws on her hind legs were as sharp as the talons on her front ones. 'Can you sheathe those?' hissed Felix, as she scratched him.

Fuzzy didn't seem quite sure how to do it, but after a couple of tries that made Felix feel as though he were carrying a porcupine, she succeeded. The fire-breather carried on snoring. Felix shut the lid of the pannier – one of the things that always annoyed him about adventure films was when the hero left a door ajar, advertizing his visit as surely as if he'd left a note. Then, his heart in his mouth, he tiptoed away and back into the forest.

They followed the path in silence until Felix considered he was far enough away from the fire-breather not to be overheard. Then he introduced himself properly, and congratulated Fuzzy on the way she'd disarmed Snakeweed.

'He was horrid,' said Fuzzy. 'Are we going back to my mum now?'

Felix nodded. 'Are you any good at walking yet?' he asked. 'Only you're rather heavy, and you do wriggle.'

'Haven't done walking,' said Fuzzy.

320

Felix set her down on the ground, and she took a few steps. She picked up the idea very quickly indeed, and soon she was tottering along beside him and looking very pleased with herself.

'Want to fly now,' she said.

'You'll have to get your wing feathers before you can do that,' said Felix.

'Want my wing feathers *now*.'

'You'll have to wait for them to grow,' said Felix.

Fuzzy gave Felix a filthy look as though this delay was entirely his fault – then she suddenly scampered off into the undergrowth, showing a surprising turn of speed for one so unversed in legwork.

Felix groaned, and gave chase.

Fuzzy thought this was hilariously funny and ran even faster, squawking with laughter.

'Come back!' Felix shouted, dodging between tree-trunks and jumping over mossy fallen branches. 'You'll get lost!' And then one of the spiky bramble-things caught at his ankle, and he fell over. He sat up immediately, and started to tear at it with his fingers. It seemed to tighten of its own accord, so he stopped fighting a losing battle, and got his penknife out of his rucksack. When he cut the stem with it he heard a faint scream; a horrible milky liquid gushed out, and the stink of rotten eggs filled the air. He stepped back sharply – which was just as well as the liquid turned to a sticky jelly, sealing the end of the stem and gluing it to a

321

neighbouring shrub.

Fuzzy had now disappeared, although he could hear her crashing through the undergrowth ahead of him. He followed more carefully, shouting every so often for her to wait for him. Eventually the crashing noises stopped, and a loud squawking replaced them. The trees came to an abrupt end, and Felix found himself out in the open on a stretch of grass. The squawking ceased as suddenly as it had started. A huge tangle of the bramble stuff was in front of him, like a hedge – but above it, a little way off, he could see the turret of a castle. Fuzzy had been caught by the hedge, and she was thrashing about and pecking at the stems for all she was worth.

'Don't!' yelled Felix. 'You'll get even more stuck!' He ran over, and the chick glared at him with her yellow eyes. She wasn't squawking any longer because the two halves of her beak were glued together with the white sap.

Felix cut the briars that held her as neatly as he could, pushing the weeping ends out of the way with a lump of dead wood. Her tail was now gummed to her body, and two of her toes were stuck together. Her yellow eyes were wide with fright – or anger, it was hard to tell which.

'I've got a nice fire going,' said a croaky old voice. 'It's got a spit above it, if you want to roast her.'

Felix spun round. One of the black birds had landed on the ground nearby, and was watching them with interest. Only it wasn't a bird – its head and torso were those of an old grey-haired crone, and the rest of it looked more like a vulture than anything else. A harpy.

'You haven't seen one of my sort before, have you?' said the harpy. 'And I haven't seen one of you, neither. You're a human being, or my name's not Scavenjit. How did you get here?'

Felix told her the truth – there didn't seem much point doing anything else. Then, and with some trepidation, he asked, 'Are you a shadow-beast?'

'*Thorns surround us*, no!' cackled the harpy. 'I'm a carrion-wing. Me and my kind clear up, see? We're refuse collectors. We got called in by a flame-bird, soon after this predator-hedge was hexed in place. Darn thing keeps sending out suckers everywhere; that shouldn't happen, strikes me the spell was cast in far too much of a hurry.' She looked pointedly at Fuzzy. 'She's my lawful prey, you know.'

'And she's also the daughter of a very good friend of mine,' said Felix.

'Oh,' said Scavenjit, looking disappointed.

'Do you know a way of un-gluing her?'

'Only if you're a prince,' said Scavenjit.

Felix decided that denying it at this stage might be unwise. 'Do you feed on the creatures that get caught by the hedge, then?' he asked.

The carrionwing nodded.

'How do you manage not to get stuck to them?'

'I'm immune,' said Scavenjit. 'That's all part of being a carrionwing, see?'

Felix glanced towards the castle. 'Is there anyone in there who knows a way of unsticking her?'

'Them's all asleep,' said Scavenjit.

Felix was about to comment on late risers, when the implications suddenly hit him. 'Are they due to sleep for a hundred years?' he asked.

'Well,' said Scavenjit, 'that's what happened last time. Being a human, you may not be too well up on this world's history. The Princess Bella? Got cursed because her father messed up some guest-list or other, pricked her finger on a spindle and went into a coma. The palace had a predator-hedge planted round it. When it was countercharmed away a century later, they found the skeletons of everything that had been unable to get out of the way. Lots of little things, of course, birds and nut-nibblers and berry-buriers. But there was a brittlehorn, and a couple of small-tails as well. This hedge, though – sloppier job altogether. Keeps on killing things, it does, and you can't just leave the corpses to rot, can you? Sorcerers aren't what they used to be. I blame printing, myself. Everyone wants what everyone else has got these days, and they don't give a thunderclap about the environment.' She jerked her head over her shoulder, towards the castle. 'That place should never have been built, if you ask me.'

'Mm-mm-mm!' fulminated Fuzzy, obviously thinking she'd been forgotten but unable to express this in words.

'Look,' said Felix, 'I've got to find a way of ungluing this chick's beak. She'll die if she can't eat.'

'The only solution I know of,' said Scavenjit, 'is to deactivate the entire spell. Wake up everyone in the castle. That'll get rid of the hedge, and any sap spillages will disappear as well.'

'How do I do that?'

'Kiss the fair lady who lies within, of course.'

It was inevitable, really. 'How do I do it, then?' asked Felix, looking at the impenetrable hedge with its vicious thorns and twisted branches.

'If you was a prince, it would open up just like that,' said Scavenjit.

'Well I'm not,' said Felix irritably.

'Thought as much,' said Scavenjit. 'You'll have to fly over it, then, and land in the courtyard.'

'Are you offering to take me?'

'*Hailstones*, no. The place is feather-proof.'

That ruled out going back for Thornbeak or Ironclaw. And Nimby would still be too wet to fly.

'Mm-mm-mm,' said Fuzzy, rolling her eyes in the direction of the lake.

Snakeweed's fire-breather, thought Felix. Clever Fuzzy. It's covered in scales, not feathers. Two big problems, though. I'll have to get it off Snakeweed somehow – always assuming he hasn't left already – and I've never even *been* on a fire-breather, let alone piloted one. Taking Fuzzy with me would slow me down – and she won't be able to cross the predator-hedge with me, if it's feather proof. Can I trust Scavenjit not to spit-roast her in my absence?

'What are your plans for the rest of the day?' he asked casually.

'Breakfast,' said Scavenjit. 'Then lunch. And after that, dinner.'

This didn't sound terribly promising. 'Is that all you do, then?' he asked. 'Eat? Don't you have any hobbies or anything?'

'Meteorology,' said Scavenjit unexpectedly.

'*Weather*? You're interested in predicting the *weather*?'

'What's wrong with that? We love storms, we carrion-wings do. The one last night was a cracker. There's not much that beats flying around in a good thunderstorm, shrieking. If we knew in advance when we were going to get a howling gale we could make preparations.'

'What sort of preparations?' asked Felix, intrigued.

'Oh, a bit of flocking and convening. It's much more fun if there's lots of you.'

So the noise last night wasn't just the wind, thought Felix. The carrionwings were out and about in it, having a party. He suddenly remembered the storm-oracle in his pocket. It was perfect; he couldn't have found anything better if he'd tried. He took it out, and cupped it in his hands. The transparent crystal clouded immediately this time – but it stayed yellow. 'Might get a bit overcast later,' said Felix, making an educated guess, 'but there won't be another storm tonight.'

Scavenjit looked at him. 'That's not one of them storm-oracles, is it?' she asked.

Felix nodded.

The carrionwing's craggy old face was suddenly suffused with longing.

'If you look after Fuzzy for me while I enter the castle,' said Felix, 'you can have it. After I get back, naturally.'

Scavenjit nodded furiously, her eyes returning to the little crystal globe. 'I can speed things up a bit, as well,' she said. 'I'll carry you back to the lake in my talons, drop you by the fire-breather and harry the japegrin for you. We can hide the brazzle chick in my own dear hollow tree for the time being.'

The hollow tree stank, but Fuzzy was in no position to complain. The journey back to the lake was terrifying, like being dangled from a parachute with a mind of its own, but to Felix's delight the fire-breather was still there. Snakeweed was just tightening the straps of the saddle. Scavenjit dropped Felix a little way off, out of sight behind a bush. Then she flew over to Snakeweed and dived into the attack, screeching at the top of her voice.

Snakeweed didn't have anything with which to defend himself, and Felix could hear him swearing, and flapping his arms around. He peeked round the bush. Scavenjit swooped again, her claws extended, and Snakeweed lost his hat. The fire-breather seemed totally unmoved by the whole thing – its hide was far too thick for a carrionwing to bother it.

'Don't just sit there, you lump of old leather!' yelled Snakeweed. 'Burn its wings to a crisp!'

The fire-breather ignored him, and started to steam-clean its tail.

Scavenjit dived again, and finally Snakeweed had had enough. He ran for cover, and Scavenjit made sure he ran in the opposite direction to where she'd dropped Felix. Once Snakeweed was out of sight Felix sprinted over to the fire-breather, trying to remember the little he knew about the creatures. You just had to instruct them, didn't you? Although they couldn't speak, they understood simple commands. They also understood abuse, and they didn't like it much; they had their pride.

Felix waited until the fire-breather had finished attending to its tail. He could still hear Snakeweed shouting in the distance, and he knew that Scavenjit would keep the japegrin out of the way until she saw the fire-breather take off. 'Excuse me,' said Felix politely, indicating the forest behind him, 'could you take me in that direction, please?'

There was a momentary pause, as the fire-breather regarded him with its blood-red eyes and considered his request. Felix wondered whether there was a password he should have used. Would the creature only respond to Snakeweed, or was it free to decide for itself? It glanced towards the forest's edge, and curled its lip in an expression of disgust. Perhaps an insult was an insult, employer or no employer, and Snakeweed didn't merit any loyalty. The fire-breather snorted suddenly, and got to its feet. Felix scrambled into the saddle and fastened his seatbelt. There was a brief gallop along the sand, at the water's edge – and then they were up in the air, and winging their way over the trees.

Before long the predator-hedge appeared below them, a dark sinuous shape twisting its way around the outside of the moat that separated it from the turrets and walls of the castle. Fortunately there was a grass verge on the castle side of the moat, otherwise the only place to land would have been in the courtyard – and there wouldn't have been enough room for the fire-breather to pull up. A few gaily-painted boats were moored to metal rings, and there was a small landing stage with some sort of sign erected on it. Felix asked the fire-breather to touch down on the side by the drawbridge, and it executed a very neat turn and complied. Even so it was a close thing, and they nearly ended up in the water.

The entrance to the fortress was protected by an iron

portcullis, but this was jammed halfway down, so Felix could walk through. He saw why almost immediately – the wise-hoof who had been in the process of lowering it by means of a heavy chain had fallen asleep in the middle of his task and was still standing there, his dark bearded head bowed on his chest. There were stone stairs under the archway, leading up to the battlements – but two guards were sitting on them, also dead to the world. Felix would have had to step over them to go up, and he didn't like to, somehow. A piece of wood was lying on the ground, with some lettering burnt into it. He picked it up and looked at it. It said: *Open all year, except on Dance-days. Entry: One silver coin, children half-price.*

The archway opened out into a cobbled courtyard, and on the other side of that was a door. There was an eerie silence that seemed out of place; this wasn't a ruin, it was a properly maintained castle, and recently built, by the look of it. The stones weren't weathered, they were new. He had seen nothing like this in Andria – there hadn't been any arrow slits in the palace, as there had never been any battles. Felix walked across the courtyard, the sound of his footsteps echoing in a faintly disturbing way. He lifted the latch of the door, and it swung open, creaking. To his left another flight of steps led upwards, but this time there was no one on them. Ahead of him was a second door, but this one was open, and he could see a great hall, with swords and shields decorating the walls. Swords and shields were strange, too.

The only weapons Felix had seen before – apart from the nomads' scimitars – were crossbows and spears and knives, which were used for hunting. The hall was full of wooden tables and benches. A few people were sitting at them, their arms on the tables, their heads on their arms. They seemed to be grouped in families; some of the sleepers were children, and the drowsiness had overtaken them in the middle of lunch. There were tangle-folk and japegrins and diggelucks, and even a party of nomads. The food was still fresh, as bewitched as the diners. Felix decided not to try any, although he was hungry and the fruit syllabubs looked delicious.

The kitchens were behind the great hall; the cooking fires had gone out, and the lickits who worked there were slumped over their work surfaces, snoring gently. A whole cuddyak had been spitted over the biggest hearth. Felix took a tentative sniff, but it smelt fine. A spike next to the serving hatch was festooned with little pieces of paper, and each one had a different order on it – two mushroom omelettes, five portions of squirtled seaweed, one melted cheese chubba. Next to it was a notice, saying, *No orders taken after sunset*. There was something very odd about all this.

Felix went back to the flight of steps, took a deep breath, and went up the spiral staircase. The first floor boasted bedrooms with four-poster beds and silver candelabras on the mantelpieces, each room grander than the last. They were, however, all numbered, and there were little notices on the walls saying, *Please leave wands at Reception*. Fluffy cream towels were folded neatly on the counterpanes, and there were new bars of soap on the washstands. It was more like a hotel than anything.

The last room was Room 13, and as Felix entered he almost tripped over a spinning wheel standing just inside the door. The curtains here were a deep blue velvet, and the paintings were all of mythical beasts – leopards and elephants and zebras. The bed was hung with gold and silver tapestries, and this time there was somebody in it. Felix walked over to the bed, knowing he'd found his fair lady.

She was older than he'd expected, but still extremely beautiful. Her hair was as blonde as Betony's, and her ears were just as pointed. She was wearing a tiara which sparkled with gems that were every colour of the rainbow, and a dress made of milky green silk. Her face looked familiar, however. He stood there, puzzled, trying to remember where he'd seen her before. But the memory refused to surface and in the end he gave up, braced himself, bent over her, and kissed her lightly on the lips.

18

Her eyes opened immediately. They were a bright emerald green, and as puzzled as his own had been a moment earlier. She sat up, and looked round. 'Where is he?' she asked.

'Who?'

'The king.'

'Your father?'

'My husband, silly.'

Felix shrugged. 'I don't know. There are a lot of people asleep downstairs.'

'He did try to stop them putting me under, you know, so they may have killed him. He was ever so brave.' She bit her lip, and looked sad for a moment. Then she smiled and said, 'That was all a hundred years ago, presumably.'

'Presumably,' said Felix, although the castle didn't look that old.

'Oh well,' she said. 'I suppose I'd better marry you, then. You're a bit young, though. Do you like dancing?'

Felix blanched. He hadn't expected this.

She looked at him appraisingly. 'You've got good legs. I love dancing. The midnight wriggle, the star squirm ... I expect there are lots of new ones now, aren't there? Tell me about them.'

That was where he'd seen her before. At the dance festival he'd attended the previous summer. He remembered the king and queen joining the tangle-children on the stage, and twining in and out of them in the most ridiculous set of moves he had ever seen, full of unexpected little hops and jumps. 'You're the Queen of Andria, aren't you?' he said.

'How clever of you to know that,' said the queen. 'And you're the prince of where?'

'I'm not a prince at all,' said Felix.

'But you must be.'

Felix shook his head.

'Are you quite sure?' Her brows drew together in consternation.

'Quite sure. The sleeping spell needed a mythical being to break it. It would have been easier if I'd been a prince, but being human was the most important part.'

He suddenly wondered what would have happened if he hadn't found her, and someone had tried to use the snail to wake her with a kiss instead. He fought back an attack of the giggles, and had to cough to disguise it.

'I'm Felix,' he said, once he was sure he could keep a straight face. 'You invited my friend Betony to dinner last year, and you gave her the book that contained the spell that cured my heart condition. And you've only been asleep for a few weeks, not a hundred years.'

The queen looked astonished. '*A few weeks?*'

'It was Fleabane who pricked your finger with the spindle, wasn't it?'

She nodded. 'Yes. He told us we were coming here for a holiday, and then he turned quite beastly. How did you know?'

'It's all fitting into place,' said Felix. 'Everyone was told you'd abdicated. But actually killing you would have been very dangerous – if any evidence was found, the population of Andria would have risen up against Fleabane, whatever the outcome. *This* was a much better solution – put you to sleep for a hundred years, in the middle of a forest. Stopped anyone finding you with the royalty location spell, as well; you have to be awake for it to work. What is this place, by the way? It looks like something from *my* world, not yours.'

'Well of course it is, soppy,' said the queen. 'It's the very latest entertainment idea, built a few months back. A mythical building. People dress up as human beings, and have pretend sword-fights on the battlements. There's a snack bar and boat rides, and you can even book a room for the night, although it's fearfully expensive. It would never have been possible before printing, of course – the advertizing campaign must have cost a small fortune.'

Felix suddenly remembered what the japegrin had said,

over lunch, on his first day in Andria. *'Did she take you to the castle? My little'un's been on at me...'* He felt let down, somehow. It was all a bit too commercial.

'Well,' said the queen, with a tinkly laugh, 'if I've only dozed off for a few weeks the king may still be around. Let's go and look for him, shall we?' She jumped off the bed, put on her velvet slippers, and skipped to the door. 'Come on!'

Felix followed her downstairs. The castle was no longer as silent as it had been – people were waking up. A baby was crying somewhere, and there were sounds of activity from the kitchen, with someone loudly complaining that the ovens had gone out. The queen found the king quite quickly, sitting in the great hall, rubbing his eyes and yawning.

'Oh goodie,' she said. She smiled at Felix. 'No offence, human boy, but the king is the best dancer I've ever met. I'm sure you'll meet someone else to marry, sooner or later. You've got good legs.'

Felix grinned. Betony had told him what the king and queen were like, but he hadn't really believed her. They were figureheads, that was all, but they were frightfully *nice*. With Snakeweed out of the way, Andria could have its king and queen again, and the guilds could get back to running the place the way they had before. There would be dance festivals and fun once more, and the library would re-open. Thornbeak and Betony could go back to work, and Thornbeak could get Ironclaw's cataloguing system up and running. He walked towards the exit, feeling very pleased with himself. He was quite sure, now, that Snakeweed had just been winding him up about his cure being temporary. He felt on top of the world. Not only had he rescued Thornbeak's chick, he'd restored the monarchy. Quite a good morning's work.

On the other side of the moat, the landscape outside had changed dramatically. The predator-hedge had completely gone, and he noticed a recently made road leading off into the forest, with a signpost pointing to Andria and Tiratattle. He could see Scavenjit's hollow tree in the distance, and when he cocked his head to one side and listened hard, he could hear Fuzzy squawking. It had worked. He had comprehensively reversed the spell; everything was all right. He realised he didn't need the fire-breather any more – the brazzles weren't all that far away, and the hedge was no longer an issue. He could leave the fire-breather here, and the king and queen could use it to return to Andria. They would keep Ironclaw's gold safe for him until he went to collect it. He went back to the great hall, and suggested it.

'What a lovely idea!' sparkled the queen. 'We'd be back in time for the fish-reels.' Seeing Felix's expression of incomprehension she added, 'It's a Dance-day that celebrates the end of net-mending week. We always do a quick turn round the floor to open the proceedings.'

'There's something else I'd like you to do, when you get back to Andria,' said Felix. 'There's an otherworld vehicle there. If someone discovered how it worked, they'd make lots

337

of them. They're bad news in my world – they're no good for the environment. I'd like you to have it destroyed.'

'OK,' said the queen brightly. 'I'm sure you know best.'

Felix said goodbye, and started to make his way back to the exit. But by now, word had got round. People kept stopping him to congratulate him, pat him on the back, offer him a glass of rainbow-juice. He was getting the full hero treatment, and he was loving every second of it. A child gave him some sweets, and a lickit handed him a pot of jellied creepy-biters. A tangle-woman stuck a flower in his cap. When he finally reached the drawbridge, the wise-hoof saluted him.

'Wait!' cried a voice.

Felix turned round, and saw one of the nomads chasing after him. He stopped.

'Bismettle Bisotti B'dil, at your service,' said the nomad. 'Your presence here is as welcome as driving rain.'

It took a moment for Felix to remember that Bismettle came from a desert region, and this was a compliment.

'Anxious to gather news from home after my enforced repose,' the nomad continued, 'I consulted the ragamucky in Room 8.'

Felix had only had fleeting contact with ragamuckies the previous year, but he did know they were brownies and that they read crystal balls for a living.

Bismettle beamed at Felix, and then, rather unexpectedly, wiped a tear from his eye. 'It can only have been you, a

338

human being, who sold your scientific instrument to my brother at a most favourable price. The very next night a vamprey took up residence in his rafters. If he had not been experimenting with the wondrous torch, he would never have seen it, let alone been able to kill it. My gratitude is greater than a cloudburst in the desert. I beg you to accept this.' He handed Felix a small lacquered box, inlaid with mother-of-pearl and malachite.

Felix opened it. Inside lay the most beautiful emerald pendant he had ever seen.

'It protects the wearer from vamprey bites,' said the nomad. 'It seems appropriate.'

'I can't accept this,' said Felix, realizing that the pendant was very valuable. He couldn't take it back to his own world, either. It was magic.

The nomad looked devastated. 'It is not good enough? Then I must beat myself with a cactus, and fast for a week.'

'It's *too* good,' said Felix, realising he'd made a big *faux pas*.

'Surely nothing is too good for the wife of a hero such as you.'

'I'm not married,' said Felix.

'Betrothed?'

Betony, thought Felix suddenly. I promised her I'd replace the shell necklace, and I've forgotten all about it. 'There is someone ...' said Felix.

The nomad smiled, bowed, and took his leave.

Felix crossed the drawbridge, and made his way over to Scavenjit's hollow tree. Scavenjit had fed Fuzzy as soon as her beak became unstuck, and the chick was in a bouncy mood. Felix gave Scavenjit the storm-oracle, and she shrieked with delight. Then, with Fuzzy trotting along beside him he went back to the brazzles, retrieving his jacket and the toadstools he'd collected along the way.

'Where have you *been?*' cried Betony, as soon as Felix reappeared. 'We've all been worried sick.'

Thornbeak was looking absolutely furious. Then Fuzzy stepped out from behind him, and her eyes widened in amazement.

'Hello,' said Fuzzy, casting a quizzical eye at Nimby, who was spread out on the grass, drying. 'Been having adventures.'

Grimspite sniffed the air tentatively, as though he couldn't quite believe what he was smelling. Felix had got used to it; Fuzzy had her very own perfume, which was a unique blend of baby's nappy, rotten fish and oily feathers.

Thornbeak was suddenly too overcome with emotion to speak. The others besieged Felix with questions, so he smiled and held up his hand, and they fell silent and allowed him to tell his story. Modesty was a family trait back home, and showing off was frowned upon – so he shrugged off their praise, and made light of his battle with the predator-hedge. Thornbeak didn't really seem to be listening anyway; she just sat and looked at Fuzzy, dewy-eyed.

Betony simply took him at his word, and said, 'It was all a bit of a cinch, then.'

'Well, not really,' said Felix, feeling his heroism was not being properly appreciated.

Betony looked nonplussed, so he tried to make everything more dramatic. It fell a bit flat, so he gave her the emerald pendant instead.

Her eyes widened in astonishment, then she flung her arms round Felix and gave him a rib-crushing hug. 'A vam-prey charm,' she said. 'I need never be frightened of those horrible things again. Oh Felix, this is brilliant. Agrimony really *will* be emerald with envy now.'

Felix then produced his bag of toadstools, the jellied creepy-biters, and the sweets, and they had a strange but satisfying brunch.

Fuzzy studied Ironclaw and said, 'You're my dada, aren't you?'

'Er … yes,' said Ironclaw. He glanced at Thornbeak, completely at a loss.

'Well give her a quick preen, then,' said Thornbeak.

Ironclaw shifted from foot to foot, looking uncomfortable. Eventually he said, 'Er … hello, Granitefuzz.'

'Fuzzy,' said the chick.

'We've re-named you Granitefuzz,' said Ironclaw. 'After an old friend of mine.'

The chick glared at him.

'Fuzzy for short,' compromised Ironclaw.

The chick burped her approval.

'She's so precocious,' said Thornbeak fondly. 'I'm going to start her on a bit of historical theory in a few days' time. Then, hopefully, when she's a bit older and the library's open again I can take her to Andria and have *two* assistants.'

'She'd be better off knowing what two and two makes.'

'Four,' said Fuzzy.

Ironclaw's expression softened to pure mush. 'She *is* rather adorable, isn't she?' he said.

'Can we get moving now?' asked Felix. 'I really do want to get back and sort out my parents.'

'Yes, of course,' said Thornbeak. 'I'll take Fuzzy back to Tromm Fell, and Nimby can take you and Betony to the Andrian Divide. Ironclaw will provide an escort, in case you run into any bother.'

Ironclaw ruffled his feathers and flexed his wings and tried to look the part. Felix noticed he had one eye on Fuzzy, and was clearly attempting to impress her with his cockiness.

'What about Snakeweed?' asked Betony. 'He may not have a wand or the gold or a fire-breather any more, but he's still out there somewhere.'

'Leave him to me,' said Grimspite.

'How are you doing?' asked Emily, appearing in the doorway and regarding Rutherford steadily with her close-set dark eyes.

'Not too well,' said Rutherford, sighing and leaning back in his chair. 'I did a UFO sightings check, but there hasn't been anything in the right area for ten years.'

'Do you still think it's something from outer space?'

'I haven't come up with a better theory. What about you?'

'I don't know,' said Emily slowly. 'I'll tell you one thing, though. The normal rules of physics don't seem to apply.'

Rutherford laughed. 'That's ridiculous.'

'You'd have said turning someone to marble was ridiculous a month ago.'

'OK. Tell me.'

'Newton's third law of motion. For every applied force, there is an equal and opposite reaction. But there doesn't seem to be. The energy's doing a sort of half-twist, and producing all sorts of weird results. One of which is turning living things to marble.'

'*One* of which?'

Emily took a deep breath. 'I can light a match with a wave of my hand,' she said. 'When I was in that summer house in the garden, I found a sheet of paper with a diagram of a hand movement, and a sort of rhyme scribbled below it. There were two versions of it, and it was obvious what it was for. I tried them both, then I tried a few of my own.'

Rutherford just stared at her for a moment. Then he said, 'Show me.'

She picked up a match, waved her other hand across it and recited: 'Don't fight; flame, light; ignite; burn bright.'

The match burst into flame.

'You flicked it with your fingernail.'

'I didn't, Rutherford,' said Emily, annoyed. 'Watch me.' She took another match out of the box, and repeated the experiment. The match burst into flame, as before.

'How do you do it?'

'I think there's a sort of mental force I exert, in opposition to the wave of the hand. I don't even have to say the words out loud – I can simply *think* them. It's a balance thing; get it right, and it ought to cancel out. But it doesn't. The match lights instead.'

'It's magic, then,' said Rutherford, smiling.

Emily didn't laugh. 'Precisely,' she said.

Grimspite watched the brazzles and the carpet take to the air, and head off in opposite directions. There had been an emotional goodbye between Felix and Thornbeak, which he didn't quite understand, but it was clearly something to do with being friends with someone. He turned into the forest and followed the path. Before too long he picked up Snakeweed's trail, and shortly after that the delectable scent of bumbled butterbugs with pukeberry sauce, and devilled creepy-biters. A restaurant, right out here in the middle of the forest? Then he remembered the castle. That was obviously where Snakeweed was going, there wouldn't be anywhere else in the vicinity that had a decent menu. The alternative would be a wooden shack, serving hunks of grimy bread with mouldy cheese – the sort of place that gives a whole new meaning to *dirt cheap*. He broke into a lope.

Lickit form was more advisable for the castle, so he transformed himself. Snakeweed was in there somewhere, he could smell him, but as he crossed the drawbridge he realized he'd have to pay to get in. He didn't have any money, so he said he was applying for a job as a chef and was waved through. As he crossed the great hall, he overheard snatches of conversation.

'Really nice, she was, not high and mighty at all.'

'Watched my little Milfoil here do his dusk hop, and told him he'd make a great dancer.'

'Andria will be back to normal now, and about time too. Snakeweed was a nasty piece of work. He never really got rid of Harshak, you know.'

'Apparently a brazzle killed Harshak yesterday. The ragamucky with the crystal ball in Room 8 told me.'

'She said Snakeweed's disappeared, as well.'

'Good riddance.'

'Did you see the queen's tiara? Beautiful, it was.'

'Waved at me as the fire-breather took off.'

'No she didn't, Mum, it was *me*.'

'You eat your spliggit, Milfoil, and less of the cheek.'

Grimspite wandered into the kitchen, and looked round. No sign of Snakeweed.

'You here for a job?' a lickit asked.

'Yes,' said Grimspite, unable to think of any other reason

for his presence. 'I've been writing a cookery book, *Dining Out on Mythical Beasts*.'

'Perfect,' said the lickit. 'We've been wondering how to improve the menu – make it more in keeping with the general theme of the place – but the only recipes we've found have been ones in children's books of myths and legends, and they don't go into sufficient detail. Fish fingers, for instance. Fish don't even have hands, let alone fingers. Look, run this lunch tray up to Room 13, would you? Got a fussy customer who doesn't want to eat in the hall with everyone else.'

That's promising, thought Grimspite, a fussy customer who stays in his room. Is it because he doesn't want to run the risk of being recognized? 'On my way,' he said, taking the tray.

He decided to play his part properly, and knocked.

'Come in,' said Snakeweed's voice.

Grimspite smiled to himself, and opened the door.

Snakeweed was sitting on the bed, reading something. 'Put it on the table,' he said, not looking up

Grimspite put the tray on the table. Then he said, 'I've come to rip you apart, Snakeweed.'

Snakeweed raised his eyes, and then one eyebrow. 'Grimspite,' he said. 'Well well.'

Grimspite leant against the door so that Snakeweed couldn't get out, and changed himself back into sinistrom form. When he was fully functional again he realized that Snakeweed had broken the spindle off the spinning wheel, and was holding it in front of him as a weapon.

Grimspite took a couple of paces forwards, estimating distances and trajectories, and then he sprang. Snakeweed sidestepped him, and jumped on to the bed. He now had a height advantage. Undeterred, Grimspite leapt at him again. Snakeweed used the mattress as a springboard, and sailed past him. Grimspite bounced on the spot where Snakeweed had been standing, hit the wall, and did a backward somersault. Snakeweed raced for the door, but Grimspite managed to cover the distance in two bounds and seized him by the ankle. They both fell to the floor, each struggling to be the first to regain his footing. Snakeweed lifted the spindle like a dagger, and aimed it at Grimspite's left eye. Grimspite had to let go of Snakeweed's leg to evade this, and Snakeweed scrambled to his feet and made another attempt to get out. Once more Grimspite intercepted him, and as the spindle swept across his vision he thought he'd misjudged it. He lunged to the right, and caught Snakeweed a glancing blow on his weapon arm. The spindle flew into the air as Snakeweed lost his grip on it, and turned end over end before it descended again, and hit Snakeweed on the hand.

The japegrin crumpled to the floor, and stayed there.

Grimspite blinked. Had Snakeweed hit his head or something? He scrambled to his feet, and peered at him. Snakeweed was breathing deeply and evenly, and appeared to have gone to sleep. There was a tiny pinprick of blood on his finger from the spindle.

Scabs and scars, thought Grimspite, is everyone else going to go back to sleep now as well? And does that include me?

He didn't feel particularly tired, however – no more tired than a life-and-death tussle usually made him. The distant kitchen sounds were still going on, too. He polished off the food he'd brought Snakeweed – no point letting it go to waste – changed back to lickit form, and took the tray back to the kitchen. Then he told them that he'd recognized Snakeweed and challenged him about the disgraceful way he'd been running Andria. Snakeweed had tried to silence him, and the rest was history.

'History's our business,' said the head lickit, 'as well as myths. I think we should capitalize on this. Put him on display. He'll stay like it for a hundred years. We can lay him out on the bed and do some nice posters round the walls, illustrating the appalling things he did. He'll be the star attraction.'

I rather like that, thought Grimspite, and I think Pewtermane and Turpsik will like it too. It's poetic justice – Snakeweed being shamelessly exploited by a business venture, instead of *him* being the one to exploit others. I wasn't all that thrilled about the prospect of disembowelling him, to be honest. That sort of thing lost its glamour a while back.

'Tell me,' said Grimspite. 'Why didn't we all go to sleep, the way everyone did last time? And the time before that, come to think of it?'

348

'Because Snakeweed was no good,' said the lickit. 'Historically speaking, the Princess Bella was supposed to be so nice that everyone went to sleep as well so that she wouldn't be lonely when she woke up. The Queen of Andria's a good sort, too. Not over-endowed with brains, I grant you, but not malicious in any way at all. Snakeweed's another matter, isn't he?'

Grimspite nodded. 'Yes. Unquestionably the most unpleasant being I've ever encountered.'

There was no reason to stay at the castle any longer. He could go back to the brittlehorn valley, and finish his cookery book. As soon as it was published he'd send the castle a copy, and they could use it to turn the restaurant into an eatery of worldwide renown. The triple-head should have one, as well. He left a few recipes for the lickit who'd shown such an interest in his work, just to be going on with, and then he strode off across the drawbridge and headed for Tromm Fell. He was really looking forward to learning about philosophy and meditation, and maybe doing a couple of poetry courses with Turpsik. Being a sinistrom didn't have to mean a life of unbridled violence; he'd been lucky enough to have a choice, and he was quite sure he'd made the right one.

19

The journey to the mountains was uneventful. Nimby got rather excited by his first glimpse of snow, and Betony had to remind him he was carrying passengers. They flew over Turpsik's valley, still carpeted with the brilliant purple flowers, and Felix pointed out her cave. There was a thin column of smoke rising from the entrance; someone else had taken up residence already. It was, after all, a highly desirable bit of real estate – running water, and plenty of space. A few minutes later they arrived at the Divide, and landed.

'Time to say goodbye again, Felix,' said Ironclaw. 'Oh, you'd better take the snail with you. Didn't need it in the end, did we?' He withdrew the box from his leg-pouch, and passed it over. 'You will be back, though, won't you?' he added. 'Now you've got the spell you can cross over whenever you like.'

Felix nodded, although whether it would actually happen was another question entirely. If – no, *when* his parents knew the full story, would they let him? The enormity of the situation facing him when he got back was hitting home; he'd been trying not to think about it too much. Whilst he'd been in Betony's world it had all seemed a bit distant. Change what you can, accept what you can't. Now the moment had arrived, like an exam you'd been aware of, but had been pushing to the back of your mind.

'Felix,' said Betony hesitantly, 'you could do with a hand applying all those countercharms, couldn't you? I'd really love another glimpse of your world.'

Take Betony with him? It would be absolutely brilliant – he wouldn't have to do it all on his own, and it would delay the inevitable goodbye. The things he could show her ... it would be such fun ... assuming everything worked out OK. But how would he get her there? He had a long coach-ride in front of him, and he didn't have enough money to pay for both of them. Ironclaw's gold wouldn't be much use at a coach station – and would she really be able to contain her amazement at all the new things she would be seeing? 'I really wish I could,' he said. 'But it's quite a journey to my house; we'd have to go by coach, and I don't have a ticket for you.'

'Excuse me for butting in like a rush mat,' said Nimby, 'but I'd love to see your world as well.'

'We could take him with us,' said Betony. 'If he promised to behave himself.'

'*I would, I would*,' said Nimby. 'I'd be the most obedient carpet ever.'

Felix felt a bit dubious. Taking Nimby across the Divide would be yet another magical invasion from the other dimension – supposing someone spotted them in flight? On the other hand, it might be less risky than travelling on public transport with an elf at his side, and Betony would take him back again when she went home. Decision time. 'OK,' he said, taking a deep breath. 'Let's go.'

Nimby squealed with delight, and flapped his fringe. Felix and Betony gave Ironclaw a big hug, which embarrassed him. Then Felix put the carpet under his arm, and he and Betony straddled the Divide.

'I'll do the honours,' said Ironclaw, and he recited the spell, thinking how elegant it was. One of the best he'd ever calculated.

Felix and Betony came to on the Pennines, and it was raining. Betony looked round. 'It's very different to Costa Rica,' she said.

Felix smiled. 'The weather's not as good.' He opened his rucksack, and pulled out his fluorescent orange cagoule. 'Here,' he said, 'wear this.'

She fingered the fabric suspiciously before putting it on, and looked very surprised when the raindrops just ran off it. 'What about you?' she asked.

'My clothes are more suited to this climate than yours.'

'I can make you a roof,' said Nimby, curling up his leading edge. 'In fact, I have to, otherwise I'll lose my voice.'

Back to the Divide

It wasn't perfect, but it was much better than nothing. They both climbed on to the carpet, which then took off.

'I want you to avoid towns and villages,' said Felix. 'We don't want anyone to see us, if we can help it.'

'I'm perfectly capable of flying in low cloud and not getting lost,' said Nimby, as anxious to please as ever. 'Would that help? I have built-in orientation sensors, once you tell me where to go. Therefore, I shall remember the route back perfectly.'

Felix laughed. 'Just don't hit any power-lines.'

'I never hit anything,' said Nimby indignantly. 'I'm a top-of-the-range carpet, remember?'

It was a boring trip, as they couldn't see much – but Felix directed Nimby with his compass and was delighted when a break in the cloud showed him the expanse of London below. The rain had stopped soon after they left the Pennines.

Betony's mouth dropped open. 'Is that a *city?*' she asked. 'It's as big as a desert, or an ocean. It just seems to go on and on for ever. And it's so horribly *grey.*'

As they approached Wimbledon, Felix felt the tension begin to rise. So much depended on him, it was really scary. The wet and dry bits of his body seemed to have swapped roles – his mouth was biscuit-dry, and his eyes felt prickly, but the palms of his hands were wet. The hair at the nape of his neck was damp, too. He looked down. It was very weird flying along above familiar roads. There was a dream-like quality to it, seeing everything from such a different

353

perspective; his school, shut up for the summer; the park, with just a solitary figure walking a dog. His initial nervousness that they would be spotted began to evaporate; the carpet didn't make any noise at all, and people never seemed to look up as they walked along. Betony brightened a little when she saw that all the houses had gardens, and she laughed out loud when she saw a plastic gnome.

They landed unnoticed in the drive, and Nimby rolled himself up. Betony just stood and stared at the house, open-mouthed, and Felix had to nudge her towards the front door.

'It's so big,' she said. 'Like a palace. Is that a stable, at the side?'

'It's a garage,' said Felix, smiling. 'For a self-propelled vehicle.' He took out his key and unlocked the front door. The door didn't want to open at the outset, but it was only due to the huge pile of mail that had accumulated behind it. They pushed their way inside, and Felix leaned the carpet against the wall. The answerphone was flashing its full-up signal, and the leaves of the pot-plant in the hall had withered and turned yellow. Betony was looking in amazement at the framed photograph of Felix on the telephone table. 'That's really good,' she said. 'Who painted it?'

'I'll explain later,' said Felix, dumping his rucksack on the floor. The excitement was making him feel twitchy. *This was it*, he was going to bring his parents back to life. He took a deep breath, and walked into the front room, where Snakeweed had turned his father to stone.

354

The statue wasn't there any more.

He stood in the middle of the room, numb with shock, just stupidly staring at the space where his father had been. Betony followed him in, cleared her throat as though to speak, and then seemed to think better of it.

'I don't understand,' said Felix eventually. His voice seemed to be coming from a long way away. 'Where is he? Has he come back to life? I thought he was going to remain like that for twenty years.'

Betony's brows drew together and she bit her lip, and he could see that she was as perplexed as he was.

He looked in the dining room, the downstairs cloakroom, the cupboard under the stairs. Nothing. He ran upstairs, and searched all the bedrooms. Still nothing. So he returned to the kitchen, and looked a bit harder at the back door. There was something strange here, all right. The lock had been forced, but the door had been bolted again from the inside. There were little chips of wood on the floor and the door itself had a white scar by the handle, where the metal was coming away. He pulled back the bolts, his mind working overtime. Someone had broken in through the back door, but locked it again as they left. It didn't make sense. He dashed out into the garden, expecting to see dots of white marble everywhere, but there weren't any. The lawn was overgrown, certainly, but it was the same expanse of green it had always been.

He was half-expecting what he found when he reached

the plum tree: nothing but a plum tree. He leant against the trunk, let himself slide down to the ground, and felt his eyes fill with tears.

Betony came and sat down opposite him on the grass, cross-legged. They stayed like that for a while, neither of them speaking.

Finally Betony said, 'I need to think about this,' and the two of them got up and went back into the house. 'It doesn't add up,' she went on. 'Not *everything* disappearing – you said there were lots of little things that had been affected as well, didn't you?'

'The spell must have worn off,' said Felix, desperately wanting to believe it. 'But where *are* they? No one's been here since I left; the lawn hasn't been mown for a couple of weeks and the houseplants haven't been watered. Maybe they've gone off somewhere, looking for *me*.'

'Spells like that don't just wear off,' said Betony bitterly. 'What about my parents? You're not the only one this has ever happened to, remember?'

Felix wasn't listening. 'There's somewhere I haven't tried,' he said suddenly. 'The garage.' He opened the hall door that led to it – but to his intense disappointment the car was still there, so his parents hadn't driven off in it. He went back into the hall.

Betony pointed at the light flickering on the answerphone. 'What's that?'

'Voice messages,' said Felix, turning it on and fast-forwarding through the boring ones. It quickly became clear that his parents hadn't contacted anyone at all; his uncle was annoyed with his father for missing a game of golf, and his mother's hairdresser had rung to complain about a forgotten appointment. It was lucky that his father was a lecturer, and his mother a teacher – no one thought it particularly odd that they'd suddenly decided to go away for a fortnight during the summer vacation without telling anyone. There were several messages for Felix himself, from friends, asking where he was and whether he'd gone somewhere even more interesting than Costa Rica this year. He felt the despair begin to overwhelm him. 'Supposing the spell makes everything eventually disappear over here? For good?' He was having trouble keeping his voice steady.

Betony went over to an ornamental candle standing on the mantelpiece, and lit it with a wave of her hand. Then she blew it out again. 'I don't think there's any difference between over here and over there,' she said. 'Nimby can fly, and the candle lights. It's a pity your parents aren't royalty, or we could have found them really quickly.' She made a face all of a sudden, and rubbed her stomach. 'Felix, we haven't eaten anything for *ages*. We need to think clearly, and personally, I don't think that clearly when I'm starving hungry.'

'There'll be something in the fridge,' said Felix, and they went back into the kitchen. The moment he saw the splintered wood on the floor again, a new train of thought entered his head. 'There's been a break-in,' he said. 'That's it. They've been stolen. They'd be worth quite a bit – solid marble stat-ues.' But at the same time he couldn't help thinking – who would want a sculpture of a woman playing cricket, and a man taking a mobile phone out of his pocket?

'Then why didn't the thief turn into marble too?'

'I don't know!' shouted Felix, the frustration taking him to boiling point.

'Make something to eat,' said Betony. 'I've got the egg of an idea, but I need to *think*.'

'What idea?'

'Felix, shut *up* and let me incubate it.'

'But ...'

Betony glared at him, so he opened the fridge. The milk had gone off, the ham had turned green, and there was a puddle of liquid lettuce in the salad compartment. He found some ready-made meals in the freezer instead, and heated them up in the microwave. Betony's eyes widened at the whole procedure, but she didn't ask any questions as Felix was too strung-up to hold a normal conversation. They ate in silence.

Eventually Betony pushed her plate away and said, 'That was *very* strange. What was it?'

'Pasta.' He wasn't in the mood to go into further detail, but he was up to a bit of sarcasm. 'Has your egg hatched yet?' he asked.

Betony glared at him. 'I don't make fun of *your* expres-sions, and you've got some really stupid ones – sorry, feather-brained ones. As if anyone would use a brazzle as an example of stupidity. Now, you know I've spent the last year helping Thornbeak with some research into magic of the past? Toadstool location spells, that sort of thing?'

Felix nodded.

'Have you still got the marble snail?'

'*Yes.*' He was beginning to see where this was leading.

'Right. I know the incantation – it's a simple one. We just need to fix it on the sort of thing we're looking for.'

'Oh, that's brilliant.'

'Hold on,' said Betony, pushing the blonde hair back from her face. 'What the old sorcerers used was a little spike of metal. We don't know what metal it was, though. They used to float it on a piece of cork in a dish of water, and it would point in the right direction. They used some sort of force that's been forgotten.'

'Magnetism!' cried Felix. 'They made a compass!' He unfastened the one round his neck, which had hung there for the last month. 'Let's try it.' He gave it a quick wipe with his sleeve, as it was rather grubby.

Betony looked at it. 'How do we get at the metal bit? It's all enclosed in that transparent stuff. We need the snail to actually *touch* it.'

'I'll break it open,' said Felix, and he ran out to the garage where his father kept his tools, found a screwdriver and a pair of pliers, and prised off the plastic casing. He found Betony some leather gloves to protect her skin, opened the matchbox, and tipped the snail on to the table.

Betony picked it up and stroked the marble against the compass needle. Her eyes were screwed tight shut with concentration, and her lips moving slightly as she recited the words in her head. Then she opened her eyes, sat back, and waited.

They both watched the compass for what seemed like a long time. Felix crossed his fingers, then uncrossed them again because he wasn't superstitious and it was silly. The needle shivered slightly. Then, quite suddenly, it swung in one direction, and then the other. For a while it oscillated wildly, apparently unable to make up its mind where to go.

'Supposing the statues are in two different places?' Felix whispered. 'What would it do?'

Betony shook her head. 'I don't know. Point to the closest one, I'd imagine.'

Gradually the violent movements subsided, and the needle came to rest.

'That way, then,' said Betony, pointing south.

'But how *far* that way?'

'I don't know.'

'It could be miles and miles.'

'We've got a carpet.'

Felix had forgotten they had their own transport. 'Come on, then,' he said, getting to his feet.

'Felix, it's getting dark. Nimby can't fly at night.'

Felix groaned with impatience. 'It's not *fair*. We come

all this way ...'

'An hour ago you thought your parents had disappeared for ever. But they can't have done, or the compass wouldn't be showing us where they are. Let's get a good night's sleep, and start off in the morning.'

'We'll have to avoid the rush-hour,' said Felix grimly, knowing perfectly well Betony wouldn't have a clue what he was talking about.

Betony gave him a filthy look. 'You want me to ask whether that *feather-brained* expression has anything to do with making rush mats so that you can laugh at me, don't you? Well I'm not going to. I know,' she said, suspecting that the best course of action might be a *distr*action, 'show me that television thing you've told me about.'

Felix's anger suddenly seemed to melt away. He had a whole evening with Betony in *his* world; he would be a fool to waste it. 'OK,' he said.

He channel-hopped for a while, finding her a soap, a news programme, a chat show, a documentary about tigers. She wasn't quite as impressed as he'd expected.

'It's not like going out looking for real tigers, is it?' she said. 'The film maker's done that already – all you're seeing is what he's already recorded. Where's the excitement in *that?*'

He took her up to his room and turned on his computer, and she typed out a couple of spells. He printed them out in green, in a handwriting font – and that did astonish her.

'*Blazing feathers,*' she said, 'did I write that? It's neater than anything a scribe could do.'

Felix laughed and they went round the house together, switching all the different appliances on and off. He took out a photograph album, and briefly explained how a camera worked. She giggled at pictures of him as a baby, and stared in wonder at snaps taken of him at the zoo on an elephant. He remembered his own camera, and took some photographs of *her*. His mother's mobile phone was still in her bag – he felt a bit intrusive, going through her things, but a mobile might come in useful the following day. He had some fun sending a few text messages to his friends, who were delighted to hear from him and sent a few back.

'Felix,' said Betony, looking at the packed bookshelves. 'Last year you said something about your civilization going from flint arrowheads and stone circles to bombs and cathedrals. Do you have any history books – with pictures?'

'Yes, loads.' He lifted one down and started to give her a history lesson, full of pyramids and amphitheatres and cannons and tanks.

'Your world's past is very violent, isn't it?' she said.

'History is written by the winning side,' he quipped. 'And the winning side likes to exaggerate its victories, and the enemy's defeats.'

She thought for a moment. Then she said, 'We don't have winning sides, or losing sides. Our history is about the development of magic, natural disasters, renegade beasts.'

'Ours is mainly battles.'

'If history's written by the winning side,' said Betony, 'they can say what they like about the other lot, can't they?'

Felix grinned. 'You'd be a good historian whichever world you were in, Betony.'

He made her up a bed in the spare room, and showed her how the shower worked.

'My clothes are filthy,' she said, looking at them with distaste.

'Right,' said Felix, 'you're not that much smaller than my mother. Come on, we'll find you some human stuff to wear tomorrow.'

Betony stared at him. 'Won't she mind?'

Felix smiled. 'She's really nice, my mum,' he said. 'If she were here I reckon she'd suggest it herself.'

Betony was awe-struck at the different fabrics and colours and styles. 'I've never worn anything except green,' she said, choosing some black trousers and a red shirt.

Felix put Betony's clothes in the washing machine. Then they had a cup of hot chocolate each, and discussed their plan of action for the following day.

'How many other spells do you know off by heart?' asked Felix. 'There may be something we can use, if things get difficult.'

Betony made a face. 'Not that many – I can cure bruises, and light candles, and I know an illusion spell. All kids catch on to illusion spells eventually, they're the basis of a lot of

party tricks, so they don't work on grown-ups. They probably would over here, though, with people who've never been bewitched before. They're not terribly powerful spells – you can only make people believe a certain amount of information.'

'Could we freeze people, with the first half of the Divide spell?'

'It wouldn't work without a Divide.'

They talked strategies for a bit longer, and then they went to bed. It had been a fun evening in the end, considering the circumstances. Felix hoped the next day would be even better. He wanted to see his parents alive and well so badly – and he really wanted them to meet Betony, too.

But he spent a restless night, dreaming of broken statues and missing chunks of marble and three-dimensional jigsaw puzzles.

The next morning they had breakfast as Nimby lay stretched out on the patio, absorbing the sunlight. Felix had defrosted some milk, so that he could serve up cereal.

'It tastes like tree-bark,' said Betony, making a face, so Felix did some toast instead.

They waited until the rush hour had passed. Then they climbed aboard the carpet, and took off.

After half an hour the compass needle had started to whiz round and round, as though it no longer knew which way to point. They were flying over a big building, and once they were past it the needle steadied – but pointing in the opposite direction to the one it had taken before.

'That's it, then,' said Betony. 'The statues must be in there somewhere.'

They went back. The whole complex seemed very security-conscious. The service road had a barrier, with an attendant in uniform in a little yellow sentry box. As they flew over, Felix had glimpsed the main doors which had an entry phone. There was a prominent alarm system on the wall above, along with a CCTV camera. Once again, though, no one had noticed them. People just didn't look up. They landed on a balcony, selecting the one about which the compass was most enthusiastic.

'What is this place?' hissed Betony, as Felix tried to open the sliding door with a gloved hand.

'It's a company of some sort,' said Felix. 'I think this is their head office. I don't know what they make; it wasn't very clear from the logo. A couple of squiggly lines, and a pentangle. The name doesn't mean anything to me, either.'

'Guess what,' said Rutherford, sticking his head round Emily's door.

'You've been voted best-dressed man in the company?' returned Emily, with a sarcastic glance at his odd socks.

Rutherford looked down at his feet, and made a face. 'They both looked the same colour without the light on,' he said.

'I'm busy, Rutherford, what is it?'

'The magic's gone out of your theory, I'm afraid.'

'How so?'

'I've been monitoring a UFO site on the Internet, and there were three reports yesterday. *Three.*'

'You've got aliens on the brain, Rutherford. I'm pursuing a different line of enquiry, as you know.'

'All three sightings were within a five mile radius of a certain house.'

'Now you do interest me,' said Emily, looking up from her keyboard. 'Were there any descriptions?'

'Yes. All exactly the same. A rectangular shape that undulated slightly.'

'*Rectangular?* Are you sure? UFOs are usually cigar-shaped, or round.'

'I know.'

'Weird.'

'Very weird.'

'However,' said Rutherford, his heart beating a lot faster all of a sudden, 'it's not as weird as the real explanation – a flying carpet that's just landed on the balcony outside, behind you, with two kids on board.'

'That's not even slightly funny,' said Emily, refusing to look.

'I agree,' said Rutherford. 'I think you'd better open the door, and let them in.'

'Stop being so childish,' said Emily. And then she heard the sound of someone trying to open the sliding door. She spun round, and Rutherford felt himself fill with pure joy as her mouth dropped open in amazement.

20

'Someone's coming,' whispered Betony.

A woman materialized on the other side of the glass. She was slightly built with brown hair and an olive skin. Her eyes were dark and intense and set a little too closely together. There were a couple of clicks as she undid the catches fastening the door, and then she slid it back. She glanced briefly at Betony, clearly noting the fact that she was wearing gloves – but, more surprisingly, she looked very hard at Felix. A man appeared behind her. He had thin sandy hair and a high forehead, and he was wearing a lab coat, odd socks, and glasses.

'I think you're looking for your parents, aren't you?' said the woman.

The man looked momentarily stunned. 'How did you work that one out, Emily?' he asked.

'Family likeness,' said Emily. She smiled at Felix, although the smile didn't quite reach her eyes. 'You'd better come in. It's a bit windy this high up. And bring your magic carpet.'

Felix picked up Nimby, and he and Betony stepped into the room. It was an office, with desks and computers and filing cabinets, and stylish leather chairs.

'The statues are through there, aren't they?' said Felix, pointing at the door. He had the compass in the palm of his hand, and he knew which way the needle was pointing. He wasn't going to reveal the source of his information, however; he had a feeling things might get tricky.

'Just … sit down for a moment,' said Emily. 'I'd like to talk to you.'

'I'm sure you would,' said Felix. 'But all I really want is the statues of my mum and dad, you see.'

'But they're not statues, are they? If you touched them with your bare skin you'd turn to marble as well. Just like the wasps, and the frogs, and the cat, and the young men who tried to burgle your house. You know how the petrification was done, I imagine?'

'Not exactly,' said Felix, filing the remark about burglars but not wishing to pursue it right at that moment. 'I do know how to reverse it, though.'

'That'll do,' said the man with the sandy hair. 'Explain the antidote, and we'll be able to …'

'Shut up, Rutherford,' said Emily.

'We haven't got time to stand around here talking,' said Betony, annoyed that none of the conversation had been directed her way. 'Come on, Felix.' She made a move towards the door.

'Oh, you can't go in there,' said Emily, quickly stepping between Betony and the door. 'Top secret, you see. Dangerous, even.'

'Perhaps I'll phone the police,' said Felix, reaching into his pocket for his mother's mobile. 'Breaking and entering, followed by theft ... or would it count as kidnapping?'

'I think it would count as acting in the public interest,' said Emily. 'The precautions we had to take when we burgled your house were considerable. We did it at night, so that we could use ultra-violet light to track down every single piece of marble. NBC suits to avoid all skin contact, a suction sampler to pick up all the invertebrates. We stopped the chain-reaction; you and the rest of the world should be grateful.'

Felix clenched his fists with fury. 'Grateful? Can you imagine what I felt when I came back and found my parents were missing?'

'Came back?' said Emily sharply. 'Came back from where?'

'An adventure holiday,' said Felix quickly. It wasn't too far from the truth, either.

'Look,' said Rutherford, 'this is all getting us nowhere fast. We've got something you want, you've got something we want. Let's do a deal. The ingredients of the antidote in exchange for your parents.'

'And the carpet,' said Emily.

'No way,' said Felix, feeling for the matchbox in his other pocket. 'You'd use your knowledge for all sorts of dreadful things.'

'Let them have the statues,' said Rutherford suddenly.

Emily turned to him. 'Have you gone mad?' she snapped.

Rutherford shook his head.

'Oh, I know what you're thinking,' said Felix. 'Firstly, you could watch us turn them back into people and try and work out how we did it. Secondly, you must have all the insects that turned to marble somewhere here as well. Thirdly, you know where I live and you could always pay me a visit and try and force me to tell you what I know.'

Emily didn't look quite as annoyed with Rutherford as she had.

'Well,' said Felix, 'I hate to disappoint you – but I only have a limited amount of the chemical required.' He took the phial of water from the prediction pool out of his pocket, and showed it to them. 'Once it's gone it's gone, and I can't get any more.'

'Where *did* you get it?' asked Emily.

'From an old man,' lied Felix, knowing that any mention of the other world would be bad news. Rutherford and Emily glanced at one another sceptically, and Felix took the opportunity to mouth, 'Time for your party trick,' to Betony.

Betony started to tap her fingers and mutter some words under her breath.

'An old man,' repeated Emily slowly, but there wasn't as much doubt in her voice as might have been expected.

'He was an inventor,' Felix elaborated. 'He died in a fire, and all his records were lost.'

'What a pity,' said Emily dreamily, although it was clear she was referring to the records, not the old man.

'So once we've turned everything back to the way it was, that's that.' He suddenly realized he had to demystify Nimby, as well. 'Even the carpet will return to being just another rug,' he lied.

'All that work we did just wasted,' said Rutherford sadly.

'I was so close to understanding the principles behind it all, as well,' agreed Emily. 'It would have been such a fantastic weapon of mass destruction.'

'I'd seen it more as an easily sustainable method of suspended animation,' said Rutherford. 'It could have made inter-planetary space travel a reality.'

'There's not as much money in space travel as there is in weapons of mass destruction,' said Emily.

Betony stopped tapping her fingers, and she and Felix edged towards the door.

Emily suddenly seemed to snap out of her hypnotic state. 'If you've got the only antidote there is,' she said, her eyes narrowing as she barred the way, 'we really can't let you use it all up on something as trivial as your parents.' She leaned sideways and took something out of a drawer, concealing it in her hand.

Felix took the matchbox out of his pocket, keeping it behind his back. Would she be prepared to kill them, to keep them quiet? What did she have in her hand? He pulled out the marble snail with his gloved fingers, and then he stepped smartly forward and pressed the snail against Emily's cheek.

She knew what he'd done straight away, and an expression of dismay crossed her face. She tried to grab the phial of water, but her arm seized up. The hypodermic syringe she'd taken from the drawer dropped from her other hand to the floor. The colour drained from her face; her hair turned white, then her clothes and her shoes.

Rutherford was backing away across the room, shaking his head, his eyes wide with fear. Felix threw the snail at him, and he became rooted to the spot, the colour leaching away as though he were being bleached. His eyes were the last things to be affected, and they carried on moving from Felix to Betony and back again until they set in one position, and the transformation was complete.

'We'll have to change them back last thing,' said Felix, retrieving the snail.

Betony nodded.

They opened the door just a crack to begin with, and Felix saw a big laboratory. On the far side were five human-sized shapes, wrapped in some sort of plastic. *Five?* Then he remembered what Emily had said about burglars. There was a big *Do Not Touch* notice stuck on them. Next to them were some crates, also wrapped in the plastic, also with warning notices. Felix looked at the compass. It was pointing directly at them. The bad news was that there were several people in the room.

'What do we do now?' whispered Betony. 'If we turn them all to marble, we'll never be able to change them all back fast enough. By the time we get to the last one, the first one will be raising the alarm.'

'Alarm,' said Felix, giving Betony a broad grin. 'Brilliant.'
He glanced round the office ceiling. Then he dragged a chair
to the centre of the room, picked up a piece of paper, screwed
it into a cylinder, and turned to Betony. 'Can you light that?'
he asked her, suspecting it was too substantial for him to risk
doing it himself and needing several goes to get it right.

Betony nodded, although it was clear she had no idea what
he had in mind. She waved her hand over the taper, and it
burst into flames. Felix took it from her, climbed on to the
chair, and held it beneath the smoke alarm. Within a couple
of seconds the most unearthly shriek started up.

Through the crack in the door they could hear a voice
saying, 'No one told me there was a practice this morning.'

Someone else said, 'There isn't.'

There was a brief pause; then there were hurried footsteps
as half a dozen people made a rush for the stairs. When the
room was empty, Felix and Betony went in. Felix started to
cut the plastic off the statues with a pair of scissors he found
on a bench. He began with the heads, for identification pur-
poses. The first one was a man in a balaclava helmet, which
was a disappointment. The second was a teenage boy, wearing a baseball cap with *Save the Whales* printed on it. The one
after that was Felix's mother, and he heaved a sigh of relief.
Then another teenager, and last of all his father. Meanwhile
Betony had found a screwdriver, and she was tackling the
packing cases. They were easier; she only had to lever up the

lids. As she opened each one, she made little noises of amazement at the variety of creatures she found.

The horrible shriek of the fire alarm continued in the background as Felix worked, but eventually the statues were freed of their wrappings. He felt a lump rise in his throat as he saw his parents again, so white and unresponsive. Supposing, after all this, Leona's countercharm didn't work? He took the stopper off the phial of water, and he was in such a hurry that he nearly spilt it. This made him realise that he was going to have to be very careful with it, and measure it out drop by drop, or there wouldn't be enough for everything they had to do. He glanced round. There was an eye-dropper on one of the benches; perfect.

The incantation was in his notebook. He took it out, and opened it. And just like the last time, the pages were blank. He wanted to scream; how could he have been so *stupid?*

'What's the matter?'

'I've been an idiot,' said Felix. 'A complete and utter *idiot.* Crossing the Divide always wipes out any writing in my notebook. It wasn't until Snakeweed ran my brazzle feather over the pages that I realized there was a way of reversing it. But we don't have one with us.'

Betony grinned. 'Good job that Emily person stole your feather as well as the statues then, isn't it?' She pointed to one of the packing cases.

Felix peered inside. Thornbeak's feather was inside a plastic envelope, labelled with the date Emily had found it, and the location. He felt tears of relief prick at his eyelids, and he took it out and stroked it over the page with the spell. The writing reappeared, on cue.

Felix put a droplet of the water from the prediction pool on his mother's arm. Then he recited the spell, and stood back. The fire alarm suddenly ceased.

'You haven't got time to stand and watch,' said Betony. 'They'll all come back now, won't they? Those people? Now that noise has stopped?'

'They'll probably send a fire inspector to take a look first.'

A hint of colour had returned to his mother's face. Felix turned to his father, and repeated the procedure. Then he went to the first packing case and tackled a wasp, a hedge-hog, a starling, a mouse, a dragonfly ...

'Look,' said Betony.

The smallest creatures were recovering first, and the chain reaction was working in reverse. A snail he hadn't even touched was crawling up the side of the case. He wouldn't have to do each and every creature – as long as they were touching one another, they'd perform the job themselves. He went to the second case, and reanimated a butterfly. The third and final case held a grass snake – this was ideal, as it was in contact with so many other things. Last of all Felix did the burglars – he didn't want to have to deal with people who might get angry and violent. Then he looked at the compass again. It was pointing back to the office where Emily and Rutherford had been petrified. This, surely, meant that they were the only marble things left untreated.

'Felix? Where am I?'

Felix spun round. His mother was standing there, looking uncomprehendingly at the cricket bat in her hands. Her brows furrowed. Then her eyes widened, and she said, 'I had this dream ... '

Felix couldn't stop himself, he had to rush over and give her a hug, and it felt wonderful. Out of the corner of his eye he noticed Betony scowling. He remembered that her parents, too, had been turned to stone, and there wasn't going to be any reunion like this for her – not for another sixteen years, anyway. He wished the spell could have worked on them, too. He felt a bit guilty, and let go of his mother who seemed a little surprised at his sudden and public demonstration of affection. Betony's scowl had been replaced by a *don't care* expression. Perhaps it was just a *mixed up* expression, which was how she felt about petrified parents in general.

'Felix?' Felix's father was also looking confused. 'What's going on?'

'It's going to take far too long to explain,' said Felix. 'You're just going to have to trust me. Please?'

Felix's father had spotted a cat that was slowly regaining its colour, and tentatively flexing a paw. He didn't seem able to take his eyes off it. A vole dashed across the floor, and took shelter behind a photocopier. 'Impossible as it sounds,' he said, 'we were turned to stone by that appalling man in purple, weren't we? The one who knew something about your disappearance last summer. I was aware of it happening, the stiffness, the coldness. I thought I was dying. And then ... nothing. Until now.'

'We need to get out of here,' said Felix. 'And I'm afraid it has to be by magic carpet. Oh, this is Betony. She's an elf.'

Felix's father was now wearing the sort of fixed smile you get when things simply can't get any stranger.

Betony took off her cap so that he could see her ears and said, 'Felix is my best-ever friend.'

'What the blazes?' said a gruff voice behind them. This was then followed by a long and imaginative list of swearwords.

'The burglars are coming back to life,' said Felix. 'Come on, we've got to go.'

'But ...' said Felix's mother.

'I think Felix is in charge for the moment,' said Felix's father, and Felix felt ten feet tall.

'Leave the door open,' said Betony, as they went back to the office. 'Then some of the animals can get out – the ones that can fly, anyway.'

Even as she spoke, the starling flew past her and out of the open door to the balcony as though the hounds of hell were after it.

'Are we ready to go now?' asked Nimby.

'Nearly,' said Felix, turning the statues of Emily and Rutherford to face the wall and dropping smidgeons of water on to them. He gabbled the spell as rapidly as he could. The last creature he returned to its normal state was the snail. It had served him well, and he put it in one of the window boxes on the balcony.

More swearing was now issuing from the laboratory, as the burglars shouted at one another. He heard the door open, as the fire inspector presumably made an entrance, and the sound of a cat yowling.

'What's the hell's going on?' someone demanded.

In reply, the speaker was treated to a stream of abuse from three different sources. One of the voices carried on a little longer than the others, shouting about animal rights and declaring that the building should be burnt to the ground.

'Let's go,' said Felix, and he, Betony and his parents climbed aboard the carpet.

As Nimby lurched into the air, Felix caught a glimpse of the scene inside the laboratory through the open door. A hedgehog was scurrying across the floor, and dozens of insects were zipping around. A magpie was sitting on a microscope, and a couple of squirrels were running along some storage cabinets and leaping from one to the other. There was a crash and the tinkle of breaking glass from somewhere out of sight. The fire inspector and the burglars were standing there, finally rendered speechless; more animals kept appearing, and the place looked like a zoo. Felix laughed until the tears ran down his face; everything was going to be all right.

Betony told Nimby to get up into the cloud, so they wouldn't be seen, and the carpet obliged. 'This has all been really exciting,' he said. 'I can't wait to get back to a proper rack and tell some of those doormats what I've been up to.'

'I'm still dreaming, aren't I?' said Felix's mother. 'It's quite nice this time, though. I've often dreamt I could fly.'

'You're not dreaming,' said Felix, worried that his mother might simply step off the carpet. 'Magic is a reality in other worlds; that's where I went last summer.'

'Yes, dear,' said his mother, smiling. 'Whatever you say.'

'*I* believe you,' said Felix's father quietly. 'I think you'd better tell me everything.'

So Felix used the trip home to tell his father about the amazing adventures he'd had, whilst his mother chatted to Betony about dreams.

'Introducing printing was a disaster,' Felix told him. 'And I only just stopped them from getting the internal combustion engine. You can't *un*-discover something, can you? Discoveries are like evolution, they don't work backwards. I remember reading somewhere that you can't stop progress. But it wasn't progress, was it?'

'That's a tricky one,' said Felix's father. 'Progress is in the eye of the beholder. Something may be beneficial in one way, and disastrous in another. But discoveries do get lost. Civilizations have come and gone, like the ones in the Americas, and simply left intriguing glimpses of what might have been. We had the Dark Ages in Europe, remember. Sometimes I think that there's a sort of hump civilization has to get over, before everyone can work for the common good. Perhaps Betony's world can find a way of getting over the hump without it causing too much damage in the process.'

Nimby spiralled down like a falling leaf, and landed in Felix's garden.

'It's such a relief to have all this out in the open,' Felix concluded. 'I'd like to go back next summer to visit everyone, you see.'

'I don't think so,' said Felix's father. 'It sounds really dangerous.'

'*Dangerous?*' said Felix, aghast. 'But I'd be dead if I hadn't crossed the Divide. That's where I found the spell that made me better.'

'I know,' said Felix's father. 'But devil-hyenas that rip you to shreds? Heavy-duty wands that incinerate things in a second? Flying around on griffins, without a safety harness? There's no end to the things that could happen to you.'

'*Please*, Mr Sanders,' said Betony. 'Things are going to be much quieter in my world now that Snakeweed's just an exhibit in – what do you call it – a theme park.'

'I'm sorry,' said Felix's father. 'I really can't allow it. You're very welcome to visit here, of course, any time you like – well, not during term-time, Felix has his schooling to consider. But you could come over for Christmas, if you wanted.'

'I make the best mince pies you've ever tasted,' said Felix's mother. 'Do you think I could fly all by myself if I concentrated really hard?'

'I think you'd better go and have a lie down,' said Felix's father.

'All right,' said Felix's mother cheerfully. She turned to Betony. 'Goodbye, dear. It's been nice meeting you. Do you know, I've got a pair of trousers and a shirt exactly the same as the ones you're wearing?'

Betony opened her mouth to reply, but Felix's father laid a hand on her arm and shook his head. Felix's mother went back into the house.

'I think it'll be best if she thinks this *was* all a dream,' said Felix's father.

'How are you going to explain the missing fortnight?' asked Felix.

'Tell her she's been ill? That she's had a dose of amnesia? If she ends up believing all this she's going to worry about you for the rest of her life. Even when you're grown up. Every time you're out of touch for any length of time she'll think you've gone back to the other world, and she'll never see you again.'

'Won't you think the same thing?'

'Yes. But I'd feel the same if you decided to become a war correspondent, or a foreign aid worker, or a deep-sea diver. And I wouldn't try and stop you being any of those things, once you're of an age to make an informed decision.'

Betony was looking annoyed. 'Why are you treating Felix's mother as though she's a wimp?' she demanded.

'Oh, I don't think she's a wimp at all,' said Felix's father. 'When Felix was ill she was tougher than me. But the difference between her and me is that she lost a brother to Mount Everest. Her fears come from real experience, unlike mine, and I don't want her to have to re-live them.'

Betony nodded and said, 'That makes sense. And I could solve the problem with an illusion spell, if you like.'

He sighed. 'More magic?'

'Magic's like science. Most sorcerers and most scientists are trying to make life better. It's only a few who use it for their own ends.'

'All right, then. What will you do?'

'Felix will tell her whatever you want. I'll mutter the spell, and she'll believe it. It can't be too detailed though, because it's a very mild hex and I'll only have a few minutes.'

'It sounds a bit like hypnotism.'

'It works on a similar principle,' said Felix.

They decided that a holiday would be the best explanation for their absence from home, and that somewhere they'd already been was a good idea because she'd have all the right memories in place. Eventually they settled on Cornwall; she'd loved the Eden Project, and the Lost Gardens of Heligan, and it was quite believable that they'd visited them a second time. Felix threw in a few invented incidents – there'd been a thunderstorm at Heligan, and she'd lost her purse in the Eden Project, but got it back again.

She had been dozing on the sofa in the living room. Felix took her a cup of tea and woke her up, and the spell worked even *better* than a dream. When they'd finished, Betony said she ought to be on her way, and Felix's father suggested his wife start unpacking Felix's dirty clothes, so that Betony could make her departure on the carpet unobserved.

Betony changed back into her old tunic and trousers, and she and Felix went into the garden.

'So when's Christmas?' asked Betony, fingering her pendant. She hadn't taken it off from the moment Felix had given it to her.

'Four months' time,' said Felix, smiling.

'Does that mean I get to come back as well?' asked Nimby, wriggling with excitement.

'I don't know how else I could manage it,' said Betony. She gave Felix a hug, and climbed aboard. Then the carpet took off, and before long it was a little speck in the sky.

Felix smiled, went back inside. He realized that his mother had started unpacking his rucksack, and stopped halfway through. She was now downstairs in the living room; he'd passed the door and seen her putting some brass ornament or other on to the mantelpiece. He carried on with the job, and at the bottom he found the small wooden statue of Leona that he'd bought in Kaflabad. For a moment he was devastated; he'd managed to bring yet another half-twisted potential hazard with him. Then he remembered that there was nothing magical about the statue; it had been carved in the usual way, from a piece of wood. It was just a harmless memento of his rather unusual summer holiday.

Blazing feathers, though. He couldn't wait for Christmas.

THE END

384